STRETCHED BETWEEN TWO WORLDS

"I wake up every morning with you on my mind, and I go to sleep with you as my last thought every night. I need you in my life, Katherine," Thomas said with all of his emotions playing across his face.

Without giving her time to reject him, Thomas pulled Katherine into his arms.

He felt her surprise fade as soon as his lips touched hers. His hands hungrily caressed her body as she clung to him and pulled him even closer.

They stood locked in each other's embrace as the fragrance of roses enveloped them.

"Thomas, I . . ." Katherine began, pushing away ever so slightly. She wanted to look into his eyes but not to break the spell that held them. She had to see that he understood when she explained her reservations. "I can't allow myself to become involved right now. In a few more months when I've finished keeping my promise to myself, but not now. It wouldn't be fair to either of us."

"Katherine, nothing matters in this world but you. You don't have to prove yourself to anyone. Nothing and no one matters."

"It matters to me, Thomas. You have to understand."

Before he could answer, a voice called from the gate. . . .

A SURE THING

Courtni Wright

ARABESQUE
BET
BOOKS

BET Publications, LLC
www.msbet.com
www.arabesquebooks.com

ARABESQUE BOOKS are published by

BET Publications, LLC
c/o BET BOOKS
One BET Plaza
1900 W Place NE
Washington, D.C. 20018-1211

First Printing: October, 1999
10 9 8 7 6 5 4 3 2 1

Printed in the United States of America

One

"Dr. Katherine Winters, you're wanted in the ER stat," the public address system blared over the roar of the hospital sounds. At four o'clock in the morning, the big city hospital was still a hub of noise with the sick and injured filling the rooms, halls, and elevators. Nurses administered medicines, changed linens, and answered the endless list of questions from physicians and families. Doctors harried from twelve-hour shifts and caring for the wounded who filled the city hospital all night rushed to one more task. They hoped that their reserve would hold up as they tried to stay awake until they could finally return home and get some sleep.

Katherine gave her face another quick look. The darkness and bags barely showed under the carefully applied concealing foundation. The light touch of blush removed some of the pallor caused by the lack of sleep and added a nice hint of color. She checked the coiled bun of thick curly auburn hair that rested demurely at the base of her neck. No wispy curls had escaped despite her having pulled off and on the cover-up for her surgical scrubs at least one hundred times during the course of the night. Her hazel eyes sparkled confidence, certainly a plus in this line of work.

As Katherine leaned against the wall in utter fatigue after twelve long hours in the emergency room, she briefly questioned her reasons for selecting emergency room medicine when she could have specialized in something sane. She could be gently tucked in her bed asleep at this moment rather than gulping down a cup of cold, black coffee. The idea of sleep seemed so far away and as much an unattainable dream to an acting chief of staff as the expensive sports cars driven by many of the rich hospital patrons.

As she shifted her weight from one tired foot to the other, Katherine wondered if she would ever make it through the night. Working the two jobs was almost more than she could handle, but she could not step down from either. A few weeks ago, the board had made its announcement regarding the permanent chief of staff. Unfortunately, she had not been the one appointed to fill Frank Harriman's shoes.

Taking the offered chart with all the grace she could muster at four in the morning, Katherine approached emergency room 3 where a child suffering from what might have been an animal bite awaited her. Before treating the five-year-old boy's wound, she held him in her lap and questioned him as his worried mother looked on attentively. When the child finished his story of sneaking out of his bed and trapping the family's terrier in his bedroom against his parents' long-standing orders, Katherine smiled and kissed him lightly on his soft cheek. Then, she examined the little bite, cleaned it off, stitched it up, and administered a tetanus shot before gently admonishing the boy about the consequences of not following his parents' instructions. Sending the youngster and his mother on their way home and back to bed, she retired to the chart room and physicians' lounge and the few minutes of required paperwork for the simple case.

Just as she placed her hand on the knob, Susan called from behind her. "Katherine," she said waving yet another clipboard, "sorry, hon, but you're needed in room 6. I tried to get someone from internal medicine, but they're all busy. You're the only one free." Handing her the case, the equally tired nurse shrugged her shoulders and retreated to the station where a backlog of work awaited her, too.

"Just my luck," Katherine muttered as she marched toward

the waiting patient. Checking her watch, she wondered if the night would ever end.

Quickly scanning the chart, Katherine read the vitals on an adult male whose car had wrapped around a telephone pole. The police had extricated him from the mangled vehicle and brought him to the nearest hospital. The triage nurse had noted that he did not appear to have suffered too much trauma from the accident, which should make this a quick check and admit case.

"Good morning. I'm Dr. Winters. How are you feeling?" Katherine asked as she pushed open the door.

"How the hell do you think I'm feeling? I just wrecked by father's damn car, and you're asking me how I'm feeling. Believe me, doctor, it doesn't matter how I'm feeling now because after he finishes with me I won't be feeling anything," the still intoxicated twenty-year-old answered.

Katherine almost felt sorry for him as she rechecked his vitals and examined the many cuts and bruises that discolored his pale white skin. The glow of the fluorescent lights gave him a slight bluish tinge. He trembled slightly from the shock of the accident and the affects of the liquor. The young man was not bad-looking, but he was definitely in need of a shower. At some time during the evening, he had vomited on himself and reeked of stale beer. He tried to maintain his tough-guy attitude even with blood and vomit streaking his baggy trousers and matting his long hair.

Ignoring his initial outburst of nerves, fear, and pain, Katherine asked as her fingers probed an especially tender spot, "What kind of car was it?"

"It was a brand new Mercedes 580. My dad is going to kill me. He told me not to drive it, but I wouldn't listen. I took it while he was sleeping. Man, I'm dead," the boy lamented drunkenly. His eyes fluttered open-and-shut under the influence of the alcohol in his system.

"You did a pretty good job of banging yourself up, too. Maybe he'll be so happy that you're still alive that he won't care about the car," Katherine offered as her skillful fingers continue their survey of his body.

"Ouch! That hurts! No, he'll kill me all right. He's my step-dad, and he'll notice. He's a good guy and all; he adopted me when he married my mom. He told me not to drive his car. He said I wasn't old enough or experienced enough. I just thought that he didn't want me driving his precious car and used experience as an excuse. Anyway, I took the keys and, well, you know the rest. You don't have to call him, do you?"

"Sorry, Jason, but the nurse already called him. He's on his way," Katherine replied as she continued to press on the area surrounding the tender spots in his abdomen.

"Hey, I said that hurts. You don't have to touch me there again," Jason said as he nervously stared at the door.

Suddenly the emergency room filled with an anxious, angry man's voice. Barging in without standing on formality, Jason's stepfather filled the small space with his huge presence. Jason's eyes widened and his body constricted from the fear that gripped him.

Casting a quick glance in his direction, Katherine could understand the boy's reaction. Jason's stepfather loomed at the foot of the gurney. All six feet five inches of his tall size forty-four frame commanded attention and obedience. He wore his stock of gray hair in a Marine-short crew cut. Even at this hour of the morning, his eyes were a sharp, penetrating blue. His mouth was a hard tight line. His body appeared ready to burst with barely controlled energy. Katherine could see why the boy would feel overwhelmed in his presence. Already she could see the belligerence and bravado slipping from Jason's demeanor. She had already sensed that Jason was only talk, the empty noise of a frightened yet arrogant teenager.

"Is my son all right?" Mr. Alexander demanded without waiting for introductions. Katherine could tell from the way he stood with his feet firmly planted, shoulders square, and hands at his sides in his perfectly tailored pin-striped suit that this was a no-nonsense man who was accustomed to quick, direct responses.

"I haven't finished my examination yet, sir, but I think Jason might have some bruising of the spleen. We won't know for sure until after I finish this sonogram. It will only take a few more minutes," Katherine responded aware of Jason's increased trembling. She was not sure if it were the result of his injuries or his father's presence. Slowly spreading the glistening goo on his abdomen, she continued without looking up from her work.

Watching the screen, Katherine slowly moved the scanner around the taut stomach. Jason winced with pain each time she applied any pressure to the area. Stopping, she looked more closely. There in the extreme corner of the spleen was a slight dark spot that indicated hemorrhaging.

"There it is. I was right. I'll arrange for Jason's transfer to the operating room. We need to repair the tear immediately. Excuse me, I'll be right back," Katherine said as she slipped past him and out the door.

"May I speak with my son while you're out of the room?" Mr. Alexander asked in a more congenial tone now that he had been satisfied that Katherine was doing all she could for the boy.

"Certainly. I'll check on his blood work while you visit with him, but please try not to upset him too much. He needs his rest," Katherine responded. Turning to Jason she added, "I'll be back in a minute."

Leaving the room, Katherine quickly checked on the results of the blood work and the ultrasound. Sensing that Jason would want someone to run interference, she quickly returned to the area outside of room 6. Resting against the window, she studied Jason's chart while she eavesdropped on his conversation with his stepfather.

Listening closely Katherine heard his stepfather say in a very angry voice, "Well, Jason, I'm glad to know that you've learned your lesson. However, your mother and I are deeply disappointed. You deliberately disobeyed my orders. When I get you

home, we'll have to figure out a way that you can work off the
cost of this unfortunate incident, young man. You won't get off
without paying the consequences of this action."

"Yes, Dad. I promise I won't do anything like this again. I've
learned my lesson for sure," Jason answered in a voice that was
so soft that Katherine could just barely hear it. He was obviously
shaken but quite relieved that his stepfather had not been
harsher in his punishment. He could have grounded Jason for
life.

"I don't doubt that you have. However, my car had to suffer
for your actions and stupidity. I'm just glad that your mother
is out of town on a business trip and couldn't be here. She would
have been beside herself. As it is, I'll have to break the news
to her very carefully. You were very irresponsible, son."

Taking her cue from the silence that filtered into the hall,
Katherine entered saying, "It's all arranged. We'll be transferring you immediately."

Jason's cheeks looked even paler than before as he opened
his mouth to speak. Suddenly, his expression changed and panic
filled his eyes. Turning his head to the side, a great torrent of
dark red-brown blood erupted onto the sheet. His body con-
vulsed with each surge bringing forth more frothy red fluid.
The air filled with the salty smell.

Springing into action, Katherine quickly produced the kidney
shaped basin. Elevating Jason's head against her chest, she held
him cradled against her body as he vomited. Returning him to
a reclining position, she quickly made notes in the chart and
signaled for the orderly who immediately began to clean the
blood from the floor.

Resting heavily against her, Jason looked apologetically from
Katherine to his father. His eyes filled with tears. All signs of
drunkenness faded quickly from his eyes. Moaning softly he
cried, "My stomach's killing me. Do something for the pain,
please, doctor. I feel awful."

Looking through the large window, Katherine saw that the
transport personnel had arrived. Looking into Jason's pinched

face, she said, "Don't worry, Jason. We'll take care of everything. Just rest. We'll roll you up to surgery right now. Mr. Alexander, you may ride up on the elevator with Jason if you would like. There's a waiting room outside the operating suite where you can sit. The surgeons will keep you posted," Katherine commented

"Thank you, doctor, I appreciate all you've done for Jason," Mr. Alexander said in a voice strained with worry. The sight of blood gushing from his son's mouth had reduced his bravado to a quivering mass. No longer did he seem to fill the room but rather he stood with his hands tightly wrapped around his body and his eyes large with fear.

"It has been my pleasure. If you'll excuse me, I have paperwork to finish. You'll be okay, Jason. Don't worry about a thing," Katherine added as she slipped out the door and down the hall to the physicians' lounge. Finally, she would be able to finish her charts and maybe catch a short nap. Maybe no one would need her for the next half hour.

Scribbling rapidly, Katherine completed the case logs and scrawled her almost illegible signature at the bottom of each. She made a mental note to try to find the time to visit Jason in his room as soon as she could steal a few minutes from the emergency room. She liked to follow up on her young patients when she had the chance. Unfortunately, Katherine's schedule usually kept her so busy that she could only stick her head into the room on her way to yet another meeting.

Laying her head on the desk for a quick nap, Katherine allowed the sounds of the hospital to lull her to sleep. Working in the hospital had taught her to relish the few stolen minutes of sleep that revived her spirits and restored the spring to her tired step. Sometimes she dreamed, although she seldom remembered the contents of her dreams for more than a few seconds after awakening. Her days and nights were so hectic that pleasurable thoughts quickly fled from her mind as she scurried down the halls rushing from one examining room or meeting to the other. The added responsibility of acting as chief of staff did not lighten her load. She had learned to divide her time as best she could between the two duties with each having her attention part of the day.

However, there were nights like this one when she had to cover the ER's night shift because of the sickness of another physician and that proved especially draining. Even now she counted off the duties that awaited her as soon as she returned to the emergency room floor. She knew that this brief respite would only refresh her for the stress of the next flood of patients.

This morning was one of those times for dreams, although this one felt more like a wish. She dreamed of lying on a raft in the middle of the small lake in which she had played as a child. That part of the farm was always so peaceful with only the squawking of the wild ducks that called the water their home to disturb her thoughts. She would lie for hours with the summer breeze cooling her skin and the water rocking the raft. When she was there, she did not have a care in the world. The gentle buzzing of the bees in the nearby flowering vines would lull her to sleep. She would move only when one of her brothers joined her on the raft. Then, she would have to share the solitude with his muscular frame.

Just as she surrendered to the calm, the pressure of someone's hand resting on her shoulder awakened Katherine. At first she thought that she was back home and her younger brother had sneaked onto the raft with her to disturb her rest. As the buzzing of her pager filtered through the fog of her mind, she realized where she was and sat up.

"Sorry to wake you, Katherine," Betsy said, lightly shaking her shoulder, "but we have a staff meeting in ten minutes. I asked one of the nurses to bring in your cases. I thought you might like to review them before we go upstairs."

Stretching, Katherine smiled tiredly at her best friend and replied, "You're right as always. Thanks. What would I do without a friend like you? Get some sleep, maybe? I probably should review what I've done in the last eleven hours. I can hardly believe that it's almost time to go home."

"A shower and a bed would look pretty good to me about now, too. Let's walk home together later," Betsy added, pushing the last straggling wisps of her hair in place. It had been a long night for both of them, and they could hardly wait to go home.

"Okay, but first, the staff meeting. Who's running it this morning?" Katherine asked.

"You'll start it until the new chief arrives. He called from the airport to say that he's running late."

"I can hardly wait. As you know, I haven't exactly been looking forward to this day. I don't care how hard I try to shed this feeling, I can't overcome the hurt of being passed over for this job. The more I think about having to work for someone else again when I have proven that I'm capable of running this hospital, the more angry I become. I realize that no one promised me a fair world, but this is really unfair. I understand the board's thoughts in this matter, but I don't see why the members did not see fit to give me a chance to make the changes they wanted. I guess I'll get over this some day, but not today. Thomas Baker is coming here to take the job that is rightfully mine, and it's not fair," Katherine remarked sarcastically.

Katherine had hoped to become the chief of staff after Frank Harriman retired. He had nominated her along with a few others, but the committee had gone outside for his replacement. It said that new blood would bring new ways of looking at things to the hospital. She had been and still was bitterly disappointed. She hated the reminder that the "glass ceiling" was still alive and well. She had worked so hard to prove herself worthy of permanent appointment to the position that Katherine still found the naming of someone else a bitter pill to swallow.

"Just remember to be polite. I've seen you when you forget to put your best foot forward," her old friend commented.

"I'll be so charming, Thomas Baker will think he's on a Hollywood set not in a real hospital. I just wish that the transition could have happened a bit more smoothly, that's all. I had hoped that last week would have been my last time chairing the meeting. It's a little awkward to have thanked everyone for their

cooperation and now to find myself in front of them again so
soon. Don't look so worried. I won't let anyone except you
know that I'm thinking negative thoughts about a man I haven't
even met except in passing when he came to interview for the
job I wanted," Katherine said with determination and resigna-
tion in her voice as she accepted her charts from Betsy.

With a chuckle and a backward glance, Betsy left the lounge.
She knew Katherine too well to continue this line of discussion.
Katherine's wrinkled forehead told Betsy that her friend was no
longer listening and would not change her ways even if she
were.

Giving her charts a quick review, Katherine remembered the
stir Thomas Baker had caused the day he first met the staff.
The women had been all aflutter when they learned that the
handsome, wavy-haired, deep-brown-eyed physician was single
and unattached. Immediately many of them had begun spinning
webs in which to entangle him at the earliest opportunity. Doctors, nurses, and technicians had all acted in a way that Katherine found profoundly unprofessional. She could hardly
believe that the women with whom she had worked for the last
five years and seen handle dreadful emergency room cases
could come unglued at the sight of a new man.

The men had been only slightly less impressed. They had
immediately started cementing the good-old-boy network with
talk of sports and business. They had jockeyed for position in
what they believed would be the inevitable staff changes as soon
as Thomas reported for duty.

Leaning back in her chair, Katherine reflected on her first
impression of Dr. Thomas Baker. His six-foot-five frame had
hovered over her own five feet eight inches. His massive hands
had totally engulfed hers as they exchanged pleasantries. His
voice had been demanding of her attention without even the
slightest hint of an accent to tell her anything personal about
him.

Katherine could understand why the other women had been
won over by his personality and charm. She had almost fallen

under his spell, too, before reminding herself that as soon as
he entered the scene as the new chief of staff she would be
forced to return to her usual position as a member of the staff.
She could not afford to like him or find him attractive since he
was now the competition and soon to be her boss. Depending
on the course he chose for her beloved hospital, he might soon
become the enemy.

Reflecting on her tenure as acting chief of staff, Katherine
reluctantly admitted that there were times when she put the managing of Boxer ahead of making the necessary social contacts
that would bolster her career. She had not wined and dined as
many of the old guard as she probably should have. She preferred to spend her time on matters that affected the welfare of
the entire hospital instead. However, those with whom she had
cultivated a relationship were firmly in her corner and thought
that she should have received the vote of confidence and the
position. Thinking back over the months, Katherine acknowledged that if she had it to do over again, she would have put
forth more effort to ingratiate herself with more of the influential members of the board.

Despite this oversight, Katherine had steered a true course
and brought a healthy institution into even greater financial stability. She had worked tirelessly for the good of the personnel
under her, the patients in her charge, and the interests of the
board. No one could fault her intentions even if she failed to
gain their total confidence. She had done what was best for
Boxer and would probably do it again without hesitation.

Muttering to herself, Katherine whispered, "Don't second-
guess yourself, kid. You did what you felt was right at the time.
No one suffered from your direction but you."

Quickly tucking the charts under her arm, Katherine navi-
gated the maze of gurneys, patients, and hospital staff before
arriving at the chief of staff's office in which they held their
weekly staff meetings. In the months since Frank Harriman's
retirement, she had begun to consider the room as her own. At
least, she had thought that way until the board announced its

plans for Thomas Baker. Yesterday, she had moved her few personal items out of the office so that the new man could move in. Now the once friendly space looked forlorn and cold to her.

Taking her seat among the others, Katherine lightly tapped on the well-worn waxed cherry surface and waited until the conversations drew to a close. She could tell that everyone was impatient for the new chief of staff to arrive. They wanted to know how their lives would change with this new man at the helm. They had all grown comfortable with Frank Harriman's laid-back, easygoing approach to management. Katherine's style had so mirrored his that they had hardly felt the impact of any change at all when she moved into his office. Now the fear of the unknown felt like an extra presence in the room.

Katherine had just finished the first case of their morning discussion session when the door opened. Sylvia Brown, the secretary to the last three chiefs of staff and a member of the old guard of hospital personnel, entered with a great show and flourish of excitement. Her lined face wore a mask of smiles, and her voice twittered like a schoolgirl's as she stepped aside with a grand sweep of her hand. A tall, handsome black man dressed in a black pin-stripped suit perfectly tailored to fit his athletic body followed at a respectable distance behind her.

"Doctors, I'd like to present the new chief of staff. Ladies and gentlemen, meet Thomas Baker, MD," Sylvia cooed as she all but fell forward on heels too high to be worn by a woman of her age.

"Welcome, Dr. Baker," Katherine replied as she instantly rose to her tired feet and walked toward the newcomer with an outstretched hand. Smiling broadly, she did her best to hide the disappointment she felt at having to relinquish her position to him.

"Dr. Winters, I'd like to thank you for all you've done to maintain order and harmony here at Boxer Hospital. I've been told that I owe the smooth transition to your skillful management. The hospital is functioning in the black with annual fund-raising campaigns underway as scheduled. You've made my job of introducing new programs and increasing the fund-raising efforts most pleasant." Thomas Baker smiled confidently as he shook Katherine's hand.

"Thank you, Dr. Baker. I owe all of my success in this short period of time to a very dedicated management team and a very supportive staff. I'm sure that you'd like to chair our traditional weekly meeting. I'll only need a few seconds to move my things," Katherine commented, scrambling to gather her cases in anticipation of a move to the other side of the table.

"Nonsense. I wouldn't think of disrupting the flow of the meeting. Continue, please. I'll pour myself a cup of coffee and take a seat at the end of the table out of everyone's way. For today, I'll simply observe the way things are done here. I don't want my presence to change anything about the smooth operation of this hospital. I'm sure I have plenty to learn from you about conducting these sessions," Thomas Baker protested as he moved to the back of the room.

Resuming her seat, Katherine felt both relieved and alarmed by his efforts to appear one of the already established team. She appreciated his consideration for her feelings and his quiet, unobtrusive manner. She had expected him to take over, to thank her for her efforts on behalf of the hospital, and then to make it clear to everyone that a new head meant immediate changes. She found his gentle manner comforting.

Yet, something in the way he had held her hand and in the calmness of his voice told Katherine that Thomas Baker was a man who made it a practice to get everything he wanted. He had an intense way of looking into a person's eyes that conveyed the message that he wanted only to please. She had the feeling that he was accustomed to little if any opposition from the ranks.

Sitting across from him, Katherine conducted her usual highly professional session as she continued with the usual Monday topics. She listened as the personnel manager discussed the impending nurses' strike and offered her suggestions on ways to reach a settlement with the least amount of disruption to the patients. She paid close attention to the financial officer's discussion of expenditures by department and made note of the areas that she thought needed immediate attention. Normally, she would schedule a follow-up meeting with the head of that department, but now she would simply hand over her notes to Dr. Baker for his attention.

Periodically she glanced up to see if he wanted to input anything to the meeting only to find Dr. Baker absently picking lint or thread from his suit, adjusting his tie, or studying the many photographs and citations that lined the walls of the huge room. She found his disinterest both irritating and reassuring. His attitude either meant that he was comfortable with the programs she had already begun or that he intended to scrap all of them and start over. If his reaction were based on the former, she would have preferred that he involve himself in the functioning of the hospital that had just become his responsibility. She was grateful for his confidence in her ability and his respect for her feelings in allowing her one last session at its head.

When the meeting ended and the other physicians and administrators left the office, the new chief of staff approached Katherine and said, "I want to thank you for running such a tight ship. Your efficiency certainly makes my transition into the job easier. I hope there won't be any hard feelings between us. I know you were also a candidate for the position. From what I've read and seen, I'm sure that I was selected instead of you because of the different perspective I can offer rather than because of ability. The 'fresh face' approach is what the hospital board wanted. I hope that we'll be able to establish a strong relationship."

"I look forward to being a member of your team, Dr. Baker. I'll leave you to get acquainted with the staff, and I'll go home for some much-needed sleep. Since Frank retired, I've been working very long hours as well as covering the night shift in the ER when necessary. I hope that last night was my final time doing that.

"Although I must admit to being disappointed at being passed over for the chief-of-staff position, I am looking forward to the relative calm of the daytime ER.

"I've learned since my arrival in Washington that there are some things against which we simply cannot fight. One of those is the unfortunate impression in this town that someone from the outside has more to offer than someone who has intimate knowledge of the inner workings of an institution.

"I harbor no grudges or thoughts of ill will against you, Dr. Baker. However, I do feel a strong desire to prove that the board was mistaken in its decision. The only way I can do that is to be the best chief of the ER that I can possibly be and to that end, I need some rest," Katherine responded tossing her sheet of notes onto the table.

With that, Katherine gathered her things and walked to the door. As she was about to depart, Dr. Baker called after her saying, "By the way, my name's Thomas. I like for my staff to be on a first-name basis. It makes the workplace more informal, casual, and familiar."

"I, too, like professional informality, Dr. Baker. However, I reserve the right to remain a bit formal until we've known each other longer than thirty minutes," she replied with a smile intended to put to rest any thoughts the good doctor might have about any other kind of relationship developing between them. She had no intention of becoming personal with the man who had replaced her in the job she wanted. Katherine did not care if the board had made the choice for the good of the hospital. She wanted nothing to do with this interloper.

Stopping at her office only long enough to drop off the case folders, remove her white coat, call Betsy, and grab her purse, Katherine left the hospital and started home. Along the way, she met Betsy at their favorite bagel shop in which she bought a blueberry bagel smeared with cream cheese, a cup of coffee that she would drink on the way home, and a morning paper for reading with her juice. Her usual routine was to spend twenty minutes running on the treadmill before taking a shower. Then she would spend an equal amount of time reading the lead paragraphs of the important articles while eating her breakfast. Finally, she would allow herself to surrender to the fatigue that threatened to consume her body.

"Well, what do you think of Dr. Baker? The women are going crazy over him. The hospital grapevine has it that he's quite available. Did he say anything interesting to you after we left?" Betsy asked in a conspiratorial voice.

"He didn't say much really, at least nothing different. Oh, he reminded me that he preferred that I address him by his first name, which I declined to do. But that's about all I can tell you about him that you don't already know," Katherine answered as Betsy stared openmouthed at her.

"What exactly is your reason for being rude to him? Why can't you use his first name? Does the name remind you of some creep who crossed your path at some time in your life?" Betsy asked with an expression of incongruity playing across her face. She could not believe that Katherine could react in that manner to such a simple request.

"I just don't want to become that familiar with someone I've only just met. I realize that people address their bosses by their first names all the time, but I'd prefer to wait until I know him better. Besides, I guess I do feel a little resentment toward him. I just need some time, that's all," Katherine responded, unlocking the door to her apartment.

"Well, I wouldn't wait too long, if I were you. While you're working to maintain a professional distance from this eligible bachelor, many of our colleagues will be beating a path to his door. There might be a few board members with the same idea, too. I would be tempted myself if I weren't your best friend and if I hadn't seen the way he looks at you. Besides, my boyfriend might not like it," Betsy commented, pulling her own key from her pocket and continuing down the hall.

"They can have him!" Katherine called after her. "He's not the only single man in Washington."

"No, but he's probably the most interesting one you'll meet

this summer," Betsy replied, watching the turmoil reflected on Katherine's face.

"Besides, how can you expect me to welcome him with open arms and practically accept him as my long, lost brother? He is the man who took my job. I don't care if it really was the board that appointed him. The bottom line is that Thomas Baker has the job that I wanted. He's the chief of staff of Boxer Hospital and I'm not. He's in and I'm out. It's just that simple," Katherine lamented, watching Betsy juggle the paper, her briefcase, and the mail while opening the door.

"I don't expect you to throw yourself at the man. I'm only asking you to give yourself a chance to like him or at least learn to tolerate his presence. You have to work with him, you know. You might as well make the best of it. Anyway, I saw him checking you out when he didn't think anyone was looking. Don't blow your chance for happiness. That's all I'm saying," Betsy said as she waved and closed her door.

As soon as Katherine entered her apartment, Mitzi, her Siamese cat, demanded her undivided attention. Purring loudly and rubbing against Katherine's legs, the cat would not stop until Katherine picked her up and stroked her silken fur. After consuming her morning half can of food, Mitzi contentedly trotted away to lie in the sunbeams that streamed through the huge living room window.

Usually Katherine fell asleep as soon as she crawled into bed, but this morning was different. Her mind raced from one unanswered question to the other. She wondered why she had been passed over for the chief-of-staff position, what Thomas had meant by his comment regarding informal relationships, and why she found herself being attracted to him despite her promise to herself to keep her distance from this newcomer.

She realized that there was an element of truth in Thomas's assessment that the board had appointed him because of its desire for an infusion of new blood and new perspective. Katherine had heard from friends in different professions that often people filling positions temporarily did not get the permanent posts. She was disappointed that the board of Boxer Hospital had followed the trend, knowing that she was capable of doing work of the same caliber. She had so much to offer considering her strong interpersonal skills. She had developed a wonderful working relationship with all the other department heads.

Katherine disregarded Thomas's comment concerning the development of an informal working relationship as simply small talk and his attempt to put her at ease with her new boss. Under different circumstances, she might have been tempted to comply with his wishes, but today, exhausted from working too many long hours, she could not muster the graciousness required of her.

Of course, Katherine found Thomas Baker interesting. He was the only new man she had met in almost five years. She had been too busy at the hospital to develop a social life; her friends had all but stopped calling and trying to arrange dinners and blind dates for her. Her parents resigned themselves to being forever without a grandchild. Some days even her cat Mitzi seemed to forget who she was and refused to welcome her home when Katherine finally returned after a long day in the ER.

Sitting on the edge of her bed, Katherine looked in the mirror over her dresser and wondered if she would be able to muster the energy to go on a date, She looked as tired as she felt. She would have understood if no one found her attractive. The long hours had taken their toll. On many occasions, Katherine looked into the mirror at what had once been a pretty face only to find dark circles around her bloodshot eyes and lines pulling down the corners of her mouth.

Naturally, under different circumstances, she would have enjoyed the unsolicited attentions of the new chief of staff. She knew all the other men who staffed the hospital from working long hours with them. They certainly offered her little challenge and definitely no new surprises. She knew their weaknesses and strengths almost as well as she knew her own. She would have welcomed the opportunity to meet someone new. Now, the timing was not right.

So now, Thomas Baker had come on the scene, a handsome man with an unblemished personal past and a bright business future. He carried himself with the detached air of a man who was accustomed to being admired for his looks as well as his professional ability. His reputation for possessing strong financial management skills had made him the best choice for the job in the eyes of the board. Katherine was confident, although no less envious, that he would do his best for the patients and staff alike. Besides, she would be there to make sure that he did.

Pulling the comforter up to her neck and settling Mitzi into her sleeping position against her side, Katherine finally fell asleep. She would need all the rest she could get. She did not know what she would face under the new chief of staff . . . either personally or professionally.

Two

The next morning at eight as Katherine returned to the hospital and her job as head of the ER, she found that someone had taped a message to her usual seat in the physicians' lounge. Opening the folded paper she read that Thomas Baker had called the reception desk at seven thirty requesting a personal tour of the facility as soon as she reported to work. With a dry chuckle Katherine muttered, "One thing for sure, that man certainly is an early bird."

Leaving the contents of her in-box on the table, she immediately made the walk to the elevator that would provide her with express service to the administrative floors. Tapping her foot impatiently as she waited, Katherine wondered why the new chief of staff had asked her to conduct the tour when he had a secretary who would love the opportunity to display her knowledge of the hospital and to fawn all over him.

As the elevator door opened, Katherine listened to the sounds of silence so unusual in a busy hospital. She had always been impressed by the difference between the environment on the eighth floor and that of the ER. Photographs and colorful prints adorned the soft pastel walls of the administrative floor and posh thick carpet covered the floor. Clusters of seating arrangements sat along the sides with pots of lush greenery sitting alongside them. Each office suite had coffee and water machines. Everyone was busy, but no one appeared rushed or hassled. In the ER, patient charts covered every available surface.

Years ago someone had nailed a white board on which they wrote physician schedules and multiple bulletin boards for staff notifications and supply forms on the gray nondescript walls. The vinyl floors were usually clean but they showed the scuffing of thousands of pairs of feet regardless of the number of times someone mopped them. There was never a sufficient lull in the traffic to wax them.

To Katherine, the administrative floors did not reflect the true life of Boxer Hospital. For that, a visitor would have to stop in the ER or any of the other bustling services. When Frank Harriman occupied the eighth floor, he made a point of spending time on each floor every day. He said that no administrator could properly manage a living hospital without knowing the forces that gave it life. When she was the acting chief of staff, Katherine followed his example by choice and necessity. As she waited for Thomas Baker to join her, she wondered if he would do the same.

Walking through each service, Katherine again introduced Thomas to the department heads, who in turn made the introductions to their busy staffs. Everyone welcomed him warmly but with a touch of reserve. They had expected him to visit their floors, but they wondered what new plans and strategies he would implement as soon as the honeymoon period ended and he began his work in earnest.

When they reached the plastic surgery wing, Betsy took the opportunity to brag about the reputation of her service. Giving Katherine and Thomas the special guided tour, she explained with pride, "Boxer has one of the finest reputations in the country for reconstructive plastic surgery. Patients from all over the East Coast fly to Washington because they know that we have more experience in the field and better facilities than most other hospitals in the country. We do our fair share of cosmetic work, too, but we've made a name for ourselves through our specialty work."

Thomas smiled his appreciation for her enthusiasm and responded, "From what I've seen from your articles in various journals, Betsy, I'd say that your skill and expertise have contributed greatly to Boxer's reputation. According to Katherine's journals, in the last six months you've purchased the newest technology for repairing severed nerves resulting from dismemberment accidents. This department and the hospital owe you considerable thanks for leading the way in reconstructive surgery."

"Thank you, Thomas. My team and I have worked hard to make this one of Boxer's premier departments. However, let me be quick to point out that everyone here has the same dedication to medicine and to the hospital. I'm sure you'll see that neonatology has wonderful state-of-the-art technology for working with especially high-risk premature infants. Gerontology has recently implemented a social services component to its practice to help the families of those patients recovering from strokes. I won't tell you anymore; I don't want to steal Katherine's talk.

"Everyone here puts forth maximum effort to do the best for the hospital. We're a team of dedicated professionals. I've never known any personal jealousy to affect our interactions. We stand together as a very cohesive unit. Well, if you'll excuse me, I'll return to my work and let you continue with your tour. Stop in any time, Thomas."

"Thank you for the hospitality, Betsy. I'll do just that," Thomas said as he matched his strides with Katherine's and continued their walk through the halls of Boxer Hospital.

After Katherine had shown Thomas through all the other departments, they turned their attention to the ER where bedlam usually reigned. Actually, to Katherine, the high energy level of her colleagues seemed very ordinary and low key, but to an outsider, the fast-walking, fast-talking doctors and nurses must have looked as if they were operating at warp speed.

As she detailed the operation of her department from its doorway, Katherine found herself almost swelling with pride for the efficiency of the massive unit. As one of the city's largest teaching hospitals, Boxer also ran one of the most efficient emergency rooms. The location of the hospital gave it easy access from downtown Washington's busy mall, the shopping areas, and the many office buildings. It was sufficiently located on the fringe of the city's heartbeat that it also attracted residential patients from the nearby apartment buildings. And, although a private facility, Boxer did its share of charity work by providing care for the city's indigent population. All of these factors contributed to the constant flow of patients through the doors and to the efficiency of the department. The physicians and nurses were part of a well-honed machine that functioned on hours of practice and repetition. They were ready for any emergency.

As they rounded the corner, the emergency room code summoning all available personal sounded on the public address system. Looking quickly at Thomas, Katherine turned to him and said, "You'll have to excuse me, Dr. Baker, but that was a general alarm from the ER. I'll leave you now. We'll have to finish this tour at a later date."

"I'll go with you. This is just the kind of thing I wanted to see. I don't believe I can know a hospital until I see it in action," Thomas replied as he quickened his steps to keep up with the hurrying Katherine.

Reaching the ER, Katherine noticed a strange orderly panic as men in dark suits with earphones stood guard at the entrances and windows, talked on two-way radios, and patrolled the almost silent room. No one talked on the telephone, chatted with patients, or moved from the bathroom to the seating areas. For the first time since she'd arrived at Boxer, the ER was still and quiet.

As she rushed to the desk, one of the dark-suited men stepped forward and demanded to see her hospital identification. From the stern expression on his face and the bulge under his arm, Katherine knew that he meant business and had the authority to command respect. With trembling fingers, she pulled the badge from her pocket and handed it to him.

Watching him examine it, Katherine asked, "I'm the chief of this department. What seems to be the problem here? What's going on in my ER?"

"The president has been shot, Dr. Winters," the secret service officer answered in clipped tones. "Boxer was the closest hospital. We apologize for disrupting your operation, but we had no other choice."

"Oh, my God!" Katherine exclaimed as she jogged to the room where her team worked frantically over the fallen leader of the free world. She did not notice that Thomas had lagged behind in conference with the officer.

Quickly showing her identification to the secret service man stationed at the door of emergency room 7, Katherine eased into the crush of assembled specialists who worked feverishly to staunch the bleeding from the assassination attempt on the president's life. Elbowing her way forward, she took her place at the table as she pulled on surgical gloves.

From where she stood, Katherine could see that President Peters had been badly injured. His jacket and shirt had been cut away to reveal a gunshot wound in the lower abdomen that had punctured the small bowel. Quickly reading the faces of her staff, she saw that the injury was serious enough to cause beads of sweat to form on the top lip of Ben Cups, her chief resident. Looking around the room, Katherine could tell that the security detail and the privileged press were aware of the severity also. Their faces were clouded with concern, and their lips were tight lines as their eyes darted from the highly skilled professionals who labored over the president and the instruments in their hands. Despite the crowd of people in the small room, an eerie silence accompanied by the gurgling of the oxygen and the beeping of the heart monitor filled the air.

Relying on her years of training and drilling for treating the influx of patients from major accidents and natural disasters, Katherine checked President Peters's vital signs. Although he was stable, she did not like the bluish tinge that colored his lips. For a while, she watched in silence as her team and the specialists led by Jonathan Dell explored the site of the bullet wound.

Suddenly blood began to spurt from the wound and the monitor began to beep wildly. "His BP is falling, Jonathan. What happened?" Katherine asked as she moved forward. She wanted to be ready to assist in any way she could.

Perspiration ran from Jonathan's forehead as he replied, "I can't see a thing. The bullet must have nipped an artery from the amount of blood that's pouring out. My vision is totally obscured."

Leaning over the prostrate president, Katherine carefully sponged the area and sectioned the wound. Probing the gaping hole in the president's side with her sensitive fingers, she found the severed artery. "I've found it," Katherine announced. "Clamp, please, Alice. If I can just slip this clamp in place for a moment, we can stop the bleeding."

"His BP is still dropping, Doctor," Alice interjected as she quickly handed Katherine the clamp and checked the readings on the monitor.

"Two more units of blood, Alice. I've almost got it. It's so slippery that I keep losing it. Wait a minute . . . just a little more. Alice, shine that light a bit more to the right. That's it. Yes, I've got it. Jonathan, can you extract the bullet now while I hold this artery out of your way?" Katherine asked as she glanced quickly at the monitor that showed that the president's blood pressure had stabilized but was not improving.

"Good going. I've almost got it, Katherine. Done," Jonathan said, dropping the slug into a pan Alice held out for him. It clinked and rolled around leaving a bloody trail before coming to a halt against the side.

"Good work, Jonathan. Now, let's repair this artery. I've almost got it sutured. Give me a bit of suction in the center here. That's it. Okay. Yes, it's done. I'm checking for any sign of leakage. No, I don't see any. Let's make a note on his chart for the surgical team to inspect the site once more while they're repairing the bowl. How are his signs, Alice?" Katherine asked as she and Jonathan worked to make the next repair.

"He's stabilizing, doctor. His BP is up to ninety over sixty-five," Alice responded.

"Good. Now, let's work on that small bowel perforation.

There might not be much we can do until we transfer him to surgery. Ted, what do you see? Any chance of repairing it here?" Katherine suggested as the nurse wiped her sweaty forehead.

"No, the best I can do without a major incision is a patch job to prevent any more feces from oozing into the abdomen," Jonathan replied, busily stitching as much as he could through the bullet entry wound.

At that moment, a man Katherine recognized from news conferences as the president's private physician entered the room. Quickly introducing himself, he checked the chart, donned a surgical scrub and gloves, and joined the team. With him looking on, the secret service men relaxed a little, but not much. They still stayed on the fringes of the ER watching the president. They looked especially incongruous in their surgical scrubs, masks, and drawn weapons.

Giving a quick nod to Katherine as the chief of the emergency room, Dr. Flowers queried, "What can I do to be of assistance?" Like everyone else in the room, he was prepared to do whatever was required to pull the president through the assassination attempt.

"Welcome to Boxer, Dr. Flowers. Stand by, if you will. We have things pretty much under control. Ted, how are you doing on that bowel resection?" Katherine asked as she prepared to pack the wound

"I've just about done all I can do. I'll be out of here in a few minutes. I've reconnected it as best I can, but it's still a mess. You'll be able to pack the wound in just a second. I've almost finished making the repairs that I can. That slug certainly ripped the bowel to shreds. From the feel of things, I'd say they will need to remove quite a bit. They will be able to see better than I can once they get him up to the OR," Ted said, making rapid stitches to prevent any more feces from infiltrating the abdomen. The surgeons in the operating room would make the lasting repair. Ted only wanted to stabilize the patient so they could move him out of the emergency room.

"Alice, give me a reading on the vitals, please," Katherine

asked as she packed the wound and readied the president for transfer to the operating room.

"He's stable, doctor. His BP is up to one ten over sixty-five," Alice replied, quickly noting the progress on the president's chart.

"Great. We're done here. Let's get him upstairs," Katherine announced as she removed her gloves.

"Your team certainly works quickly and efficiently, Dr. Winters. My compliments," Ted Flowers said with respect in his voice.

"Thank you, doctor, my people train for this kind of disaster, although we pray that we'll never need to put our skills into play," Katherine answered, shouting over the noise of the secret service radios. She had not taken the time to look around the emergency room, but she could imagine that her staff would have made a very favorable impression. They had always performed well under pressure.

Throwing her bloody gloves and scrubs into the hamper, Katherine turned to the waiting orderlies and secret service men and instructed, "Take the president up to operating room 1. The surgeons are standing by to receive him."

Immediately, the two-way secret service two-way radios began to crackle as instructions for transporting the president and securing the elevator and halls passed from one agent to another. Almost as quickly, the orderlies gathered the pole holding the blood and saline solution and the monitor and began pushing the gurney into the empty hallway.

After the president left the emergency room, Katherine could almost hear the collective sigh of relief as everyone returned to their usual pace. Now that the waiting room was empty of secret service men, it was strangely quiet. For the first time, Katherine wondered about the missing patients and about Thomas, who she had left standing alone while she worked feverishly over the fallen president.

Reading the unasked question in her eyes, Thomas said, "The secret service men routed all emergency traffic to another hospital while the president was in the ER. That should give you some time to clean up, debrief, and relax before you open for business again."

Nodding in agreement and turning to her emergency room team, Katherine said, "Ladies and gentlemen, I would like to commend you on a job well done. You have certainly risen to the challenge of working in a pressure-cooker environment with the eyes of all the world on you. You made me very proud of you."

Giving themselves a much deserved round of applause, the emergency room staff threw their blood splattered scrubs in the nearest receptacles and began setting up for the usual flow of patients. The gunshot wounds, the traffic accident victims, and the sick would return as soon as the Secret Service loosened its grip on Boxer.

With a sigh and a stretch Katherine commented, "I bet the Public Relations Department worked overtime on that case, too. They must be swamped up there. I don't envy them having to work with a White House that wants to release as little information as possible for security reasons and the press that wants all the news that's fit to print.

"As much as the president's team would like to keep this incident quiet, the public has a right to know about the assassination attempt and the president's condition. Boxer is caught in the middle. Naturally, we want to abide by the desires of the White House, but we need to give out the information. It certainly makes good press to publicize that your hospital saved the life of the President of the United States. Regardless of how tired I am at this moment, I would not change places with the people in Boxer's public relations department for anything.

"At any rate, they must have been up to their ears in telephone calls and interviews while we were busy. As hectic as it was down here, I would not want to have the responsibility of cooperating fully with the needs and demands of the Oval Office, the thirst of the press for a hot story, and the desires of the people to be informed.

"This certainly has been a day I don't ever want to repeat," Katherine concluded as she ushered Thomas into the lounge for a cup of much-needed coffee. In the turmoil of the emergency surrounding the assassination attempt, she had forgotten that he had accompanied her to the emergency room. She had not felt the need to include him in her work. Realizing that he would be in the way, Thomas had spent his time in conversation between the head of the secret service team and the public relations office and served as the liaison between the board and the White House. Not having been invited to join the emergency room team, Thomas had concentrated on the area in which his skills as an arbitrator were most needed during the crisis.

Thomas took the offered cup of strong black coffee and replied, "I had overlooked the possibility that the president or some other dignitary or head of state might be a patient at Boxer. With all the military hospitals in the area, I had thought that all of their treatment would have been directed to one of those facilities, but in an emergency, it's very possible that Boxer might be the closest one as it was today. That's even more reason why we must remain on the cutting edge of technology. We must be ready for any emergency and any patient."

"Boxer has always been one of the best hospitals in Washington, and I'm sure that under your leadership it will continue to be. At the same time, it has also been one of the most employee-sensitive facilities, too. I'd hate for us to lose sight of that benefit of working here," Katherine said as they sipped their coffee and listened to the sounds from the ER. She had hoped that her discussion had not been too forceful and overly proud of the hospital that consumed all of her life.

Looking at Katherine's tired, strained, beautiful face, Thomas decided that he was not ready to leave the ER yet. He wanted more time in her company. Thinking of small talk as a diversion from the chaos of the morning, he asked, "What do people in this town do for leisure? I know the ER staff is very dedicated, but there must be some downtime during which people relax a little. Where do you go for entertainment? What do you do to have fun?"

"Well, as you're already aware, you have membership in a country club that comes along with your position as chief of staff. It has a fabulous golf course and tennis courts that I suggest you enjoy to the fullest whenever you can steal a few minutes from your busy schedule.

"We also have picnics during the summer and a Christmas party. Usually, we get together by department, which seems to work well since we spend so much time together anyway. Most of our friendships seem to be based on department affiliation, so I guess it's only natural that we should play together.

"We do challenge other departments in softball games. I often take on Betsy's department since she and I are best friends. Surgery has a pretty good team, too.

"The picnics that are organized by department or as an entire hospital activity are probably the most fun. We tend to let our hair down quite a bit at those. We hold them in Rock Creek Park from early morning until late at night so that everyone gets a chance to come. There's always plenty of food, good times, beer by the keg, and music."

Pouring another cup of the strong brew, Thomas asked, "What about the theater? I've heard that Washington has been getting some good shows lately. Is that true?"

"Oh, definitely. I've never had much luck in arranging my time so that I can attend the theater or the opera. As head of this department, I've had to cover when other people have been absent. I find that it's very difficult for me to plan anything long term," Katherine replied. She wondered why Thomas would ask her about Washington's social life when he had a secretary who could make any arrangements he would like. If she had been the suspicious type, she would have thought that he was sounding her out for possible dates. As it was, Katherine decided that Thomas was only making small talk so that they could get to know each other.

As if reading her mind Thomas suggested, "I'm quite fond

of the theater. Being from New York, I usually take in several shows each year. I'd appreciate it if you could find the time to attend one with me sometime. Since I'm new in town and don't know anyone, you'd be doing me a great favor. We could work around your schedule, even purchase tickets at the last minute. I'm very flexible."

"Thank you, Dr. Baker. I'll keep your generous invitation in mind. Perhaps now that you're onboard, I'll be able to delegate my work and have a little free time. Speaking of work, now that the president is safely in the operating suite, things will soon begin to return to normal down here. I'd best return to my desk. I have my entire in-box to read," Katherine said, easing into the flow of people who were beginning to visit the ER from the other floors of the hospital. The word had spread that the president had been a patient and was in surgery at that moment. The curious wanted to see where he had lain in the ER.

"The pleasure has been all mine, Katherine. You certainly know how to give an exciting tour. Perhaps we might grab a quick lunch together soon. I'd better see how things are going in surgery and public relations. I saw an entire battalion of the press corps outside. They seemed to be mingling with employees and the usual knowledgeable spectators," Thomas replied, entering the elevator and pushing the button that would speed him to the surgical suite.

"Keep me posted, please. I'm available to help out any way I can," Katherine responded as the door closed between them.

Returning to her in-box, she forced herself to forget that the spotlight should have been on her and not on Thomas. Her ER had saved the president's life. She should be the one to face the world with the updates on his condition.

"Excuse me, Katherine, but I thought you'd like to know. The president has come out of surgery and sends his thanks to your skillful emergency room staff. He was resting peacefully in the intensive care. It won't be long before he's transferred to his suite of rooms," Edward Ramsey said as he poked his head into the lounge.

"Thanks, Ed. I appreciate the news," Katherine answered, relief flowing through her body.

"What can I say? We make a good team. By the way, Thomas Baker is holding a press conference in a few minutes. We're expected to be there," Edward replied as he saluted. Looking a bit tired from the strain of operating on the president, the chief of surgery smiled and quickly left Katherine to her work.

"I'll be there as soon as I finish this last case," Katherine responded with as much interest as she could muster. If it had not been for the board's decision, she would be the one giving the speech. Katherine did not hunger for public attention, but she did feel that as the chief of the ER staff that saved the president's life, she should be the one to face the press.

Taking her place among the other department heads who lined the auditorium walls, Katherine tried to push away the irritation she felt at having to watch Thomas deliver a speech that by rights should have been hers. If the president had been shot only a day earlier, she would have been the one to stand squinting into the camera lights in readiness to fend off the inquiring press.

Katherine watched as Thomas entered the room. From his expression, she could tell that he was taken aback by the crowd that filled the hospital's large auditorium. He was not a local of Washington, where photographers seemed to grow on every corner, and his reaction showed that he had never seen so many cameras, microphones, or reporters. Looking around the room, she, too, was impressed by the massive amounts of equipment and the number of journalists who lined the aisles, filled every seat, and pressed against the back wall. Only once in her tenure had there been quite so much news coverage when emergency crews had brought the survivors of a bomb explosion at a nearby association to Boxer.

Clearing his throat and tapping lightly on the microphone at the speaker's podium, Thomas waited until the roar of voices decreased. Speaking slowly and with confidence he issued the statement he had been rehearsing for the last hour saying, "Ladies and gentlemen of the press, this has indeed been an eventful and frightening day for Boxer, the nation, and the world. My staff has been called upon to labor under the most trying circumstances and has risen to the challenge of performing with the eyes of the world on our emergency room and surgical suite. I am very proud of their performance and of the news that I will share with you today.

"I am very happy to announce that the president is out of danger and recovering nicely. We removed a thirty-two caliber slug from his abdomen that had severed his small bowel. After removing approximately six inches of intestine to repair the shredded area, we closed the incision of approximately eight inches upon seeing no further damage to the surrounding tissue. He was transferred to the recovery room and then to the intensive care unit where he is still being monitored. He is alert and joking with my staff. His personal physician was with the president the entire time and is still at his side. Although he is a bit groggy from the anesthesia, he is in complete control of his faculties.

"Our plan is to transfer him to his room later this evening. He should be discharged in approximately one week. At this time, there is nothing more I can tell you about his condition as the president is progressing well and as expected. Mr. Franklin of the White House press corps will answer any questions you might have. Thank you."

Walking past the assembled staff, Thomas smiled and waved as they applauded his speech. Scanning the crowd, he found Katherine in the midst of them. She, too, appeared pleased with his effort on behalf of the hospital. As he approached, she smiled and gave him a thumb's up.

As Thomas reached her side, Katherine offered, "Nice job, Dr. Baker. That should keep the press off our backs for a while. I've issued the usual statement to my staff that all questions from the outside are to be referred to the public relations office.

Things have pretty much returned to normal in the emergency room with a steady stream of patients beginning to arrive. The White House has lifted the restriction against ambulance traffic, although security is still tight."

"I suppose we'll have to live with the presence of the Secret Service in the hospital the whole time he's a patient here. We'll have to take the intrusion in stride. As long as they don't interfere in our ability to provide care for the president and our other patients, we can live with them for a while.

"Katherine, I realize that we've gotten off to a rocky start. This would have been your press conference if I hadn't been hired. I just want to tell you that I'm incredibly impressed with your professionalism and your ability to manage the ER. I had the opportunity to watch you perform today and to demonstrate your skill. You motivate your staff by becoming one with them, yet you maintain the appropriate distance that never lets them forget that you're the boss. That takes talent and the awareness of people's needs. I'm very impressed by what I witnessed today."

"Thank you, doctor. My staff and I were simply performing the job we have trained hard to do. I'll admit that there was the extra stress of working on the president, but he was still only an injured man who needed our attention.

"But, you're correct. This would have been my press conference just as this would have been my hospital if you had not arrived on the scene. Although I will do nothing to sabotage your plans for Boxer, I feel it is only fair that I tell you that I will do everything in my power to prove to the board that I should have been given that position and not you.

"When you leave here, this place will mean nothing more to you than one more success on your résumé. For me, this is home and these people are family. I've worked too hard to turn it over without a fight. Maybe I'll get lucky and the board will see the error of its ways before your tenure is up. Boxer might be mine again even sooner rather than later" Katherine declared with determination. She could not allow his warmth and obvious interest in her to cloud her determination to reclaim her position at Boxer.

"Very well, Katherine, I'll remember that. I like a good battle. But I want you to keep something in mind, too. if I leave here after my job of stabilizing Boxer is done, I intend to take you with me. I've never met anyone, man or woman, with your energy and determination. In the few hours that I've been here, I've read about your accomplishments and seen you in action. I want you on my team personally as well as professionally. You're on notice, Katherine," Thomas replied with as much conviction as Katherine.

"I'm flattered, Dr. Baker, but not moved," Katherine responded as she turned and walked through the thinning crowd. She had work to do and had allowed Thomas Baker to distract her from it long enough.

Chuckling, Thomas returned to his office. He had never met anyone quite like Katherine Winters, MD. Instantly he knew what she would do if she were in his place. Picking up the telephone, he ordered flowers for each department of the hospital as his way of thanking them for a job well done. He requested that the florist send special arrangements to the ER, operating area, intensive care unit, and the public relations department.

Before he hung up, Thomas added another saying, "I'd like something special delivered to Katherine Winters, MD. Yes, she's the head of the ER. No, I don't want roses. I'd like something that will last a long time. Do you have any dried flowers? Right. Some nice sturdy lotus pods would be just fine. Send them with a card that reads, 'To auspicious beginnings.' Thanks."

Katherine was not amused when the arrangement arrived two hours later. She sat in the physicians' lounge staring at the card and wondering what her next move should be. She had to show this man that she could not be bought for the price of bunch of dried seed pods despite the fact that the arrangement was quite elegant in its austerity. She had not missed the underlying message of its relative permanence either. Thomas was again sending the hint that he meant to make their duo a lasting relationship.

When Betsy dropped in later on her way to the lab, she looked from Katherine's sour expression to the large display of dried flowers. Unable to refrain from teasing her friend she laughed, "I'd say you have an admirer with a need to give you a forceful message."

Katherine only gave her a sideways glance as she continued to work at the little table made even smaller by the large arrangement. "Not funny, Betsy," she said, as she reached for yet another case to review.

"I wonder where he'll take you to dinner. Let's see. What restaurant has a name that would continue this thought? Too bad we don't have any place called the 'Now and Forever' or 'The Eternity' or 'Beyond Tomorrow.' Or he could buy you some of those candies called 'Now and Later,' " Betsy mused with great enjoyment at Katherine's increasing irritation. Not waiting to hear Katherine's sarcastic reply, she hurried down the hall to finish her errand.

Katherine did not look up as the sound of her friend's footsteps and laughter blended with the other noises of the ER. She had too much to do to waste time thinking about Thomas Baker, and she refused to allow Betsy's pathetic attempts at levity make her any angrier than she already was.

Three

She should not have worried about the adjustment to the new chief of staff. As the weeks passed, Katherine found herself learning to appreciate Thomas's quick, although somewhat unusual, sense of humor and skillful management of the bottom line, although she never lost sight of the goal she had set for herself. She looked forward to the leisurely tone of his Monday morning meetings. She thought the others were growing to appreciate him, also, although no one as yet was ready to say that Thomas had replaced Frank Harriman or her in their affection. They still maintained a wait-and-see attitude toward him. Everyone was aware that there was always a honeymoon period when someone new came onto the job. They reserved passing judgment until after he had been among them for a while.

Katherine knew that Thomas was a smart, savvy man. As an African-American, he had not risen to his level of power and authority by being naive, gullible, or inept. He would know that he could not immediately affect change. She was sure that he was aware of when to jump into a situation and when to stand back. She had watched him reason that he had to wait until the management team learned to accept him and felt confident that his guidance before he took action. His patience would serve him well. She knew that after he had gained their trust, he would suggest the strategies that would enable Boxer to move successfully into the future.

Katherine estimated that Thomas would wait approximately

two months before slowly beginning to implement his changes. By that time, the department heads would have begun to think that he was one of them and that his suggestions matched their own. She would be waiting when he made his move.

Katherine still could not bring herself to address him by his first name, although everyone else did. He referred to her using her given name just as he did with all of the other department heads. She was the only one who continued the old style of formality. Despite the favorable reception Thomas had received from some of the other members of the Boxer community, Katherine would not let down her guard.

She knew that her hesitation was not merely professional. Katherine found herself being drawn to Thomas more every day. He had made his attraction to her known in many ways, too. From the casual but repeated invitations to lunch in the cute bistro-style restaurants in the neighborhood to offhand references to movies he would like to see, she could tell that Thomas was only waiting for her to give him the nod. She did not want to let down her guard and give in to her emotions until she proved to him that she was a forceful manager. Despite the change in authority at the top, she needed to demonstrate that she was worthy of the position he now held. She knew that he would not be the chief of staff for more than a few years. She wanted the position when he left. Katherine did not want to give the board an excuse for passing her over this time.

Yet, on days when the Washington sky was especially blue, Katherine found it difficult to remain remote and distant. When she saw him casually strolling across the hospital grounds with the sun playing on his warm brown skin and sparkling in his hair, she wanted to drop her resolve and go to him. However, she knew she could not do that and remain true to herself. Before she could welcome his embrace, the intellectual challenge of his conversation, and his comradery, Katherine had to become comfortable within herself and with her return to the ER.

In the days following his arrival, Katherine had put her own plans into effect. She had begun cultivating the most influential

A SURE THING 45

members of the board. Carefully so that she could not be accused of doing anything unethical behind Thomas's back, she invited a few of them to visit the ER and see it in action.

The three men and two women arrived attired in either black or navy suits and represented the most influential bankers and attorneys in Washington. They carried briefcases that appeared to be integral parts of their bodies. Their faces reflected neither curiosity nor disinterest. It was clear that they came to visit in answer to an invitation that they could not decline as board members in good standing. It was their civic duty to pay a call on their hospital.

Katherine had prepared an impressive film of life in the emergency room as a supplement to her brief talk and tour. She had dug into her department's budget and hired an advertising firm to prepare the script. They had spent over a week in the ER capturing just the right footage to tell the story of the dedicated staff. She was determined to make a lasting impression on the board. When Thomas Baker left Boxer, they would know without a doubt that Katherine was the perfect person to assume command of the hospital.

As Katherine thanked the somber-faced board members for taking time from their busy schedules to visit Boxer, she wondered if all of her effort would have any effect on these people who did not smile at her corny opening joke. At least it would save her the embarrassment of standing in front of them for longer than absolutely necessary. Already their penetrating gazes were making her feel very uncomfortable. She could almost read the silent criticism on their stony faces.

Squaring her shoulders, Katherine continued with her prepared talk in which she clearly outlined the changes she had implemented to make the ER even more efficient. Speaking clearly and slowly, she said, "The emergency room of today is very different from the one of the past. Modern technology has given us the tools with which to respond more effectively to the traumas experienced by our patients. Portable EKG, EEG, and x-ray machines have provided us with on-the-spot analysis

and improved diagnostic capability. Greater coordination with
the labs has afforded our patients quicker response time in assessing their vital statistics. Continuous training of personnel
has exposed my staff to all the latest techniques available to
physicians who practice emergency room medicine. In other
words, we are an emergency room staff that is ready for anything, as we proved in the recent presidential assassination attempt.

"Now, let me share our story with you. If you'll focus your
attention on the screen, you will see a video that will share with
you the typical day in the life of the emergency room. After
you view the film, I'll take you on a personal tour during which
time my staff will be available to answer any questions you
might have concerning our operation."

Motioning to the technician at the back of the small auditorium, Katherine took her seat on the sidelines. From her angle,
she could watch the faces of the board members as they viewed
the film. She hoped they would be as impressed by the performance of the staff as she was.

As the images flickered across the screen, Katherine occasionally peeked at the assembled men and women. Their faces
transformed from being closed and unmoving to wide-eyed as
the scenes played out before them. She watched as they gasped
at the sight of startlingly red blood flowing from deep cuts and
gunshot wounds. They recoiled at the sounds of pain emanating
from the sick and injured who arrived on stretchers and on foot.
They all but cheered when scenes of treating little children with
severed fingers played across the screen. One of the women
wiped tears from her eyes when the episode about the premature
delivery of a crack baby appeared. The infant looked so helpless
and fragile, and the emergency room physician loomed so large
despite the incredibly gentle care he provided.

When the film ended, Katherine rose and returned to the
podium at the front of the room. From the smiles on the faces
of the board members, she could tell that the film had done its
job. She mentally made note to use it as a fund-raiser to show

to the many financial patrons of the hospital. From the reactions of this target audience, Katherine realized that the video would open many checkbooks and start the flow of black ink.

"Ladies and gentlemen, if you will follow me, I will take you to the ER where you will have the chance to see the staff in action firsthand. I would like to remind you that nothing you will see will have been staged for your entertainment. I have not planted actors in the ER for your visit. Therefore, you might see things that are upsetting. However, that is the nature of life in an emergency room. Now, if you will follow me, I will take you on your tour," Katherine said, motioning toward the exit at the back of the room.

Katherine did not speak as she led the five board members down the hall. Unless one of them posed a question, she intended to allow her speech, the video, and the sights in the ER speak for themselves. There was nothing she could say that would increase the impact of actually visiting the ER.

As she had hoped, the ER was packed. Homeless with festering sores on their dirty feet waited in the reception area beside children with broken arms, old people with bruises from falling down, and drug abusers suffering from withdrawal. Despite the cooling air from the air-conditioning, the room had a unique smell of body odor, medicine, vomit, blood, and stale food. Watching the faces of the five visitors, Katherine could tell that they missed none of the elements that added to the ambiance of the ER.

"This place is a mob scene. Is it always like this?" asked John Baxter, a prominent attorney and the chair of the hospital's employee benefits subcommittee.

Scanning the room, Katherine answered, "We do have some days with light traffic, but this is fairly representative of our average day. We work hard down here twenty-four hours a day, seven days a week. There are no holidays in the ER, Mr. Baxter."

Delicately touching her nose with a handkerchief, Elizabeth Palmer asked, "Does it always smell like this in here? Can't anyone do something to freshen the air?" Ms. Palmer was the chair of the facilities management subcommittee and was the person to whom Katherine had repeatedly submitted budget figures for a new ventilation system for the ER.

"Unfortunately, we're part of the main hospital's air-conditioning system. As a result, the smells from the kitchen flow through here to mix with those of bodily fluid, feces, and unwashed bodies. I've asked for a separate system that was specifically designed for emergency room applications, but my budget requests have not been filled. Perhaps when the committee meets again you might describe the conditions under which we work every day now that you've experienced it firsthand," Katherine replied as she mentally ordered the new air filtration system.

Suddenly the door to the ambulance bay opened and two paramedics rushed into the ER pushing a stretcher on which lay a motionless boy. His lips were decidedly blue and his arms and legs twitched convulsively. Froth had accumulated at the corners of his lips and trickled down his cheeks. His eyelids fluttered and his eyes rolled upward.

Immediately the ER team sprang into action as the nurses and doctors transferred the boy to the gurney and strapped monitors to his chest. Ron Holmes, the internal medicine specialist dedicated to the ER, listened as the paramedic recited the information they had on the patient, "We found him lying on the street. There are no signs of injury or trauma. His pulse is weak and thready. There was no identification on him and none of the spectators who gathered around us knew anything about him."

As Dr. Holmes started working on the boy, Katherine allowed her attention to shift from the scene in emergency room 3 to the faces of the board members. All five of them stood motionless at her side. This was their first visit to the ER despite all their years on the board. Now, they found themselves watching real-life drama play out before their eyes. Katherine wondered if the sights would be more than they could handle.

Standing next to Katherine, Elizabeth Palmer whispered as

if talking in her sleep. Leaning closer, Katherine could hear that she was repeatedly reciting a prayer for the boy's recovery and the physician's skill. Her eyes never left the face of the stricken boy as her lips moved over the familiar words.

Mark Evans was equally as moved. Katherine knew from his biography that he was the father of a ten-year-old boy. She could imagine that he was probably thinking about his own son, who could find himself in the same situation from sudden illness.

Marilyn West, the other woman in the team of visiting board members, suddenly clutched her throat and gasped, "Oh, no, the boy's heart stopped. Look, they're turning on the paddles. This is too much. It's just horrible. How can you stand this every day? Oh my!"

Returning her attention to her staff, Katherine excused herself and joined them in working over the child. As a pediatric emergency room specialist, she felt that her expertise might come in handy. She could do more for the boy as a member of the team than she could by standing on the sidelines with the visitors. As she walked away, the hum of the electroshock machine momentarily drowned out Elizabeth Palmer's whispered voice.

"How does he look, Ron?" Katherine asked as she donned her scrubs and slipped her hands into the gloves that would protect her from hepatitis and AIDS infection.

"Not good. We're having one hell of a time stabilizing him. I'm going to pump his stomach now. The blood gases show that he ingested a handful or two of pain killers. Maybe that will give us a chance to save him. I sure wish we knew something about his boy," Ron answered without looking up from the tube he slowly inserted into the child's mouth and down into his stomach.

Immediately, the contents of the boy's stomach began to spill out into the pan. Counting aloud, one of the nurses said, "Thirty capsules. They look like extra strength over-the-counter pain killers. This kid was determined to get someone's attention."

"What a shame! I wonder what could drive a kid to do something like that. From the way he's dressed, I'd say that he's from a caring home. I can't even imagine what must have pushed him to this. Call psych and order a consult, please. When he wakes up, we'll need to get the name of his parents from him if we can. He's going to be one sick kid for a few days and will need his family with him," Katherine ordered, looking down on the lifeless child. His coloring had begun to return and the twitching had ceased.

While they worked, Katherine had totally forgotten about the board members who stood with their faces pressed against the glass. Her main interest at the moment had been in saving the boy's life, not in obtaining the air filtration equipment or in winning the favor of the board. Now that he was out of trouble, she again turned her attention to her visitors.

"Sorry, folks, I didn't know that we'd have this much excitement down here during your visit. I hope this hasn't been too much for you," Katherine said as she rejoined them.

"How's the boy? Will he be all right?" asked Marilyn West, who had almost rubbed her hands raw with worry.

"He'll be fine once the effect of the pills is out of his system. From our count, he ingested more than thirty pills, but he'll pull through without any adverse side effects. Our biggest problem now is locating his parents. Social services will take care of that for us.

"If you've seen enough, I've ordered a bit of lunch for us. Let's return to the conference room, shall we?" Katherine urged as she started walking out of the ER with the board members silently following her. She was pleased not only with the performance of her staff but with the reaction of the visitors. The morning had been an even greater success than she had originally hoped.

As Katherine led them back through the winding halls to the conference room, Elizabeth Palmer walked beside her. In a voice still trembling from the sights she had just witnessed, she said to Katherine, "Submit your budget request for the air filtration system again, Dr. Winters. I'm sure my committee will be more supportive this time."

With a sly smile, Katherine replied, "Thank you, Ms. Palmer. I'll do that as soon as I return to my office. I hope your visit to the ER hasn't been too taxing."

"Oh, no, but it certainly has been an eye-opener," she responded.

Katherine had to force herself to contain her feeling of euphoria over her success with the visiting board members as she nibbled at the lunch of artichokes and spinach salad. She had executed her plan perfectly with the unexpected help of the little boy's attempted suicide. Unfortunate as it was, his case had tipped the scale for the ER and made her efforts much easier.

For the first time in her career, Katherine had played the game of politics. She had courted a select group of influential board members and won their favor. She had stressed her department's efficiency, its need for funding, and its personal side with just enough balance to be credible without appearing overly emotional about her work or her staff. She had encouraged the visitors to experience the department at work, which proved to be a touch of brilliance.

As she watched the guests try to eat with stomachs that rebelled against the food after the sights and smells of the ER, Katherine almost smiled at her success. It had been so easy, yet a lesson that she had taken so long to learn. If she had only played the game sooner, she would be the chief of staff and not Thomas Baker. Tucking this new awareness away for the future, she ate hungrily of her salad and relished the moment.

As Katherine sat in her office trying to catch up on her paperwork, Gwen Tomer from social services arrived. Since they were colleagues and old friends, she did not wait for Katherine to offer her a seat. She immediately sank her tired frame into the soft upholstery and sighed deeply.

Folding her hands in her lap, Gwen said slowly, "Thanks to the combined efforts of the police and my department, we have found the boy's parents. It seems that the child has been under a physician's care for depression and had run away from home following an argument with his mother. The distressed woman had searched everywhere and reported him missing to the police, who coordinated the two reports. The parents now sit in their son's hospital room. It's really a sad case. Sometimes, I hate my job. If I weren't a strong woman, the things I have to see would send me to a shrink."

"Stress is an occupational hazard for both of us, Gwen. Thanks for getting on this case so quickly. That boy needed his parents with him. You done good, girl," Katherine remarked as she studied Gwen's haggard face. Her friend was the mother of two children and suffered great pains of empathy when a child was involved in one of the cases referred to her.

Forcing herself to rise from the comfortable chair Gwen said, "It has been a day. See you later, Katherine."

Later that evening Katherine joined Betsy for a quick dinner of pizza and salad in Betsy's apartment. She happily shared her news to her friend saying, "I guess I've finally learned how to play among the big boys. It took me long enough. I sure wish I had involved myself in the political side of hospital operation while I was acting chief of staff. Thomas wouldn't be sitting in my office now if I had."

As Betsy watched Katherine struggle with the conflicts between her interest in Thomas and her need to demonstrate her managerial abilities, she saw what Katherine tried to deny to herself. Katherine's competition was not Thomas, but her own drive and ambition. She could not accept the board's rejection of her because it stung her pride. Katherine had to prove, not to the board or to Thomas, but to herself that she was capable of managing a challenging unit like the ER. Betsy knew that her friend would be happy only when she could look at her accomplishments and feel pride. She hoped that Katherine would come to the realization quickly, before she threw away the opportunity for love that waited for her in the person of Thomas Baker. Plaques noting accomplishments were reassuring, but a special someone was so much easier to take to bed.

* * *

Katherine had estimated the amount of time Thomas would wait before beginning his changes to the management of the hospital almost to the day. By early summer, he had taken the first steps and caused quite an upheaval. She returned after a long, peaceful four-day weekend to find the hospital in turmoil with almost no one speaking to anyone else. Someone had spread the word that Thomas Baker intended to rotate department heads and perhaps lay off a few, causing everyone to worry about pink slips, security, and duplicitous behavior as colleagues jockeyed for the remaining positions. The feeling of hospitality, congeniality, and collegiality that usually filled the hospital and especially the ER had vanished overnight.

"What happened? Everything was just fine four days ago. Everyone was tired and overworked as usual, but at least we were still speaking to each other," Katherine asked Betsy as soon as they had a moment to themselves.

"The same atmosphere is upstairs in my department, too. Everyone says it's because of Thomas Baker. They're blaming him for the sudden change. You've read his memo. I guess I can see how some people might be a little concerned about the rotations, but I'm not sure what caused the job scare. I don't think rotating people is such a bad idea, personally, but you can't convince the majority of the people to like it," Betsy answered, licking the last drop of yogurt, honey, and fruit from her spoon.

The two friends sat in silence as Katherine mulled over the situation. At that hour of the afternoon, almost no one ate in the hospital cafeteria except those people who had missed lunch and were too hungry to wait until dinner. They had the huge room to themselves except for a cluster of nurses at the other side who were too engrossed in their own conversation to look up when Katherine and Betsy entered.

Until Thomas arrived, Katherine would have felt comfortable going to Frank Harriman with concerns about employee reaction to a well-intentioned memo he had written. Now, however, since she did not know Thomas Baker that well, she felt hesitant. Katherine was concerned that he might think that she was criticizing his managerial skills if she offered suggestions or comments, although she had welcomed conversation with the department heads when she was the acting chief of staff.

Finally deciding that there was only one course of action, Katherine pushed back her plate of half-eaten, tasteless hospital chicken salad and rose from her chair. Looking down at Betsy's concerned face she said, "I guess there's only one thing for me to do. I have to sit down with Dr. Baker and let him know the chaos he has caused. I really don't want to force an encounter with him. I'm still hoping that we can establish a hands-off kind of relationship so that we can both have our own space. I'm sure that the intent of his memo was not to disturb the troops, but it has happened and he needs to straighten out the confusion. Wish me luck."

"I'm sure you won't need it. He'll understand that you're only looking out for his and everyone else's best interest," Betsy answered consolingly. Watching her best friend walk away, she momentarily considered talking her out of meeting with Thomas Baker, but she did not. She knew that if anyone could stop the spread of panic among the hospital staff, Katherine was the one to do it. Besides, if they worked together to convince the other heads of the feasibility of this project, with luck a relationship might develop between them.

The walk to the chief of staff's office had never seemed so long or so lonely. In all the months Katherine had rushed down that hall, she had never been alone. Happy, laughing people had always filled the space as they gathered in little conversation groups, stood around the candy and soda machines, and visited in the courtyards that branched off from the busy thoroughfare. Now, however, no one lingered. The once bustling corridor looked like one of the old television western portrayals of a ghost town.

To her surprise when she entered the office door, Katherine

found that not even his secretary, the faithful Sylvia Brown, waited to greet her. Frowning, she quickly glanced at Thomas's calendar, which lay open on the abandoned desk, and found that he should be available for a conference with her. Mustering the last of her resolve, she knocked on the heavy paneled door and waited.

"Yes?" Thomas Baker's booming baritone answered. "Come in."

"Dr. Baker, if this is a good time for you, I'd like a moment or two to talk with you. There's something we need to discuss regarding personnel," Katherine ventured as she walked across the once familiar mauve and blue geometric patterned carpet to the desk. He sat with his jacket off and the sleeves of his shirt rolled up to the elbow, revealing muscular forearms and broad shoulders.

"The name's Thomas, Katherine, and I am free at the moment. What can I do for you? I've just been going over your journals for the last six months or so. They're very complete and quite informative," he replied, motioning to the blue leather sofa where he joined her for their conversation.

"I'm glad they're of help to you. I tried to keep accurate notes on everything of importance during the time I served as the acting chief of staff. But I'm not here to talk about that right now, although I'm available any time you feel a need for clarification. I came to see you about the worry and concern many members of the staff have expressed over the pending reassignments. You know, Thomas, people become content in their jobs and really don't welcome change," Katherine commented, charging right into the discussion.

"Thank you for your concern, but I'm aware of the reactions from the staff. As soon as the memo made its rounds, people began bombarding me with their concerns in voices that could not be mistaken for friendly. However, regardless of their reactions, the plans stay as outlined. A shake-up is healthy; it forces us to take a step back and to assess how we go about our jobs. Some people might find that they've reached a time when a more permanent change would be to their liking. Others will discover that they could benefit from additional training. A few will decide to revamp their original departments to reflect the new procedures they've learned. I think a vast majority will find that the skills they've honed all these years will hold them in good stead in a new environment."

"If I might ask, Thomas, what was the reason behind the reorganization? Have you seen any problems within the departments? I thought everything was sound," Katherine ventured carefully, aware that his ego had been bruised by the vehement challenges of the other department chairs.

"Efficiency and money . . . plain and simple. Although the hospital has been operating in the black and making a modest profit, the board wants to make more, to expand the facility, and to move to a cutting-edge position. That's why they brought me onboard. I have a pretty good reputation for getting things done. They wanted someone who does not have any emotional attachments to the hospital to take a close, hard look at all departments and decided where services can be modernized, eliminated, or expanded. No department will be exempt, although I'm only starting with a few at a time. Soon I'll get around to studying the others. I suspect that I'll find a good solid conservative organization that just needs the right infusion of properly directed funds to set it on its ear. That's what I found at the other hospitals at which I've worked. I can't imagine that this one will be any different," Thomas replied with a calculated offhanded indifference that made Katherine's anger rise. He was talking very impersonally about the hospital that for the last few months had been the center of her life both day and night. She had given every free minute of her time to running Boxer during her tenure and did not appreciate his quick dismissal of her efforts.

If he had been concerned about the rapid changes or if he had regretted the worry he had caused the staff, she would have found his actions less offensive and his tone less cold and calculating. But now with Thomas taking this tone about the future of the people and the hospital Katherine held so dear, she found him to be a cold, manipulative tyrant, which confirmed the reactions of the others.

Katherine felt trapped and stifled by being in the same room with him. Suddenly the colors were too closing and too demanding of immediate attention. She could not understand how she could ever have taken comfort in these surroundings. She no longer wanted to give him the benefit of the doubt in his treatment of her friends. She could see his motives too clearly now, and she did not like what she saw. Katherine found it reprehensible that she and the others would be put through so much turmoil simply for the bottom line with so little concern for the welfare of the staff or the patients. She had expected him to show concern for the people who made Boxer Hospital great, not just the figures at the bottom of a ledger.

Unable to maintain her composure in the face of what she considered to be total disregard for people, Katherine spat out the mouthful of angry words. They left behind a sour taste and a sense of loss for the years of tranquillity she and the others had enjoyed under Frank Harriman's leadership. "You can't possibly care so little about the welfare of the people who make Boxer Hospital the remarkable place it is to work. We have a sense of family here and of commitment to each other as well as to the hospital and patients. I'm in favor of doing almost anything that will make the hospital more profitable except sacrificing the integrity and fellowship of the people behind the bricks and mortar," she said, as fire flashed in her eyes.

"There are some things, Katherine, that need to be done although they appear to be rather ruthless in the doing. I trust the board of director's vision for Boxer and will do everything possible to make their plans become reality. I don't expect to win any hearts in doing what's right for the hospital as a viable future-looking institution. I do plan to implement the restructuring with as little disruption to the people and patients as possible. It's my job here, just as it was at the other hospitals.

"You misjudge me if you and the others think that I don't

care about the employees. In the short time I've been here, I've seen the cohesive manner in which people here pull together. I find the comradeship quite heartwarming. Believe me when I say that it does not exist in many other hospitals. Often, I've had to build togetherness before I could effect change. However, here at Boxer I see a strong united institution that only needs a little encouragement to become even stronger.

"When my tenure is over and Boxer is stronger, you and the others will wonder why anyone ever raised any objections to the changes. You'll see that by implementing my suggestions and by putting in place a more aggressive fund-raising campaign, Boxer will become the leader in hospital care that the board sees as its future. In the meantime, it is imperative that everyone pull together to accomplish the desired results. If we work together, there will be less unwanted disruption. My goal is not to lay off people, although that may be part of the solution. I simply want to move forward in a manner that will satisfy my charge from the board.

"On a personal note, I'm sorry if our relationship has been affected by the dynamic of change in the institution. Since the first day I met you, I had hoped that we would be able to separate our professional life from our personal one. I was hoping that we might be able to become more than just coworkers," Thomas replied with a cool, calm tone in his voice that made Katherine's anger flare even higher.

"Our relationship? The only bond that exists between us now or ever is the determination to do the best we can for Boxer Hospital. Our approaches to people are diametrically opposed. There is no possibility that anything could ever exist between us, Dr. Baker, on any level other than professional," Katherine responded, rising from her chair and slowly backing toward the door.

"Again, I'm sorry to hear that. I had heard so much about your sensitivity toward others and your devotion to Boxer that I had hoped to earn your respect and, perhaps, affection. Maybe when you see the results of a few more months of my guidance, you'll have a change of heart. I'm not an ogre and I'm far from unfeeling. I hope that after you've had some time to consider my proposals for the hospital, you'll see that my suggestions will not be as far-reaching and unpleasant as they appear at first look. In any instance of change, employees must accept new working conditions, layoffs, downsizing of workforce, and scheduling adjustments. It's only natural.

"Contrary to what your colleagues believe, I'm not trying to be punitive or disruptive. I'm only doing what's best for the hospital in the long run. If something doesn't change now, there will be no tomorrow for Boxer. If you can think of another way to accomplish the same results, let me know. I've only made suggestions; they're not cast in stone. However, if someone does not offer alternatives, my suggestions will become directives.

"Concerning us, I hope you'll see me differently after we've worked together for a while. I greatly admire what you've done here and your passion for life. I hope that some day soon, we can see past our differences to our similarities. We are quite alike, you know. My approach isn't as caring as yours; I'm more bottom-line oriented, whereas you're concerned with the welfare of the individual. We'd make a great team if you'd only give me a chance," Thomas rebutted with a new gentleness in his voice.

Katherine, although seething with the anger she shared with her colleagues toward him, could hear the genuine warmth and professional respect in his voice. She almost wondered if she had misjudged him. After all, he had turned around other hospitals and led them into the new age of technology. When he spoke of their future, his eyes had taken on a softness she had not seen before. Yet Katherine could not allow herself to soften toward him when she had so much work to do.

Drawing the mantle of her rage around her shoulders, Katherine stated calmly, "Allow me to be up front with you on this matter, doctor. I intend to do everything I can to make Boxer my hospital again. What you've done to date in dealing with my colleagues in this manner has only helped my efforts. We are an organization of feeling, thinking people. We will not be pushed into accepting an edict that is neither to our advantage nor to that of the hospital that we serve so devotedly. We do not deserve this treatment and will not stand by and complacently accept it.

"You have drawn the battle line, doctor. I will do everything in my power to assist my friends in formulating a strategy that will represent our direction for Boxer. We will offer it to you as a counter to your ill-conceived plan. We are a dedicated group of professionals, doctor. I hope that you will give us the audience that we deserve. Good day, Dr. Baker."

Without waiting for him to respond, Katherine turned and left Thomas Baker to stare helplessly at her retreating back. If he had been able to view her face, he would have seen a bright glow of purpose emanating from her eyes and a tight line of immediacy at her mouth.

By the time Katherine reached the physicians' lounge in the ER, the majority of her anger had turned to determination. She had decided to meet with the other department heads to design a foolproof strategy that would show Thomas Baker that Boxer Hospital did not need him. If the board wanted a more technology-driven, modern approach, they would rise to the challenge and make the changes themselves by tightening their budgets and implementing their own strategies before he handed down plans that were insensitive to the needs of the people who comprised Boxer. She would show him that they had gotten along just fine without him under Dr. Harriman's administration and hers and that they did not need him now. If the board wanted cost containment and a dramatic fund-raising effort, all it had to do was ask. Katherine and the other department heads could accomplish more with kindness and respect for the members of the staff than Thomas could with his broad-brush approach.

Yet, having been the chief of staff, Katherine understood the force that compelled Thomas's actions. She knew that he had to take immediate steps to affect the changes the board demanded. His job and reputation were on the line as much as hers or that of any other department chair.

The sincerity on Thomas's face had touched Katherine's heart. She wanted to believe that he would be flexible in dealing with the department chairs if they could offer a viable counterproposal. She had been impressed with Thomas since the first day she had met him and had hoped that he might have been equally impressed by her. He had acted as if he were on a professional level. Today he said that he was on a personal one as well. Katherine wanted to believe him on both counts.

Four

Katherine sat down at the small desk in the corner within earshot of the ER's heartbeat. She preferred this little space to her office down the hall in which she felt isolated from everyone. Thoughtfully, Katherine drafted a note to her colleagues, inviting them to join her that night at her apartment for a light supper and a meeting. She thought that they should gather away from the hospital and ever-present gossip spreaders. She would serve something quick and easy to prepare and then open the session much the same way as she ran the usual Monday morning briefings. Katherine wanted to set an unhurried, casual tone for the evening to help settle everyone's nerves. All of the department chairs would have the opportunity to vent their frustrations, offer suggestions, and take the advice of the assembled colleagues in a congenial fashion without the threat of the pendulum swinging in their direction.

When she had finished the short personal notes, Katherine personally delivered each one. No one was at all surprised that she had taken steps to unite the department chairs in solving their own problems. Actually, they welcomed the opportunity to share concerns in a private setting. With that task accomplished, she returned to the lounge to write the next day's schedule and review patients' charts.

Stopping first at her office, she picked up the overflowing in-box. In her short absence of four days, quite a number of projects had accumulated that needed her immediate attention.

Carrying the in-box to the comfort of the old sofa, Katherine
attacked the work that waited for her. From the corridor, she
occasionally heard the clatter of a dropped chart or metal pan.
The voice of the public address system became a constant but
ignored companion. Periodically one of the other doctors would
enter the lounge, change clothes, and leave quickly and quietly
so as not to disturb her. Usually, however, she was alone.

Katherine loved the constant flow of energy that filled the
ER during the day. She much preferred it to the stop-and-go
pace of the night shift. She was much relieved to be back on
her regular schedule now that vacations were over and bouts of
viruses had run their course among the doctors. The return to
her normal shift was one positive thing she could contribute to
the appearance of Thomas Baker at Boxer Hospital. Working
only one job instead of two gave her more time to herself.

In all fairness, as Katherine briefly reflected on Thomas's few
months as the chief of staff, she could say that he had given
the institution a new sense of calm, at least until the distribution
of his memo. While she was in charge of the hospital, everyone
constantly speculated as to her future in the job and the upheaval
that replacing her would cause. The decision to name him to
the post settled some nerves and rattled others. His charm and
flair had certainly unsettled her. Katherine had never found herself so instantly attracted to anyone and was not certain that she
liked the sensation even now. She needed to be in complete
control of her emotions when dealing with him.

She was so engrossed in her thoughts that she did not notice
that the last intruder into the physicians' lounge had not left
and stood watching her work. When he cleared his throat, she
looked up with a start and said, "Oh, I didn't know anyone was
here. When I'm working, I tune out everything and everyone.
Do you need me, Dr. Baker?"

With a slight nod of his head he replied wearing his most
beguiling smile, "The name's Thomas, and I've come to see if
you'd have lunch with me. I'm meeting with some of the old
dowagers of the hospital's service board and would like some

direction on how to approach them. If you're not too busy, I'd like your help."

Ignoring his repeated reference to his first name, Katherine replied, "I'd be happy to assist you in any way you'd think beneficial. I'll be free in about thirty minutes if that would be a good time for you, Dr. Baker."

"Thank you, Katherine. I'll continue my rounds and meet you here in half an hour," Thomas answered with only the slightest change in the brightness of his smile. She could tell from the glint in his eyes that he was determined to get on her good side.

Watching him leave the lounge, Katherine sighed. She had to admit to herself that Thomas Baker certainly was a handsome man. Under more favorable circumstances she would have been drawn to those shoulders, his height, his soft yet commanding baritone, the sense of humor darting through his sparkling brown eyes, the direct assessing gaze, and the dimples that played at the corners of the kissable lips. But not today, not now, and maybe not ever. Their relationship would have to remain strictly professional and unbending. She had too much to prove in her professional career, and he had a hospital to run. Considering the turmoil his memo had created, he was the enemy of the moment.

Still, Katherine found Thomas Baker difficult to push from her mind. Although she hated losing the appointment to the chief-of-staff position to him, she could not hold it against him. He was known throughout the hospital industry for his ability to lead dependable, solid hospitals into the new age. He had the reputation for being able to turn any tradition-grounded monolith into a leading-edge competitor. She knew that he was a manager who possessed stellar credentials.

For her part, what Katherine lacked in experience she made up for with her energy, drive, and devotion. She would have appreciated the opportunity to help move the hospital forward. She loved Boxer Hospital and had turned down numerous job offers from other larger facilities in the Baltimore-Richmond

corridor to remain within the solid gray walls. She had wanted
to remain at its helm.

What irritated Katherine the most was that she had proven
to the board that she could manage the thriving hospital in a
successful manner. She had directed the staff under her leadership to run Boxer as Frank Harriman had always done and as
the hospital's reputation dictated that it should be governed. if
the chairman of the board had only told her that he wanted a
new approach rather than the continuation of tradition, she
would have changed her focus. Katherine felt that she was
equally as capable as Thomas Baker of plotting a new course
for the new millennium.

After witnessing the success of her video, Katherine realized
what she should have done to secure the chief-of-staff position.
If she had only given some of her time to the winning of the
board's devotion, she would not have been overlooked. However, knowing that Thomas's tenure was limited, she continued
to put into play the strategies that would position her for the
job when he left. This time, she would not be overlooked.

Returning to her in-box, Katherine tried to push the irritating
appeal of Thomas Baker and the equally frustrating task of
working under him from her mind. She still had a lot to do and
only a few minutes left in which to complete everything that
demanded her attention. Yet, try as she might, she found it difficult to concentrate now that he had invaded her inner sanctu-
ary. She could not stop her mind from returning to him. In her
subconscious, she heard the repeated lament that a good man
was hard to find. Here he was a wonderful prospect, and because of the work tension between them, she could not take
advantage of the opportunity to seize the moment and the man.
As the fragrance of his aftershave lotion lingered in the lounge,
she almost abandoned her resolve.

Finally, giving in to the reality that she would not get any
more work done that morning, Katherine rose from the comfortable sofa, gathered her files, and returned to her office. After
depositing her in-box and white jacket on her desk, she checked

her reflection in the mirror on the inside of her closet door. Her brick red linen suit with black trim flattered her figure perfectly and accentuated her trim waist and pert bust. The serviceable two-inch black heels gave definition to her shapely legs while protecting her feet from the trauma of standing all day. Giving her shoulder-length auburn curls a final check, she picked up her purse, turned out the light, and left the office.

Retracing her steps, Katherine stopped at Betsy's office where her friend was busily sorting through her mail. Never too busy to chat with her best buddy, Betsy looked up and immediately put down her pen. She could tell by the look of concentration on Katherine's face that something important weighed heavily on her shoulders.

"Hey, what's up?" Betsy asked as Katherine slipped into the chair beside her desk.

"I'm having lunch with Thomas Baker in a few minutes to give him the inside scoop on the hospital's old guard," Katherine responded with an expression on her face similar to that produced by sucking on lemons.

"Whose idea was that?" Betsy asked. She could not imagine enjoying lunch, dinner, tea, or even a snack with someone whose main responsibility in life was counting pennies. She was afraid he would ask her for a contribution not only to the hospital's ongoing capital campaign but also to the cost of lunch.

"You can be sure that I didn't suggest it. He stopped by about thirty minutes ago to ask for my help. He has a meeting with them later today and wants to know their hot buttons before offering himself to the lions," Katherine answered as she picked imaginary lint from her suit.

"You couldn't think of an excuse to get out of it?" Betsy queried, watching her friend struggle with unvoiced conflicts. She suspected that more lay beneath the surface of Katherine's concerns than simply the decision of the correct fork or the most appealing appetizer.

"I guess I could have, but he probably needs the information.

When I first took over the chief-of-staff position, I would have liked a little forewarning before my first session with them. Unfortunately, no one offered any true insight into dealing with them. Yet, I survived without it. For that matter, he could, too," Katherine reasoned without looking up from her impeccably lint-free suit.

"So, what's the real problem? I don't think I've ever seen you like this. It's more than just the passing on of information to the man who's filling the chair you once sat in that's bothering you," Betsy blurted out unable to wait any longer for Katherine to get to the real reason for her visit.

"You know as well as I do what the problem is, but I'll say it straight out. I'm attracted to him. That's what's bothering me. He's the kind of intelligent, challenging, handsome man I've been looking for. Now that I've found him, we're on opposite sides. What is it my mother always says? 'If it weren't for bad luck, I wouldn't have any luck.' Well, that's the way I feel right now. We've met too late, and there's nothing I can do about it," Katherine lamented, her beautiful face a storm cloud of emotions.

"That's not entirely true. The first thing you can do is to forget your determination to show Thomas Baker who the boss is around here. He knows you did a fabulous job as the interim chief while the board undertook the candidate search. I'm sure he's aware that you really wanted the job and would have made a great permanent chief. I know your pride was injured when the board selected him, but you should put that aside. He hasn't done anything to justify your hostility toward him. Even this rotating department head idea isn't as dreadful as some of our colleagues want to pretend that it is. They'll learn quite a bit about their managerial style from the change. Your reaction to him is simply your pride speaking," Betsy counseled carefully. She knew that Katherine was particularly vulnerable at the moment. It was not like Katherine to fidget with her clothing or sit restlessly during a conversation. She acted as if she had some urgent matter distracting her mind from giving full attention to the discussion. From her behavior, Betsy concluded that she did.

"I know, but I have to make this point. Pride or not, I wouldn't be able to live with myself if I didn't prove to him that I can run the ER better than he ever anticipated. That way he'll see what I could have done for the hospital if the board had only given me the opportunity. I know I'm being obsessive about this, but I have to do it. Besides, I'm planning for the future. You never know when I might decide that my turn is now not later. I only hope he's still interested after the fight is over," Katherine conceded, walking toward the door, adjusting her skirt one last time.

"So do I. You don't want you to throw away this chance for happiness. Who knows when or if you'll have another one," Betsy added as casually as she could. She and Katherine had been best friends long enough for her to know that Katherine had to follow her own intuitions. Usually they steered her in the right direction. Maybe that would be the case this time. Besides, Betsy could say nothing that would convince Katherine that her course might not be the correct one.

Katherine had almost reached the physicians' lounge when Thomas appeared among the clutter of gurneys that lined the hall. His lively step and broad smile told her that he was looking forward to their luncheon meeting. As he matched his long, powerful stride to hers, Katherine once again remarked on the perfect way they fit together. She could not help wondering how dancing with him would feel. She could only imagine the strength of his arms around her body as he guided her across the floor. Maybe when she resolved this conflict that lay between them, she would find out.

Thomas had made luncheon reservations at a restaurant near the hospital that served Greek cuisine. As they entered, the aroma of souviaki, lamb rubbed with garlic, and mousaka greeted her nose and caused her mouth to water. The menu overflowed with all of her favorites, making it difficult for her to narrow her choices. Finally, she decided on a tempting lamb stew with grilled eggplant and a Greek salad. Thomas ordered the mousaka and offered to share it with her. She would order a piece of baklava for later and one for Betsy, too.

Settling into the thick cushions of the corner booth, Katherine watched as Thomas skillfully selected the wine. She did not know a chardonnay from a burgundy and always admired the knowledge of those who did. She had planned to take a course in cooking with wine and selecting the appropriate one for each course, but she never had the time or the opportunity. She promised herself that some day she would treat herself to a bit of leisure to do some of the things she had always dreamed of doing. Wine tasting evenings, cooking classes, and craft weaving courses were just a few of the many interests she would like to cultivate.

As soon as the waiter took their order, Thomas sat back in his seat and looked intently at Katherine before he spoke. He had rehearsed the conversation he would have with her regarding the hospital's old guard one hundred times since devising that plan to be alone with her. He knew she would not accept his invitation to lunch unless he disguised it as related to work. Even then he had been a little worried that she would refuse. He had felt her anger all too clearly when she left his office earlier than morning. Yet he could not wait until her disapproval dissolved; he had to act promptly. He did not want to run the risk of losing her to another man.

Thomas had seen the way the other men looked at her as a highly trained and respected professional and as a gorgeous woman. Although he realized that Katherine appeared oblivious to their interests, he knew that her reaction could change at any minute now that she had some free time on her hands. When she took the time to assess the men in their small community, Thomas wanted to be sure that Katherine looked in his direction.

Feeling more than a bit awkward, Thomas began the conversation by saying, "Katherine, I want you to know how much I appreciate your professionalism during these trying transitional weeks. I had heard about and become impressed by your ability to manage the hospital even before had the opportunity to watch you in action. You had so skillfully assumed the acting chief-of-staff position that no one felt the usual tremors when a change in administration occurs. Everyone including the board members liked your energy, drive, and management savvy. Several people on the hiring committee told me that the only reason they did not permanently promote you to this position was that they needed my expertise for the express purpose of moving the hospital forward into the twenty-first century. You simply did not have the experience in raising money that the transition from the traditional hospital to the facility of the future required.

"When I accepted this job, I made it clear that I have no intention of making my tenure at Boxer into a permanent arrangement. Since leaving the operating room and taking on the role of a problem solver, I have not set down roots at any hospital. I enjoy the challenge of stepping into an institution, assessing its strengths and weaknesses, and putting it on the path to a brighter future. I am not a day-to-day administrator.

"Until I met you, nothing and no one had been able to make me want to change my mind. I have always known that I would be ready to settle down if I ever met the right woman. Your independent spirit certainly leads me to believe that you might be the one to give my life purpose and direction.

"You see, all of my friends have long ago married and are happily raising children. They have abandoned the endless stream of boring parties and unsatisfactory liaisons in favor of attending their children's soccer matches and spending quiet nights at home. They have given up introducing me to their single women friends and have learned to think of me as a confirmed bachelor.

"Still, I could tell that they hoped that by including me in their family birthdays and Christmas celebrations I would see their happiness and want the same for myself. So far, very much to my dismay, their scheming and plotting have not worked; I have not found the woman who would make me feel complete.

I am not especially proud of being a bachelor; I simply am one. Luck and love have not smiled on me. Until I met you, I did not really believe that they would."

Katherine sat quietly with her hands folded in her lap watching a cavalcade of emotions parade across Thomas's handsome face. She wondered where this discussion would lead. She had seen some of the same expressions play across his chiseled cheeks when they first met. Then, too, she had wondered what secret thoughts caused him to knit his brows and furrow his forehead as his eyes alternately sparkled and dimmed as he engaged in introspection.

Now, she waited to see what he would reveal of his own volition and in his own time. They were engaged in a battle of wits. As much as she would have liked to reach out to him, she could not forget that he was the opponent. She had always heard that in conflicts of love and war, the combatants often found it difficult to determine which was the more powerful force.

When Katherine did not respond, Thomas continued to wrestle with putting his thoughts into the unfamiliar words as he stared into her unblinking brown eyes. Slowly he began again. "I sensed from the careful journals you kept and your efficient handling of that first staff meeting that you could be as warm as you could be professional. I watched you maneuver around the many personalities and egos that filled the room.

"Over time, I've learned that you would make an invaluable asset to my team as I lead Boxer Hospital into the new century. I also determined that you have the respect of everyone who works with you. You are indeed a formidable opponent. I had hoped that, despite the rumors of discontent among the ranks, we might be able to move our relationship forward. Unfortunately, it has remained coolly professional, an arrangement I had hoped to change. You see, I've decided that it is time for me to make the first careful move toward winning your confidence and shaking up the status quo that exists between us."

"So, what do you expect from me?" Katherine queried. "I've already told you that nothing can happen between us as long as I have unfinished business. I will help you in any way I can in your capacity as the chief of staff of Boxer, but I cannot foresee any change in our relationship. I appreciate your kind feelings toward me, but I am afraid that at this time I am not free to reciprocate. I cannot at this moment afford to make room in my life for romantic entanglements." She was neither shocked nor dismayed that Thomas had come so close to telling her the extent of his admiration. She had long suspected it. However, she could do nothing at this moment to give him encouragement.

"I appreciate your honesty. This is not what I wanted to hear. However, I will respect your decision and will leave you to pursue your career . . . at least for the time being," Thomas continued, trying to keep his disappointment from showing in his voice. "Well, then, I suppose we might as well turn to topics of business. I could use your help in dealing with the old dowagers whose hearts I have to win in order to ensure their financial support. I hope I have more luck with them than I have had with you."

Smiling slightly to reassure him that professionally at least she was in agreement, Katherine began, "You'll be surprised when you meet them. Several of them aren't so very old, actually. Ms. Augusta Maine is the daughter of a cosmetics baron; she's young and filthy rich. She accepted me, but she much prefers the company of men who will wine, dine, and dance while they flatter her insecurities and encourage her philanthropic generosity. She has an obnoxious, spoiled Basenji that you'll have to learn to like if you want to court her wallet.

"Then there's Jasmine Gaylord whose dear, departed husband left her with more money than she can possibly spend in a thousand lifetimes. She's athletic and loves the outdoors, especially hiking and horse racing. She'll expect you to take her to the track and cover her bets. I've never seen her win, but she loses so graciously that it's a treat to watch. Oh yes, she loves to ride to the hounds and will expect you to join her. Her checks to the hospital are always more than enough to cover her losses and the cost of a couple of new MRIs.

"Finally, you'll have to spend some time with Patrice Miller. She has a fiery temper and the language to match. She made it to the top on her own. If I remember correctly, she developed a powerful bug repellent that sold like wildfire and made her a fortune. She's rough around the edges, but she's the most fun and honest of the 'Three Sisters of Charity,' as we fondly refer to these young benefactresses of Boxer Hospital. She loves to go to movies, ball games, and wrestling. You'll like her.

"Well, I guess I've told you everything you wanted to know and then some. I hope my litany hasn't bored you, too much," Katherine concluded. She had not realized that she had talked for so long until she noticed that Thomas sat smiling at her. He seemed pleased and amused at her facility in providing the necessary tidbits for working with the supporters of the hospital.

"Not at all. I've enjoyed hearing about them. Your insights are exactly what I needed to hear. Now tell me about the older set. What do they like?" Thomas asked, encouraging Katherine to continue so that he could watch the movement of her sensuous lips and listen to the lilt of her melodious voice. He was falling under her spell and he liked the feeling.

"There's nothing interesting to tell you about them. They're all the usual three-piece-suit types. Sylvia has complete dossiers on them. For the most part, all you have to do is send them copies of the annual report and periodic friendly updates on fund-raising efforts and the manner in which the hospital spends their generous gifts. They're very happy with that. They haven't much time for anything else. They're usually too busy managing their own businesses or traveling to spend much time with the operation of Boxer. They only want to know what we need and how much it costs. They're generous to a fault and never question any request that we make of them," Katherine answered as the waiter placed an overflowing plate on the table before her. Even if her stomach and nerves could handle the food, she would never be able to eat all of it.

"Thanks, that's good to know. I'll ask her for a complete rundown on each one of them. I'm meeting with the older ones as a group later this evening. I haven't set up anything with the others yet. I wanted to talk with you first," Thomas responded. Looking down at his plate, he was overwhelmed, too, but not at the size of the portion. He felt a sense of regret that he would have to turn his attention away from Katherine's beautiful face and bewitching lips. He loved listening to her talk; her enthusiasm was highly infectious.

They ate in uncomfortable silence, as if something unspoken stood between them and prevented them from opening up to each other. Katherine was afraid of allowing the man with whom she would soon be engaged in battle to know her feelings toward him. Thomas feared that he would frighten her and interfere with her sense of fair play if he spoke any more of his feelings aloud. Both were plagued by their insecurities about what might turn into a meaningful relationship if time and circumstances provided the opportunity.

As they waited for the check, Katherine seized the moment to pose the question that had been at the heart of her agreement to lunch with Thomas. She had hoped that after she answered his questions, he would answer some of hers. Setting aside her coffee cup she said, "Since our earlier conversation I've had the opportunity to revisit your memo regarding the changes in staffing. I can understand the reaction of some of my colleagues and still sympathize with the fact that they are quite concerned about the wholesale disruption to the flow of their departments if they implement what you've requested. However, I do also see the position in which the board has placed you in this matter. Considering both sides I must ask you if you think it's wise to do so much so soon? I'd like to suggest that you consider an alternative that I'll be more than happy to propose to my peers. Perhaps you could raise the funds you need for technology expansion from among the 'Sisters' rather than by asking the staff to undergo personnel and equipment budget cuts."

Thomas felt almost relieved now that she had voiced the topic of her concern. Folding his arms on the table, Thomas leaned forward and said, "I have no plans to abandon my stated course of action without cause, but I am pleased to know that you felt that you could approach me. None of the others has spoken to me; they had preferred to stay within their ranks and complain loudly but to no one in particular, least of all to me.

"After my earlier confrontation with you, I am happy to see that you have cooled off a bit and might be willing to serve as the mediator between myself and your department head colleagues. I am relieved to know that I have not misjudged you, Katherine. Since the first day I met you I knew that you would be an invaluable asset to me in many ways.

"I see no possible way to raise the amount of funds with which to undertake this major overhaul without asking people to sacrifice. The most costly area is, as you know, personnel. I haven't asked anyone to fire staff members, although I've been tempted to go for maximum results. I've simply suggested that overtime be eliminated and that everyone works a little harder to cover the shifts where we now use temps. If everyone pitches in, there won't be any further need for cost reduction. That's what I tried to explain to your colleagues while you were on leave. If you remember, I also made an effort to clarify my intent to you this morning," Thomas explained carefully. He wanted Katherine to be able to relay his intent accurately to the others. He knew they would listen to her. Besides, he needed her to believe that he wanted only the best for Boxer Hospital.

"I don't think the department heads will understand that they have to ask their staffs to work longer hours for less money. That's asking quite a lot of people. I'll certainly have a hard time selling the idea that the purchase of expanded and improved technology, which might possibly replace people's jobs in the future, is worth sacrificing salaries in the present," Katherine retorted still somewhat unable to see both sides.

"I'm not asking anyone to do anything I wouldn't do myself. I've asked all departments to schedule me into regular work sessions to help out during this crunch. In addition to doing my own job, I'll be spending time in obstetrics, pediatrics, the ER, and all other departments. That's quite a sacrifice for me, too," Thomas replied, leaning closer so that Katherine would not miss the seriousness in his tone and demeanor.

"Somehow I don't think anyone will feel sorry for you, considering you make many times more than they do, have a private car at your disposal, and have free membership to exclusive country and men's clubs. If I were in a clerk's position, I'd find it difficult to sympathize with your 'sacrifice.' I still think that a more conservative approach and the involvement of the 'Sisters' would accomplish your goals with the least amount of disruption," Katherine responded without trying to hide the sarcasm in her voice. Against her will, she found the heady scent of his aftershave appealing.

"I suppose I'll just have to prove to everyone that I only mean to do what's best for the hospital and for them. I don't expect you and the others to either believe or trust me immediately. I have to earn your confidence. This is simply the first hurdle. Unfortunately, our honeymoon period has been cut short by the need to move the hospital into the future. To do that, we have to raise funds and cut costs. It's a fairly simple concept, really, and one that I've put into place in many other institutions. Once the new technology is in place, everyone will forget the hours of argument and resistance. But, as I said earlier, I'm all too happy to entertain suggestions from others. My door is always open. I'm not opposed to doing anything that you can sell to me as a viable solution," Thomas stated, folding his napkin and placing it beside his plate. From the expression on Katherine's face, he could tell that their lunch and conversation had ended. Despite his best efforts at reconciliation, she had remained hesitant to join forces with him. He could understand her reluctance and wondered if he would have responded any differently if the roles had been reversed.

Rising from the table, Katherine and Thomas slowly exited the restaurant. Thomas lightly touched Katherine's elbow and added, "We are both correct in our positions on the changes at

Boxer. I am asking a lot of people, but they will have to understand that they either have to make the changes willingly in the present or lose many jobs in the future. They need to understand that I will be right beside them to help ease their fear about the changes that I have proposed. Still, I am confident that we must take these initial steps toward a stronger tomorrow."

Katherine was equally correct in her assessment of the reactions of her colleagues and their staffs. Her strong interpersonal skills had enabled her to take the pulse of her colleagues and staff. "I hope you're right, doctor. My colleagues have voiced very real hesitations. I will do whatever I can to make Boxer even healthier than it is today. However, like the others, I will not sacrifice people and their futures in order to do it. There must be an alternative. We must find it. I cannot allow faithful employees to suffer for the sake of change, regardless of how necessary it might be," Katherine said as she left Thomas standing by the elevator door.

As she returned to her office, Katherine knew instinctively what her next move had to be. The dinner tonight with her colleagues would set the tone for future interaction with the new chief of staff. She would have to put aside her own conflicting emotions regarding the changes Thomas suggested and her feelings of irritation at no longer being the head of the hospital in order to help her friends formulate the best possible counteroffer to Thomas's suggestions. She would have to call upon all of her bargaining skills to reach this compromise.

Katherine dreaded the rift that would develop between Thomas and the department heads if something was not done soon. She knew that the only way they could show him how much they disliked the changes was to mass together in protest and to offer an alternative suggestion. She would do her best to keep the patients from suffering while she worked to position her suggestions with both sides of the struggle.

On a personal level, Katherine hoped that the show of force would not hurt her potential for a relationship with Thomas. She had grown to respect and admire him and actually hoped they could progress to being more than simply colleagues one day when the environment was conducive. However, as long as he was intent on pressing the changes on a reluctant management, she would have to oppose him and join with the others regardless of the personal peril. Besides, she still had a need to prove to him that she could manage as well as he could. Perhaps by serving as a mediator, she would be able to demonstrate her expertise in personnel management as well as financial planning.

Five

That night as Katherine readied her apartment for the meeting, her mind and heart were not on the agenda. She kept thinking of the luncheon with Thomas. Although they had mainly discussed hospital business, they had spent a rather pleasant time together. Granted, several moments had caused her a great deal of frustration, but for the most part, she had enjoyed the freedom to share her thoughts and concerns with him. Katherine hoped that she and the other department heads could think of a way to avoid a confrontation with the chief of staff. If they could only devise a plan that would accomplish his goals for the hospital and theirs for the people in their charge, everyone would be happy.

Placing the last pad of paper on the table in the dining room that would serve as their conference room, she acknowledged that everything was ready. Promptly at eight thirty the doorbell rang and her colleagues began to appear. Betsy was the first to arrive from her apartment down the hall. She was as hopeful as Katherine that they could draft a counterproposal that would appeal to Thomas's sense of fair play as well as his need to cut costs. As the daughter of a corporate vice president, she had seen firsthand the devastation that conflict within the ranks of management could cause on morale and profitability. Josh Katz, Fred March, Rebecca Poore, and Toni Ivy arrived together a few minutes later. Each brought folders containing lists of areas within their departments that would be affected by Thomas's proposed cutbacks. Katherine could clearly see that they were armed for a fight if their proposals were not accepted.

Katherine had prepared a pleasant meal to be shared by her colleagues as the first order of business. She ushered everyone into the kitchen where plates of spaghetti, bowls of salad, and baskets of steaming garlic bread waited on the counter. The cheerily set table with its red checked cloth, flickering candle, and perky daisies invited them to enjoy their food. Everyone chatted animatedly as they spooned out the delicious smelling food. Katherine hoped that the weight of the meal and the strength of the Chianti that Betsy poured with a heavy hand would lull them into a relaxed state and help the evening's discussion proceed smoothly and calmly. For dessert, she would serve a chocolate cheesecake with raspberry sauce, another treat meant to please even the most discerning palate. She hoped that contented people would be easier to sway to her way of thinking than those whose hunger had not been satisfied.

To her relief, everyone ate in silence with only brief moments of very congenial conversation interrupting the flow of fork to mouth. Considering the gusto with which everyone attacked the food, Katherine decided that at least the meal portion of the evening was a success. She hoped that the discussions would progress as smoothly as the pasta vanished from their plates.

After everyone had relocated to the dining room table, Katherine called the meeting to order as she had done so many Mondays in the conference room before Thomas came to Boxer Hospital. Immediately, they all started to speak at once. They all waved sheets of paper containing all the relevant figures that proved the point that Thomas's plan was detrimental to the well-being of their departments.

Speaking in a soft yet commanding voice, Katherine tried to calm down the hot tempers. Standing to get their attention she said, "People, we can't possibly make any progress unless we slow down and listen to each other. We must proceed with some sense of order. Betsy, you tell us what's happening in surgery."

As the noise level dropped, Betsy opened her folder, spread out her sheets, and began to describe the situation in her department. As she spoke, Katherine looked around the table at all the heads nodding in agreement. With the exception of the exact dollar amount, Betsy presented a picture of her department's destruction that the other heads could easily second. They concurred that if they put Thomas's proposed changes in place, his efforts would lead to the demise of Boxer Hospital as they all knew it. They also agreed with Betsy's assessment that they had to find a way to save money while safeguarding jobs, services, and morale.

"Well, it looks as if our case should be easy to argue," Katherine concluded after she had presented the financial and emotional impact Thomas's plan would have on the ER. "I'll inform him of our thoughts during my appointment with him tomorrow morning. I'm sure he'll be agreeable to our views. His ultimate concern is the hospital's bottom line. He doesn't strike me as being the kind of person who initiates change simply to stir up the troops. From what we've just proposed, we can reach the same results with less disruption by implementing our approaches. I think we should compliment ourselves on a job well done. I'll contact each of you as soon as I leave his office in the morning."

Ushering the heads to the door, Katherine felt her confidence waning. She had not wanted to tell them that their plans appeared to be satisfactory steps toward cost containment, but they would not accomplish the desired long-term savings. They really needed to tighten their belts even more to make the far-reaching goals with which the board had entrusted Thomas. Between tonight and her appointment with him the next day, she would have to think of another way to produce the funds he needed for the technological plans he hoped to implement. Katherine knew that if she went to bed at all that night, she would not sleep well.

* * *

The next morning as Katherine drove to work, she devised what she hoped would be a foolproof plan. After her meeting with Thomas, she would call the "Sisters" herself and set up a casual luncheon that she would host on his behalf under the guise of passing the baton of leadership. She would invite all three at the same time so that the rendezvous would not appear to be a date with any one of the lovely, supportive ladies. In addition, she would arrange for him to escort each woman to a function appropriate to her particular interests. Like all major benefactors, they appreciated it when someone gave them special treatment. Besides, Katherine knew that they would readily respond to the opportunity to outshine each other in front of an eligible bachelor. Knowing the feeling of competition that existed among the "Sisters," Katherine felt confident that she would have no difficulty selling the concept to them. She hoped convincing Thomas to play along would be as easy.

Taking her customary seat across the conference table from Thomas, Katherine delivered her soft-sell pitch. She skillfully combined the projects outlined by her colleagues with her scheme of manipulating the sense of competition among the major benefactresses of the hospital.

As Katherine spoke, Thomas listened to the plan that she said would generate the funds he needed to modernize the hospital. This would not be the first time he had wined and dined major contributors in order to open their wallets, although he had never had to concentrate his attention on three women at one time and with equal vigor.

If all went well, he would be happy, the board would be happy, and from the sounds of it, the department chairs would be happy. If Katherine's plan failed, everyone would finally agree to implement his restrictions and budget cuts.

When Katherine finally paused, Thomas commented, "I'm not a shy man, but I usually prefer to meet people the old-fashion way through an introduction made by a mutual friend. This new way of simply throwing one's self into the arena at a singles bar does not appeal to me. This idea of yours of calling on the

'Sisters' without the benefit of a formal introduction does not sit well with me. Business or not, I find the cold-call approach to interacting with other people to be forbidding and off-putting. Considering what you have told me about each of the ladies, your introductions and presence might make the purpose of their association perfectly clear. The last thing I want is for one of the 'Sisters' to think that my interests are anything other than strictly for the good of the hospital."

"Don't worry, doctor. I'll be with you as much as is feasible. However, you must establish yourself as the focus of their attention. They already know me and have given generously every time I have approached them. It's your turn to convince them to support the hospital one more time. You have to sell them on the benefits of your programs," Katherine added before returning to her planned presentation.

"Although I am willing to give your suggestions a chance, my plans are still the ones with the greatest potential for success," Thomas argued gently.

"Initially and on the bottom line. However, your plans of layoffs would not work to your advantage in the long run. Morale would drop and employee energy would wane. Before long, you would have to initiate changes to recover the money lost to lower patient attendance and a decrease in reputation. You would spend hundreds of thousands of dollars on advertising to convince the public that Boxer was as good as ever and an equal amount on training to ensure that personnel worked at the level advertised. So, you see, my solution prevents all of that extra effort while still maintaining morale, employees, and community."

As she spoke, Katherine knew that as soon as Thomas raised the money the hospital needed and put his modernization plans into effect, he would leave. He had been hired to rejuvenate the hospital, and when that was done, someone else would step into the position of chief of staff. He would pack up and move to another hospital that needed his problem-solving expertise. Katherine considered it foolish to think about falling in love

with a man whose presence was temporary at best. She did not
want to be another crossed out name in his little black book.

Besides, if her plan worked and her efforts to win the board
to her side succeeded, Katherine might have moved into the
executive suite even sooner than she had originally planned.
She had resolved to allow nothing, not even her interest in
Thomas, to keep her from attaining her goal. She wanted and
would have the chief-of-staff position at Boxer.

"How soon before you put this plan of yours into motion,
Katherine? I need to sign some contracts with networking
providers and don't want to take any action until I know that
the financing is behind me," Thomas inquired, interrupting her
thoughts.

Quickly and decisively Katherine replied, "I'll get the ball
rolling as soon as I return to my office. Is this afternoon for
the group luncheon good for you? The 'Sisters' are usually in
town on business early in the week. If I call immediately, they
might be available on short notice."

"Fine. I'll look forward to it. I hope your scheme works. If
it doesn't, I'll be forced to implement my suggestions immediately. Please make sure the other department heads understand
that I'm being flexible, but I won't be foolish about this. The
hospital needs the technology and need the funds with which
to purchase it. In this case, the means to the end don't matter
to me in the least. My only concern is the bottom line. It's that
simple. If I can accomplish the job using your plan, I'll do it.
If not . . . well, just make sure they understand. By the way,
you'll see to it that the 'Sisters' know that the time I spend with
them is not personal. I have absolutely no interest in forming
alliances with any of the ladies," Thomas said, walking with
her to the door. The nearness of her slight body was almost too
much for him to endure. He had to force himself not to submit
to the overwhelming desire to pull her into his arms and bury
his face in the sweetness of her neck.

"I'm sure our plan will come off without a single glitch. The
'Sisters' are very dedicated supporters. They'll do anything for

Boxer Hospital, even if it includes digging deeper into their already generous pockets. I'll see to it that they understand that your meetings with them are strictly professional. However, I will not be responsible if one of them becomes romantically inclined in your direction. You are the youngest, most available male chief of staff we've had at Boxer in their memory," Katherine responded while trying to retain her professional composure. Thomas's hand on her elbow sent pleasurable tingles coursing through her body.

Standing at the door, Katherine could feel the electricity pass between their bodies. She felt herself being drawn into his arms. If only the timing was different and there was no hospital between them, Katherine would have responded to the urging from her body rather than followed the dictates of her mind. As the intercom buzzer sounded, she breathed a sigh of relief. Reluctantly, Thomas released her and walked toward the telephone. As the buzzing sliced through the silence, she hurried down the hall to share the news of her success with her colleagues.

As she had predicted, the "Sisters" were anxious to meet Thomas. Patrice Miller scolded Katherine in her usual straightforward way for not having introduced them sooner. She had heard quite a bit about Thomas's good looks and business skill and wanted to check him out for herself. She was all too happy to meet for lunch that day and to accompany him to a baseball game the next evening.

For her part, Augusta Maine canceled her long-standing dinner date with old girlfriends from college to meet Thomas for a light supper and dancing at the country club that night. She, too, had heard all about him and wondered when he would get around to introducing himself. After her conversation with Katherine, Augusta phoned her manicurist and hairdresser, made an emergency appointment with both, hopped into her Jaguar, and spent the rest of the morning making herself beautiful and alluring. She had no intention of having a first encounter with a man like Thomas Baker with her hair in a scarf, regardless of how flattering the style was to her perfectly heart-shaped face. She certainly would not appear for lunch in the company of other women against whom she could be measured without looking her best.

Jasmine Gaylord was busy at her horse farm, but she said that an errand to the bank would bring her into town that afternoon anyway. She invited Thomas to join her at the farm for a weekend of riding and mingling with the Virginia horsy set. She encouraged Katherine to come along, too. Jasmine had someone in mind for her to meet during her visit.

Although Katherine suspected that he would be reluctant to accept with a day of riding on the agenda and that he would have preferred dinner and the theater, when Katherine relayed his invitation, Thomas graciously accepted for the good of the fund-raising campaign. Katherine silently relished every minute of his discontent. He was learning what it meant to manage a major hospital in a city like Washington, where everyone expected to be placed on a pedestal.

Seeing his stricken expression at having to ride a horse again after fifteen years, Katherine gleefully detailed the events that awaited him over the next few days. "Don't worry," she said with a chuckle, "Jasmine keeps some lovely gentle mares for people who either have never ridden or who haven't been near a horse in ages. They're delightful, well-broken ladies who would never think of throwing you. I hadn't been on a horse since before college, and I survived my weekend with her. You'll love it."

"I'm sure I will," Thomas snorted. "I knew I'd have to kiss a little butt for the benefit of the hospital, but I didn't think that horses would be involved. If I'd known, I might not have taken this job."

Katherine sensed that Thomas was less than happy that he was the center of her entertainment that morning. More than that, she was aware that he did not look with anticipation at being back in the saddle again, literally. He had alluded to an unpleasant experience that had hurried him off riding forever and had made reference to having been dumped in a freezing creek. He had muttered more to himself than to her that he could still hear the laughter of the other guys now and could still feel his clothing turning to icicles on his body as they galloped back to the barn. If the picture had not been so humorous, Katherine would have felt sorry for putting him through the ordeal even for the good of the hospital.

Covering her mouth with her hand to stifle her laughter, Katherine left him in his office to nurse his memories. One day she would have to ask Thomas to share them with her. But for now, duty called in the ER. Now that everyone, with maybe the exception of Thomas, was happy at Boxer, she could concentrate on making her department the crown jewel she knew it could be. Katherine still intended to prove to the world that she should be at the helm of the hospital and not Thomas.

The morning passed so quickly that Katherine had little opportunity to think about Thomas and his upcoming sessions with the "Three Sisters of Charity." Besides, she did not consider them to be more than business meetings and certainly not dates. When she did allow herself the fleeting moment to reflect on them at all, she felt a twinge of something akin to jealousy. Rebuking herself soundly, she returned her attention to the taut abdomen of her young patient who groaned in pain every time she touched his right side. She quickly pushed any further thought of Thomas from her mind.

Thomas's day, however, did not move as quickly. He sulked and simmered about allowing Katherine to talk him into meeting the "Sisters" on a quasi-social basis. He had originally planned to invite them to tour the hospital as he would any other supporter. Yet Thomas had found that when Katherine delivered her counterproposal, he could not reject her logical offer. He hoped that the plan she presented would work. She had shown considerable resourcefulness in developing it. He liked that quality in a woman and in a partner. He would hate to have her plotting against him when it appeared that they would make such a lovely pair if they ever had the opportunity.

When she had shared her information on last night's meeting,

Thomas had easily been able to imagine the flow of events with
Katherine listening attentively as each department head vented
steam over his or her area's proposed changes. Her light touch,
her ability to maneuver people without their awareness, and the
softness of her voice had combined to make her the perfect
intermediary, the person all parties involved could trust to look
out for their welfare. She knew how to finesse people into doing
exactly what she wanted without having to resort to muscle and
brute force. With a chuckle, he conceded that she had certainly
worked her magic on him.

He envisioned her taking her usual careful notes and then
recapping the general consensus from the comments made by
all present. Thomas had once watched her work with her own
department and liked her style and the ease with which she
made people see the importance of their opinions and concerns
in the planning process. She was skilled at formulating plans,
testing the water, and making quick modifications on the spot.
He could learn a lot from her if given the time and opportunity.

Thomas was sure that Katherine had maneuvered the department chairs into complete agreement on their counterproposal,
with each one thinking by the end of the meeting that he or she
had developed the strategy personally rather than collabora-
tively. After all, by the end of theirs, she had convinced him
that calling on the "Sisters" separately and socially was the best
way to appeal to their hearts and wallets. If she could win him
over, Thomas could only imagine how lost the others felt when
they found themselves in her grasp. In the hospital industry,
many considered him to be a hard sell and a real tough guy.

Looking at his watch, Thomas eased from his overstuffed
chair and headed down the hall to collect Katherine for what
was destined to be the most trying meeting of his career. He
did not look forward to being the entrée in a meal served to
three of the hospital's most devoted supporters.

Katherine was especially cheerful as she introduced Thomas
to Jasmine, Augusta, and Patrice. The ladies were blatantly flir-
tatious and interested in him, showing a side of their personali-

ties that Katherine had not seen when she first met them. They tried to outdo each other in showing support for Boxer hospital, winning Thomas's affections, and politely putting Katherine in her new position of support staff to the chief of staff.

If Katherine had not been so entertained by their actions, she might have felt envy and jealousy as they lavished attention on Thomas. As it was, she could barely refrain from laughing at their antics and at his discomfort. Katherine sensed from the telling glances he shot in her direction that she would have to do him many favors once this fund-raising campaign ended. Despite her determination not to become emotionally involved with him, Katherine hoped that some of her compensation could be in the form of candlelit dinners for just the two of them.

Looking around the small, intimate dining room, Thomas could not quite believe that he had allowed Katherine to arrange anything so obviously contrived as this luncheon and the events that would follow. The women were at their best as they regaled him with stories about their lives and the history of Boxer Hospital. He was forced to smile appreciatively at each new anecdote.

Once the ordeal of the luncheon ended and the ladies returned to their scheduled activities, Katherine and Thomas strolled back to the hospital from the bistro. Reflecting on the success of the afternoon, she asked, "What did you think of the 'Sisters'? Each is a very lovely lady in her own way. They're generous to a fault and very interested in the success of Boxer's fund-raising campaign. They seemed quite impressed by you also, I might add."

"Let's just say that I know how women in beauty contests must feel after spending the afternoon on display. The ladies uncovered every blemish in my physical and moral character in one short afternoon," Thomas replied as he pushed the elevator button and stepped inside among the other staff members returning from lunch.

"Yes, but just think of what you accomplished for the hospital," Katherine said with a barely disguised smile flickering at the corners of her mouth. She turned and hurried back to the ER. She had been away far too long. Besides, she did not want Thomas to see the enjoyment his discomfort gave her.

Later that evening as he glanced at his reflection in the mirror while he quickly changed into the dinner jacket and trousers that he kept at the hospital, Thomas decided that he was not such a bad "blind" date candidate. At forty, his hair already carried gray streaks of distinction at the temples and a bold blaze over his left eye. His barber had tried to convince him to dye his hair, but he had refused. Looking at himself in the exquisitely tailored jacket, he acknowledged that he cut a rather dashing figure even with the gray. Now if Augusta Maine would only act as generously at dispersing her money as the silver that sparkled in his hair, he would be well on his way toward raising the funds the hospital needed. Turning into her driveway, he knew that in very short order he would discover her intentions toward the hospital and him.

Katherine had told Thomas that Augusta Maine was wealthy and generous, but she had neglected to say that she was also breathtakingly beautiful when attired in evening clothes. Earlier in the day, she had been impressive as she stood a tall, thin, five feet ten inches. But tonight, Augusta had the carriage of an Egyptian goddess. She appeared to float across the carpet in a gossamer haze of pale blue silk as she entered the elaborately appointed formal living room complete with grand piano, colorful tapestries on the wall, and thick Turkish rugs on the glistening oak floor. Candles sparkled in silver holders everywhere, giving the room an aura of mystery. The sweet yet intoxicating aroma of flowers filled the air as she glided past. Thomas was not sure if the perfume emanated from her or the roses that filled the myriad of vases.

As Augusta extended her well-manicured hand, Thomas could see that the candles were not the only things that sparkled in that room. On her ears, shone large pear-shaped diamonds.

Around her neck winked an even larger stone on a slender platinum chain. Her hands were bejeweled with fiery rocks. Augusta certainly was a woman who believed in wearing her wealth rather than in keeping it locked in the safe-deposit box.

Somehow all the glitter and diamonds looked right on her. On other women, all the sparkling jewelry would have seemed ostentatious in their display, but Augusta carried her wealth so well that the diamonds looked appropriate and almost necessary. Had she been dressed in jeans and tennis shoes, the diamonds still would have been the perfect accessory for her.

"Well, Thomas Baker, so Boxer Hospital's new savior has come to wine and dine the first of the hospital's dragon ladies. Even if we had not lunched together this afternoon, I would have known you anywhere. For once, the rumor mill was correct. Let's go. I'm starved." Augusta smiled and purred as she hooked her arm through his and led Thomas past the attentive butler and into the night air.

Service at the country club with Augusta Maine on his arm was superior to its usual astounding quality. In all the times Thomas had dined there since arriving in town, he had never had so many people attending to his every need. He was not sure whether it was her beauty or her money that drew them like flies, but waiters fell over themselves to take their bar and dinner orders. Busboys constantly refilled their glasses and often spilled water as they stared at her. The wine stewards repeatedly verified their pleasure with his selection and almost made himself drunk from sampling new wines to enliven their dinner. The headwaiter frequently abandoned his post at the door to supervise their service personally, as if the overly attentive waiters were not giving enough of themselves.

Thomas was impressed by more than simply the service. Augusta was probably the most beautiful woman he had ever met. Her deep, rich mahogany skin shone with health and carefully applied makeup. Her black hair glistened from the careful application of conditioners and hung precisely under her chin with not a single strand out of place. Her lips pouted just enough to accentuate the hollows of her cheeks and the dimples that played mischievously whenever she smiled. Her nails were stylishly long yet sophisticated in shape and polish color and freshly manicured, making perfect companions to her long slender fingers. He had found her stunning in her linen and silk afternoon slacks suit, but in her evening attire, she was beyond comparison.

Looking at her, Thomas could easily understand how she had become accustomed to being pampered and spoiled by her father and all the other men who had entered her life. He had heard about her reputation for mistreating her companions and for leading their hearts on a merry chase. Something in her smile told him that the men probably enjoyed the punishment. At any rate, he did not intend to add his name to her list of conquests. His interests in her were purely professional and for the good of the hospital. He intended that they would remain that way.

When the orchestra struck the first notes of a waltz, Thomas rose and asked with a slight bow from the waist, "Would you care to dance? I can't promise that I won't step on your feet. I haven't waltzed in quite some time."

"Don't worry, Thomas. I'll be able to follow your lead and make you look good no matter what happens," Augusta replied with a cocky smile. She threw her head back in a hearty laugh that exposed her perfect pearly white teeth and long graceful neck. Thomas found his eyes drawn to the swell of her exposed bosom above the deep décolletage of her gown. With a chuckle, he reminded himself that this was a business venture and nothing more. As Augusta eased seductively into his arms, Thomas could tell that he would have to be careful around her. If not, he might feel her fangs.

Around the time that Thomas and the first of the "Sisters" should have been making their first turn around the dance floor, Katherine began to have misgivings as to the wisdom of sending him for an evening with Augusta Maine. She was known as a temptress who used her wealth, beauty, style, and elegance to gather men, use them, and then discard them. All of which she did quite publicly and with little feeling of remorse. When scolded for her brazen behavior, she had been known to respond that men did it all the time. She did not see any reason why she should not engage in the same practices. Besides, she reasoned that she had so much money that no one would dare shun her for her actions. And she was right. Everyone talked about her, but they all quickly forgave her behavior whenever they needed someone to chair a fund-raiser or write a check to a favorite charity. Augusta's generosity was as well known as her dalliances with men.

Yet Katherine could not help but wonder if she had made a mistake in insisting that he see Augusta alone. Katherine was aware of the growing affection that she and Thomas shared for each other, but as long as Boxer's financial situation and Thomas's position as her replacement as chief of staff lay between them, they would not be able to become a couple. Still, she did not want him interested in anyone else while they bided their time.

Shrugging off her worry and settling into her favorite chair with a cup of cocoa, Katherine quickly pushed thoughts of Thomas and Augusta from her mind. This was the first evening in a long time that belonged to her without any crises looming on the horizon. She intended to make the most of it and not let anything, including her concerns for Thomas, interfere with her relaxation. Besides, he was a grown man and could take care of himself. At least, she hoped he could.

Six

By the time the waltz had transitioned into a tango, Thomas found that he was actually enjoying himself. All the years of tedious dance lessons that interfered with football practice had finally paid off as he glided around the floor with Augusta in his arms. Her body melted into his as they dipped and oozed to the sultry rhythm. She fairly pulsated with passion as the music reached her core and moved her to insinuate her hips seductively. Thomas was almost embarrassed, but not quite.

This would definitely go down in the books as the blind date to remember. He would have loved to be able to tell someone about the feel of this sultry vision in his arms, but he could not. The first person with whom he thought to share his impressions was Katherine. As a student of human nature, he was aware that the last thing about which one woman wanted to hear was the virtues of another even if there were no romantic involvement between any of them. He forced himself to think of her as an undulating sack of money rather than as a woman. Still, the image of shimmering gold coins rippling through his fingers was almost as stimulating as the feel of the blue silk and Augusta's warm flesh under his fingers.

When the music stopped, Thomas sighed deeply and escorted Augusta back to their table. Tiny beads of perspiration dotted his top lip from the nearness of her. Katherine had been right. Augusta was a handful and definitely a woman to watch. As

Thomas sipped the cool champagne, he did just that as her catlike eyes hungrily devoured his face.

"Well, finally the hospital has a chief of staff with energy and stamina. A real man, not dear old Harriman or the woman doctor Katherine Winters. It's about time. I've had enough of port wine by the fire in the reading room or tea in the sunroom. At last, they've sent me someone who is worth the money I spend on that place every year. That's what this is all about, isn't it . . . my money? I shouldn't try to fool myself into believing that this is a real date. What exactly does the hospital need this time and what's it worth to you," Augusta purred, licking her full bottom lip as if something sweet clung to it.

"You're absolutely correct. This isn't a date. Although I'm having a fabulously good time, we do need to talk dollars. The capital campaign needs your support and so does a major technology upgrade. I've been charged by the board with bringing Boxer Hospital into the new millennium in the black with money to spare and new medical and surgical technology that will make every other hospital in this country green with envy. As the chief of staff, the success of this fund-raising campaign drive is vitally important to me. So, Augusta, we're here tonight in this grand dining room with this lively music wearing these somewhat uncomfortable clothes so that I can ask you to open your checkbook and write the biggest check you ever have to Boxer Hospital," Thomas replied without holding back. He saw no reason to be coy with a woman whose hand rested invitingly close to his crotch.

"My, my, you certainly are direct. Is this all the foreplay I get from you? A couple of dances, a bottle of champagne, a fabulous meal, and a hard sales pitch. You're a slam-bam kind of guy, aren't you? Well, so am I. I like a man who says what he wants and doesn't hold back. You show promise, Thomas. Now, I'll give Boxer what it wants from me if I get what I want from you. While you've been analyzing my financial portfolio, I've been studying your social register. You're single, never married, ambitious. You run five miles every day and work out at the gym every other. You have no unpleasant vices and do nothing to excess. You've lived a fairly discreet life and have not left behind a line of broken hearts. All of which makes you an ideal catch. Therefore, Dr. Baker, if you want money from me, you'll have to work for it. I have a list of demands that I don't think you'll find too difficult to satisfy. As a good faith gesture, I'll have my accountant send you my usual donation to the hospital in the morning. The rest you'll have to earn." Augusta winked and smiled wickedly as the tips of her nails lightly stroked the inside of Thomas's thigh.

Gently cradling her mischievous hand in his and skillfully maneuvering it to the top of the table, Thomas smiled with a controlled effort and said, "I'll do anything within reason for Boxer, but I cannot be bought. When I'm with a woman, I pick up the tab because that's what I do as a gentleman. I buy her flowers, I take her dancing, and I treat her like a lady not a hooker. What you're implying cheapens you and degrades me. I find you attractive, but I won't trade my personal self for the hospital's purse. Besides, I've found a perfect woman for me, only she doesn't know it yet. Therefore, Ms. Augusta Maine, I will accept your usual donation to Boxer and call it a night. Any additional money you might desire to donate to the hospital will come from your generous heart not because of anything that might develop between us in the way of payment for services rendered. Now, it's getting late and I have a full day planned tomorrow. This has been a very interesting evening. I'll take you home now."

Rather than being offended, Augusta responded, "Even with my hand in your crotch you manage to remain true to yourself. It looks as if Boxer finally has a no-compromise man at the top. Good for them. The stuffy old board finally had enough sense to select a chief of staff with spunk. But, you can't blame a girl for trying. Despite the rumors about me, I get lonely sometimes. Unfortunately, the only people I know are ones who like me only for my money. I've made that same offer to countless men, and every one of them has accepted it. But you're cut from a different cloth. I find that endearing, a little risky in business, but endearing. Very well, Dr. Baker. Call my accountant tomorrow and tell her the full amount you want. You'll have it the same afternoon, no strings attached. I like you, Dr. Baker. Good luck with the capital campaigns. Let me know when you want to go dancing again. I think I'll stay here a little longer. I haven't any reason to rush home, and my day doesn't start until the afternoon. I'll have my chauffeur pick me up when I'm ready to leave. By the way, if your love interest doesn't pan out, give me a call. I'm not a bad person to get to know. I do have some good qualities."

Bowing over Augusta's outstretched hand, Thomas replied, "I'm sure you have many, the least of which is a generous heart. You'll find the right person to share your life one day, if you give people a chance, but offering them money for their affection isn't the way to do it. Good night, Ms. Maine."

Thomas turned and walked from the room, leaving her sitting at the table sipping her champagne. To his relief, he had spent a profitable evening with the first of the "Sisters of Charity" and survived. He hoped that the others would be as agreeable.

Sitting in the hospital-provided car with his head resting against the soft leather upholstery, Thomas outlined what he would tell Katherine in the morning. He was tempted to call her tonight with the details of his evening, but he decided not to disturb her. She had been looking a bit tired and needed the rest after spending long hours in the ER.

He could almost read her expression as he described the dinner and dancing. He had not quite figured out how he would go about telling her of Augusta's strategically placed hand. Maybe he would leave out that little detail when he told her of the generous contribution Augusta had made to the hospital. Yet if he did not say anything about the attempted and almost successful seduction, Katherine would know that he was withholding information from her. She knew about Augusta's reputation with men and had warned him to be careful around her. He would have to think of the perfect approach before Katherine's nine o'clock appointment with him.

Katherine . . . now that was his idea of a woman. She was not cloying or clinging. She had her own approach to doing things. She was determined and strong. She knew what she wanted and went about getting it. She was not at all like Augusta, who used her sexuality and bank account to lure men into her trap for her own selfish motives. That was one woman who was too much like the black widow spider for his taste. He did not mind being consumed by passion shared with a woman, but he definitely did not want to be devoured by his partner. With Katherine, Thomas thought more of a give and take and a sharing of souls would exist. He had every intention of finding out as soon as he could arrange for them to have some time alone together without patients and Boxer between them.

Contrary to Thomas's beliefs, Katherine was not asleep. She had tried to go to bed after finishing her cocoa, but she found that her mind was much too restless. She kept picturing him in the arms of Augusta Maine, on the dance floor with Augusta Maine, in rapt conversation with Augusta Maine, in bed with Augusta Maine. Each new vision caused her eyes to pop open one more time. She tossed and turned so often that she ripped off the sheets and had to remake the bed.

"I never should have sent him off alone with that woman," Katherine fussed at herself as she tucked in the top sheet. Thomas didn't know how conniving Augusta could be. He thought he was worldly and quite sophisticated, but he had never played in that woman's court. She'd probably finished him off early and was simply sitting back picking the remains from her teeth right now. Even if she left him with a shred of his dignity intact, she would have left her imprint on him. Katherine didn't know what she could have been thinking. She should have gone with him on his first visit. She could have introduced them, set the stage, eased over any awkward moments.

But no, she was too busy thinking of herself. She wanted an evening at home to relax. Now, she hadn't had a minute of peace since his date with Augusta started. She wondered what time he'd get home, if she released him from her clutches long enough for him to go home. "I bet he'll be useless in our meeting tomorrow morning," Katherine speculated.

Clutching her pillow, Katherine paced her bedroom with great vigor. Her steps were as erratic as her thoughts as she tried to formulate a strategy for introducing the topic of Augusta into the conversation tomorrow. She wanted to know all the details, but she did not want to appear too interested in Thomas's personal life. She was quite curious about the outcome of the dinner. She wondered if Thomas had managed to secure the funds the hospital needed as he maintained the position of respect and dignity of the office of chief of staff.

"This is ridiculous!" Katherine stewed as she threw herself and her knotted up pillow onto her bed. Her cat Mitzi looked ready to bolt from the room at any minute. She had never seen her owner look and act so upset. "I don't know why I'm being so silly." Surely Thomas had not risen to this position of power without knowing how to avoid the traps laid by men and women. He certainly should know how to assess the enemy's vulnerable points and strike at them. If he didn't, that was one more reason why she should be the chief of staff.

"She was acting just like a high school girl over a guy who meant nothing to her. What did she care if Augusta Maine ate him alive and spit out the leftovers for all of Washington to see? What he did to acquire money for the hospital was of no concern to her. He was the boss. He was the man. He sat in her office, rode in her car, and ran her hospital. She'd say he had it pretty good. If Augusta proved to be a bit more than he expected, he'll know better than to meet her without a body shield next time. It was not her job to take care of him. She'd already saved his hide once by arranging this truce with the department heads.

She was the one who diverted a strike by them. She was the one who proposed an alternative strategy. He owed her . . . she certainly didn't owe him anything, including her loyalty.

So why was it that she couldn't get to sleep? Because she was a fool, that's why. She had this tall, handsome, take-charge man to get under her skin when she should have resented him. She'd lowered her defenses and softened her exterior armor to the point where he had been able to penetrate her fortress. She had promised herself that she would not fall for him and already she'd broken her word to herself. She'd compromised her position and forgotten that her goal was to regain the top management spot at Boxer.

"From this moment onward, I will not let this happen," she promised herself aloud. She would not bleed for him when he showed the scratches inflicted on him by Augusta. She would not sympathize, considering she'd told him to be careful. This was a new day! "I am in control of myself, not Thomas. I am going to sleep. Good night, Mitzi."

With that, Katherine turned out the light and willed herself to fall asleep.

The next morning both Katherine and Thomas looked as if they needed rest. Anyone seeing them would have thought that they had been out together. Instead, each one had been at home tossing and turning and thinking about the other.

Katherine arrived at Thomas's office promptly at nine o'clock with a cup of very strong, black coffee steaming in her mug. Thomas immediately ushered her to the conference table in the corner where his mug of equally strong coffee waited. As if anticipating a need for more, he set the entire pot at the center of the table as he pulled up his chair and opened the first file requiring their attention.

The air was thick with the unmentioned topic as they discussed the budget of the ER, personnel matters, and patient concerns. Katherine wanted to know all about the evening with

Augusta, but she had promised herself that she would not bring
up the topic unless he did. She did not want to appear overly
interested in Thomas's activities or concerned about his welfare.
Thomas wanted her to ask him a leading question so that he
could tell her about his success. He had decided to omit the
part about Augusta's wandering hand and proposition, but he
needed Katherine to show interest so that he could open the
discussion. Both showed their frustration by pouring yet another
cup of coffee and remaining silent on the topic that really interested them.

When the business part of their meeting ended, Thomas
glanced at the calendar he knew by heart and said, "I see I'm
taking Patrice Miller to a baseball game tonight. I assume we'll
be sitting in the hospital's box seats. Is there anything I should
know about her that you haven't already told me? I'm prepared
to dress casually, eat stadium food, and swear openly. This
should be a much more enjoyable evening than last night."

"Oh, why? What didn't you like about spending the evening
with Augusta at the club?" Katherine asked with what she hoped
was just enough interest. She did not want to appear too anxious.

"I really can't quite put my finger on it, although I don't
think Augusta had any problem doing just that. The food was
great and so was the service. The orchestra played beautifully,
and she danced like Ginger Rogers. She was also incredibly
generous with her attention and her finances. Augusta said that
her accountant would send over her donation to the capital and
technology funds later today, but it was here when I arrived.
You might want to take a look at it. But, at any rate, the awk-
wardness of a first meeting is over," Thomas replied in an offhand manner. He wanted to appear nonchalant about his
dealings with Augusta and about his success with the campaign.
He watched attentively as Katherine's eyes adjusted to the enormity of the figure printed on the check.

"You must have made quite an impression to cause the lady
to part with this much money. Old Harriman and I never saw

this large a single contribution in all of our efforts. I won't ask what you had to do to win her favor, but I'm sure the hospital will appreciate your sacrifice," Katherine remarked with her teeth closed. It took all of her strength not to throw the check into Thomas's face and storm from the room. To think she had lain awake all night worrying about him, hoping that Augusta had not hurt his ego too badly, and all the time he had been playing up to her. Now it looked as if she paid well for his services.

"Well, I was given the responsibility of turning the tide on the flow of pink ink spewing from Boxer before it turned to red. I'm sure the board won't question my methods. Now, tell me about Patrice Miller," Thomas said as he extracted the check for ten million dollars from Katherine's outstretched fingers.

Settling into her chair with the mug of hot coffee between her hands, Katherine told Thomas all she could remember about Patrice, saying, "She's a chemist or at least she was before she developed that bug repellent that sold so well. She holds a number of Ph.D.'s in different fields of chemistry and biology. In addition to the spray, she filed patents for anticorrosives used by the Navy on submarines and shatterproof stain resistant glass employed in the cockpits of almost all planes. She's very down to earth and 'normal' for someone who thinks and lives so completely in the world of the sciences. Unlike Augusta who has had numerous husbands and is always on the look out for more, Patrice has never been married and appears perfectly content with that status. She's a lot of fun in a clean, wholesome way."

"Great. I look forward to an uncomplicated evening. Would you care to join us? It gets a little difficult to maintain conversation at a ball game. Your being there would help keep things moving along," Thomas asked, genuinely interested in having her company. He did not want to spend another evening trying to decide what to share with Katherine. It was much easier to have her along so that she would see firsthand what transpired between Patrice and himself.

"No, thanks. I've already planned my evening. Besides, I

really don't like baseball. You can tell me everything about your evening when we see each other tomorrow. I'll go with you to Jasmine's because of your fear of riding and my passion for it, but I'll take a permanent rain check on attending a baseball game," Katherine quickly responded.

"Fine. I must admit that I was extremely reluctant to approach the 'Sisters' on an individual basis asking for contributions so early in the relationship. But it looks as if you were correct in your assessment. If Patrice proves to be as generous as Augusta, the hospital's financial worries will be over and a confrontation between management and the board will have been diverted. That plan of yours certainly seems to be working," Thomas said with a yawn and a stretch.

Not wanting to take a chance on hearing anything she might not want to know, Katherine rose, gathered her papers, and walked to the door. "Don't forget to buy Patrice a little something from the souvenir vendors . . . a hat or some kind of baseball trinket. She would like that," she called with her hand on the knob.

"Thanks for the tip. Don't forget your cup," Thomas replied as he walked toward her with it in his hand.

Before Catherine could balance all of her stuff and turn around, Thomas stood behind her. His nearness made her heart flutter. She tried desperately to push down the blush that rose from her chest to her neck and threatened to consume her face. She did not want him to know the effect he could have on her.

Spinning around with a cheerful smile pasted on her brightly flushed face Katherine sputtered, "Thanks. I don't know what I'd do without this mug. It's the third one I've bought this month. I keep putting them down and not remembering where. I'll see you later. Enjoy the game."

"Right," Thomas managed to reply as he looked into her upturned face. He had never stood this close to her before. Katherine was even more beautiful up close. He was totally overwhelmed by her nearness as her eyes flickered gold sparks into his.

As he placed the empty mug into her hand, Thomas's fingers lightly brushed against Katherine's, causing rivers of fire to flow through both of them. Her lids fluttered slightly as his face moved almost imperceptibly closer to hers like a moth being drawn to a flame against its wishes. She dared not move for fear of frightening him away.

Just as their lips were about to touch, the intercom between Thomas and his secretary sounded. Its shrill buzzing broke the silence and the mood, snapping them back to the reality of their lives. Hastily taking her mug, Katherine quickly backed out of the room and closed the door. For a moment, Thomas stood transfixed in time and space as the fragrance of her perfume lingered in the air.

When the intercom buzzed again, Thomas pulled himself away from his pleasant thoughts to answer it. The moment was gone, shattered. He hoped it would return again some day.

Katherine shook off the spell of Thomas as she marched to her office. She was late for rounds in the ER, but she had to settle her nerves or she'd subject her colleagues to her tumultuous emotions.

Katherine could not believe that she had almost allowed him to kiss her. She had wanted him to do it and done nothing to stop him. As a matter of fact, she had encouraged him by blushing like a schoolgirl. She scolded herself as she rushed down the hall. It must have been the caffeine in the coffee. It was capable of making her face turn that obnoxious bright shade. Surely, it could make her want to throw herself into his arms. She would have to remember to avoid caffeine when she was at work. She did not want a close call like that again.

Passing the coffee machine, Katherine paused for a minute. She thought to herself that something must be wrong. This machine and the one in Thomas's office were identical. The pot on the left was always and automatically the decaffeinated canister. The machine was programmed to take only the smaller of the two carafes designed for decaffeinated coffee. Her first cup had come from the pot on the left. She had watched Thomas

bring the full pot to the table after taking it from the left side
of the coffee machine.

Slipping into her lab coat, Katherine mused that she must be
coming down with something. She still felt hot and flushed. It
must have been because of the fatigue that numbed her body
and the lack of sleep last night. That was the only way she could
explain the blush that burned her cheeks when she only drank
decaffeinated coffee. She was definitely floating under the affects of something but it was not caffeine.

Seven

That night Thomas met Patrice Miller at the ballpark. Unlike Augusta Maine, Patrice refused to allow him to pick her up at her house. She said that she would be in Baltimore shopping and did not see any reason why she should have to return to Washington for him to pick her up to take her back to Baltimore. Anyway, just in case she did not enjoy his company, she would have her own car and would be able to leave on a moment's notice.

From that and Katherine's description of Patrice, Thomas had expected a very liberated woman, a woman who held her own door and maybe his, a woman who spoke her mind and would tell him when and if he could express his opinions. He was not surprised when she finally arrived.

Patrice entered the box about halfway through the third inning and caused quite a stir among the men seated there. Her tall, elegant carriage bordered on regal as she eased her way through the press of people milling around the skybox. She wore her thick, black hair in a river of curls that cascaded down her back. Although her attire was simple, she commanded everyone's attention by the way she moved in the beige slacks and cream silk blouse. Her only adornment was a simple gold necklace from which hung an ornate "P," which she fingered constantly. Her nails were short but newly polished in a subtle almost nude shade of pink that complimented her fair skin tone. She wore no makeup on her perfectly chiseled face and needed none. From the top of her head to her feet, she exhibited no sign of imperfection.

"Dr. Baker," Patrice said almost timidly as she approached, "I'm dreadfully sorry for being late. I was at Pimlico and lost all sense of time. I do hope I haven't missed anything. How are the birds doing?"

"It's the bottom of the third and they're in the lead. Not exactly inspired playing, but I can't ask for much more than that. Why were you at the track? Was something important happening, a big race perhaps?" Thomas asked as much from real curiosity as from a desire to fill the void in conversation. Patrice did not look like the type who would frequent the paddock.

"My mare is running in a claiming stakes race tomorrow, and I wanted to see her last workout. She has been clocking some impressive times lately. Don't look surprised, doctor. You'll find that there isn't much in the way of a sport that I don't like. I'm sure my file told you about all that. You have me at a disadvantage since I know very little about you. What are your interests? I've read that you're single and a golfer, but that's about all I know. What's your handicap?" Patrice asked with genuine interest. It was well known in her social circle that, although she had never married, she enjoyed men who were athletically fit and could keep up with her appetite for all things physical.

My golf game is mostly social, although on a good day I can do pretty well. I play a little tennis and I run for exercise and enjoyment. I've entered the Marine marathon a few times. I didn't embarrass myself too badly. At least I finished before nightfall, which is more than I can say about some people," Thomas replied with a chuckle. He did not add that he had sprained a muscle in his groin and had to lay off running for a month after that race.

"Well, I'll have to see for myself. One Sunday you'll have to come out to the farm with me. We'll get up early for a brisk run along the bridle path and then have a light breakfast. Afterward, we'll play some tennis. I like a man whose interests in sports are varied. When you tire of one activity, there's always another," Patrice said without taking her eyes from the game. Since arriving, she had not missed a single pitch. Thomas could see her level of dedication to sports in her ability to divide her attention between his conversation and the activity on the ball field without missing a beat in either.

So far, the play on the field had been less than inspiring, with neither side hitting especially well and nothing spectacular happening in the pitching arena either. When the star batter came up to the plate, all of that changed. Suddenly, a hush fell over the skybox and the stadium. No one moved. Patrice raised her right hand as a sign to Thomas that she intended to give her full attention to the game.

Planting his feet, the batter waited for the perfect pitch as the people in the stands held their breath. The pitcher shook off the first signals from the catcher and accepted the next. He wound up and let fly a fast ball that curved off the right corner of the plate. "Strike one!" the umpire shouted as the crowd booed.

"Don't worry, Hector, you'll get another good one. Shake it off!" Patrice shouted, her voice mingling with the thousands of others in the park.

Readying himself again, the pitcher threw a sinker that dropped just as the batter swung with all his might. "Strike two!" the umpire motioned, his voice drowned out by the chorus of boos that filled the stadium.

"Strike? That was not a strike. We need a new umpire!" Patrice booed along with the others. Thomas, who was not exactly a baseball fan, almost smiled at her annoyance but decided against it. The expression on her face said that she took her baseball seriously and would not react well to his inability to see what she considered the umpire's glaring deficiency as a major flaw in the man's character.

Once again the deafening hush fell over the crowd. The batter bent down and picked up a handful of dust that he rubbed onto the handle of his bat. Taking his stance once again, he waited as the pitcher wound up and fired. This time the ball missed its mark but almost hit the batter.

"Ball!" shouted the umpire.

"Well, at least you got that one right!" Patrice shouted back, rolling up her shirt sleeves and unbuttoning the top button of her blouse. Tiny beads of perspiration glistened on her top lip and forehead. Sitting on the edge of her seat, she was ready for the next pitch.

The pitcher fired another wild ball toward home plate. Again the umpire shouted "Ball" as Patrice and everyone else in the stands cheered the poor effort of the pitcher and their team's good fortune.

Now the stands came alive. Conversation broke out among the spectators in the skybox. Patrice's eyes sparkled brightly with her excitement. She clutched Thomas on the forearm and waved her hands enthusiastically as everyone waited for the next pitch.

When it came, the batter swung, but tipped it back into the stands. With a full count against him, the stands grew silent once again.

Patrice nervously chewed on her knuckle until the skin was red and swollen. With the bases loaded and two men out, the batter must have been feeling the pressure. If he could only hit a home run, he could put the team ahead of its opponent by a score of four to zero.

The pitcher shook off the catcher once, twice, and finally accepted the pitch on the third offer. Patrice gripped Thomas's arm as the batter took his stance and stared intently at the pitcher's mound. It was time for the show down.

"Let her rip. Hit it out of the park!" Patrice whispered, afraid to speak too loudly. She did not want to break the batter's concentration.

As the pitcher wound up for the pitch, a sickening hush fell over the stands. The batter focused all of his concentration on the ball as it sailed straight toward him on a straight and true line. No curve ball and no sinker could fly like a fast ball over the center of the plate. It was his pitch . . . he could hit this one out of the park. He could taste the adrenaline, smell the victory, and hear the applause.

But there was none. The bat never made contact with the ball. The batter swung and missed his favorite pitch. He had become too sure of himself or too cocky or maybe a speck of dust had gotten into his eye at that very moment. It did not matter why he had not hit the ball. All that mattered was that the inning ended with the score still tied zero to zero with three men on base.

The fans tried to rally their spirits, but it was no use. The inning was over. They would have to wait until the bottom of the fourth when the home team would once again come up to bat.

"Damn, but I'm hungry. Baseball always makes me hungry. Let's take a walk. You can buy me a dog while we talk. I can tell that you're not exactly a baseball fan. I know that you didn't bring me here to watch the game. How much does Boxer need this time?" Patrice asked as she took Thomas by the arm and led him into the stadium and the crush of people.

Thomas was relieved to be out of the box. Patrice was correct. He did not especially enjoy the game, and they did need to talk business. Buying her a stadium deluxe chilidog with raw onions, cheese, and extra hot peppers and a plain extra crispy almost black one for himself, he explained his purpose as they strolled along the concourse of overpriced shops.

"I'll come right to the point. Boxer needs a complete technological upgrade to all of its equipment in addition to the capital expansion project already under way. As a major supporter of the hospital, I've come to ask you to open your heart one more time," Thomas replied, matching his pace to Patrice's as she looked into each store.

"Well, I guess it was simply a matter of time before the old equipment broke down. Technology isn't much different from a racehorse; you overuse it and it reaches a point where it just can't cut it any longer. I had to put one of my studs to pasture for that very reason. He just couldn't produce a foal worth the effort anymore. Some people said I should put him down since he couldn't contribute to his upkeep any longer. But, you know, I simply couldn't do that. Well, of course, I'll help Boxer, but what's in it for me? I already give that hospital a fortune every year. What will I get out of it this time?" Patrice asked. Unlike Augusta, she did not give any indication of what she requested in return for her money.

"The undying gratitude of the board and staff of Boxer," Thomas responded instantaneously.

Throwing her head back in a hearty laugh, Patrice said, "That's the best answer I've ever gotten to my suggestive proposals from a man. Either I'm slipping or you didn't understand my question. Let me reword it. I'm a single woman in need of a man's companionship. You're a single man who might have the same needs. We seem to be reasonably compatible. We could start with an occasional dinner to see if we liked each other and progress from there. What do you say, Dr. Baker?"

Before Thomas could respond, a voice from the crowd called his name. "I knew I'd find you two in the shopping concourse. There wasn't a chance you could pass up the team merchandise, was there, Patrice? How are you? It's been a while since we've chatted," Katherine gushed as she trotted up to join them.

Thomas smiled at the sight of her in jeans, T-shirt, tennis shoes, and baseball cap. He had not known that Katherine was such a fan of the sport. If he had, he would have insisted that she join them. Patrice would have had someone with whom to talk about the game.

Patrice, however, did not share his enthusiasm for Katherine's appearance. She had counted on having him all to herself. So far, he had not responded to her proposal. From the expression on his face as he gazed at Katherine, Patrice suspected that she did not stand a chance with him. Even if Katherine were unaware of his interest in her, she could see that Thomas seemed quite smitten.

"Well, you hospital people certainly have your timing down

to a science, don't you? It's good to see you again, Dr. Winters, although I would have preferred that you had arrived just a little later. I had just asked Dr. Baker exactly how much my contribution to the hospital meant to him. I guess I have my answer. How much did Augusta Maine ante up? A little bird told me that she coughed up about ten million. Put me down for the same. I can't have that woman outdoing me. My accountant will be in touch. I've seen all I care to of these shops. Let's return to the game," Patrice said with the annoyance she felt only slightly disguised in her voice.

As they settled themselves in the skybox once more, Katherine leaned over and whispered, "What did Patrice mean when she said that she had been trying to ascertain the importance of her contribution to you? I don't remember her ever putting it quite that way when she and I did business."

"Let's watch the game. I'll tell you later," Thomas replied. He needed the time to formulate the response he would give to Katherine concerning Patrice's proposal. He would have to explain very carefully that he had not done anything to elicit her proposition any more than he had suggested anything to kindle Augusta's interest in him. He knew from his experience with women that he would have to tread very carefully on this subject.

Although Katherine enjoyed baseball, she could not keep her mind on the game. She had a suspicion that Patrice had tried to proposition Thomas. However, she did not know if he had given her a reason to think that he might be interested. After all, he was a perfectly healthy man and would undoubtedly feel flattered by the advances of beautiful, wealthy women. She could understand Patrice's interest in him, too. When she took the time to think about him, which to her surprise happened more often lately, she found him attractive and appealing, too. If she could be drawn to him, surely other women would be also.

Not that his social interaction with other women mattered in the least. Katherine had convinced herself that she had no real desire to move their relationship to another level despite the intimacy they had almost shared earlier in the day. She told herself that she was merely curious in a clinical sort of way. Her reaction to him was on a par with her desire to understand the life cycle of a virus so that she could develop an antidote to it.

Still, as she watched Thomas out of the corner of her eye, Katherine grudgingly had to admit that he did have a noble chin and well-defined cheekbones. His skin was certainly smooth despite the heavy clean-shaven beard. His appearance was impeccable even at a baseball game at which a more relaxed presentation was certainly the norm. His shoulders were distinctively broad but not at all vulgar in a suit. His legs were long and athletic but not lumpy with muscles. He appeared to be in good physical condition and quite well toned. Overall, Thomas made quite pleasant company.

Thomas's communication skills were certainly adequate, although some of her colleagues did not agree. Only once concerning the issue of the downsizing of departments had he spoken in a way that had offended others. Even then, Katherine chalked that episode up to a driving desire to do what was right for the hospital. He had shown a delightful ability to be flexible when the department heads presented an alternate plan. No, she could not complain about Thomas Baker.

As the seventh inning ended and the eighth progressed with the score tied, Katherine became increasingly tired. She longed to be in her bed sound asleep rather than sitting here chaperoning a nondate between her boss and a member of the hospital's board. Despite the loud stadium noise, she found herself dozing only to awaken in time to do the wave. She was not having a good time and should be at home curled up in her bed with her cat at her side.

Finally Katherine could stand it no longer. Leaning across Thomas to bid Patrice good night, she said, "I have to call it a night. I'm on duty in the ER at seven tomorrow. Thank you so much for your generosity toward the hospital. Your contribution will make so much possible."

Patrice barely disguised her delight at Katherine's leaving as she cooed, "It's been wonderful seeing you again. Let's not wait a year before we take in another game together."

Thomas, on the other hand, was not happy to see Katherine leave. "Why don't you stay a little longer? You can get someone else to cover for you. You must be getting hungry. We could stop for a pizza on the way back to Washington after the game," he almost pleaded with her to stay.

"If I stay any longer, you'll have to book a hotel room for me. I drove myself up here, remember. I have to leave now while I'm still awake. I'll see you in the morning," Katherine responded, picking up her cap and bag. Her keys jingled from her fingers as she climbed the skybox stairs and disappeared into the mezzanine crush.

"Before I make a total fool of myself, tell me something Dr. Baker. Is there anything going on between you and Dr. Winters? I thought I picked up some vibes between you, but I'm not quite sure. If you two are an 'item,' I'll back off. What's the scoop?" Patrice asked.

Thomas could tell from the expression of sincerity in her voice that she was truly interested in getting to know him better, unlike Augusta Maine who only wanted to use him. Unwilling to comment on a relationship that was only a wish in his heart, he quickly ran over his calendar of events for the weekend. Although he did not look forward to spending the day in the horse country with Jasmine Gaylord, he certainly appreciated having the commitment with her as an excuse for not seeing more of Patrice.

"Our relationship is strictly professional. However, I'm not free this weekend. I still have one more member of the board to approach for a contribution. Boxer's fund-raising effort has to take top priority with me for a while," Thomas responded graciously. Patrice was certainly an appealing woman, but until he could reach some level of understanding with Katherine, his

mind was too busy with thoughts of her to entertain the idea
of forming a relationship with anyone else.

"Too bad, but I understand and appreciate your devotion to
Boxer. There are times when I put everything else aside, too.
Well, give me a call if you're ever up my way. This game is
over. It's time for us to head home. If you don't hear from my
accountant tomorrow, give me a call and I'll get right on it,"
Patrice accepted his rejection in the same spirit with which he
had given it. Sadly, she acknowledged that her woman's intui-
tion had been correct. Even if Dr. Baker did not admit the existence of a relationship, she could tell that some kind of spark
or chemistry passed between them. She spent a lot of time
watching people and was seldom wrong when she picked up
their vibes.

Thomas walked Patrice to her car on the huge lot before
returning to his waiting limousine. Taking his seat, he closed
his eyes and thought about the success of his visits with the
"Sisters" and the difference in personality between the two he
had already met. Augusta was flashy and aggressive; Patrice
was subtle but direct. Augusta exuded an almost melancholy
passion and joy of living, as if she worked at having fun. Patrice
grasped life and lived it while not missing an opportunity to
add to its wealth. He wondered what kind of person Jasmine
would be. He would find out soon enough.

Despite Patrice's winning personality, she could not begin to
compare to Katherine, whose sense of grace and compassion
for humanity combined to make her such a wonderful person.
Patients and colleagues always complimented her ability to listen and make people feel loved and valued. She possessed a
way of making people feel so comfortable with her that they
immediately wanted to open their hearts and share their secrets.
She empathized without becoming maudlin, sympathized without being mushy, and listened without being condescending.

Thomas had heard about these wonderful attributes from people who knew of her ability to manage the ER and the hospital
long before he took over the chief of staff's job at Boxer. Since

arriving, he had seen her in action and learned to value her gentleness firsthand. She had saved the relationship between his office and the department heads. He already knew that without her devotion to Boxer and commitment to her colleagues and patients, he would have fallen flat on his face.

What Thomas did not know was Katherine's level of devotion to him. He believed that she would have yielded to him in his office earlier that day, but the call had interfered. He hoped that another opportunity would appear for him to test the waters. Before he took the next step, he needed to be certain that she was willing for him to occupy a space in her heart. Until then, he had no choice but to wait and hope. Maybe tomorrow or the next day he would be able to find out where he stood with her.

Katherine's drive down the busy highway was anything but pleasant. It was not the lateness of the hour but rather the thoughts that echoed through her mind with every rotation of the tires that made the distance seem so long between Baltimore and Washington. She had driven this road so many times but never had she heard it speak to her. Now, the closer she came to Washington and the more distance she placed between herself and Baltimore, the louder she heard his name. Over and over the road shouted "Thomas" and made her question her decision in leaving him at the baseball game.

As Katherine pulled into the driveway of her apartment building, she was almost convinced that she had made the wrong decision. By the time she opened the door of her apartment, she knew she had.

Flopping down on the sofa with Mitzi at her side, Katherine loudly chided herself for her decision. "I could have stayed until the game ended, Mitzi. Yes, I was very sleepy, although I'm completely awake now. I should have forced myself to stick it out. Now, once again, I've left Thomas with another woman. Somehow, I don't remember Patrice being that attractive either.

Whenever I met with her, she wore jeans and beat up tennis shoes. Her hair was always a wreck, and she never wore makeup. She certainly has changed a lot in the last year. I definitely made a mistake this time. She's more his type than Augusta is, too. Well, Mitzi, there's nothing like throwing a man at your competition. You should be very happy that you don't have this problem," she said stroking her cat's slick fur. Mitzi always seemed to understand everything Katherine shared with her without asking for any additional explanation. She was certainly a good listener and confidant.

Katherine went about the motions of getting ready for bed without giving any thought to the actions themselves. After she had given Mitzi a late night snack and tidied up the kitchen, she checked the locks and turned out the lights. Although she was extremely tired, Katherine was not sure that she would be able to sleep with her thoughts a jumble of confusion.

Pulling up the covers, she stared at the ceiling and mindlessly watched the blades of the ceiling fan revolve. As they turned, Katherine felt her mind gradually slowing down and her body growing heavy. Slowly she sank into the much-needed sleep. Her last thought was of Thomas. In her presleep dream, he had pulled her into his arms. She had not resisted as his lips pressed against hers. She had not wanted him to stop as his hands caressed her back and shoulders and his fingers tangled in her hair.

The next morning awakening refreshed and ready for a busy day in the ER, Katherine bounded out of bed and out of the apartment before Mitzi could protest the speedy departure and the lack of morning scratching. She was determined to push any thoughts of Thomas Baker from her mind. He had plagued her mind enough already. She had work to do and goals to meet. She would no longer allow herself to be sidetracked by treacherous thoughts about him. She still had to prove to him and to the members of the board that she could have run the hospital with as much ease as he was doing.

After scanning the charts from the previous night and running her eyes over the department's budget, Katherine felt ready for her morning meeting with Thomas. Actually, she was more than ready. She had just completed a very detailed budget review that showed her department performing in top financial condition. It was actually under budget thanks in no small part to her cost-containment practices, which she'd accomplished without schedule changes or workforce reductions.

Gathering the copies of her report and her memo pad, Katherine took the elevator to the eighth floor and the office of the chief of staff. She walked down the hall with confidence as the heels of her sensible shoes tapped a bold tattoo. She felt good this morning and ready for anything.

While she waited for him to appear, Katherine looked around the conference room that should have been hers. Nothing had changed since Tomas had taken possession of the offices; everything down to the plants in the windows and the prints hanging on the walls was exactly as she had left it. She did not know if Thomas simply did not care about decorating, if he did not object to her taste, or if he knew that his tenure would be so short that changing anything would be a waste of money. The reason did not really matter—all that concerned her was the mark she had left on the ambiance of the room. Katherine knew that she had affected other aspects of the hospital, also.

Folding her hands behind her head as she sat in the comfortable chair, Katherine thought of the innovations she had made for the betterment of the institution's environment. Under her direction, a day care center had opened in the north wing, enabling parents to spend quality time with their children during their work hours. She had staffed it with teachers who specialized in early childhood development so that the children could have instruction as well as nurturing. It was such a success that other hospitals in the city had followed Boxer's example and opened their own centers.

She had also instituted a mentoring program so that staff new to the hospital would find a friendly face to which to turn in the first few awkward months of getting acquainted with the hospital. Everyone commented on the improvement in morale as soon as the program started. The "old timers" suddenly felt a new purpose in coming to work every day and the new employees found a ready ear for their problems and concerns. Again, other hospitals had heard of the success of her program and initiated their own.

Her latest coupe was reflected in her budget. Simply by asking the members of her department to tighten their belts and to treat the hospital's funds as if they were their own and to conserve, she had encouraged them to reduce spending. Her people understood that if they pinched pennies, recycled what they could, and used less of disposable items they could and would save money. Katherine knew that as soon as her figures became known throughout the hospital all of the other department heads would follow in her footsteps.

Rising, she walked over to what she referred to as the "wall of honor" on which hung the photographs of all the chiefs of staff. Thomas's was the most recent addition to the long line of men who had held the position. Katherine wanted hers to be among them one day. It should have been there already.

"Your photo will look lovely on that wall some day," Thomas said as he entered and closed the door behind him.

Katherine spun around at the sound of his voice. She had not heard him enter. The last thing she wanted was to be discovered gazing with envy at the photographs. The last person she would have wanted to find her was Thomas.

"Will I? What makes you so sure that I'll be offered the position? Why are you so sure that I'll accept? I have my pride, you know. I know I'm still young and considered by many to be green, but they should have given me the job instead of you. It should be my photograph up there now and not yours. You'll see and so will the others," Katherine said with more than a little anger in her voice.

"Katherine, I know you can do this job. You've proven it many times. I've told you before that there were two factors against you in the board's decision-making process. The first is that you really are too young for the position. After you finish running the ER and are about thirty-five, you'll be ready for this job. At thirty, you simply can't command the level of confidence that a person of forty can. Give the hospital time and give yourself time. You'll find your way here without any trouble," Thomas responded, trying to sound convincing. He knew that Katherine felt as if she had been ignored by not being permanently promoted to that spot. He wanted her to understand the board's position so that she would stop thinking that he was in any way responsible and holding him at arm's length.

"And, what's the second reason?" she asked taking her seat at the table.

"At this time in the hospital's life, the board felt that it needed someone with considerable experience in fund-raising. Like it or not, I'm the one who can do it. I've already raised twenty million in two days. Not bad for the new guy on the block," Thomas added, assuming his seat at the head of the table. "Shall we begin our meeting now?"

"Shall I remind you, Dr. Baker, that I'm the one who suggested that you introduce yourself to the 'Sisters' and that they were a soft touch? Perhaps you should give a little credit where it's due. Those women are very generous toward Boxer. All you had to do was open your arms to receive their gifts. Even I with my youth managed to appeal to their generosity," Katherine replied with her voiced tinged with anger.

"Were they as generous with you? I seem to remember that the figures you reported were somewhat lower than mine. Am I mistaken?" Thomas countered as he gave the indication that at any minute he would search for the elusive numbers.

Conceding reluctantly Katherine said, "You are correct. However, if I had only played the game more effectively, I could have achieved the same results. I'm more knowledgeable now about the importance of politics in every endeavor. I was naive enough to think that I could simply present the facts and that they would obtain the desired results. I know better now. When the opportunity arises, I'll do better this time."

"I don't doubt that you've made considerable progress in your education. However, the figures speak for themselves. My contact with the 'Sisters' has been very profitable for Boxer," Thomas concluded as he settled into his chair. He felt satisfied that he had successfully made his point.

"While we're talking about figures, I'd like to share my department's budget with you. If you look at the bottom line, you'll see that we're in the black by quite a healthy margin. Let me point out that this is due in no small part to the ability of my people to pull together when the times get tight," Katherine explained, gesturing with her pencil and displaying a great deal of pride and irritation in her voice.

"That's remarkable. I'm sure the others will follow your lead. When will you have copies of your report available for their perusal?" Thomas asked. He wanted her to know that the full weight of his support was behind her.

"They're ready now. I wanted to share the results with you first. I'll have my department's secretary deliver copies to everyone as soon as we finish our meeting. By the way, how was the rest of the game? Sorry I had to leave you, but I couldn't stay awake any longer," Katherine said feeling a bit more confident now that Thomas had looked so favorably on her figures.

"We won by one run. We didn't stay much longer either. I had finished what I needed and as Patrice said, 'the game was over.' But, you know, a funny thing happened as I walked Patrice to her car. She commented that she thought there was something going on between us. I didn't know how to reply really. I've never had a woman ask me if I'm available. They usually assume that since I'm single, I'm fair game," Thomas commented in an offhanded way. He hoped he was convincing in his effort to sound nonchalant about the topic.

"Really? That was rather bold of her, don't you think? And what did she mean by saying that the 'game was over'? Did she think you were entertaining yourself with some kind of man-woman amusement at her expense or was she referring to what she assumed was our relationship?" Katherine asked with more than a little irritation in her voice.

"Considering she thought that we had something developing between us, I guess she could have meant both scenarios. What should I have told her . . . about us I mean? Something almost happened yesterday if I remember correctly. If my secretary hadn't buzzed me, who knows what would have occurred," Thomas stated, hoping that Katherine's answer would match his thoughts.

"What is there to say about us, Thomas? We were both very tired and overworked. We had been working together on serious matters. Obviously, we have a good professional relationship. I suppose it would be possible for an outsider to misconstrue the nature of our association and make assumptions about the extent of our relationship based on the relaxed manner in which we conduct ourselves. I'm sure that there aren't too many people who are as dedicated to their work to the same level that we are. Naturally, that devotion throws us together in a way that might be suggestive of something more to those who don't know us. What did you tell her about us?" Katherine answered, avoiding his question by asking one of her own.

"I told her basically the same thing you just said. I'm relieved to know that we're on the same page with this easy, relaxed working relationship. It clears the air considerably to know that we understand each other on this topic. It should also keep any misunderstandings from developing between us, especially where people of the opposite gender are concerned. Now that we're on this topic, you know that we're both expected at Jasmine Gaylord's this Saturday for a day with the hounds and horses. I'll need all the support and backing you can give me to get through this one. I told you how I feel about those animals," Thomas confided with a broad smile that conveyed his understanding of the full meaning of their conversation.

"Don't worry, I'll be there to help you in any way I can,"

Katherine responded giving special emphasis to her words. "Jasmine did say that we'd be riding to the hounds that morning. Do you having the proper apparel?"

"Are you kidding? All I have is business suits, tennis wear, and a few pairs of jeans. What will I need?" Thomas asked with real concern in his voice. It was one thing to be expected to ride a horse for the good of the fund-raising campaign. It was another all together to jump over a fence on one.

"There's a sporting goods shop in Georgetown that sells everything you'll need. We'll get you outfitted at lunchtime. You'll look stunning. No one will notice that you don't know what you're doing. I already arranged for you to have a gentle mare as a mount. You can always linger in her living room until everyone rides off. You can pretend a migraine if you really need an excuse," Katherine added with a helpful smile.

"Good idea. I'll remember that. If I ride out with everyone else, I'll definitely return with a headache and more," Thomas replied, looking anything but confident.

Suppressing a laugh, Katherine gathered her paper, saying "Well, if we've completed our business, I'll return to the ER now. I'll see you at lunchtime."

Rising, Thomas followed her to the door, where he gently placed his hand on Katherine's shoulder. Looking deeply into her eyes, he said, "I really appreciate all of your help in establishing the contacts with the 'Sisters.' You've been a great asset to me. Without you I couldn't have raised the funds. I find that I'd be quite lost without you in many ways."

Returning his gaze with one that was equally as steady, Katherine replied, "I'd do anything to help this hospital . . . you, too, of course. We do work well together, don't we?"

"Katherine, I don't only mean professionally. You've become very important in my life. Patrice was correct in sensing something, at least on my part. I find myself thinking of you first thing in the morning and last thing at night. I accomplish a task, big or small, and immediately think of sharing it with you. When I think of something funny, I want to share it with you.

The other day, I remembered the punch line of a joke I'd heard at the club and almost called you at home to tell you. I overheard people in the elevator talking about a great sounding movie, and immediately I thought of taking you to see it with me. Lately, I find that I compare all women to you. I'm not talking about only their physical appearances but the way in which they carry themselves, their energy level, and their drive. And, you know, they can't measure up. You're one in a million, Katherine. Do you see any chance we might see each other outside of work?"

Katherine felt as if she were being stretched between two worlds. With a catch in her voice she replied, "Thomas, a relationship with you at this time simply would not work; it would only complicate matters and serve to confuse me even further. I need to prove to the board and to you that I could make the ER profitable. I haven't gotten over the pain of the board's rejection of me in hiring you for the position that I know I could have done with ease. I filled it well on a temporary basis, and I still don't understand why they passed me over for you. I understand that I'm young, but I could have done the job. Try as hard as I can, I just can't get over the fact that all of my work proved nothing. Anyway, I have so many thoughts running through my mind and so many things that I have to do that I can't become involved right now. I'm not even sure what my own future will bring. I can't become involved with anyone and have to worry about his life, too. Caring for you would only get in my way. I'm so sorry."

"You have nothing to prove to me or the board. Everyone recognizes your abilities; no one questions your performance record. Please don't let the hospital stand between us. One thing I've learned over the years is that an institution will survive without the people who give their blood, sweat, and tears to it; it will simply hire someone new. It's a loving relationship that makes us whole, not corporate responses. You can't take any portion of this place to bed with you at night. Boxer Hospital won't rub your shoulders when you're tired. It won't serve you breakfast in bed. It won't need you the way I do," Thomas replied with such longing in his eyes that Katherine felt herself wanting to melt into them and block out everything else.

"Thomas, I . . ."

He did not wait until she finished her sentence. Pulling Katherine against him, Thomas covered her lips with his and held her tight as if the force of his need for her would keep her with him forever. The scent of his spicy aftershave lotion filled her senses and mingled pleasurably with the warmth of his arms.

Katherine discovered that her limbs had grown weak. She clung to him with all her strength. She could not have returned to the ER if she had been called. Her entire being wanted to capture this moment and make it last forever. This handsome, strong, caring man had entered her life, and she did not want to lose him.

Suddenly, the buzzer on the conference room telephone began to sound. At first, neither of them responded. Its intrusive voice remained on the outskirts of their world as their hands memorized the shape of each other's shoulders and the feel of each other's skin. They drank deeply of the taste of each other and pushed aside all else.

But the insistent buzz soon proved too demanding. Slowly, they forced their bodies to separate and their hands to part. As Thomas answered the telephone, Katherine slipped from the room.

"Katherine!" he called but she was gone. She needed the noise of the ER to clear her head.

An important message from the ARABESQUE Editor

Dear Arabesque Reader,

Because you've chosen to read one of our Arabesque romance novels, we'd like to say "thank you"! And, as a special way to thank you, we've selected two more of the books you love so well to send you absolutely FREE!

Please enjoy them with our compliments, and thank you for continuing to enjoy Arabesque...the soul of romance.

Karen R. Thomas

Karen Thomas
Senior Editor,
Arabesque Romance Novels

3 QUICK STEPS
TO RECEIVE YOUR FREE "THANK YOU" GIFT
FROM THE EDITOR

Send back this card and you'll receive 2 Arabesque novels—absolutely free! These books have a combined cover price of $10.00 or more, but they are yours to keep absolutely free.

There's no catch. You're under no obligation to buy anything. We charge nothing for the books—ZERO—for your 2 free books (except $1.50 for shipping and handling). And you don't have to make any minimum number of purchases—not even one!

We hope that after receiving your free books you'll want to remain an Arabesque subscriber. But the choice is yours to continue or cancel, anytime at all! So why not take us up on our invitation to receive your free gift, with no risk of any kind. You'll be glad you did!

Call us
TOLL-FREE
at 1-888-345-BOOK

CHECK OUT OUR WEBSITE at www.arabesquebooks.com

FREE BOOK CERTIFICATE

Yes! Please send me 2 free Arabesque books. I understand I am under no obligation to purchase any books, as explained on the back of this card.

Name _____

Address _____ Apt. _____

City _____ State _____ Zip _____

Telephone ( ) _____

Signature _____

Offer limited to one per household and not valid to current subscribers. All orders subject to approval. Terms, offer, & price subject to change.

Thank you!

AB10A9

Accepting the two introductory free books places you under no obligation to buy anything. You may keep the books and return the shipping statement marked "cancel". If you do not cancel, about a month later we will send 4 additional Arabesque novels, and bill you a preferred subscriber's price of just $4.00 per title (plus a small shipping and handling fee). That's $16.00 for all 4 books for a savings of 25% off the publisher's price. You may cancel at any time, but if you choose to continue, every month we'll send you 4 more books, which you may either purchas at the preferred discount price. . .or return to us and cancel your subscription.

THE ARABESQUE ROMANCE CLUB
c/o ZEBRA HOME SUBSCRIPTION SERVICE, INC.
120 BRIGHTON ROAD
P.O. BOX 5214
CLIFTON, NEW JERSEY 07015-5214

AFFIX
STAMP
HERE

This fall, BET Arabesque Films will create 10 original African American themed, made-for-TV movies based on the Arabesque Romance book series.

The list includes some of the best-loved Arabesque romances, including Francis Ray's *Incognito*, Donna Hill's *Intimate Betray* Bridget Anderson's *Rendezvous*, Lynn Emery's *After All*, Felici Mason's *Rhapsody*, Monica Jackson's *Midnight Blue*, Dianne Mayhew's *Playing with Fire*, Donna Hill's *A Private Affair*, Jacquelin Thomas' *Hidden Blessings, and* Donna Hill's *Masquerade*.

And now BET is offering you the chance to win a cameo appearance in one of these upcoming productions! Just think, you can join some of today's hottest African-American movie stars—like Richard T. Jones, Loretta Devine, and Holly Robinson—in the creation of a movie written by, and for, African-American romantics like yourself! All you have to do is complete the attached entry form and mail it in. Just think, if you act now, you could be in one of these exciting new movies! Mail your entry today!

PRIZES

The **GRAND PRIZE WINNER** will receive:

- A trip for two to Los Angeles.
  Think about it—3 days and 2 nights in L.A., round-trip airfare, hotel accommodations.

- $500 spending money, and round-trip transportation to and from the airport and movie set...sounds pretty good, right?

- And the winner's clip will be featured on the Arabesque website!

- As if that's not enough, you'll also get a one-year membership in the Arabesque Book Club and a BET Arabesque Romance gift-pack.

5 RUNNERS-UP will receive:

- One-year memberships in the Arabesque Book Club and BET Arabesque Romance gift-packs.

WIN A CHANCE TO BE IN A BET ARABESQUE FILM!

Yes! Enter me in the BET Arabesque Film Sweepstakes!

NAME _____

ADDRESS _____

CITY _____ STATE _____ ZIP _____

TELEPHONE _____ AGE _____

SIGNATURE _____ (MUST BE 21 OR OLDER TO ENTER)

ARABESQUE FILM SWEEPSTAKES
P.O. BOX 8060
GRAND RAPIDS, MN 55745-8060

AFFIX
STAMP
HERE

Eight

Katherine was so busy in the ER that she could not accompany Thomas to the sporting goods store at lunchtime. A truck had jackknifed on the beltway while traveling at tremendous speeds. It had careened into many other vehicles, causing a considerable number of injuries but, fortunately, no fatalities. The overflow from the neighboring hospitals had been brought into town to Boxer by special buses. People who needed her care and attention had besieged the usually busy emergency room, making it more chaotic than usual.

Even Thomas had taken off his jacket and donned a white lab coat when he saw the mass of people. He had been out of the trenches of practicing medicine for quite some time, but he found that the adrenaline rush that came from working so closely with dedicated people helped him remember how to give some of the basic first-step care. He proved himself to be a pretty good triage nurse.

Katherine was impressed by his ability to mingle with the other doctors and get into the work. She had often worked with chiefs who would oversee but not roll up their sleeves. She was relieved to see that Thomas was not one of those. His already impressive standing in her book soared even higher.

When the mayhem in the ER returned to its usual roar late in the afternoon, Thomas slipped into his jacket and prepared to leave. He motioned to Katherine, who was still busily suturing a gashed forehead. With a sad smile, she shook her head, telling him that she would not be able to get away. As much as she would have liked to have accompanied him, Katherine was not ready to trust herself with him alone again. She wanted the crush of people around them as security from her own feelings and his.

When the ER had erupted in activity, however, Katherine had taken a moment to call Thomas's secretary and given her the name and address of the store at which he could purchase all he would need for the weekend. She had phoned the shop's owner, who happened to be an old friend of hers, and told him that Thomas would be arriving at lunchtime. She had instructed Frank to outfit Thomas in everything he would need for a day of looking as if he knew a little something about riding a horse. She even suggested that Frank look through his consignment section to see if he could find any articles in Thomas's size. She wanted him to appear to have spent some time in his life among the horsy set. A few grass stains on the jophers, scuff marks on the boots, and pulls to the tweed of the jacket would give the appearance that Thomas had some experience in the saddle. Frank had been very willing to help and promised that Thomas would not leave his shop until he looked just right for impressing a society horsewoman with a big bank account and a generous heart.

By the time Thomas returned to hospital, Katherine's shift had ended and she had already left for the day. He was disappointed that he would not be able to show off his new duds, but he reconciled himself with the fact that she would see everything tomorrow at Jasmine's farm in Middlebury. Anyway, he wanted to model the outfit for her approval, not simply open the box and show it off. Frank had done a credible job of turning a hospital administrator into a huntsman.

As they had arranged, Thomas picked up Katherine at around eight o'clock that night for the drive out to Jasmine's estate. Jasmine had asked all of her guests to arrive the night before the hunt so that they could all be ready for coffee and juice early and breakfast immediately following. She did not want to take the chance that anyone would arrive late and hold up the keeper of the hounds . . . bad form, and all that.

Thomas drove his own car rather than using the hospital's limousine for this outing. Although they were not officially on a date since the trip to Jasmine's was for fund-raising purposes, Thomas wanted to set a more relaxed tone. He hoped that Katherine would think of him as a man and not a boss once they were away from the hospital and that infernal buzzer.

Initially, Katherine felt awkward as she sat upright on the thick-cushioned soft leather upholstery of his posh convertible. She was not sure how to react to him. The kiss in the conference room had changed their relationship whether she wanted the metamorphosis or not. She could not turn back the clock. She could not erase the feel of his hands on her body. She could not remove the memory of his kiss from her heart. She would have to wait and see what developed as the days progressed. The only thing about which Katherine was definite was her determination to follow her initial course. She had to prove her worth and would not stop until she had.

As they motored past Tysons Corner and McLean, the Friday night traffic began to dwindle to almost nothing. The wide highways no longer ran past major shopping malls, business centers, and housing developments. The road wound through expansive pastureland and past massive homes set off by tree-lined drives and fences. In the distance, Katherine could see deer grazing in the summer night. The breeze felt fresh against her cheek and was totally unlike the heavy city air they had left behind them in Washington.

"Oh look at the lovely fireflies!" she exclaimed as the fields came alive with tiny flickering lights.

"They're called lightning bugs where I come from. We used to catch as many of them as we could, put them into old jelly jars with holes punched in the lids, and use them as night lights. The girls would pull off the light and attach it to their ears or fingers as jewelry," Thomas said with a slight hint of nostalgia in his voice for his childhood days.

"How awful! I grew up on a farm, and we usually just watched them. They were always among the first harbingers of summer along with strawberries. I think it's cruel to catch them. See how pretty they are as they flicker in the fields? That's a memory of growing up in the farmland of Maryland that I'll always cherish," Katherine responded, feeling a need to defend her way of life.

"Look, when you spend your formative years in Manhattan the way I did, you don't find the little bugs too exciting or romantic. The only lightning bugs I saw lived in the grass at the summer camp to which my folks sent me to keep me out of trouble. Besides, they're just bugs doing what bugs are programmed to do . . . they're flashing their lights to attract a mate. When you look at it that way, it's simply an example of biology at work," Thomas replied.

"I think that's rather romantic. The male bug has to shine his light to attract his woman. The male peacock has to display his feathers to win his lady. It's only human men who feel that all they need to do is swing a well-aimed club and all the women will literally fall at their feet. Maybe the other males of the world have the right idea," Katherine rebutted with a laugh, enjoying their good-natured banter so much that she hoped they would never arrive at Jasmine's.

Thomas laughed so hard at her description of the human courtship ritual that he feared he would drive off the road. Sadly, he had to acknowledge that it was often too true. Romance unfortunately gave way to quick dating, sudden marriages, and years of regret. That was why he had promised himself that he would not marry until he found the woman with whom he could share a fulfilling life. Now, at forty, he knew he had found her.

By the time they reached Jasmine's home, Katherine and Thomas had sung every summer camp song he could remember and all the Motown oldies that crossed her mind. Neither could recall a more pleasurable drive in the country or an instance in which their faces had been more painful from smiling.

As they pulled from the main road, they were struck silent by the grandeur of the home that loomed at the end of the long winding driveway. The imposing white brick structure dwarfed even the White House in size. Its columns rose stately and strong as symbols of the strength of the family that lived inside. The stable in the distance to the right was equally as immense as the main house; even the horses lived well in this paradise.

Parking in front of the multicar garage beside the cars of the other guests, Katherine and Thomas tried not to walk with their mouths gaping at the spectacular gardens illuminated by spotlights that cast a luminous glow over all the flowers. Even at ten o'clock at night, the landscaping was breathtakingly beautiful. Not a weed or a stray flower appeared anywhere.

Even before they could ring the bell, the butler opened the massive mahogany door and ushered them inside. After instructing them to leave their bags in the large foyer with its chandelier sparkling overhead, he led them to the parlor where Jasmine and her other guests sat before the fire sipping brandies and scotches.

Jasmine immediately greeted them. Katherine was impressed by her simple elegance as Jasmine floated toward them with her hand extended in welcome. The gold bracelets at her wrists made a gentle clicking sound as she seemed to hover above the deep pile of the exquisite Turkish carpet. Its blues, greens, browns, and mauves perfectly matched the hues in the tapestry-upholstered sofa, the leather chairs, and the paintings that graced the dark paneled walls. The room was casual elegance on a grand, mind-boggling scale.

"Dr. Winters, how lovely that you could join me this weekend. I remember how much you enjoyed yourself last year. You were the first to reach the hounds if I remember correctly. This must be Dr. Baker. I'm delighted to meet you. I hope you'll both make yourselves comfortable. These are a few of my oldest friends. We always get together to open the hunt season. Dr.

Winters, you really must tear yourself away from that stuffy old hospital and ride with us," Jasmine cooed as she directed them toward the assembled friends. Making quick work of the introductions, she poured brandies for the new arrivals.

"Perhaps this year, now that Thomas is onboard as the chief of staff, I'll have more free time. I'd love to ride more often. Perhaps I could have my parents ship my horse to a reliable stable down here," Katherine answered. Although she had not been born with a silver spoon in her mouth, she felt quite comfortable with the horse set. She had long ago discovered that people who loved animals managed to overlook position and wealth in order to enjoy each other's pride in the beasts. She found it especially true of people who loved riding horses whether in competition or friendly foxhunts.

"I'll give you the name of one that's very near here before you leave. They'll make room for a friend of mine. And you, Dr. Baker, do you enjoy riding also? I've heard very little about your personal life. Everyone spends so much time talking about the improvements you're making to the hospital that it's almost as if you have no other identity," Jasmine inquired, handing each of them ornate snifters of heavenly scented brandy.

Katherine had to bite her tongue to keep from laughing. She knew that Thomas could not tell the truth and blow his cover; he needed to fit in with Jasmine this evening in order to ingratiate himself with her. If she knew that he hated riding and planned to escape from the task of doing it tomorrow, she might not be quite as generous. Sipping her brandy and peering at him over the rim of her glass, Katherine watched as he maneuvered his way out of a potentially sticky situation.

"Unlike Katherine, I did not grow up on a farm. My experience with horses or any animals for that matter comes from my time at camp. I'm a city boy at heart. I love the smell of the country and the experience of being where nature resides free of the restrictions of traffic. I'm certainly looking forward to tomorrow," Thomas answered, skirting the issue but sounding quite sincere as he carefully sidestepped the horse pile hazards.

"The weather will be glorious," chimed in Buffy MacIntyre from her perch on a nearby chair. "We'll have simply the best time."

"At my age, it's the end of the hunt that I look forward to the most," her husband commented from where he stood beside the fireplace. "Nothing upsets my old knees more than being jostled over miles of terrain on the back of a horse. Now, don't get me wrong, I still enjoy the thrill of the chase, but I'd rather do it from the seat of a car."

Everyone laughed at his candor. For one of their own circle of acquaintances to say that age affected even their love of the hunt made them all feel more human and vulnerable. They knew that someday their favorite weekend activity would have to end.

When the grandfather clock in the hall struck eleven, Jasmine rose and suggested that they call it a night. The hounds would be ready for the chase at eight o'clock. The horses had to be ready and the riders up no later than seven thirty for those riding horses not their own and seven forty-five for those using their own mounts. The paddock would be ready for warm-up jumping at seven for early birds. She would provide tea, coffee, and juice in the breakfast room starting at six thirty.

Katherine could feel the energy and the excitement of the hunt flowing through the room. She doubted that she would get much sleep. The thought of riding either steeplechase or the hunt always excited her. She could remember the sleepless nights when she was a little girl on the farm. The horses they rode were not as sophisticated as the ones Jasmine owned, but the feel of soaring over a jump and galloping through the open fields on a muscular animal always made her heart pound.

Casting a sideward glance at Thomas as he concluded his conversation with Robert Whitaker, a local banker of great wealth and renown, Katherine saw that his face already wore a drawn expression. His level of anticipation did not exactly match hers. To the contrary, at that moment, Thomas was thinking that an attack of dysentery would be preferable to the experience that awaited him in the morning. He decided that if he

survived the morning's ride, he would have to make sure the
board and his staff understood the sacrifice he had made for
Boxer Hospital.

Although Katherine would have liked a few minutes alone
with Thomas to finalize their strategy for the next day, she graciously allowed Jasmine to lead her toward the wide curving
staircase that connected the public rooms on the first floor with
the bedrooms on the second.

Walking arm in arm like old friends, they chatted animatedly
about the Fortune 500 report, the current state of Blue Chip stocks,
and the most recent findings reported in the *Journal of American
Medicine*. Katherine was amazed at Jasmine's recall of the little
items that they had discussed last year. She imagined that Jasmine's
apparently genuine interest in her guests was what made her one
of the Washington area's most sought-after hostesses.

"I'll see you in the morning, Katherine. Let me know if
there's anything you need. I think I've anticipated everything,
but ring if you find something not to your liking. Sleep well.
We have a busy day planned for us tomorrow," Jasmine gushed,
ushering Katherine inside and closing the door behind her.

Katherine found herself standing in the same incredibly appointed room as last year, only Jasmine had redecorated, making
it even more superb. The king-size four-poster Louis XIV bed
with its heavy drapes and posh spread beckoned to her. She
knew from last year's experience that the mattress would be so
soft that she would feel as if she were sleeping on a cloud.

Jasmine had replaced the former but definitely not old carpets with new ones that matched the bed coverings. Highly polished, shimmering wood floors glowed in shades of brown
around the edges of the carpet. The wallpaper picked up one of
the subtle colors and repeated it in a pattern that closely resembled the rainbow effect of hair ribbons. The same heavy drapes
hung at the French doors that overlooked the pool in the distance
and the formal gardens directly below. On cool summer nights
like this one, they were left open so the breeze and the smell
of the roses in bloom could blow into the room.

Taking a quick shower in the magnificently appointed bath-room equipped with bidet, massive shower stall, separate toilet facility, double sink, makeup sink, and whirlpool tub, Katherine wished she had more time to enjoy the luxurious bathroom. Maybe tomorrow after the hunt and before the dance to which they had also been invited, she would be able to relax and luxu-riate in the rose-petal-scented room.

Toweling off with the thickest, softest towels she had ever felt against her skin, Katherine wondered if Thomas were en-joying his sojourn among the rich and famous as much as she was. Pulling her nightshirt over her head and stepping out into the bedroom, she discovered that a maid had entered while she was in the shower and turned back the bed for her. A rose bud in a crystal vase and a brandy nightcap sat on a little silver tray on the bedside table.

Easing between the sheets, Katherine allowed the fragrance of the night in the country to fill her being. The sound of the crickets was as familiar as her mother's voice. She had been lulled to sleep by songs from both when she was a little girl. Although excited about the hunt, she could not stay awake. The warmth of the shower, the music of the night, and the softness of the mattress relaxed her body and removed all the tension from her limbs. The hospital was suddenly far away. Her last thought was of Thomas on horseback. With a soft chuckle, Katherine turned over and fell fast asleep.

Thomas, however, was not enjoying himself in the least. After Jasmine had deposited him in his room down the hall from Katherine's, Thomas had discovered that he was wide awake and filled with anxiety. Pacing the fabulously thick carpeting that filled his room with masculine deep blue and brown tones, Thomas could not settle either his mind or his body. The next day would be a challenge on two fronts. If he survived the horses in the morning, he would have to face Jasmine in the evening. Something in the way she had stroked his arm as she ushered him to the room had told Thomas that the dear lady had more up her sleeve than simply her checkbook.

Thomas needed to speak with Katherine. She would have suggestions on how to avoid both pitfalls. He had thought of either phoning or visiting her room, but he decided against doing either. He would not take the chance of compromising her reputation by being seen entering her bedroom. Although the sight of her in her nightclothes would certainly make him feel better, he did not want any of the other guests to think that they were engaged in a relationship that was more than professional. He thought better of calling her because the jangling of the bell would be too disruptive at this hour of the night. He would have to wait and hope for a few words of advice from her in the morning.

As for Jasmine, well, he had handled some pretty determined people in his time and managed to escape without getting caught in their webs, schemes, and entrapments. He hoped that he would be as successful with her. His only real worry was that Katherine might misunderstand. He did not want anything or anyone to interfere with their budding relationship.

In a fit of sneezing, Thomas slipped into bed. "Now, I remember another reason why I didn't like camp," he muttered to himself as the fragrance of country air, flowers, grass, and trees filled his room.

Katherine was up early the next morning. By seven she had sipped a little juice for energy and taken several practice jumps on a spirited stallion named Fortune's Fool. He was not the mount she had ridden last year with such great success, but he was a fiery animal just the same. He tossed his head in the breeze, pawed at the ground, and snorted with impatience to start the hunt. Katherine felt much the same way as she guided him over jumps, learned his preferences, and put him through his warm-up paces. She was ready for the exhilaration of riding with the crisp morning air on her face and a strong animal's muscles straining under her.

By seven thirty all of the other guests had assembled . . . except for Thomas. She wondered if he were going to make a late entrance and beg off because of a headache. If he did, she would keep his secret and not let anyone know about his fear of horses.

As Katherine guided Fortune into the pack of other horses and riders assembled in the driveway, Thomas and Jasmine appeared. Jasmine waved and said gaily, "Look who I found straggling downstairs at the last minute. This workaholic has been on the phone to the hospital and almost missed the ride. With weather and horses like this, that would have been a shame too large to imagine."

Thomas smiled bravely at the unwanted attention and walked toward the mare the groom held for him. Watching Jasmine, he took a deep breath and pulled his memories of the required riding classes from summer camp into the foreground of his mind. Grabbing the pummel with his left hand and the back of the saddle with his right, he inserted his boot into the stirrup, sprang a little, and successfully pulled himself into the saddle on the first try. With a sigh of relief, he willingly accepted the groom's assistance in adjusting the stirrups to fit his long legs and in tightening the girth around the trim little mare. Pulling his hat down securely on his head, Thomas was as ready for the hunt as he would ever be.

As they walked their horses into the pasture, Katherine eased into position beside him. Before she could speak, Thomas said with a definite pout in his voice, "Jasmine stopped by to get me when she didn't see me with the others. She made me abandon my phone calls and join the group. I didn't have the chance to feign a headache."

"You look great. The clothes are perfect. No one would guess that you're not one of the horse set. Actually, you appear more comfortable than Buffy's husband. His knees are already bothering him. Just relax. You might find that you enjoy the ride," Katherine commented, trying to ease Thomas's mind.

"I'm okay now because we're only walking. I'll be fine at a canter, too. But I'm not too sure about a gallop, and jumping is out of the question. I've never done it," Thomas grumbled in a low voice.

"A gallop is a very comfortable gait. All you have to do is relax and let your body merge with the horse. When you take a jump, lean forward low on the horse's neck and hold on with your hands and knees. It's simple. If you don't want to jump, try going around the obstacle. You might not have too much luck, however. I think most of our route is over fences, fallen logs, and creeks. Don't worry. I'm sure Jasmine gave you a great jumper. She'll do all the work," Katherine tried to reassure Thomas, but she could tell that it was not working.

Thomas was not overly concerned with his appearance at the moment, but he did strike an attractive figure in his brown and gray tweed jacket and buff-colored jophers. The snug pants set off his muscular thighs perfectly and his arms showed good conformation through the jacket. Even the boots appeared well molded to his feet. The outfit appeared well used and was from the consignment section of the Georgetown shop. No one would have assumed that until a few minutes ago they still carried price tags.

If Thomas had not been so petrified, he would have noticed that Katherine looked stunning in her attire as well. She had owned the togs since her high school days and had worn them in many county fairs. She loved the feel of the soft leather boots and the smell of the jacket that over the years had picked up a decidedly horsy smell that no amount of dry cleaning could remove.

At exactly eight o'clock the master of the hounds released the fox. The braying of the hounds, which had been loud, became deafening as they waited to give the scurrying fox a fair head start. Although they never harmed the animal, they followed the practice of allowing it to run ahead a safe distance before releasing the dogs that would lead the riders on the chase.

At the sounding of the bugle that marked the beginning of the hunt, the dogs raced after the fox, followed by the horses and riders. Katherine felt the rush of expectation, the flow of energy, and the power of the horse as they moved from a trot to a canter and then settled into a gallop. The rolling green of the fields spread out before her. The singing of the birds provided a symphony to accompany the pounding of the horses' hooves.

Again this year, Katherine took the lead as she and Fortune sailed over the fences and forded the streams, effortlessly following the braying dogs. She felt exhilarated as each stride carried her closer to the goal. The clean smell of the country air in her face made her smile as she ducked under low-hanging branches. As she splashed through the little creek, the spray of water wet her boots and sent a cooling spray into her face. Her heart pounded with almost crushing force as she galloped over the soft green sod and jumped the fallen logs along the path to finding the fox. She did not concern herself with the fact that Jasmine followed in her wake. In a hunt, every woman had to take care of herself.

Glancing quickly behind her, Katherine saw that Jasmine on her chestnut stallion was slowly closing the gap, but she could not see Thomas anywhere. Although she hoped that he was safe, she could not turn back to search for him now. The desire to ride to the first-place honors stirred too strongly in her breast with the same force as her determination to regain control of Boxer Hospital. She and Fortune's Fool were of one mind . . . the hunt was of utmost importance.

Giving her horse his head, Katherine pressed herself against his surging muscles as Fortune's Fool cleared yet another fallen tree, sailing over it with room to spare. The beautiful jumper seemed to laugh at the other horses and riders, who slowed as they approached it. The call of the hounds was so compelling that nothing could stand in his way.

After almost two hours of furious riding, the braying stopped and the dogs gathered panting around a vine-covered log. Pawing at the ground and barking furiously, they called angrily to the inhabitant. Reining her lathered horse, Katherine pushed the stray hair from her face and wiped the mud from her cheeks.

"Good ride. You've beaten me again. It's a bit embarrassing, considering you're riding my horse on my property. However, you win so graciously that I hardly feel the sting. I'd hate to see what you could do on your own mount," Jasmine said as she joined Katherine.

"You'll have to come up to my parents' farm for a rematch. Our horses aren't as sleek as yours, but they hunt well enough." Katherine laughed, accepting the sportswoman's handshake as a sign of Jasmine's appreciation. Each knew the other was a skilled competitor.

They waited together until the master of the hounds arrived to investigate the hole. The others gathered around as he proclaimed the hunt over and the hound aground. Trumpeting his horn, he called the dogs and riders to attention and signaled the return to Jasmine's house and the waiting breakfast feast.

Riding back with Jasmine at her side, Katherine searched the woods and fields for Thomas. Seeing her worried expression Jasmine said, "Maybe he turned back. I don't really think he was having a very good time. Thomas doesn't strike me as a horseman. That's a gut reaction, but from the way he sat the saddle, I'd say he hasn't ridden much in his lifetime."

"No, he hasn't, but he was willing to try. Thomas wanted very much to impress you. He thought that by joining you in your favorite sport, he would do just that. Maybe that wasn't such a good idea, but at least he tried," Katherine replied as she defended Thomas's actions in passing himself off as an able horseman.

"Oh, I'm impressed all right, but not because he tried to ride a horse. I find his business acumen sexy, not to mention his sense of humor and his ability to fit into any situation. That's more important than riding to the hounds," Jasmine offered, cantering beside Katherine.

The two women rode in silence for a time, each one deep in thought. Suddenly, Katherine reined her horse and pointed, "Look over there. Isn't that Thomas?"

Throwing her reins to Jasmine, Katherine ran to the figure

lying on the ground. Without moving him, Katherine carefully examined Thomas's limp body for breaks and obstructions in the airway. Finding none, she checked his reflexes as well as she could without her medical bag. As he started to stir, she sat back with a sigh of relief.

"I knew I shouldn't have tried that last jump. I was doing just fine, moving slowly, but keeping up until then. How's the horse? Is she all right? I seem to remember that she stopped but I didn't," Thomas said weakly, trying to make a joke out of a potentially dangerous situation. Being thrown from a horse was not a laughing matter. In her practice of medicine, Katherine had treated several people who had been paralyzed by landing the wrong way and snapping their necks.

"Thomas, don't move. One of the men will ride back and call an ambulance. You should have an x-ray. At the very least, you might have a concussion," Katherine said, trying to hold his powerful shoulders to the ground.

"No, that won't be necessary. I simply had the wind knocked out of me. There's no need for an ambulance or an x-ray. The last thing I want to do is disrupt everyone's weekend fun. I'll be fine as soon as I catch my breath, but I must say that I appreciate the concern. It almost looks as if it borders on love," Thomas teased as he eased his tall, stiff frame into a sitting position. Aside from a little soreness in his shoulders, he felt remarkably well for someone who had just sailed over the head of a horse. Fortunately, he had landed in a thick bed of leaves that broke the impact of his fall.

"You must be feeling okay. You're already beginning to make suppositions based on my natural concern for my boss," Katherine retorted with a laugh. She was not ready to admit to herself or Thomas the extent of her feelings toward him, but she did not mind if he guessed.

"Thomas," cooed Jasmine, unable to remain outside of the action any longer, "you gave us such a scare, you bad boy. You really shouldn't try to do things that are beyond your experience level. It's so unnecessary for a man of your professional status.

Now, let's get you back to my house and into a warm bath. I know just the thing to make a new man out of you. A good soak will do wonders for those stiff muscles. After that, I'll arrange for my personal masseuse to give you a massage. You'll be ready to dance away the evening in no time at all."

"Thank you, Jasmine, I'm feeling much better already. If someone can help me into the saddle, I'll ride back. We're late for breakfast," Thomas replied, aware that Jasmine's voice had hinted at the possibility of personal attention from the hostess.

Katherine had caught the subtle undertones in her manner, too. She looked with a watchful eye as Jasmine rubbed Thomas's temples a little too suggestively with his head resting on her exposed cleavage. She instinctively knew that more than Thomas's health would need monitoring over this potentially long weekend.

Nine

Regardless of any ulterior motives, Katherine had to admit that Jasmine was a superior hostess. The hunt breakfast was plentiful and filling, according to the dictates of tradition that called for a heavy meal following the ride. Thick slabs of only the best country-cured ham shimmered next to perfectly scrambled, fried, and poached eggs on elegant platters. Eggs benedict with divine hollandaise sauce tempted the palate of those with little regard for fat grams. Waffles, pancakes, corn bread, spoon bread, and biscuits all dripped the sweetest butter. The chef sweetened the meal with a delicious compote of fresh blueberries, raspberries, and blackberries to which he added strawberries. After eating all of that, the guests retired to the drawing room to read the paper and sip coffee, tea, or cocoa.

In between tending to their culinary needs, Jasmine doted on Thomas. Her masseuse stood ready as soon as Thomas called to say that he was ready. Jasmine herself brought him a hot cup of strong black coffee and held it for him to sip as he lounged by the picture window in his room.

"Thomas, you gave us such a start. Promise me that you'll never do anything like that again. You really don't need to ride to the hounds to impress me. You've already shown that you're a superior businessman. I'm sure your performance is equally as stellar in all aspects of your life. If you're feeling up to it, you might give me a demonstration tonight . . . dancing on the patio after dinner . . . or anything else you would care to suggest,"

Jasmine cooed, lightly trailing her fingers across Thomas's hand. Her lips pouted temptingly and her eyes glinted under their half-closed lids.

"Dancing under the stars sounds lovely, Jasmine. You'll have to save me a waltz or two. I'm sure I'll be feeling just fine by this evening," Thomas answered, aware that Katherine stood at the open doorway. From the slight tightness in her jaw, Thomas could tell that she observed Jasmine's skillful flirtation with more than a little interest.

"I had envisioned you as the tango type," she responded as her tongue quickly darted between her red lips.

"Jasmine," Katherine interjected, entering the bedroom, "I'm not sure that Thomas will be up to dancing this evening. As his physician, I might suggest that he take it easy for at least twenty-four hours. He did take quite a spill."

"I wouldn't think of putting undue stress on his body. Of course, my invitation to dance naturally depends on his good health. Dancing, when done properly, can be so . . . physical. I'll leave you now, dear Thomas, and check on my other guests. Katherine, feel free to stroll the gardens, read in the library, or whatever else tickles your fancy. Dinner is at eight, black tie. My other guests will begin arriving at seven for cocktails. I'll see you both later," Jasmine twittered as she left the room. The coffee cup and spoon did not even rattle in her hand.

"You're looking much improved. How's the soreness? Are you sure you don't want to take a quick trip to the hospital?" Katherine asked, perching lightly on the seat of the extra chair.

"I'm fine. Don't worry about me. Two lovely, talented women have given me wonderful care. I don't need anything else. What I think I'll do is sit by this window for a while or maybe have that massage. I brought some work with me. After I finish it, I'll take a walk. Would you like to accompany me? I should be ready in about an hour. You can never tell when I might need medical attention," Thomas said with a boyish smirk on his face. He was obviously enjoying the attention.

"Not that I think you'll need my professional services, but

I'll be in the library should you feel lonely. If I remember correctly, Jasmine has a rather extensive collection of first editions. They should keep me busy while you're working. When you're ready for your walk, I'll be waiting," Katherine responded with a quick smile. She would have loved to kiss the corners of his lips or stroke the back of his neck, but she dared not show that level of affection. She did not fear Thomas's reaction as much as she did her own. She was not ready yet to admit that she wanted him in her life.

"Katherine," Thomas called as she reached the door. "Thanks for caring so much about me. Between your efforts and Jasmine's I couldn't have had better care even at Boxer."

"Anytime you decide to show off your jumping skills again, just let me know and I'll be there," Katherine commented as she left the room. She would have been happier if he had left Jasmine out of the words of thanks.

After she left, Thomas called the masseuse who arrived promptly and performed his magic on Thomas's stiffening muscles. The skilled practitioner kneaded and rubbed until the flexibility in Thomas's back and shoulders had returned almost to normal. Recommending a long, hot soak, the man gathered his lotions and towels, folded his table, and left.

Following his suggestion, Thomas drew his bath and sank slowly into the steaming water. Immediately, he could feel the rest of his stiffness fade as the soothing heat penetrated his muscles. He was determined to restore his body to its former condition before the evening. The thought of twirling Katherine around the dance floor as her lithe body pressed against his was more than enough to accelerate the healing process in any normal man.

Katherine's memory had indeed been correct. Jasmine did own an incredible collection of first editions that she stored in a special book cabinet. Easing it open, she slipped on a pair of the cotton gloves kept for handling collectibles and extracted a copy of Alexandre Dumas pere's *Three Musketeers*. Katherine then settled into one of the comfortable wing chairs for an hour of reading and translating French.

The anticipation of time spent in leisure with Katherine empowered Thomas to work more quickly than his usual rapid pace. Correspondence and reports that usually would have taken him the full ninety minutes only required half the time. At first, he experienced difficulty keeping his thoughts focused on the work and not on her. However, knowing that if he finished early she would be waiting forced him to concentrate.

As soon as he capped his pen, Thomas left his room and walked quickly down the stairs. He was only slightly sore from being thrown from the horse, but he had a slight headache. Reaching into his pocket for the little tin of aspirin he kept with him at all times, he quickly dry swallowed two of them. Nothing would interfere with his afternoon alone with Katherine, not even a mild concussion.

When he entered the library, Thomas discovered that Katherine was not alone. Roger Whitaker had joined her. Thomas had seen him at breakfast but had been too preoccupied with the attentions of both women to pay the tall, trim banker any real attention. Now that Thomas saw him again, he noticed that the man had penetrating gray eyes, boyish freckles, and gray-flecked sandy hair. His appearance was that of a much younger man. To be the CEO of a bank, Roger had to be at least fifty.

Thomas," Katherine called, smiling broadly as he entered the room. "I'm so happy you've joined us. How are you feeling?"

Great. Only a slight headache, but I've taken care of that," Thomas answered. He would have been feeling substantially better if he had not seen Katherine extracting her hand from Roger's. Thomas did not fancy himself the jealous type, probably because he had not been strongly enough drawn to anyone to experience that emotion. Now, however, he felt a quick unsettled nagging at his inner core. He was not sure that he liked it.

"It's good to see you moving about. You gave all of us quite a scare. Not too long ago a friend of mine was paralyzed after a fall like that. Riding can be much more dangerous than people think," Roger commented as he resumed his seat next to Katherine. He seemed completely unaware of anything other than a professional relationship existing between Katherine and Thomas.

"I don't plan to ride again ever. This is one city slicker who has learned his lesson about horses," Thomas answered him before turning his total attention to Katherine. "What have you been reading," he asked, lifting the unopened book from her lap.

"Nothing actually. I had planned to tackle Dumas, but Roger's conversation was so engaging that I never opened it. Here, let me return it to the case. I'm ready for our walk whenever you are," Katherine said as she rose from her chair. Thomas noticed that Roger could not keep his eyes from following her. The slightest smile of appreciation pulled at the corner of his mouth. Again Thomas felt that little biting at his core.

"I've noticed a lovely garden below my bedroom window. Let's start there," Thomas offered as he waited for her to join him at the door.

"See you at dinner, Roger. Maybe we can finish our conversation then," Katherine called over her shoulder.

"I'd like that, Katherine, very much."

Something in Roger's tone caused another little feeling of acid burn to eat at Thomas's core. He made a mental note to position himself as Katherine's shadow the entire evening.

As they strolled through the gardens, Katherine and Thomas shared stories of their childhood. Katherine had grown up on a farm with two brothers and an assortment of farm animals. Thomas was an only child from Manhattan. She had played in the sun and the meadows all summer; he had gone to summer camp and sneezed. She had learned to ride, shoot, and fish; he had studied the piano. She was fluent in French, Spanish, and German; he had a passable knowledge of Latin. Despite the differences, they discovered many similarities, also. Both of them had decided at an early age to enter medical school, both had found complete professional satisfaction in working with patients, and both were devoted to Boxer.

By the time they had explored all of the gardens and ventured into the meadows, Katherine and Thomas had learned that they were even more interested in each other than they had originally thought. Sadly, Katherine admitted to herself that Thomas was indeed the man for whom she had been searching. She felt frustrated that fate had thrown them together at this worst possible time and in the worst possible circumstances. She had to satisfy this burning need to prove herself as a manager of the hospital before she could think of forming a relationship with Thomas. Watching Thomas cut one of Jasmine's prize roses for her hair, for the first time Katherine questioned her decision.

Thomas was more determined than ever to hold tightly to this elusive treasure who had entered his life. He understood Katherine's driving ambition, but he had goals of his own. He wanted her in his life and would not allow her to keep him at arms' length any longer. Time was a precious commodity that should not be wasted. He wanted every minute of his life to be filled by her. Now seemed to him to be the perfect time to start using it wisely.

"Katherine, we've been stepping around our emotions for some time now. It's time that we discussed them openly and without that interfering buzzer. I've watched you manage the ER's finances and interact with staff members and the board. I'm aware of your skills as a physician, your warmth as a person, and your determination as a manager. Everything about you fills me with admiration. I'm not a very demonstrative man, but I want you to know just how much you mean to me. I wake up every morning with you on my mind, and I go to sleep with you as my last thought every night. When something happens, you're the first person with whom I want to share my news. I need you in my life. I love you, Katherine," Thomas said with all of his emotions playing across his face.

Without giving her time to reject him, Thomas pulled Katherine into his arms. He felt her surprise fade as soon as his lips touched hers. His hands hungrily caressed her body as she clung to him and pulled him even closer. They stood locked in each other's embrace as the fragrance of roses enveloped them.

"Thomas, I . . ." Katherine began, pushing away ever so slightly. She wanted to look into his eyes but not to break the spell that held them. She had to see that he understood when she explained her reservations. "I love you, too, Thomas, but I can't allow myself to become involved right now. In a few more months when I've finished keeping my promise to myself, but not now. It wouldn't be fair to either of us."

"Katherine, nothing matters in this world but you. You don't have to prove yourself to anyone. Nothing and no one matters," Thomas replied. He had to make her understand that she was perfect exactly as she was.

"It matters to me, Thomas. You have to understand."

Before he could answer, a voice called from the gate saying, "Katherine! Thomas! I've been looking all over for you two. Roger said I'd find you here. I have some people for you to meet, Thomas. They're very interested in the improvements you're implementing at the hospital and might be encouraged to provide some funding. I'll keep Katherine entertained while you speak with them. You'll find them in the parlor. Now, hurry along."

"Thanks, Jasmine. Katherine, let's finish this discussion at dinner," Thomas said as he allowed the butler to lead him inside.

As soon as Thomas vanished into the darkness of the interior, Jasmine linked her arm with Katherine's and propelled her around the boxwood garden. "I've missed our little chats, Katherine, since Thomas took over the chief-of-staff job. You've neglected your old buddy. I was so looking forward to you telling me everything about him. He's wonderful . . . so complicated, so complex. He isn't married, isn't attached. He doesn't drink. Sounds too good to be true. Do you know anything unfavorable about him? He's just the kind of man I'd like to include in my stable if you don't mind the analogy," Jasmine purred.

When Jasmine was being coy and charming, Katherine found her difficult to swallow. This was one of those times. Jasmine wanted something badly enough to take the chance of including Katherine in her conspiracy.

Unlike some of her friends, Katherine did not enjoy the camaraderie of other women. She much preferred the no-holes-barred approach of men. Women often talked around a situation rather than facing it head on. Jasmine was trying to manipulate her out of some dirt on Thomas, and Katherine did not want to be involved. Besides, Katherine wanted Thomas for herself, even if she had not been able to say the words even to him.

"He appears to be exactly as we see him. I haven't heard anyone say that there's anything duplicitous about him. He is a wonderful boss, a kind colleague, and a great dancer," Katherine answered, hoping that Jasmine would be satisfied with that tidbit.

"Well, as long as no one has any claims on him, Thomas Baker is fair game," Jasmine confided with a wink that sent a chill over Katherine's body.

As they entered the house, Jasmine excused herself and went to check on the arrangements of the evening's cocktails and dinner. Katherine took the opportunity to be alone with her thoughts.

Sliding into a tub filled with hot water and rose-scented bubble bath, Katherine let her mind return to the feel of Thomas's arms and lips. She wanted him in her life with the same urgency that he craved her, yet she could not be content until she finished the task that still lay before her. She hoped that he would understand. At the very least, she needed to unscramble the jumbled mess of thoughts that plagued her often-tired mind.

Thinking of him also brought thoughts of Jasmine who had

made her interest in Thomas perfectly clear. She suspected that Jasmine had picked up some of the vibes between them. Katherine had to admit that she had not tried to conceal her concern as he lay lifeless in the grass. Jasmine probably read her face and knew the unspoken truth. Katherine was sure that Jasmine was only putting her on notice of her intent to win Thomas's affections if she could.

Suddenly, a cold fear gripped Katherine's heart. She had told Thomas that their relationship would have to wait and that he was not as important as her dream. With Jasmine planning her strategy, she could lose the only man she had really wanted in her life . . . the only man she had loved.

"Why does life have to be so complicated?" Katherine muttered to herself, splashing the water with angry fists. "Why can't I have Thomas and the professional life I crave at the same time? It's so unfair. People like Jasmine have it all. She's wealthy, beautiful, and free to set her goals for anything she wants."

The ringing of the telephone on the table beside the tub jarred Katherine out of her sulk. "Yes?" she answered as the soapy water dripped onto the gold flecked mauve tile.

"Hi, Katherine, it's Roger. It's time for cocktails. I'll meet you downstairs in five minutes," Roger's happy tenor voice sounded in her ear.

"Thanks for the call, Roger, but I'll need more like fifteen. Don't wait for me. I'll see you there," Katherine responded without enthusiasm and hung up without waiting to hear his response. The last thing she wanted to do was give Roger any encouragement to think that she might be interested in him. She definitely did not need any further complications in her life.

Hopping from the tub and toweling as she pulled her black lace slip dress from the closet, Katherine ignored the annoying ringing of the telephone as it sounded once again. Finally, when she thought that she could stand it no longer, she answered saying, "Yes, Roger, I'm on my way."

"Roger? Sorry, but you'll have to settle for me. I only wanted to know if you were ready to mingle a bit, but it looks as if you have other plans. I'll see you downstairs," Thomas said with obvious annoyance in his voice. He hung up before she could explain.

"Damn! What a mess I've made of things," Katherine spat as she crammed her foot into the high heels that she knew accentuated her leg muscles but would make her feet ache in thirty minutes. She closed the door behind her and quickly hobbled down the steps. At the landing, she stopped long enough to put on the other shoe and adjust her face. Catching a glimpse of herself in the mirror, Katherine saw that, to her surprise, she actually looked quite put together and composed.

Cocktails were only a partial disaster with Roger breathing on her arm at every turn. Dinner, however, proved unbearable. Jasmine had seated Thomas directly to her right with Katherine at the other end of the table. Not only could Katherine not engage him in conversation, but she could also do nothing to distract him from Jasmine, who constantly poured attention and herself on him. If she had leaned any further forward in that suggestively low cut dress, he would have known everything about her down to the identifying marks on her belly.

The thing that unnerved Katherine the most was not Roger's attention to her but Thomas's apparent fascination with Jasmine. Katherine knew she had to do something but positioning herself where she could do it would take skill and diplomacy. Jasmine had seated her far enough away from Thomas that there was nothing she could do during dinner. She would have to wait until after dinner to execute her plans.

Immediately after dinner, Jasmine ushered her guests onto the patio where a quartet played an assortment of waltzes, fox trots, polkas, and tangos. Without giving Thomas the opportunity to slip away, she claimed him for her partner for the first dance. Fixing him with a definite "come hither" stare, Jasmine pressed herself against Thomas as they began to dance a sultry, suggestive tango that left both of them breathless.

Katherine watched helplessly with Roger constantly by her

side. She could not make a scene and commit the unpardonable act of cutting in on her hostess. She had no choice but to wait until Jasmine grew tired or felt a need to favor her other guests with her radiance. In the meantime, Katherine had to be content with the attentive, doting Roger.

Actually, Roger was a wonderful dancer. His moves were fluid yet controlled, indicative of many long hours in dance classes. He virtually glided across the floor to the waltzes and insinuated himself in a very sexy tango. Had Katherine's heart not been so totally consumed by Thomas, she might have found Roger's flashing eyes, eager smile, and quick wit quite charming. There was no denying the appeal of his boyish good looks and his athletically contoured body.

Katherine chided herself for not reacting more favorably in the garden. If she had, Thomas would be with her now and not with Jasmine. If she had not answered the telephone calling Roger's name, Thomas would not have spent the dinner hour sending looks of doubt and confusion in her direction. Her position beside Roger at the table did not help matters one bit. Thomas was free to speculate and imagine anything he chose.

Scanning the smiling people on the patio, Katherine tried to catch Thomas's attention as he stood sipping his drink. The glow of one of the many spotlights that illuminated the lawn and silhouetted the trees cast an almost surreal feeling on the setting and made the liquid in his glass appear silver. While she watched, Jasmine floated toward Thomas and appeared to envelop him as she pressed her body against his and swayed to the music of the waltz.

Katherine tried to call out his name but found that her throat had constricted to match the pain in her heart. She could not tear her eyes away from them as Thomas and Jasmine swayed, stepped, and dipped in synchronized steps to the music she no longer heard. Only Roger's hand on her arm managed to break the spell as she became one of the phantoms on the patio.

The rest of the evening passed in slow motion for Katherine as either Roger or another of Jasmine's guests kept her company.

She danced every dance, sipped the offered drinks, and carried on mindless small talk under the spell of a strange automatic pilot that kept her functioning outside of herself. Katherine could not break the spell that held her prisoner. She could not leave the patio. She had no will of her own as long as Thomas remained locked in Jasmine's controlling, manipulative embrace.

The music and the scent of flowers clung to everything and everyone until there was no separation between them. Katherine watched as couples strolled into the garden to return with bouquets of freshly cut flowers, daisy chains around their necks, and lily of the valley boutonnieres. Laughing, smiling people did not recognize that her smile was not real and that her laugh was artificial.

Slowly the guests began drifting to their cars for the drive home. The ones who had arrived the preceding evening took to their beds with warm words of praise for the hostess who had produced such a delightful evening. Katherine joined them as they walked up the stairs. She paused long enough at her door to bid Roger good night. She did not see Thomas as she closed the door. Since Jasmine was nowhere in sight, Katherine did not tax her brain in wondering where Thomas might be.

The clanging of trays as the wait staff cleaned up and the closing of doors as the quartet packed up to leave were the only sounds that broke the silence of the night. That, too, stopped soon and all was quiet.

One of Jasmine's efficient household help had already turned back the bed and placed a mint and a rose on the pillow. Sinking into the luxurious comfort of the mattress, Katherine realized for the first time that evening that her feet ached terribly. Removing her shoes she patted to the bathroom where she filled up the bidet. As so many others were doing that night, she used it to soak her tired feet. Slipping between the covers, she willed herself to sleep as the chorus of crickets provided the serenade.

* * *

The next morning everyone ate heartily of the massive Sunday breakfast served formally in the dining room. To Katherine's dismay, she found that Jasmine's attention toward Thomas had not faded with the daylight. She still kept him at her side, and she continued to anticipate his every desire. Thomas appeared to have recovered from his initial embarrassment of last night at Jasmine's public demonstration of affection. Now, he allowed her to spoon extra portions of fried apples onto his plate. Katherine cringed at the visible inroads Jasmine had made toward winning the heart of the man she loved.

When the time finally came for them to leave, Katherine and Thomas loaded their bags into his car, expressed their gratitude to their hostess, and said their goodbyes to their fellow guests. Publicly, Thomas thanked Jasmine for her generous contribution to the hospital. Privately, Katherine wondered what kind of concessions he had to make to secure it.

The trip back to Washington was long and tense. Neither of them had anything in particular to share. Suddenly people who had been so compatible were now so distant. Thoughts, suppositions, accusations, and pain consumed each of them.

Thomas had planned to take Katherine to dinner upon their return to town. Now, after that disastrous two hours of absolute silence, he sadly left her at the door of her apartment. Katherine had dreamed of inviting him up for a light supper. She had planned to prepare a meal of spicy chicken on a bed of lettuce and sprinkled with toasted sesame seeds. She has sliced the chicken, marinated it, and toasted the seeds before she left. She only needed about ten minutes to finalize the preparations. Following the heartbreaking show on the patio last night and again at breakfast, she decided to call Betsy to share it with her. At least with Betsy, if she felt like crying, she could without having to explain her reasons. After all, sometimes a woman just needed to cry.

As soon as Katherine heard the elevator door safely close behind Thomas, she petted Mitzi, grabbed the pot of spicy chicken and the lettuce and rushed to Betsy's apartment. She knew her friend would be there waiting to hear all the details of the weekend. Katherine had hoped to have only good news to share. She had imagined them laughing at the funny mishaps. Now, she had to ask Betsy to help her plan a strategy for winning Thomas's affections.

The friends ate in almost total silence. Katherine had seasoned the chicken perfectly, but neither of them noticed the taste of their favorite meal. Betsy felt so badly about Katherine's pain that she thought she might burst into tears at any minute. Katherine worked so hard at putting on a brave front that she dared not look at Betsy's pinched face. Their usual peaceful, harmonious time together was missing its usual energy.

As soon as they had placed the dishes in the washer, Katherine and Betsy took their cups of coffee to the living room for an evening of strategizing. Before dinner, Katherine had relayed the grisly details of the posthunt activities. While Betsy ate her meal, she chewed over the possible courses to chart. Both of them knew that it would not be easy to win Thomas back with another woman and an institution standing between them.

"This is what I think I would do if I were in your shoes. I would keep my standing appointment with him after the staff meeting on Monday. After briefing him on the past week's activity in the ER, I'd start the conversation by again thanking him for doing the driving to Jasmine's place. Then, I think I'd ask him about the amount of her contribution. After all, he attended the hunt weekend with the hopes of asking her for more than her usual contribution. Up to that point, you would be on safe ground," Betsy said as she carefully laid out her part of the strategy.

"And then what? After we finish discussing the business portion of the weekend, how do I bring the conversation around to the personal aspect? That's where we're having problems. I had thought to take the direct approach, to hop in with both feet. What I fear the most is that I might hop into the proverbial pile of manure. I don't know what really happened between them, but I can guess. Thomas thinks that Roger and I became more than friends, especially after I said that I could not allow a relationship to develop with him. This is all a big mess," Katherine moaned with her head in her hands.

"Well then, you have nothing to lose by taking the direct approach. I'd go right to the point and have it out with Thomas. If everything is as bad as you say it is, you can't make it worse. If the relationship is salvageable, an open discussion will make it stronger. Either way, you'll know where you stand," Betsy consoled. She hated to see Katherine so distressed.

I know you're right, I'm simply being cowardly. I really don't like confrontations of any kind and especially not personal ones, but I'll tackle this thing head on. By this time tomorrow, the lines will have been drawn in the sand, the air will have been cleared, and all will have been settled, I hope. No matter what happens, I'll be happier than I am at this moment. At least I'll know where I stand with Thomas," Katherine agreed as she gathered her belongings and headed back to her apartment.

Ten

The next morning before Katherine could have her meeting with Thomas, the ER erupted into a hotbed of activity as hundreds of patients flooded the facility. A fire in one of the dormitories of the university with which the hospital was affiliated sent students running into the early morning air. Katherine ordered two tents set up outside on the lawn. The first served as a triage center from which the more seriously injured were funneled into the hospital. The second was the treatment point for those who were less seriously injured. It also functioned as a refuge from the broiling sun while the students recovered from the shock of awakening from their sleep to find their rooms filled with smoke.

As the patients flowed into the tent, so did the rumors. Some said that a disgruntled student had deliberately set the fire. Others reported that a contraband hot plate had touched a curtain and ignited it. Still others speculated that someone's careless cigarette had caused the flames that destroyed the building and all of their clothing, books, computers, and belongings. The only thing that Katherine knew with any certainty was that the students had inhaled great quantities of billowing black smoke that could cause permanent damage to their lungs.

Katherine and her staff worked tirelessly to evaluate and treat everyone who passed through the doors. To handle the enormity of the emergency, any physician who was not otherwise engaged was called to the ER. Every available pair of hands was needed to handle the frightened smoke-stricken students, deal with the inquisitive press, and notify the worried parents. Administrators from both the hospital and the university rolled up their sleeves to help.

Katherine's eyes burned from the students' smoky clothes and her feet ached from standing all day. However, she stood ready as the next stretcher rolled into emergency room 1 where she had spent most of her morning. If she had taken the time to think about the sights that greeted her, she would have been distressed by the sheer numbers. As it was, Katherine only knew that she had treated so many burns, breaks, cuts, and smoke cases that all the faces had become one soot-covered blur.

Pulling on yet another pair of gloves, Katherine cut away the charred clothing that mingled with the raw flesh on the young woman's leg. The patient lay motionless but alert. Her right leg was totally numb from the sedative Katherine had administered to dull the pain.

"Alice, get me some gauze and the burn salve, please. Call the burn unit and tell them that I'll be sending up another one in about half an hour. I'll need some saline solution, too," Katherine ordered. She and Alice had worked together for so long and so efficiently that the needed supplies appeared almost as soon as she requested them.

Almost wincing at the sight, Katherine carefully used a saline bath to coax the fabric into releasing from the mutilated flesh. Bloody water flowed from the leg onto the protective sheeting, but the material of the summer-weight slacks remained embedded in the skin of the girl's leg.

Carefully taking tweezers and a moistened cotton swab, Katherine slowly and painstakingly picked at the fabric bits. Slowly lifting a corner of one of the fragments, she applied more saline solution to the area until a small potion of the cloth pulled free of the mangled skin.

Pausing to allow her nerves and stomach to settle, she studied the face of her young patient. The girl showed no sign of pain or any reaction to the tugging motion as Katherine removed the fabric bits. Her eyes were closed and her breathing normal despite the shock she had endured.

"I certainly hope they catch the guy who did this," Alice remarked angrily as she carefully bathed the blistered skin with saline.

"So do I, Alice. I can't remember treating so many victims of a single fire. We've only been treating the worst of the cases. There are plenty more waiting for us," Katherine responded as Alice wiped the perspiration from her brow.

"This is the worst fire-related accident I've ever seen. These poor kids have gone through hell. I can't imagine what they went through. It's a miracle that more of them weren't seriously injured," Alice commented as she produced another bottle of saline solution.

Collecting herself, Katherine again drenched the site and pulled at the remains of the cloth. This time a larger portion lifted from the skin, revealing a mass of blood and swelling flesh. Depositing the shriveled fabric in the bowl in Alice's hand, Katherine moved to another section of the leg and began the painstaking process again.

Finally, when the ache in her back had become unbearable and the stench of burned flesh had embedded itself in her nose, Katherine extracted the last shard of fabric from the girl's leg. Applying special salves, she prepared the young woman for transfer to the overworked burn unit. From the looks of the leg, she did not think that the patient would suffer any mobility problems as long as the area was kept moist and flexible.

Removing her bloody gloves, Katherine checked the girl's vital statistics. She was relieved to see that all of her signs were stable. As the girl's eyes fluttered open, she asked, "How's my leg? I can't feel a thing. Is it all right?" Her eyes were now wide open with fear.

Katherine responded softly, "Your leg is just fine. I've removed all the fabric that burned into your skin. Your leg will be disfigured, but you shouldn't loose mobility. We're moving you up to the burn unit now. You'll be fine."

"Thank you, doctor," the girl replied groggily as the anesthesia thickened her tongue. "You should have seen that fire. The smoke was terrible. I tried to open my door, but I couldn't from the heat in the hall. When the smoke came under my door, I had to take a chance. I guess I waited too long because all I saw was flames. Everywhere I looked there was nothing but fire. It reached to the ceiling, consuming everything in its path. I thought that kind of thing only happened in movies, but it's true. It even had fingers that reached out to me and the furniture in the hall and the posters on the walls. It ate everything. I hope I never see anything like that again. I just knew I was going to die.

"Then, when the flames grabbed my pants leg, I panicked. I forgot to drop and roll. All I could think about was running from the flames that were chasing me. With every step, the flames on my leg spread upward. All I could do was stand and watch them. I was too scared to think about anything. All I could hear was the roar of the fire behind me.

"One of the other girls on my floor saw me. She knocked me down and beat the flames out with her hands and pulled me to my feet. My leg was hurting so bad that I could barely limp on it. The fire had melted my pants. When I saw the fabric stuck to my skin, I freaked out. I just started screaming. She dragged me out of the building, too.

"I don't really know her well, but you can bet she'll become my best friend after this. I owe her my life."

Katherine watched as the gurney eased into the elevator. She wondered how the girl would feel in few days once the shock of the fire had faded and the truth of her disfigurement had sunk into her psyche. Quickly Katherine made a note at the bottom of the girl's chart to the burn unit physicians suggesting a consultation with plastic surgery. Slipping the chart into the slot at the foot of the gurney, Katherine smiled and waved goodbye.

In the lull between patients, Katherine toured the emergency room. Each suite was filled and everyone was hard at work.

She knew that her staff would rise to the challenge of the disaster and did not wonder who was performing which task.

She had been too busy stitching wounds incurred during the stampede of frightened students and ordering x-rays of possible broken limbs and smoky lungs to give much thought to Thomas. She did not see him as he cleaned out the wound of a senior who had been trampled by his floor mates in their haste to flee the burning building. As the morning stretched into afternoon and then into evening, Katherine was not aware that Thomas had joined the throng of ministering angels. All she knew was that their talk would have to wait until another day. When Katherine did finally realize that Thomas had joined the throng of ministering angels, the morning had stretched into afternoon and then into early evening. Their talk would have to wait another day.

Pushing the door open, Katherine stepped into the sunlight for the first time since arriving at the hospital that morning. As she approached the triage tent, she discovered with a great sense of relief that only ten patients with minor injuries awaited treatment. The scene in the next tent was equally as heartening. Only twenty students sat around the parameter of the makeshift examining room. They waited for the four physicians to clean and stitch or bandage their sprains or cuts.

In the last tent, Katherine poured herself a glass of fresh, cold orange juice and sat down next to a student wearing a bandage on his naked foot. Sipping her juice she asked, "What happened to you?"

"I stepped on some glass as I lowered myself from my second-story room. I figured that it was either the glass or the fire. Since that wasn't much of a choice, I jumped. I would have made it if someone hadn't left that beer bottle on the ground under the window. I got a pretty good cut that required a few stitches and a tetanus shot, but it beats being burned," the young man replied. He was quite calm and almost cocky about his successful escape.

"Well, I'd say that you're one of the lucky ones from the number of kids I treated who received serious burns. I hope they find out who or what started that fire," Katherine commented as she dragged her tired body from the bench.

"Me, too. If I ever get my hands on the guy, he'll have hell to pay. All of my stuff was in that room. My CDs, my clothes, my books . . . I've lost everything except the shirt on my back. But I guess it could be worse. Some of my friends are in pretty bad shape. See you, doc," the young man replied as he limped off in the direction of the front entrance and Katherine trudged toward the emergency room door.

Despite her fatigue, Katherine smiled sweetly at the reporters who thrust their microphones and cameras in her face as she entered the emergency room. Delivering a brief reply, which she knew would warm the hearts of the public relations department, she said, "Boxer, as a dedicated member of this community, has done its part to relieve the pain and suffering of the young fire victims. At this time, it would appear from the few who remain to be treated that the nightmare day is finally over."

"How many students did you treat, doctor?" asked one reporter whose face Katherine had seen in the hospital during other emergencies.

"I couldn't begin to give you a precise count. We set up the tents to handle as many as possible on an outpatient basis. Only the more seriously injured were treated in the ER and admitted. However, I think it's safe to say that anyone who did not have an early class was in some way given medical treatment by the staff of this hospital," Katherine replied.

"After a day like this, doctor, what's next for you," inquired yet another reporter who was in search of the more personal angle.

"I have a report to write and then I'm going home for a bath and a meal. Other than a glass of juice, I haven't eaten a thing since breakfast. If you'll excuse me, I'll get to that paperwork now," Katherine answered as she slipped into the physicians' lounge.

Typing madly, Katherine managed to complete her report in record time. Anything that she might have forgotten today, she would handle tomorrow when her mind was fresh and her body rejuvenated. Exhausted, Katherine threw her blood- and soot-soiled coat into the laundry hamper and grabbed her bag. Casting a look in the mirror, she discovered that her face was almost as streaked with sweat and soot as her patients'. Scrubbing quickly, she removed the bulk of it from her skin, but she could do nothing for the smell that clung to her clothes and hair.

Barely able to walk the few blocks to her apartment, Katherine was oblivious to the passersby who looked at her bedraggled appearance as they continued on their way to the subway. She did not even notice the roses and daylilies blooming in the yards along her route home. Her mind was on the agony and pain she had tried to soothe in the long hours she had worked nonstop in the ER. She did not hear the twittering of the birds either as she moved through the teaming streets. Her usually quick, light footsteps were leaden with fatigue and anguish. She had never seen so many people in need of medical care in one place at the same time. Not even in the gore of automobile accidents had she seen the sheer number that flowed through the ER that day.

As she approached her building, Katherine became aware of the feeling that someone familiar was with her. Turning, she looked into Thomas's equally strained face. She was happy to see him. She managed a tired smile as she said, "Good afternoon, doctor. You're going the wrong way, aren't you? Shouldn't you be heading more toward the Kennedy Center? By the way, where were you during the fire disaster? I didn't see you in the ER."

Taking her arm Thomas replied, "Which question should I answer first? You didn't see me because you didn't look up from your suite in the emergency room all day. I divided my time between the ER in room 6 actually and the public relations office. You're not the only one in demand by the press. Yours is not the only pretty face in town, you know.

"Now, the second question you asked me. I thought I'd escort you home and then to dinner. We didn't have a chance to talk today, and there's quite a lot between us that we need to be said.

If you're not too tired, maybe we could linger over dessert and coffee while we work through a few things. I'd like to get our relationship back on solid ground before the events of the past weekend fester between us. Are you up for dinner?"

"I am very hungry, but I feel terribly grubby and in desperate need of a shower. Do you mind waiting?" Katherine suddenly found that she did indeed have an appetite. Thomas's invitation has started her heart beating a little faster, too. She felt renewed energy that only a few minutes ago she did not think she could muster.

"I'll sit right here until you return. I can't stand the idea of being inside after the day we've spent. Don't take too long. I'm starving," Thomas replied as he walked toward the bench in the little park next to her building. Although exhausted from the day's ordeal, he had already freshened up in his private bathroom before the latest round of meetings with the press. His carefully selected suit reflected the professionalism of his position in the hospital and helped to assure everyone that the hospital had successfully handled yet another medical crisis.

As Katherine ran up the steps to her apartment, her mind raced from one topic to the other. There were so many things that she wanted to discuss with Thomas that her tired brain could not focus on one. She had rehearsed her talk with him this morning as she showered for work, but now she could not remember anything that she had planned to say.

Scooping Mitzi into her arms, Katherine quickly fed the hungry cat and then rushed to the bathroom. Throwing her slacks, shirt, and undergarments in a pile on the floor, she dashed into the stream of still cold water that felt refreshing as it pounded her tired back and shoulders. As the water began to warm, she could feel the tension drain from her body.

Toweling off before the mirror that hung on the back of her bathroom door, she took a quick look at her reflection. Despite the shadows around her eyes and the lines of fatigue, Katherine thought she looked pretty good for someone who had not sat down since eight in the morning.

Pulling on a shape revealing spaghetti strap summer dress,

Katherine ran her fingers through her shower-fresh hair, put a touch of blush on her cheeks, and a dab of lipstick on her lips. Satisfied that she looked respectable for an impromptu dinner date, she grabbed her purse and darted down the steps. Her thin strapped sandals made a soft clicking noise on the steps as she rushed toward the park where Thomas sat twirling a dandelion between his outstretched fingers.

"I hope I didn't keep you waiting too long," Katherine said as she stood looking down on his broad shoulders.

"On the contrary, I was wondering if I'd be able to change that quickly if someone were waiting for me," Thomas replied and motioned toward the little bistro up the street where they would dine alfresco at one of the little tables that lined the sidewalk.

They walked the two blocks in silence with each one deep in thought. Katherine hoped that Thomas would begin the conversation and clarify his relationship with Jasmine without her having to ask about it. He hoped that she would be the first to break the silence by disclosing the nature of her relationship with Roger.

Although they had eaten business lunches together at the same little restaurant, it looked very different to Katherine in the dusk as candles flickered on every table. Taking their seats at a table in a secluded corner, they studied their menus and ordered with very little small talk between them. The seriousness of the topic that lay unspoken between them overshadowed any attempt at lighthearted conversation.

Finally, unable to stand the silence any longer, Thomas cleared his throat and nervously began to say, "I'll get right to the point, Katherine, and say that nothing is happening between Jasmine and me. She's a delightfully attractive divorcée who is very supportive of the hospital, as you know. She generously donated a million dollars to the capital campaign for which there are no strings attached. Her attention to me on the night of the party and then again on Sunday morning were quite innocent, although suggestive of a deeper understanding between us. I am in no way personally indebted to her. Now, might I ask about your new friendship with Roger? He appeared quite devoted to you last weekend."

"Roger is a very interesting man, but, I haven't even heard from him since we left yesterday and I doubt that I will. We danced and shared dinner conversation, but that's all that happened. It looks as if we jumped to conclusions without having all the facts, doesn't it? Had we been diagnosing a patient like that, he would have died," Katherine commented. She stared into Thomas's face intently trying to understand the emotions that played across his brow.

With a soft chuckle Thomas said, "Does this mean that we can get back to where we were before the weekend at Jasmine's? I was hopeful after the ride to her home that we'd be able to move forward and allow our friendship to develop into something more substantial, more lasting."

"I think it's fair to assume that all is well between us, at least it is from my perspective," Katherine replied with a tired smile as she allowed Thomas to take her hand into his. The warmth that transmitted from his body into hers was strangely comforting. She found herself believing that everything between them would, indeed, move smoothly from that moment.

As they ate a dinner of linguine with clams and mussels, mozzarella cheese and tomato salad, and fragrant garlic bread, a roving violinist played the haunting strains from romantic movie theme songs. Thomas lifted his glass of Chianti and proposed a toast saying, "To new beginnings and bright tomorrows!"

Looking into his eyes, Katherine believed that anything would be possible with Thomas at her side. Even the goals that she had set for herself would be within reach with the emotional conflict that had existed between them smoothed away. She wanted to believe that she saw nothing but golden horizons in their future.

Walking back to her apartment building, Katherine and Thomas strolled along holding hands and sharing stories of their childhood. It was almost as if the memory of the misunderstanding between them had faded away. She had never been happier or felt more sure of her direction than she did at that moment. Thomas found his step lightened by their renewed commitment to each other.

Without even asking, Thomas slipped the keys from Katherine's fingers and opened her apartment door. Mitzi greeted them with apprehension at first, but she quickly warmed to him as Thomas scratched the hard to reach spot between her shoulder blades. Katherine smiled, relieved to see that her cat approved of Thomas. When Mitzi remained aloof, she knew that the relationship was doomed to failure. So far, the feline barometer had reacted favorably to only one of her male friends, and he was simply her buddy, not at all someone with whom she would think of becoming romantically inclined.

Thomas's presence seemed to fill the large two-bedroom condo. His shoulders made the large living room appear small and cramped. His legs severely reduced the floor space as he sprawled on the blue leather sofa. The room that Katherine had previously envisioned as tastefully decorated now looked fussy and overdone. She was amazed at the change he made in her space, yet she found the transformation oddly comforting.

As she returned from the kitchen with tall, chilled glasses of soda and slices of pineapple, strawberries, and melon, Katherine saw that Mitzi had curled up on Thomas's lap for more of the scratching he had begun at the door. She purred contentedly as Katherine and Thomas sipped their drinks and nibbled the fruits in a strangely peaceful silence.

Katherine had always found the atmosphere strained the first time a date visited her apartment, but, with Thomas, it felt natural that he should be there. He did not seem a stranger or an intruder despite his size. As she watched his long fingers stroking the sleeping cat, she wondered how long this feeling of tranquility would remain unbroken. She hoped forever.

Yet the voice of her determination would not remain silent. Despite her happiness at being with Thomas, Katherine had a

goal that she had to attain and a purpose that she had to fulfill.
She had promised herself that before she settled into a relationship she would prove her managerial ability. Katherine would
not be swayed from that goal. She had to reclaim the chief-of-
staff job that had been ripped from her fingers.

Sensing the oneness of their shared silence, Thomas gently
pulled Katherine against his shoulder. His fingers lightly caressed her face and neck as he pressed his lips softly against
hers. His movements were slow and deliberate. There was no
hurry. They had this night and many more in which to explore
each other and share their affection. He only wanted to show
Katherine that he cared deeply for her; he did not want to pos-
sess her. Besides, from what he had learned of Katherine in the
short time they had been together, Thomas doubted that anyone
would or could ever own her. She was definitely the kind of
strong-willed, determined woman who controlled her own destiny rather than allowing someone else to dictate her actions.
He would take his lead from her. When she was ready, he would
show her the depth of his emotions.

Katherine's tired body responded to the warmth of his hands
and the sweetness of his kisses. Slowly, she began to relax
against him as her fingers stroked the back of his neck above
the collar of his shirt. She sighed deeply and took comfort in
the smell of his maleness. Suddenly the hospital seemed far
away. Katherine found herself becoming a woman in the arms
of the man for whom she cared deeply. She was no longer the
head of a department with a budget to meet, personnel to supervise, and a boss to impress.

Thomas felt Katherine relax in his arms and knew that the
barriers she had erected between them no longer stood in the
way of their happiness. Pulling her more closely against him,
he allowed his restrained desire for her to dictate his actions.
Lowering his lips to her neck and bare shoulders, he gently
placed burning kisses along the line of the straps that hugged
her soft flesh. Teasingly, he traced the place where the gold
necklace rested. Allowing his fingers to take increasing free-

doms with her yielding body, he gently stroked the nipples as they strained against the fabric of her little dress.

Moaning softly, Katherine tightened her fingers in his hair and held him fast to her. She had never been kissed by anyone who made her feel the way that Thomas did. She had never longed to meld her flesh with that of a man with the intensity with which she wanted to give herself to Thomas. He had captured her heart long ago; she was now willing to give him her body.

Thomas, too, had never wanted to make love to a woman as he desired Katherine. It was not simply the desire to couple that emboldened his hands and lips. He wanted to share himself totally with her, to make his flesh one with hers, and to feel their hearts pounding in tandem. He longed to lie beside her for the rest of his days and to know that she would always be a part of his life.

Rising from the sofa, Thomas pulled Katherine to her feet beside him. He needed to feel the full length of her body pressed against his. His hands and arms lovingly possessed her as he breathed in the scent of roses that emanated from her warm flesh.

Laying her head on his shoulder, Katherine matched her breathing to his as her arms encircled his waist. The nearness of him made her feel secure and protected from the harsh realities of the world that threatened to invade their little space. She pushed to the recesses of her mind any thought of Boxer Hospital. For the moment, they were all that mattered and all that existed.

Lifting her face so that he could gaze into her eyes, Thomas whispered, "Katherine, I love you. Let's not ever let anything or anyone come between us."

Tears of joy filling her eyes, Katherine nodded and replied, "I love you, too, Thomas. Nothing else matters but us and our love."

Bending slightly Thomas scooped Katherine into his arms and carried her to her bedroom. Mitzi looked up from her perch at the foot of the bed. Stretching languidly, she meowed, jumped from the bed, and left the room. She seemed to understand that even the presence of a pampered companion would be intrusive at that moment.

As Katherine watched, Thomas quickly removed his clothes and neatly folded them before placing them in the nearby chair. His every action was deliberate and meant to prolong the moment of their union. It was a test to see how long he could control the passion and desire that burned within him. Only when he stood naked before her did he unwrap the special present that Katherine offered him.

Slowly sliding the straps of her dress from her shoulders, Thomas kissed the bare flesh of her neck, shoulders, and breasts. Easing the fabric over her hips, he helped Katherine step out to reveal her black lace panties. Laying the garment on the nest of his clothing, he returned to the thrill of her flesh under his hands.

With his tongue, Thomas outlined the swell of each breast and the hard little bud of each nipple. His hands tugged at the film of nylon that covered her womanhood until her panties fell onto the floor at her feet. His lips burned a line from her belly button to the thatch of hair below.

Katherine sighed and gently massaged Thomas's shoulders. Pulling his mouth up to her lips, she darted her playful tongue around his warm mouth and tasted his sweetness. Easing back to the bed behind her, she lowered herself onto the cool sheets as the ceiling fan breathed a refreshing breeze over her warm body.

Gazing down on her, Thomas could hardly believe the happiness and love that filled his heart to overflowing. For so long he had been looking for a woman with Katherine's passion for life and love, and now he had found her. This wonderful gift lay ready for him, offering herself to him with all her love spread open for him to savor.

Joining her body with his, Katherine felt the quickening of their hearts as their movements reflected the urgency of their need for each other. No longer able to move slowly and deliberately, they thrust their bodies in a frenzied primal dance. Their desire for the satisfaction that came from loving totally and abandoning all pretenses drove them to lock their arms and legs around each other. Their breath came in quick grunts and moans indistinguishable one from the other.

Finally, in a meshing of one soul with the other, they shuddered from the release of their passion and lay spent in each other's arms. Neither wanted to let go of the other, neither felt the need to speak, and neither desired to move. The sound of the fan and the rushing of their breath filled the room.

Slowly, they became aware of the passing of time. The darkness had deepened into the stillness of night. The streets of Washington had grown silent. The streetlights shone their full brightness. In the distance, prowling dogs barked at their own shadows and marauding cats hissed at the full moon.

When their bodies finally separated, Katherine lay with her head on Thomas's shoulder as his arms encircled her lithe form protectively. The breeze felt soothing on their moist skin. Her fingers traced the pattern of the hairs on his chest and his played in the curls that lay disheveled on her shoulder.

As their eyes grew heavy, Thomas reached for the sheet and pulled it over their nakedness. As they snuggled tightly against each other, Katherine waited for the customary thump on the bed that signaled Mitzi's return for the night. Patting the cat on her head, she allowed the gentle rise and fall of Thomas's chest to rock her to sleep.

The next morning as the sun streamed onto the bed, Katherine eased out of bed and into the shower. She dressed soundlessly, pulling on the navy blue slacks and matching cotton sweater that she would wear to work that day. Giving her hair a quick finger combing, she left the bathroom to awaken Thomas and feed Mitzi.

Much to her surprise, Katherine found that Thomas had already risen, dressed, and made the bed. Following the smell of freshly brewed coffee and warm toast, she found him in the kitchen. Mitzi waited expectantly as he scrambled eggs and cooked bacon.

"Good morning," Thomas said cheerfully, "I know this isn't health conscious eating, but I had a taste for real eggs and greasy bacon this morning. None of the egg substitute and turkey bacon would do for our first breakfast together. I bought these at the nearby market while you were in the shower. I hope you don't mind. By the way, you're beautiful in your sleep and you snore. Not loudly, a gentle puffing."

Katherine laughed, feeling genuinely happy and relaxed as she watched him move about her kitchen as if he knew where she stored everything. Even Thomas's familiarity told her that they were made for each other. Wrapping her arms around him from the back she sighed. "I don't mind one bit. As a matter of fact, you can feel free to make our breakfast every day. Can't he, Mitzi?"

Even the cat looked pleased to have Thomas standing over the stove as she rubbed against his legs. She meowed contentedly as she waited for him either to drop a scrap of food or decided to share a morsel with her. It was not often that she and Katherine ate breakfast food with Katherine's busy schedule.

As they ate sitting at the little table in the kitchen with the vase filled with flowers, Katherine mused contentedly, "You've thought of everything. Be careful or I'll get used to this treatment. I spoil easily."

Taking her hand and looking deeply into Katherine's eyes, Thomas responded, "I hope you do. I want to spoil you and give you everything your heart desires. Just give me the chance and I'll make you very happy, Katherine."

"You already have, Thomas." Katherine smiled with tears sparkling in her eyes.

With Mitzi sitting at their feet contentedly munching the little treats they generously handed to her, Katherine and Thomas dined leisurely until the reality of the day returned. After quickly scrubbing the frying pan and the dishes, Thomas pulled Katherine into his arms and pressed his lips possessively against hers. For yet another moment, time stood still as they clung to each other. Slowly they released their grips and separated.

"I'll see you tonight," Thomas said with a happy smile on his face. He felt as if he were saying goodbye to his wife as he reached for the doorknob.

"Or sooner. I seem to remember a postponed appointment with you, Dr. Baker," Katherine teased as a reminder that they had work to do together.

Thomas chuckled as he dashed down the stairs, very aware that he still had to go home and change before he could report to the hospital and his first meeting of the day. His schedule was crammed with appointments. After yesterday's dormitory fire, all of his meetings had been rescheduled for today. As he rushed toward his car and the drive home, he smiled with the knowledge that one of his appointments would be with Katherine. He wondered if she would still refuse to address him by his first name at work after this change in their relationship.

Katherine had to move quickly, too. She had scheduled a debriefing session with her staff members to assess their reactions to their performance during the emergency. Often during the course of the year, the hospital ran training sessions to keep employees at the peak of their emergency preparedness. Her department always performed well since it lived on the brink at all times. But yesterday had not been a training session. She thought that everyone had responded well, but she wanted to hear how the others felt about the energy level of the day.

Checking Mitzi's bowls, Katherine gave her cat a loving scratch and dashed out the door. She did not want to be late to her own meeting. However, Katherine knew that she would have great difficulty keeping her mind on matters of business. She could not push the taste, feel, and smell of Thomas from her mind.

Eleven

Katherine floated through her morning on a cloud of contentment. The members of the ER staff wondered what had come over their usually business-oriented head. Winking at each other, they concluded that she must be in love with someone unknown to them.

The press that always lurked around Boxer waiting for a newsworthy story was surprised by the change in Katherine, too. She had always treated them kindly when they visited the ER, but today the reception was warm and almost friendly. Chuckling and casting sidelong glances at each other, they decided that she must have found a way to relax after yesterday's hectic hours that they had not tried.

Completing her staff meeting in record time, Katherine rushed upstairs to the conference room to await her usual session with Thomas. Arriving exactly at ten o'clock, she threw open the door and entered without thinking that the room might still be in use. To her surprise, she found Thomas in an intense discussion with Jasmine.

Immediately, Katherine felt her face grow hot, her hands become clammy, and her heart begin to pound furiously. With great effort, she managed to control her desire to physically remove not only the engaging smile from Jasmine's face but Jasmine's person from the conference room. Resisting both urges, Katherine spoke with great effort through lips that felt rigid in their effort to smile.

Speaking with as much grace as she could muster Katherine said, "Jasmine, how nice to see you again. I didn't know you would be here this morning. I didn't expect to see you again so soon. Let me take this opportunity to tell you again just how much I enjoyed my weekend and the hunt."

"Katherine, it is such a pleasure to see you. I was just telling Thomas that we needed to have a little reunion lunch today since I find myself in town on business. If you're free, you could join us. We're not going far, only to the little bistro up the street," Jasmine purred in her usual throaty voice.

Katherine grabbed for the nearest chair at the mention of the restaurant that she now considered their special place. Looking first at Thomas and then back to Jasmine, she managed to keep her composure long enough to say, "I don't know if I'll be able to get away. The fire yesterday left me with a ton of work."

"Well, do try to join us, Katherine dear. A threesome would be so nice," Jasmine responded unaware of Katherine's discomfort. Turning her full attention to Thomas, she immediately forgot that the other woman was in the room.

Thomas, however, had noticed the sudden change in Katherine's appearance. He hoped that she did not think that he had invited Jasmine to his office. Thomas had been just as surprised as Katherine when she had appeared. He had been waiting in the conference room for his ten o'clock meeting with Katherine when Jasmine had unexpectedly arrived. She had deposited herself into the chair near his as if he had been expecting her.

Katherine sat immobile as she watched Jasmine and Thomas continue their conversation. It sounded completely focused on the hospital, but Katherine could not be certain, knowing that anything was possible with Jasmine. Her emotions were in such a state of turmoil that she barely heard their words over the mutterings of her own internal struggle. Katherine knew that she had to trust Thomas or else their relationship would never grow. However, seeing Jasmine in his office with her hand so freely resting on his shoulder, her suit jacket open to expose her ample bosom, and her chair pulled suggestively close to his did not make Katherine feel exactly confident. She wanted to believe that the meeting was entirely professional, especially since Jasmine had also invited her to lunch with them. However, Jasmine's demeanor was entirely too friendly and too provocative.

"Well, I'd best be on my way if I'm to finish everything in time for our luncheon," Jasmine cooed, rising from her chair and coaxing her skirt down her trim body. "If you change your mind about joining us, feel free to come along. There's always room for one more, Katherine, although you might find our conversation frightfully boring. Goodbye, Thomas dear. I'll see you at noon."

Katherine tried to focus her thoughts through the haze of Jasmine's perfume, but she found that her emotions interfered. She had always prided herself on being a calm, collected kind of woman. She was a woman who never jumped to conclusions. She always thought of herself as a woman who never made snap judgments. Now, she found that she did not even know herself. Katherine felt as if she were looking at a total stranger. She had become a woman capable of jealousy and feelings of inadequacy because she had allowed a man into her life and heart.

Pulling herself together, Katherine methodically arranged her folders on the conference room table in the order in which she intended to discuss their contents with Thomas. She hoped that her emotions would be easier to control than her fluttering hands as she took a seat opposite the one Jasmine had recently vacated. As she opened her notes, she could feel Thomas's eyes intently watching her every move. She hoped that her actions looked natural, although she felt more like an automaton than a real woman with each move of her hand.

Thomas watched as Katherine took meticulous pains in an obvious effort to control her emotions. He realized that he would have to take a direct approach in dealing with this delicate subject. He was quite concerned about Katherine's reaction to Jasmine's visit.

"Katherine, I didn't know that Jasmine would be here today.

I would have told you if I had. I'm sure seeing her was quite a surprise," Thomas began as he continued to scan her face. The downward turn of her mouth worried him. He had seen that same expression on Katherine's face at Jasmine's house on Saturday. He did not want to be frozen out of her life again.

"Shock, I think shock is more the word especially since you only last night told me that there's nothing between you two. It's amazing how quickly you could forget the woman with whom you made love last night in favor of the one from the weekend. There's something I wanted to ask you last evening, but I suppose I was too carried away by your attention to think about it. However, I'm certainly earthbound now. Did you sleep with Jasmine, too, or is that expression of familiarity something she bestows on all her perspective husbands? Never mind. Don't answer that. I don't know if I'd believe the answer anyway. I should have known better than to mix business with pleasure. For all these years I succeeded in avoiding office affairs and now I find that I'm engaged in a threesome in which I can't possibly emerge the victor. Let's get on with business, shall we?" Katherine said with a minimum of pauses but a maximum of effect.

"We need to finish this discussion before we move to our business for the day, Katherine. I don't want Jasmine's presence to affect our professional dealings, and I certainly don't want her to interfere in our personal lives. I told you how much I need you in my life and how much I love you. Jasmine means nothing more to me than any other member of the board. And, no, I did not sleep with her. There hasn't been a woman in my life and definitely not my bed since my last relationship broke up four years ago. I haven't wanted that kind of involvement or the possibility of that level of pain again until I met you," Thomas said with his emotions clearly visible on his face and in his voice.

Despite her desire to believe him, Katherine could not bear the thought of being hurt. Yet, she did not want to inflict pain on him either. Softly she responded, "I suppose I could be mistaken about your reaction to Jasmine, but I'm not wrong about her interest in you. Every fiber of her body screams that she's interested in you. Knowing that Jasmine collects husbands as well as horses, it's not difficult for me to guess that you're at the top of her acquisitions list. Please be careful, Thomas. Our relationship is too new and too fragile for any missteps."

"You have to believe me when I say that I would never do anything to damage our relationship. Jasmine only stopped by to tell me about a major fund-raising dinner dance the board has planned for next month as part of the anniversary celebration. She suggested it yesterday at the meeting I missed because of the ER overload, and the other members jumped at the idea. I'll share the details with you as soon as I have them. Now, can we put Jasmine out of our minds?" Thomas said as he rose from his chair and slowly pulled Katherine into his arms. He could feel the tension fade from her body as she surrendered to his closeness.

"I know I shouldn't be suspicious. Jealousy is so unattractive." Katherine sighed as she nestled into the strength of his arms.

Lifting her face to his, Thomas pressed his lips slowly and softly to Katherine's. The force of their affection immediately spread over them enveloping them in a protective cocoon. Suddenly, an annoying buzzing sound filled the room. Laughing, Thomas held Katherine's hand as he answered the intrusive telephone. Both wondered if the day would ever come when his secretary would not interrupt their stolen moments of affection.

Suddenly, Thomas's expression changed from playful to worry. Every muscle in his body tensed as he listened to his secretary's voice. Hearing only the snippets from his side Katherine could not make out what had caused the sudden transformation. She waited impatiently until he hung up the telephone and turned toward her.

Before Thomas could open his mouth, the fire alarm began to blare in the hall. Propelling Katherine toward the door, he said, "There has been a fire in the A wing kitchen. It's mostly under control, but the fire marshal has insisted on evacuating everyone from this wing of the building. Just when things were looking so good for the hospital and the money was being directed to futuristic goals, something like this happens. I certainly hope it's not too severe."

Over the clanging of the alarm Katherine yelled, "I hope no one was hurt. Surely the hospital's insurance will cover the repairs."

"All we can do is wait and see. At this point, I'm grateful that none of the patients was injured. It could have been so much worse. As soon as we can return to the building, I'll check out the damage for myself," Thomas shouted back as they joined the others on the fire exit.

As they joined the others on the lawn, Katherine was amazed by the orderly fashion in which the staff had evacuated the ambulatory patients who now sat basking in the sun and resting under the trees. The ones who could not be moved had been relocated to other wings of the hospital behind the safety of the fire doors.

Because of the possibility of massive loss of human life, four hook and ladder trucks as well as three ambulances waited in front of the hospital to be called into action. To Katherine it seemed as if every fire fighter in Washington swarmed in and out of the doors. Their yellow jackets sparkled in the sun, giving the onlookers a feeling of confidence at their presence.

Joining Thomas in conversation with the fire marshal, Katherine listened attentively as he said, "Dr. Baker, the kitchen's in a bad way. It wasn't a grease fire as you'd expect but an electrical one. Good thing you folks have two kitchens because this one needs rewiring that's going to keep it out of commission for quite some time. I'm sorry to be the one to give you the bad news, doctor, but I always say that the direct approach is better than being hit by a surprise. You'll be able to see the damage yourself in a few minutes. My men have everything pretty much under control."

"Was anyone injured?" Katherine interjected as she studied the concerned faces of the men.

"Fortunately no one was hurt. One of the cooks saw the sparks flying from behind the wall in time to throw the main breaker. If he hadn't acted so quickly, I don't know what would have happened," responded the fire marshall. Touching the brim of his hat, he walked off, leaving Katherine and Thomas standing together on the grass.

Surveying the patients in their wheelchairs and gurneys, Katherine was indeed relieved that the fire had not been more extensive. She could imagine the scope of the tragedy they would have encountered if it had spread. The cook's quick thinking had averted a real disaster.

Although she could breathe a sigh of relief, she could see from the furrow on Thomas's brow that he was busily calculating the expense of repairing the kitchen and returning it to working condition. With only one kitchen in operation, the meal delivery would function at a snail's pace. The hospital would have to work quickly to repair the damage or else elective surgery patients would schedule their operations at other hospitals, causing the hospital's bottom line to suffer even more.

Returning from his last inspection of the kitchen, the fire marshal spoke into his megaphone saying, "Ladies and gentleman, I have inspected the kitchen. The fire has been extinguished and it is safe for your return. However, I ask for the continued safety of the kitchen staff that you not visit the fire site unless it is absolutely necessary in the performance of your duties. The staff will be very busy removing debris and repairing the faulty wiring. Although intended as moral support, your presence would only impede the repair effort. Thank you."

Turning to Katherine, Thomas asked, "Would you like to accompany me on my inspection of the kitchen? I would welcome your suggestions for coping with this mess during the repair phase."

"Of course, Thomas, I think the ER can survive without me for a few more minutes. We were very fortunate that our wing was not included in the evacuation," Katherine responded as she studied his worried face. Without even seeing the damage to the kitchen, she knew that the repairs would be costly.

The smell of burned wires accosted their noses as Katherine and Thomas entered the kitchen. An entire wall had been damaged and charred black. The fixtures had been melted by the heat of the flames and lay in twisted heaps. The counters and cabinets provided vivid reminders of the extent of the damage as they lay in blackened mounds in the center of the floor. Broken crockery, scattered cooking utensils, dented and fire-distorted pots and pans littered the floor.

Stepping carefully over the debris, Katherine and Thomas surveyed the surreal site that had once been the hospital's second kitchen. Exposed wires dangled from the ceiling like octopus tentacles, chunks of plaster and tiles had been strewn around the floor. Even the clocks had stopped working in this space where time had been suspended at ten o'clock.

As the ceiling tiles shifted into their unfamiliar positions on the floor at their feet, Katherine cast a quick look at Thomas's forlorn face. He had worked hard to put his futuristic plans for Boxer into action only to have old technology pull him back to the reality of the day-to-day operation of the hospital. It would be hard for him to reconcile his need to regroup and perhaps abandon his forward motion in favor of retrenching for a while. She wondered what course of action he would decide to take.

Katherine was the first to speak as the remnants of the once sparkling chrome and white kitchen lay in ruins at her feet. Calmly she said, "Thank God no one was injured. The cook's quick action really saved us a bundle. Imagine what would have happened if he hadn't noticed that sparking wall. The entire place might have gone up in flames. What a mess!"

Thomas turned to Katherine as if reading her unspoken thoughts and said, "Well, Katherine, I'm left with no choice but to resort to drastic measures. There's no way that our operating budget even with the help of our insurance coverage will be able to handle a repair of this magnitude. The deductible alone will have a drastic effect on any future technology up-grades unless I cut costs wherever possible.

"I'm sorry to say this, but the quickest, surest way to save money is through cost containment and that means jobs. There's nothing else I can do. I'm calling an emergency department heads meeting for two o'clock this afternoon. By then I will have spoken with the board and the insurance adjuster. I'm sorry, but my hands are tied on this one." Not waiting for the opposition he knew Katherine would raise, Thomas turned and picked his way through the rubble.

Katherine watched his retreating back. Although she did not like the approach she knew Thomas would take to solving this dilemma, Katherine agreed with him that something drastic had to been done. There was no time to waste with subcommittee reports. The situation demanded immediate attention or else the entire hospital would suffer the consequences. Returning to the ER, Katherine dreaded the two o'clock meeting.

As all the department heads settled around the conference table, Thomas entered flanked by the chairman of the board of directors of the hospital and members of the financial subcommittee. Involving Douglas Myers in the discussion was Thomas's way of overriding any objections to his plans before anyone could voice them. He knew that what he was about to propose would not be well accepted by anyone on his staff. However, he could think of no other immediate way to solve the financial crunch the kitchen fire placed on the hospital.

Inviting everyone to take a seat and positioning Douglas Myers on his right, Thomas opened the meeting by saying, "Ladies and gentlemen, as you are all aware, the hospital suffered a fire today in the A wing kitchen. The insurance adjuster has only just left us with the distressing news of our portion of the repair bill. Let me assure you that the figure is astronomical. It succeeds in depleting any and all discretionary funds as well as reducing our annual giving account. All monies that can be diverted will be.

"However, we still have a huge shortfall that must be eliminated now. The restoration of the kitchen is not a project that can be placed on the back burner, no pun intended. We must take action now or see the erosion of our patient base as all but emergency services slowly transfer to other hospitals. With only one kitchen in operation, we will be greatly handicapped in our ability to serve meals in a timely fashion.

"Therefore, I am asking you to support me in the proposal that I am about to present to you. I know that this is not a subject that will set well with most of you. However, I do not suggest it lightly. There is no other solution that I feel will produce the same rapid results. We must act immediately regardless of the personal hardship that our actions might cost.

"To that end, let me outline my program to you. First, all personnel normally assigned to the A wing kitchen will be shifted to the main kitchen during the repair effort. The kitchen manager is in the process at this moment of designing a schedule that would allow for the maximum food preparation time with the least disruption to patients. He is hoping to begin the day earlier and shift meals by one hour.

"However, knowing that this will not alleviate all of our problems, I have support from the board for the following action. The first four floors of the A wing will be closed until the repairs have been completed. All patient services on those wings will be terminated and all patients will be relocated within the hospital if appropriate or moved to other hospitals. I have already spoken with the chiefs of staff at our neighboring hospitals and received their agreement to receive our patients. The transfers will begin this afternoon and continue tonight until everyone has vacated those floors. For safety reasons as well as financial ones, it makes sense to relocate those patients.

"As of tomorrow morning, hospital staff normally assigned to those floors will be notified that their services will not be needed for the duration of the repair period. Again, I realize that this is drastic, but the hospital needs the funds that will be saved by reducing our personnel load during the repair period. As soon as the kitchen has been restored, we will rehire all of them. I know that this will place a hardship on many of our people, but I see no other recourse in this unfortunate time.

"I realize that the measures that I have suggested are not popular ones, however, in light of this disaster, they are the only ones possible. This is a temporary but necessary action to solve this crisis. I look forward to your support. If you have any questions, Douglas Myers and I are available now and in the days to come to answer them."

Thomas looked across the table at shocked expressions. Never had anyone heard of a hospital layoff of such massive numbers of staff or transferring such large numbers of patients. The move was bold and fraught with potential danger. The pink-slipped personnel might find other jobs and not return to Boxer, which would reduce the hospital's ability to respond quickly to emergency situations. The patients might prefer the care they received at the other hospitals and not return to Boxer for other procedures. Thomas was taking a considerable gamble with the hospital's reputation as a caregiver in order to rescue its financial situation.

Katherine was the first to speak up. As she listened to Thomas outlining his decisions, she had weighed the impact of her opposition to his strategies against the effect it would have on their relationship. She quickly decided that she could not sit by and allow him to go unchallenged regardless of the personal risk. She had to keep the people who made Boxer a great hospital in their jobs. They had worked too hard, risen to every challenge, and given their all for the hospital. Katherine could not let them face financial hardship if she could serve as their intermediary. She could not and would not allow Thomas to do this to her people.

"Dr. Baker," Katherine began, "although I agreed that drastic actions are necessary, I cannot in good conscience give consent to the laying off of valuable, devoted Boxer personnel. These people have worked here for years. They are the backbone of the hospital's success. The nurses and physicians are second to none. Surely we can find temporary positions for them in a hospital of this size."

"No, Dr. Winters, Dr. Baker is correct." Douglas Myers interrupted. "We cannot allow sentimentality to get in the way of sound business reasoning."

"We will lose valuable, highly skilled employees if we implement this plan," Katherine argued. "They will find other jobs during the months of repairs. We cannot expect them to sit idly by. They have mortgages to pay and children to feed. They need their industry to keep their skills sharp."

"Dr. Baker's right. We can't expect them to go on welfare and wait for us. We need to assess the cost of training replacements in the full picture before we take such far-reaching steps," Betsy offered.

"The cost of training new hires in Boxer's procedures must be weighed against the potential savings of terminating all of these people," echoed Ben Carson, chief of the obstetrics and gynecology floor. His people were among those scheduled for termination in the morning.

"I'm sorry, Ben, but I can't go along with you on this one. The way I see it, our greatest expense is in insurance, salaries, and pension for our personnel. The cost of training them is negligible in comparison. I'm with Dr. Baker on this one. This is the only way we can save the hospital."

"I don't agree, doctors. We must look at this more carefully. Don't forget to factor in the effects on moral. We're asking for real trouble if we do this. Just give us a week, Dr. Baker. That's all we need to study the options more fully," Katherine pleaded.

Seeing that the line was clearly divided between those who believed as Katherine did and those who sided with him, Thomas nevertheless had to act immediately and decisively. The hospital was at stake and any hesitation could mean its financial ruin. He knew that the board, mindful of the anticipated dispute among the department heads, had put the weight of its support behind him.

"I'm sorry," Thomas replied as the eyes of his opponents

bore into him, "but I have already made my decision. The pink slips for your personnel have been delivered to your offices and the press announcement is ready. I have not acted without considering your concerns, but I have found that we have no other recourse. I would like to ask that you encourage your employees to support the decision of this office and the board on behalf of the hospital."

As the muttering increased, Katherine rose and gathered her things. Looking around the room at Thomas's long-faced supporters, she knew that as the former chief of staff, she had to take a stand against what she knew to be unjust treatment of unfortunate personnel. She would not want the same thing to happen to her or her staff. She had to work quickly to find another way to the desired results.

"Dr. Baker, I cannot agree with your decision. In the hours before you put this potentially disastrous strategy in place, I will endeavor to propose a countersolution. I regret that it has come to this, but I also see no other recourse. I must do what I can for the people who served me with great dedication while I was the acting chief of staff," Katherine announced, moving toward the door.

As she turned the knob, Katherine took a last glance at Thomas. She knew what she had risked in opposing him, but she had to follow the dictates of her heart. Boxer was and always would be her hospital. She had guided it once in time of need and would do it again. Katherine hoped that Thomas would eventually understand that she had as little choice in her decision as he had in his.

The scowl on Thomas's forehead said that he was not pleased with her decision to oppose him. As he watched her leave, taking with her half of the board's subcommittee and a sizable portion of the department heads, he wondered what she would propose as a solution and what action she would take if he did not agree to it.

* * *

That night, Katherine again hosted a meeting of people who shared her opposition to the direction in which Thomas was moving Boxer hospital. By eight o'clock her apartment was filled with nurses, doctors, orderlies, and support staff who had been issued the pink slips and board members and other medical personnel who had not received them but who were in opposition to Thomas's actions. Instead of a pasta dinner, she served chips, cookies, and sodas to the more than one hundred people who sat on the floor, furniture, and window seats in her living room.

As Betsy took notes, Katherine outlined their strategy for the next day. Standing before them, she directed, "We will meet at seven thirty in front of the hospital. Each one of us will be responsible for one tasteful sign. We are to write nothing slanderous or offensive on our posters.

"Our goal is to slow down Dr. Baker's implementation of his plan and force him to listen to our counterproposal. We do not want to alienate him or any of the department heads or board members. We want to keep our jobs rather than to give him reason to believe that his actions are justified. I have assigned everyone to a time slot after the mass demonstration at seven thirty. Please arrive at your post on time.

"For the first day or so, I would like to ask that as many of you as possible remain on the grounds as support for those who are walking the line. The larger the force, the more effective the results. We hope that our boycott will keep the work from starting on the kitchen repairs and force Dr. Baker to take note of our opposition.

"Now to the business at hand, we need to formulate an alternate strategy that will allow Boxer to make the necessary repairs and continue its forward motion. Let's hear some suggestions, people. Considering the amount of brain power we have in this room we should be able to come up with several possibilities."

"We could rent a hall and host a dance," Mark Evans, one of the earlier visitors to the ER and Katherine's latest convert offered. He had been so impressed with Katherine's efforts in the ER that he would give his support to any program under her competent direction.

"No, that would cost money that we don't have. True we'd make plenty, but we don't have the initial investment. How about a 'Christmas in the Summertime' yard sale day? That wouldn't cost the hospital anything and would bring in quite a bit. We could invite the entire neighborhood to participate," proposed Elizabeth Palmer. She, too, had been won over by Katherine's performance in the ER the day she visited.

"I don't know. We're on really short notice. A lot of people could be out of town. What if no one shows up?" posed Marilyn West. She enjoyed a good time as much as anyone, but she wanted to be practical. It would be embarrassing to hold an event and have no one come.

"Wait a minute," said Mark Evans. "I like both ideas. Why don't we combine the two? As all of you know, I own a restaurant barge. I'll donate my establishment for the cause of making money for Boxer. We'll charge a hefty fee for the dinner dance tickets. I'll only take enough to cover the cost of supplies and staff; I won't charge the hospital a rental fee. We'll make a sizable amount. If we combine that with a neighborhood yard sale, everyone will feel a part of the effort to save jobs and restore the kitchen. If we talk some of the others who couldn't be here tonight into digging into their pockets, we could get a Ferris wheel and a cotton candy machine and make it a real carnival. What do you say?" He urged. He was a major supporter of Boxer Hospital. Some people said he had more money than the Queen of England or the Pope. Whenever he proposed something, the others usually joined him.

"Let's do it," Tony Moore, one of the pink-slipped physicians seconded. "It would be a lot of fun and really good public relations for the hospital, too."

"Great, that's settled. By the time we arrange for the permit and the band, we will have boycotted the hospital for almost two weeks. That's long enough to make our point. Beyond that, some of us will begin to experience financial difficulty making bill payments. Let's plan on hosting this as a weekend affair. That way, we'll catch as many people as possible. It will be a great celebration of the spirit of the personnel of the hospital to pull together in times of adversity. Is everyone in agreement?" Katherine asked, scanning the room for dissenters.

Seeing none she said, "Okay, then. Our meeting is adjourned. I'll see all of you on the north sidewalk at seven thirty tomorrow morning."

Betsy hung back as the others left. She wanted to have a few minutes to speak with Katherine in private and to help her clean up her apartment. When the last person had left, she asked, "Do you really think the boycott will work? Thomas looked pretty determined to proceed with his plan."

"He's a reasonable man. As long as we can offer something that will satisfy his needs, I think he'll go along with us. He conceded to our demands once before. Don't worry, he'll see our way this time, too. Thomas is a bottom-line person. He doesn't care how we arrive at the figure as long as we do," Katherine concluded as she picked up the plate of cookies.

"What about your relationship with him? This might be the straw that destroys it, you know. You can only push a man so far before the relationship shatters," Betsy suggested reluctantly, following Katherine into the kitchen. She carried a heavy plastic trash bag filled to the brim with paper plates, napkins, and cups.

Silent for a few minutes, the two friends worked to gather the mess that covered the counters and kitchen table. Stuffing everything into the bulging trash bag, they lugged it to the door and into the hall. Hoisting it, they eased it down the trash chute.

"This will definitely be a test, but I think we'll make it. Regardless of the outcome, I had to do this. Boxer means too much to me," Katherine responded. She linked her arm through Betsy's and walked back to her front door.

Looking her buddy in the eye and seeing the determination and drive that burned there, Betsy commented, "I hope you're right. When cold weather comes, I'd hate to see you with only the cat for comfort."

Watching her friend walk down the hall to her apartment, Katherine reflected on Betsy's last statement. She hoped that she had not made the wrong decision. Knowing that it was the only choice open to her, Katherine called, "I'll see you at seven thirty."

"With bells on!" came Betsy's reply as she waved and vanished through the door.

Twelve

Thomas and the rest of his supporters did not have long to wait to see the results of the meeting at Katherine's apartment. As the next morning dawned, a picket line formed outside the hospital. Katherine and her supporters marched in orderly formation along the sidewalk on which the previous day they had stood watching the fire department pass judgment on the safety of the hospital. Her energy and devotion to the hospital had propelled them to take action against the tide that threatened their future. Now they massed over one hundred strong, waving signs and banners. Their voices echoed in the silent street as members of Washington's press corps snapped away.

For the sake of the hospital and her relationship with Thomas, she hoped that the boycott would not last long. She could already see the results as the repair men who had been scheduled to work on the fire-damaged kitchen refused to cross their picket line. As she took her place among them and lifted her sign for everyone to read, Katherine had a plan to propose that she knew would work if she could only gain Thomas's ear.

Temporarily pushing Thomas from her mind, Katherine surveyed the reaction to the statement she and her coworkers were making. Cars slowed down on the busy street during rush hour to read their signs. The drivers flashed their lights or gave a thumbs up in support as they drove away. Most pedestrians waved and spoke kind words of encouragement. However, some encouraged them to remember that health care should take priority to personal feelings. When Katherine or one of the others explained why they were boycotting Boxer, the objection quickly turned to support.

As the morning slowly turned to afternoon, Katherine hoped that their boycott was having some effect on Thomas, too. Ne had not come out to speak with them yet, but she hoped that he would soon. Even without Thomas's presence, the morning had been a great success.

The reaction of the press was highly favorable and plentiful. Camera crews from each station recorded their peaceful, quiet marching. Reporters interviewed Katherine, members of the board, and several of the affected personnel. Their initial questions and follow-up showed genuine concern and respect for their opinions and rights. Overall, the community at large supported their fight to retain their job security.

Thomas stood looking out his office window at the assembled hospital employees. He had known that Katherine and her supporters would boycott his decision, and he was proud of their actions. Boxer Hospital was a strong, committed community of professionals who not only provided the best hospital care possible for its patients but who worked together beautifully as a team. Now, as he watched staff in white jackets take turns in the line marching shoulder to shoulder with those in casual attire, he felt a renewed sense of pride and a nagging regret.

In his professional career as a hospital administrator, Thomas had often found it necessary to make unpopular decisions in order to achieve favorable bottom-line results. He had always made them swiftly and without regret. However, he had not been able to distance himself from the employees of Boxer and only see them as figures on a ledger because of Katherine. Thomas had been affected not only by her beauty but by her deep love of the hospital, its people, and its patients.

From the first time he had watched her rush to the aid of an injured child, he had felt her warmth. His first day on the job as he had read her journals, he had learned of her professionalism. The first time she, had rallied the department heads to resist his edict and offer a countersolution of involving the hospital's most generous benefactresses in a vigorous fund-raising campaign, he had learned of her managerial strength.

Now, as he watched the orderly demonstration, Thomas saw Katherine's ability to inspire people once more. Even if she did not suggest the boycott, he knew that she had provided the picketers with a place in which they felt safe voicing their opposition to his proposed changes. She was their champion, their leader, and their friend.

Although he had the title of chief of staff, Thomas knew that Katherine had the devotion of the people that he would never command. If they were ever given the opportunity to work together, they would make a powerful team. His financial acumen and her managerial skills would really put Boxer over the top.

Making a note on his calendar to propose the possibility of a joint chief-of-staff position with the board at his next session with them, Thomas forced his mind to focus on the job at hand. He had practically saved enough money by laying off employees even after paying their severance to compensate for the shortfall between the insurance payment for the fire damage and the available funds in the hospital's operating account. Remembering the effectiveness of the first capital campaign involving the "Sisters," he had decided to contact other equally generous supporters of the hospital. He felt confident that there must be others who would be as generous as the ladies if he only asked for their support. He had learned from Katherine that people sometimes only needed a little encouragement to dig deeper into their pockets for a good cause.

Thomas was concentrating on the format of the contact he was about to make, that he did not hear the gentle knocking on the door until the rapping grew in intensity and penetrated his thoughts. Wondering why his secretary had not paged him, he realized that the morning was over and that it was already twelve thirty. He had been at work, as was his custom, since seven.

Looking up, Thomas called, "Come in. It's open." He hoped

that whoever had chosen to disrupt his tranquility would quickly state his business and leave.

"Thomas, I think we need to have a talk," interrupted the voice as its owner rushed into his office. "That group of rabble must be stopped. It's embarrassing to the hospital and disquieting to the patients."

Looking up, Thomas studied Douglas Myers's agitated face. Speaking slowly and softly so as not to further upset the chairman of the hospital's board, Thomas replied, " 'That group of rabble' as you call them are our staff. We riffed them, remember? I can't see that they're hurting or upsetting anyone except maybe you. What makes you think that they are affecting our quality of patient care? They certainly aren't keeping anyone awake. If I didn't occasionally look out the window, I wouldn't even know they were still there."

"Wouldn't you be disturbed if you knew that your physician had left a picket line before coming to your bedside? I don't have any problem with the staff we riffed boycotting against us, but I don't like it that several of the ones still on the payroll have joined them," Douglas Myers said, collapsing into the nearest seat.

"From what I've been told, they join the line during their breaks. They only want to show support of their colleagues. I don't see anything wrong with that. As a matter of fact, if I weren't the chief of staff, I'd join them. We have taken a very strong step in cutting their jobs. I realize that the move is only temporary, but it's still a hard pill for them to swallow. They've heard of employees in other companies who were told that the changes were stopgap measures only to find that their futures were put in limbo indefinitely. I'd be upset with the hospital administration for a drastic act of cost containment like this, too," Thomas replied, twirling his pen between his long fingers. He was beginning to regret not being one of them. Sitting in that lofty position of power could get dreadfully lonely.

"Thomas, are you beginning to regret our decision?" Douglas Myers asked, excitedly pacing the floor.

"No, I don't regret it. We had no other choice for the good of the whole hospital but to lay off the few who were affected by the repairs. No, I'm not having second thoughts at all. My job is to run this hospital with the bottom line in mind. We were pushed to the wall with no other immediate possibility for raising the funds available. Our hands were tied. Our capital was committed. We had to take this step.

"However, I am capable of understanding their side, too. They feel justifiably hurt and betrayed. I just hope that they will remember that this is only temporary. However, you can't take a promise to the bank," Thomas responded. He had learned years ago not to second-guess his actions. He deliberated, weighed the facts, and made decisions based on them. Once made, there was no turning back.

"I hope the patients don't panic. What a mess. If only the staff had understood our position," Douglas Myers stated shaking his head. He finally lighted again on one of the chairs in a dejected, exhausted pile.

Again Thomas spoke slowly. He could see that the chairman of the board was almost to the breaking point on the first day of the boycott. He could imagine how upset the poor man would be if it continued for a long time. Assuming a professorial tone, he said, "There's still time. We're open to negotiation and suggestions. If they want to move things along at a faster rate, Katherine and the others will find a way. She won me over once before. I'm sure she can do it again.

"By the way, as long as we're discussing Katherine, I'd like for you and the board to give some consideration to what I'm going to propose to you. right now.

"As you are aware, Katherine has fabulous leadership ability. She's young, but her interpersonal skills are among the finest I've ever experienced. She definitely makes up for what she does not know about the financial element of running a hospital with her enthusiasm for and love of Boxer and her ability to work with people who are both her superiors and her subordinates.

"I'd like to see my job split between the two of us. My strength is financial management and that's why you hired me. However, I'll be the first to admit that people are my weakness. I see the bottom line and don't worry too much about the employees over whom I have to tread in order to make the changes to strengthen it.

"Katherine would be a perfect complement for me. She needs to learn to toughen up a bit if she wants to be successful on the financial end, but she has the interpersonal skills at her disposal. With her empathy for people, the two of us would make a dynamic team. Give it some thought, Douglas. You might just find that the two of us together are better than one of us alone."

Rising slowly from his seat like a man much older than his sixty years, Douglas Myers retorted, "Considering she's dragging Boxer through this embarrassing show, you must really think highly of her. I'll think about it once this debacle is over. Good afternoon, Thomas."

Returning his attention to the script of the conversation he had been trying to write before the chairman of the board interrupted him, Thomas again concentrated to the exclusion of everything around him. Just as his thoughts began to flow in a coherent manner, someone knocked on the door again.

Looking up with a great deal of irritation, he called, "Come in. The door's open. I might as well be trying to work at Union Station."

"I'm sorry to bother you, Thomas. I can return later if you'd like, but I didn't think you'd mind seeing me without an appointment," Katherine responded as she pushed open the door and walked into the angry lion's den.

"Katherine, I didn't expect you until tomorrow morning. I thought you'd let me stew until after the evening news. I've been quite impressed by the orderly manner in which you've handled this boycott. From what I can tell, none of the hospital's services have been negatively affected. All of the department heads have reported that, for the most part, it's business as usual. I'd like to thank you for that consideration. I appreciate the devotion that the staff feels for its members and the need to show that concern publicly. As long as the hospital and the patients do not suffer, I see nothing wrong with staff joining the picket line. I'd do it myself if I weren't the chief of staff and the enemy." Thomas smiled as he waved her toward the vacant chair.

"You're not the enemy, Thomas, and everyone understands that. I explained your side to them. We simply don't agree that your decision was the right one. We think you can produce the same results without affecting people's paychecks. I've come to offer you a counterproposal," Katherine replied as she slid into the seat.

Being outside had given Katherine's cheeks a healthy rosy glow. Looking at her, Thomas had to use all of his willpower to refrain himself from pulling her into his arms. He could imagine that her skin smelled soft and dewy with just a light touch of perspiration that would bring out the fragrance of her perfume. He forced himself to listen and respond as if she were simply an employee rather than the woman he loved.

"Let's hear it, Katherine. As you know, I'm always open for suggestions," Thomas said. He pushed back from his desk and crossed his arms comfortably over his chest.

Thomas was not the only one who had to remind himself about the nature of this meeting. Katherine, too, had to force herself to remember that she was in Thomas's office as the spokesperson for a group of dedicated staff and board members who had stood outside in the sun protesting the treatment of their colleagues and friends. She had a job to do, and she would not allow her desire to melt against Thomas's strong shoulders to get in her way.

Carefully, Katherine began outlining their plan by saying, "We met last night in my apartment and agreed upon a plan that we think would accomplish your financial goals, our personal ones, and unite the community. One of our group, a board member to be precise, owns a floating restaurant. He has offered it to us free of charge as the site of a dinner and dance fund-raiser. He will absorb the rental and employee cost as his contribution to Boxer. We'd make a bundle.

"We also entertained the idea of making this a full-community event by hosting a small carnival on the hospital grounds. Some people might not be able to afford the price of the dinner dance tickets, but they could attend the carnival. People with children who are reluctant to hire baby-sitters for the dance could bring the kids to the carnival and share the hospital experience with them. We thought we'd give some tours of the less congested area as a good will outreach sort of thing.

"The way I see it, you'd have what you want most, a healthy bottom line, and we'd have what we want, employees back on the job and off the picket line. What do you think, Thomas? Will your supporters on the board go for it?"

"I can't speak for the board, although I do see merit in your suggestion. I especially like the idea of encouraging the community to join us and to see Boxer as more than simply a caregiving facility. I'll pose it and let you know. Douglas Myers left here only a few minutes ago. From the jangled state of his nerves, I would think he would readily accept anything that would remove Boxer from the public eye," Thomas replied. Regardless of the board's reaction, he was very pleased with Katherine's suggestion. He could readily see the ease of implementing it and the good fellowship that would come from it.

"Good, I'll be expecting your call. In the meantime, Thomas, we'll keep our picket lines up. We've tried to maintain as much silence as is possible when you have this number of people walking together. We hope that our presence hasn't upset any of the patients," Katherine commented as she placed her hand on the doorknob. "Well, I'll wait to hear from you tomorrow. Goodbye, Thomas."

"Katherine, do you have to leave so soon?" Thomas asked, quickly walking toward her. "We haven't had any time to talk about anything other than business."

"What more is there for us to discuss? Until this is all cleared up and everyone is back on the job, we really don't have anything to say to each other. I cannot afford to be accused of maintaining divided loyalties and neither can you. It's better this way. We need to keep our distance. If all works out well, the boycott won't last long," Katherine answered with her heart practically showing on her sleeve.

"Why don't we meet for dinner? There are plenty of little out-of-the-way restaurants where we wouldn't be seen together. Our integrity would not be challenged if we spent a few hours together," Thomas coaxed. He was unwilling to go even another day without having Katherine in his life.

"I'm sorry, Thomas, but I already have plans for the evening. A group of us from the picket line are meeting for dinner at the little bistro down the street. It's sort of a planning session," Katherine replied. She opened the door.

"At our bistro? You're having a meeting at the one we enjoy together?" Thomas asked with an expression of disbelief on his face that Katherine would actually set foot in their restaurant without him.

"Sure, the same place to which you took Jasmine, if I remember correctly. Yes, as a matter of fact, I'm sure you did. Yes, it was the same little place, our little restaurant. Have a good evening. Goodbye, Thomas," Katherine responded with a gloating sound in her voice as she left him staring after her.

The impact of Katherine's seemingly innocent words were not lost on Thomas. He knew that she was giving him a not too subtle message that she could make it just fine without him. The problem was that he was no longer confident that he wanted to continue his ascension in the corporate world without her.

Dialing Douglas Myers' number, Thomas decided that he would have to present Katherine's counterproposal immediately. Her strength increased geometrically with every moment in the limelight. He did not want to take any chances that Katherine would push him out of her life entirely. She had given him a warning that he intended to heed.

While Thomas pitched Katherine's counterproposal to Myers and the board, Katherine and her friends dined together and fleshed out their plans. By the time everyone arrived, all the major arrangements had been made and all that remained was the fine-tuning. It did not take them long to decide on the color scheme for the decorations and flowers for the dance or the banners to deck the hospital. The menu fell into place easily with them relying on the excellent reviews the restaurant had already received in the dine around section of the newspaper. The most difficult decision centered around where to set up the pony ring at the carnival.

Leaning back in her chair after a filling pasta dinner, Katherine studied the faces of her colleagues. They had all been congenial coworkers before the boycott began, now they had become friends as they united against the hospital for the restoration of jobs. Not all of them at the table had been directly affected by the reduction in force, but they all believed that the hospital had reacted too quickly and too harshly.

"What's next?" Betsy asked as she folded her napkin.

"We've presented our case to Thomas who is currently placing it before the board. All we can do now is wait. Our logic was perfectly sound, and our plan is quite workable. We'll have to bide our time until we hear from them. I don't think it will take long. I passed Douglas Myers in the hall after he left Thomas's office. He looked quite upset. As a matter of fact, he barely spoke to me. I don't think Thomas will have a particularly difficult job of selling our counterproposal," Katherine replied, reflecting on the angry way in which the chairman of the board had breezed by her with barely a nod. He was not the kind of man who liked to air the hospital's dirty linen for all of Washington to view. She was sure that he was already fed up with the media attention of only one day.

"I hope you're right," Marilyn Ford interjected. "My family's budget can take a few days without a paycheck, but more than a week would be hard on us. Besides, I'd rather be in the hospital emptying bedpans than standing outside. Even on bad days, I'd rather be working than picketing."

"I agree with Marilyn. Let's hope they come around soon. I don't believe I'm saying this, but I miss the sound of whining children," echoed Bill Bradley. Both he and Marilyn were nurses in the pediatrics, which had been consolidated with general medicine.

As they left the bistro, Katherine wished all of them a peaceful good night. Linking her arm through Betsy's, she walked with her toward their apartments. The night air was wonderfully clear. Even with the bright lights of Washington casting their glow on the world, they could still make out the stars that twinkled in the cloudless sky.

"Our proposal will work, won't it, Katherine?" Betsy asked as she inhaled deeply of the sweet air.

"Definitely. You'll see, Betsy. The board will come around. Just wait until the members see the article in the paper tomorrow. A reporter interviewed me for what he thought would be a trash Boxer article. Instead, what he will print is a glowing depiction of life in the hospital and the dedicated staff that is only picketing to preserve its right to work for the good of our patients and the hospital's reputation. That article will soften the heart of even the coldest board member.

"Besides, our proposal raises the funds Thomas needs for the repairs without displacing anyone. The board will come around. It's in everyone's best interest for us to work together peacefully.

"Don't worry, Betsy. I think tomorrow will be our last day. Well, good night. I'm tired. I thought I was prepared to stand all day after working in the ER all these years, but running between the emergency room and the picket line all day has tired me out. I'll see you in the morning," Katherine said. She hugged her best friend good night.

"I'll meet you on the line, boss!" Betsy replied as she gave her best imitation of a teamster and closed her apartment door.

As Katherine snuggled into her sheets, she was not the least concerned that Thomas might not be able to convince the board to accept their counterproposal. She felt confident that he would be able to sway Douglas Myers to their reasonable offer. Besides, if he could not, the article would.

The article generated an even greater outpouring of support than Katherine had anticipated. As she watched the line of cars slowly creep past the hospital, it looked to her as if everyone who could drive had decided to show their support that morning. The steady stream of vehicles with their lights on despite the bright morning sun attested to the effect of her words on the hearts of the residents of Washington. She had not seen so much congestion on the streets except during the blooming season of the famous cherry blossoms.

Katherine had to admit that the headline was eye-catching. Perusing the article for the fourth time as she stood on the sidewalk, she was impressed by the boldness of the print and the emotional punch it delivered in its subtle way. She read, HOSPITAL WORKERS STRIKE FOR THE RIGHT TO SERVE BOXER AFTER FIRE DESTROYS KITCHEN.

If that were not enough to soften the board, the first paragraph clinched it. "The staff at Boxer Hospital took to the streets this morning to protest the loss of jobs after one of the kitchens was destroyed in a fire. The hospital administration in a cost-cutting measure designed to provide the needed funds to pay for the repairs, laid off more than one hundred nurses, physicians, and support staff. The spokesperson for the group of displaced employees, Dr. Katherine Winters, the former acting chief of staff, commented, 'We are not asking for improved benefits or increased pay. We simply want to return to our jobs and to give the community the quality of service that has long been the hallmark of Boxer's tradition of excellence.' "

The rest of the article followed the same line of discussion and painted the picture of a dedicated workforce that simply wanted to continue doing what it did best in a place that it valued. Katherine was quite pleased and knew that the board would be also.

"Good morning, Dr. Winters. I see you've achieved stardom," Thomas commented as he stopped on his way into the front door. He had walked to work this morning rather than driving from his apartment. He wanted to see the congestion for himself after hearing about it on the radio. If he had driven, he would have been a part of it rather than a witness to it.

"It's not me, it's the dedicated staff of Boxer. You certainly look fit this morning and rather rested. I trust that your conversation with Douglas went well," Katherine replied, quickly diverting the attention to the issue rather than herself.

"I did indeed. He probably didn't rest too well since it was his job to poll the others. I should hear from him early this morning. If all goes as expected, are you prepared to end this boycott?" Thomas asked, watching the employees of Boxer walk past with their signs held high so that the slowly moving traffic could read them with ease.

"We are ready to return to work as soon as you tell us that everything is back to normal. We never wanted to take this action, Thomas. We always had Boxer's best interest and our jobs at heart. All any of us wants to do is work with patients and provide the quality care for which this hospital is so famous. Just say the word and we'll return," Katherine said as a handy photographer snapped a photograph of the protest leader and the chief of staff.

"Shall we kiss and make up for the benefit of the press?" Thomas asked teasingly.

"Let's save that for the announcement . . . or later," Katherine responded with a throaty chuckle. "I, for one, have work to do. You'll know where to find me if you need me."

Shaking his head, Thomas walked into the hospital. As he had expected when he first met her, Katherine had proven to be a formidable, determined opponent. He was happy to have her in his life.

As he stepped off the elevator, Thomas was immediately accosted by a weary Douglas Myers. "Where have you been?" he demanded irritably. "I've been waiting here for you for fifteen minutes. Is that any way to treat the chairman of the board?"

"Douglas, if you had told me that you were coming this morning, I would have been up here sooner, but you didn't. So just reign in your attitude. I was outside talking with Katherine. They're ready to return to work as soon as you give the word. What'll it be?" Thomas rebutted without the slightest trepidation. He had known too many chairmen to allow this one to bully him around.

"The board reached a unanimous decision last night to adopt the counterproposal offered by Katherine's side. I've called a press conference for ten o'clock. I'm sorry that I was snappy. This thing has taken all of my time and energy and left me exhausted. As soon as this meeting is over, I'm going home to bed," Douglas Myers conceded. He detested any kind of conflict between people and had not meant to be unpleasant in his dealings with Thomas, who he considered the finest chief of staff at any hospital.

"Good work, Douglas. Why don't I treat you to a cup of coffee and a donut while we wait?" Thomas offered. He felt sorry for the man who had to come out of his cloistered existence to deal with this problem when he would rather remain on the sidelines.

"Oh, no thank you. I couldn't drink another cup. I'm so wired now that I can hardly sit still. I need to stop by to see the public relations people now anyway. They want to interview me as part of the press conference material. I don't know how you can stand these long hours, I'm exhausted. I'll take my banker's life any day over this hectic one. I'll see you in the auditorium at ten," Douglas replied as he quickly left Thomas's office.

Chuckling softly, Thomas glanced out the window at the people on the hospital's lawn. Katherine stood in the midst of them smiling and waving. It was obvious that she enjoyed being one with them. Thomas wished he had that quality.

As he returned to the stack of papers on his desk, he realized that he never would be as easygoing and open as Katherine. She fit into every situation and relished the company of people. He, on the other hand, preferred solitude and work to mingling. Everyone had strengths and his was efficiency and the masterful direction of the financial life of a hospital. Thomas again noted that they would make a wonderful team if the board would one day buy off on the idea.

Joining Katherine and Douglas in the auditorium an hour later amid the flashing lights of the press, Thomas was once again struck by her poise and confidence. Katherine stood at the podium beside the almost quivering Douglas Myers as he announced the end of the brief but highly effective boycott. Smiling slightly, she did not gloat but accepted his defeat graciously and listened to his brief statement. Clearing his throat, Douglas said, "On behalf of the board of directors of Boxer Hospital and the chief of staff, Dr. Thomas Baker, it is with great pleasure that I announce the agreeable conclusion to the boycott. We have met and come to an agreement on terms that will immediately restore order to our hospital. All employees involved in the reduction in force will return to their former positions in accordance with their customary work schedules. Patients who had been relocated within the hospitals will again be housed in the appropriate areas. During the restoration of the fire-damaged area, we will do everything in our power to minimize the inconvenience to our patients and staff. Thank you for your kind and generous outpouring of calls and messages to the hospital."

When it was Katherine's turn to speak, she stepped forward and took possession of the microphone. Unlike Douglas Myers who stuttered and stammered uncomfortably through his presentation, Katherine faced the assembled faces and spoke with dignity and assurance. "Ladies and gentlemen, I would also like to thank the press and the community for their support at this difficult time. No organization wants to see its members pitted against each other, but sometimes in any family this happens. We are healthier for having aired our grievances and addressed them openly.

"Rather than instituting a reduction in force to help the hospital overcome the tremendous burden of the fire damage, we will celebrate Boxer's position in the community with a carnival and dinner dance next weekend. We hope that everyone will attend one or both functions. The money raised from these events will help defray the cost of the repairs.

"Again, I join with Douglas Myers, Boxer's chairman of the board, and Dr. Thomas Baker, the chief of staff, in thanking you for your support."

As the cheering filled the pale blue room, Katherine smiled, waved, and stepped back from the podium until she stood beside Douglas and Thomas. Together the three of them accepted the applause of the reinstated employees who enjoyed the return of their livelihoods and their colleagues who could now turn their attention exclusively to the performance of their jobs. Everyone knew that, although Katherine had proposed the countermeasure, the receptive board and chief of staff made the agreeable conclusion to the boycott possible.

As the flashing of the cameras dwindled, they all returned to work. They had more than enough to do considering the patients who needed to be relocated to their original rooms and the plans for the gala weekend that still had to be put in place.

Thirteen

The next week flew by in a flurry of activity. The previously quiet hospital was anxiously awaiting the celebrations. The planners scheduled little intimate teas and luncheons to whet the appetites and open the checkbooks of the major contributors. Banners fluttered in the summer breeze announcing the block party. The hospital's three guilds had hung lanterns and streamers on the lawn and in the trees. The board had mailed invitations to the dinner dance onboard a ship to all major contributors. The preparations had finally reached their final stages for the big event. Everything was in readiness for the big weekend.

Katherine and Thomas spent what little free time they had together. The hospital's committee chairpersons had managed to snare everyone for duty. No one was spared the poster making, volunteer soliciting, and decorating duties. Between working their usual duties and their heavy volunteer schedules, they saw even less of each other. Yet the time they shared was quality and filled with charming candle-lit dinners, strolls through the neighborhood, picnics, and evenings at the theater.

However, the excitement was so infectious that they hardly noticed as the time sped by. Everyone suddenly needed to make plans, purchase clothing, and order flowers. Katherine and Betsy had purchased new formal gowns to wear the night of the dinner dance, although both of them owned perfectly presentable ones that hung invitingly in their closets. They wanted

the evening to be special in every way. Betsy was dating a radiologist and wanted to make a stunning impression. She
thought that the new lavender silk with its slight train would
show off her figure and highlight her complexion more than
any of her old gowns possibly could. Katherine had bought a
copper-colored strapless that accentuated the color of her hair
and made her eyes glow.

The Saturday of the opening festivities was sunny and hot.
Katherine had not been to a carnival in years and felt like a
child as she strolled from one ride or arcade game to the other.
At one stand, she won a perky little gold fish and at another a
small stuffed bear. She ate cotton candy and funnel cakes until
she began to worry about being able to fit into her new dress.
Before she left the hospital for the day, she allowed Betsy to
talk her into eating a foot-long hotdog with everything on it.

As Katherine rested her tired feet, she watched the kids who
swarmed onto the hospital grounds. Some of them were patients
from the pediatrics floor, but many came from the neighborhood. They all had a good time whether in quick moving wheelchairs or on foot. She loved the sound of their laughter and
noticed how different the hospital felt as their voices resounded
in the air.

Thomas joined Katherine for a glass of lemonade and several
chocolate chip cookies before they went off duty. He had been
busy with financial matters for most of the day, but he had
stolen away long enough to enjoy the Ferris wheel and some
cotton candy. As he surveyed the hospital complex from the top
of the ride, Thomas was pleased with what he saw. He had
worked hard to raise the funds for the new wing for which
construction had just started that morning. He knew that Boxer
was on the right track to a strong future. He considered himself
very lucky in his success and in having someone with whom
to share it.

Glancing to his right, Thomas saw his future sitting beside
him. He chuckled as Katherine covered her eyes when the wheel
stopped to pick up new riders. He held her tightly against his

chest as it began to turn and she squealed with mock horror.
When the ride ended, he kissed her lightly on her smiling lips
for everyone to see. He was proud to have a woman like Katherine in his life and did not care who knew about their relationship.

Jasmine was probably the only person on the entire parking
lot who saw or cared about the kiss, and she was livid. She had
plans for Dr. Thomas Baker and they did not include Katherine
Winters, whose happy, smiling face made her feel as if she
would puke. Jasmine was not accustomed to competition and
did not welcome obstacles in the way of her success. She wanted
Thomas all to herself. By the end of the evening, she would
have him.

Everyone who knew Jasmine was aware that she was a ruthless hunter and collector of treasures, both animate and inani-
mate. She always prided herself on getting exactly what she
wanted when she wanted it. No one and nothing ever stood in
the way of her success. Her string of husbands stood as proof
of her accomplishments. They were successful corporate presi-
dents and bankers who should have known better than to be
taken in by her wiles, but they succumbed with barely a whim-
per. The promises she made and kept were more than they could
resist. Although they knew her reputation and had seen her in
action, they were lured by the delicacy that offered itself to
them. They overlooked the danger of her powers until it was
too late to turn back. By the time they realized the truth, they
were hopelessly hooked and at her mercy.

To her credit, Jasmine was very kind when it was time to
remove the men from her life. She did not parade their faults
for others to see, and she did not embarrass them in public with
accusations of their inadequacies. She slowly over the course
of several months pointed out their deficiencies as husbands
and her waning interest. By the time her attorney served the
separation papers on them, they had learned to accept the inevitable and to welcome the possibility of protecting their im-

ages from public scrutiny. They left thinking that Jasmine was indeed a lady of the highest standards.

For her part, Jasmine had never intended to embarrass them publicly. She never wanted anyone who might find himself on her list of perspective husbands to think that she would treat him in the same manner. She was content with slowly moving them out of her life as she surveyed the horizon for her next prospect.

When she met Thomas, Jasmine had just divorced again and was on the prowl. She had not found anyone in her usual social circle interesting enough to make even the bottom rung of her list. She had decided to branch out into the previously uncharted waters of the respectable medical and business communities. Her usual targets had been born with silver spoons in their mouths and worked simply as a means of daily entertainment. This new tier worked in order to eat and have a decent livelihood. It consisted of highly motivated, upwardly mobile men who would benefit from her connections in the old-money crowd. When she heard about Thomas, Jasmine knew that she had found the man she could help as she taught him the finer things of life that only living with her could provide. He would appreciate her efforts in assisting his climb in fame and power. And, when she inevitably divorced him, he would leave with tender memories and a feeling of gratitude toward her.

Jasmine had not counted on an "office romance" complicating her plans. None of her other husbands had been reluctant to abandon the women who had populated their lives before she came on the scene. They had all too quickly thrown them aside. Unfortunately, she sensed that Thomas was different. He seemed genuinely infatuated with Katherine. Jasmine had long ago decided that when she wanted something or someone nothing would stand in her way. She would simply have to rise to the challenge and remove Katherine from his mind. After all, Katherine had little to offer him. She was a farm girl with no real contacts. She had done a credible job as the acting chief of staff before being replaced by Thomas, but she truly was no real threat. Jasmine, on the other hand, knew that she could offer Thomas a future and invaluable connections.

Seeing them together made Jasmine's blood boil, and her sense of competition increased one thousand percent. She could hardly wait until the evening's grand ball. She would show Katherine who the best woman was for the job of being Thomas's benefactor, supporter, and wife. Until then, she pasted a smile on her lips as she flitted from one cluster of friends and influential people to the other. She would graciously put aside her own plans until the evening when she would be in her element. Until then, she would allow Katherine to bask in the glow of Thomas's affection, knowing that soon he would belong to her.

Katherine suspected nothing of Jasmine's plans as she carefully styled her auburn tresses so that just the right number of tendrils escaped to look seductive but not messy. Satisfied with the results, she fastened a single strand of perfectly matched pearls around her neck and a matching bracelet onto her arms. The cream color of the pearls reflected the healthy glow of her skin. At her ears, Katherine wore a cluster of pearls and diamonds.

She had carefully selected her lingerie to compliment the copper gown. The luxurious silk panties made her flesh tingle with the softness of the fabric. Unlike her usual utilitarian white cotton, these undergarments made Katherine feel rich and pampered. The silk stockings that she slipped onto her shapely legs completed the aura of decadence.

Finally, Katherine eased into the copper gown as she carefully pulled it over her hips and adjusted it over her strapless bra. It hugged her curves and showed off her athletically tuned figure to perfection. Gazing at herself in the mirror, she thought that Thomas did not stand a chance that night. Something grand would definitely happen at the ball . . . or immediately thereafter.

Giving Mitzi a goodbye scratch, Katherine picked up her bag and gloves at the sound of Betsy's impatient knocking. Knowing that Thomas would be busy at the ball, she had agreed to meet

him there. Betsy and her date, Frank, would drive her to the
floating restaurant where she would meet him as soon as the
receiving line disbanded. The rest of the evening would be theirs
to enjoy.

Walking up the gangplank, Katherine was again struck by
the beauty of Washington and the majesty of the Potomac River.
All along its rippling current, the running lights of small boats
flickered as their captains sailed toward their slips and the tranquility of dinner on the water. Houseboats and cruisers began
easing into their spots with their crews shouting greetings from
one vessel to the other.

Along the shore, Washington's harbor was alive with activity
as the fish merchants began closing up their stores and the hungry hoards began pouring into the restaurants that peppered the
waterfront. Cars of all description discharged passengers as diners arrived happy with the anticipation of the evening on the
wharf.

The laughing voices of the hospital's revelers greeted Katherine as she stepped onboard the yacht that served as a floating
restaurant for hundreds of happy diners. Because of the size of
their gala, the hospital had contracted to have the entire vessel
at its disposal. When it finally cast off for the dinner cruise,
they would have the scenery of Washington all to themselves.
The smoothness of the river and the coolness of the evening's
breeze promised a delightful sailing.

Thomas stood buried in happy, smiling people as Katherine
walked down the stairs of the ballroom. He and the members
of the board made an impressive sight as the candles flickered
on the tables, the chandeliers glowed overhead, and the leaves
of the potted plants fluttered in the breeze.

Katherine thought Thomas looked the most handsome of all
the men who escorted women in their evening finery and jewels.
He stood an elegant six feet five-inches in his beautifully tailored conservative tuxedo. His broad shoulders towered over

those of the other members of the board as he greeted the assembled guests, shook hands, and chatted amiably with the friends of the hospital who had gathered to give financial support to the technology campaign and the annual giving fund.

Beside him to the right stood the chairman of the hospital's board and to the left its various members in order of seniority. Jasmine, by virtue of being the chairperson for the evening's festivities, stood next to Thomas. She beamed contentedly at the success of the evening as the well-heeled guests flocked through the doors. The cash register in her mind clicked noisily with each hand she shook. Occasionally, she lightly and possessively touched Thomas on the arm and smiled up at him.

As Katherine passed through the line, Thomas gave her cheek a warm kiss in addition to the formal handshake. Whispering into her ear he said, "Save the first waltz for me. I can hardly wait to hold you in my arms. I won't be much longer. Save a space for me at your table, too. I'll be there as soon as I can steal away."

Gazing into his smiling face Katherine answered with a tease in her voice, "Don't take too long. I'm a sucker for a good waltz. Some other handsome man might steal me away. Don't forget that I have to do my share for the hospital, too. We wouldn't want someone to spend the evening unattended, unhappy, and unrelieved of a fat check."

Thomas chuckled and gave her hand an extra squeeze before sending her along the line. He marveled at her quick wit, her fabulous figure, and her wonderful personality. He could hardly wait to shake loose the obligations of being chief of staff so that he could take her into his arms and twirl her around the floor for everyone to admire.

Katherine, Betsy, and her date Frank quickly made one of the tables at the front of the room theirs. From where they sat, they could watch the other celebrants enter. Katherine was quite impressed with the turnout as former members of the board, major contributors to the fund-raising efforts, special friends of the hospital, neighbors, and dignitaries of the Washington com-

munity poured into the ballroom dressed in their finery. If all
had simply given modestly, the affair would have been an out-
standing success at two hundred dollars per ticket. However,
knowing that many had not only purchased the tickets but had
also made the suggested additional contribution to the fund of
their choice, she was even more impressed.

Katherine watched as the wealthy of Washington floated
down the burgundy carpet of the ballroom to come to rest quite
circuitously at their chosen tables, many of which had been
reserved in advance. They wore the latest in elaborate and exquisitely fashionable evening apparel from the top fashion de-
signers. Each gown was worth enough to make a sizable dent
in the cost of a new piece of machinery. On their ears and hands
glittered jewelry that on most nights sat in safe-deposit boxes
in their banks or in wall safes. Around their necks were chokers
or strands of diamonds that sparkled in competition with the
chandeliers. The only items of finery missing were the tiaras
that had long ago been abandoned for social functions and reserved only for occasions of meeting royalty.

Even the men appeared to have pulled out all the stops. Many
of their tuxedos were new and of the latest style. Their shirts,
if studded, sparkled with onyx or diamonds down the front. If
they wore the new, banded collar, the single top button was
often a diamond stud. They walked with confidence in the preferred black patent leather loafers. Even the cigars, which they
only fingered since smoking them was inappropriate, were part
of the latest fashionable craze.

Looking around the room, Katherine saw faces she had not
seen since the Christmas ball of two years ago. Then, she had
been in the receiving line shaking hands until her fingers went
numb She chuckled at her memory of listening to suggestive
comments from young and old men. She wondered if Thomas
were hearing the same offers of amorous evenings and fabulous
trips in exchange for a contribution toward a new MRI or much
needed optic laser.

At the prescribed time, the receiving line broke up and the

members took their places at the head table. The chairman of the board lightly tapped the microphone to signal the official beginning of the dinner and his speech. Those in attendance still on their feet scurried to their tables leaving behind promises to finish conversations that they would forget before they had consumed their appetizers.

Douglas Myers, the chairman and the richest, most influential man in town, spent little time in getting to the point of his brief speech as he said, "We are here tonight to spend a few hours with friends and to make a major contribution to this hospital. I am confident that we will do both with equal amounts of enthusiasm. Enjoy your meal and the delightful music of this spectacular quartet."

Katherine heard very little of what he said as she watched Jasmine. Wrapped in a gossamer silk gown that clung to her body and accentuated every curve, Jasmine sat so close to Thomas that she was practically perched in his lap. She only stopped monopolizing his attention long enough for Thomas to hear Myers's brief address. As soon as the last of his words stopped echoing through the microphone, Jasmine resumed her animated and, from the expression on her face, intimate monologue. As a twinge of jealousy coursed through Katherine, she found herself speculating on the topic and on the location of Jasmine's invisible hands.

Despite Jasmine's entertaining show at the head table, Katherine had to admit that the food was fabulous. She had never tasted such succulent shrimp in an almost translucent clarified butter and garlic sauce. The mussels and linguine with saffron and tomatoes were equally as taste tempting. The roast capon with chestnut dressing accompanied by asparagus and princess potatoes was exquisite. For dessert she delicately munched on a sinfully rich chocolate cake served in a pool of fresh raspberry sauce. Looking at Thomas, Katherine wondered if he had enjoyed his meal as much despite the constant attentions of Jasmine who never stopped her chattering into his right ear.

If his expression had not been so similar to the one she saw during especially boring department debriefings, Katherine would have wondered if Thomas were enjoying the attentions of his dinner partner. In fact, as Jasmine continued her obvious attempts at seduction, Katherine began to think that Thomas might actually be pretending to be disinterested. She could not image that the fragrance of Jasmine's perfume, the nearness of her bare shoulders, and the constant mingling of her fingers with his would have no effect on Thomas's ego and, of course, his lust. Any man would have loved to have been in his position with a fabulously attractive, wealthy woman pouring her attentions on him.

Although she abhorred jealousy as a sign of insecurity, Katherine could feel her own emotions heading in that direction. After all, she had witnessed Jasmine's actions at her estate at Middleburg. As she watched, Jasmine very inappropriately tickled her glossy, red fingertips along the top of Thomas's shirt collar. To stop her, he gently picked up her mischievous hand and cradled it in his before placing it beside her plate. All of his actions were executed slowly without drawing the attention of anyone at the head table. Katherine wondered if any of the other guests had seen him and decided that she was probably the only one whose eyes were glued on him.

Katherine could barely stand watching the display of affection even if she should discover that it was only one way. Turning away with a strange lump creeping into her throat and a burning feeling behind her eyes, she found herself looking directly into the face of Roger from her weekend at Jasmine's home. She had not seen him enter the room. The display at the front table had prevented her from seeing him slip into the empty chair beside her.

Smiling at her, Roger crooned, "This certainly is my lucky evening. I hadn't planned to attend the dance until Jasmine talked me into becoming a supporter of the hospital and her escort for the evening. I knew she would abandon me as soon as she found the man on whom she planned to focus her attentions. She did not wear that gown for her old buddy Roger.

Obviously, I was correct in my assessment. But, as I said, I'm feeling especially fortunate at the moment to have found you here. I had hoped we would have a chance to spend an evening together. But listen to that music. I just love the tango. Let's dance; we can talk later."

Katherine did not have time to object as Roger scooped her into his arms and led her to the dance floor. Executing complicated moves before he pulled her tightly against him, she saw Thomas's expression of surprise to see her in Roger's arms. As he watched her dance to the sultry rhythm in the arms of another man, his jaw tightened ever so slightly. Katherine hoped that he would feel the same tinge of jealously that she did as she watched him with another woman.

Thomas did indeed feel an unaccustomed and unpleasant sensation. He had always prided himself on being above the more common reactions brought on by seeing the object of one's affection with someone else. This time, however, he found that he was not immune from the age-old emotion of jealousy as he watched Roger press his hand into the small of Katherine's back, dip her provocatively against his thigh, and meld his body into hers. Thomas wondered how long he would have to wait until he could cut in. He searched his mind for the rule of etiquette governing smashing the faces of hospital contributors.

When he could stand the sight of Katherine in Roger's arm no longer, Thomas rose to his feet. As if anticipating his purpose, Jasmine said with a bewitching smile, "Thomas, dear, I thought you'd never ask me. I'd love to tango. It's one of my favorite dances."

Unable to ignore her and aware of the rudeness and damning social blunder he would commit by walking away from her, Thomas took Jasmine's offered hand in his and mutely guided her to the dance floor. Slipping his arm around her lithe body as she melted against him, he skillfully tangoed his way around the floor. The years of dance lessons his mother had insisted on his taking in preparation for events like this one held him in good stead. Not once did he step on her foot or become tangled in her long graceful legs. In fact, he was aware that they made a strikingly handsome couple. The only thing Thomas regretted was the expression of dismay that played across Katherine's face as she and Roger joined the other couples who had stepped aside to give them more space.

Jasmine basked in the attention from the onlookers who stopped their conversations and their dancing to watch as she and Thomas took possession of the floor. She reveled in the way his tall lean body dominated her own trim one and masterfully propelled her through the intricate steps. She smiled with a sense of victory as they responded to the heat of the tango with new warmth of their own. Jasmine had known that if she could only engage him in something other than a sedate waltz, Thomas would be hers. She only hoped that the pained expression on Katherine's face was only an acknowledgment of defeat and not a declaration of war.

As the music came to an end, the applause of the watching diners erupted. Jasmine beamed with delight as she and Thomas took their bows of appreciation before heading back to their table. Catching Katherine's eye, she shot her an especially meaningful glance as she tightened her grip on his arm. Katherine had no choice but to stand by and watch Thomas being swept away by one of the hospital's most generous patrons. She could not afford for the sake of the institution and her job to alienate Jasmine.

Just as the quartet sounded the first few notes of a cooling waltz, the yacht lurched, throwing everyone off balance. A collective sound of surprise filled the ballroom as people tried to regain their footing after being thrown against tables and pillars. Waiters, who had been unobtrusively clearing the tables, dropped their trays amid a clatter of silverware and the tinkle of breaking glass. Katherine, too, righted herself after being deposited in the lap of a portly gentleman who did not appear to mind her presence one bit. Apologizing profusely, she continued to make her way to her empty table.

Again, the yacht lurched. This time the sound of surprise became a gasp of fear as the vessel shuddered and stalled. The dance floor listed ten degrees as glasses, candles, and vases slid off the tops of tables. Katherine had to cling to the table to keep from tumbling out of her chair.

"What's happening?" questioned an obviously frightened older woman. Her eyes were huge with fear as she clutched her shimmering silver bag.

"Have we hit something? Is the boat sinking?" asked the portly gentleman with real fear in his voice. Now that Katherine was no longer sitting in his lap she could see that he was almost seventy. Despite the extra pounds that his wealth had secured, he looked very worried and vulnerable as the listing continued.

"Oh, no!" wailed a woman as she tried to stand only to fall flat on her buttocks as the boat pitched to an even steeper angle.

"Don't panic, everyone! I'm sure the captain has everything under control," Thomas shouted above the rising tide of tremulous voices. He was afraid that they would start running for the upper decks and fall into the water.

As he spoke, the vessel took a third and more violent lunge that threw seated people onto the floor and flung across the room those unfortunate enough to be standing. Screaming voices filled the dining room. Thoughts of the *Titanic* and old movies of sinking ships sent a wave of panic through everyone as they clawed their way to the doorway. No dinner cruise had ever perished on the Potomac. They did not want to be the first.

The hallway was almost instantly filled with women who ran barefoot in glittering gowns, men who clawed their way in stocking feet and tuxedos, and wait-staff trained in emergency preparedness who suddenly forgot their instructions and only wanted to escape what appeared to be a sinking vessel. Above all the crashing of glass, screaming of women's voices, and breaking of furniture, Katherine could hear the death knoll of the ship and the sound of the alarms that notified everyone on the water that the vessel was in extreme danger.

Looking around, Katherine tried to find Thomas as the smell of smoke filled the room and brought tears to her eyes. "Thomas!" she called above the din as flames consumed the heavy drapes and sent the last remaining passengers fleeing for their lives. No one wanted to be trapped below deck in the inferno of a sinking ship.

As Jasmine darted past her, Katherine grabbed her arms and turned her around toward her. Jasmine's eyes were wild with fear. She closely resembled a horse Katherine had once seen after it had been caught in a barn fire on her parents' farm. The woman's eyes were huge with little sign of coherent thought behind them.

"Where's Thomas?" Katherine shouted at her as she shook Jasmine by the shoulders hard.

"I don't know. He just left me standing there all alone. I've got to get out of here. Save yourself. This boat is going to sink, can't you see? You'll die if you stay in here. The smoke and flames will kill you," Jasmine said before she managed to free herself from Katherine's strong grip.

"I won't leave Thomas," Katherine called after her hastily fleeing back. Thick, black smoke billowed from the front of the ballroom obscuring almost all of her view. Katherine grabbed a napkin and sopped up some of the water from the broken glasses on the floor. Pressing the cloth to her face, she staggered against the pitch of the vessel into the heaviest of the smoke.

Struggling with each step, she fought her way to the table where only minutes earlier Thomas had sat with Jasmine. Calling his name frantically, Katherine did not find him anywhere. The heat and flames from the blazing curtains caused her to abandon her search as sparks ignited the carpets. Turning, she groped her way to the back of the room with the flames lapping at her heels.

As she reached the stairs, Katherine stopped one last time. Choking on the smoke and peering into the flames, she saw someone lying prostrate at the side of the room. Struggling against the tide of overturned chairs, broken dinnerware, and shattered glasses, she rushed forward. Reaching the lifeless figure in a black tuxedo, she turned over the unconscious man. Looking through the tears that poured from her stinging eyes, Katherine made out the face.

"Thomas!" she cried in horror. Katherine knew that she had to get help. Frantically scanning the room through the smoke, she realized that no one would come to her aid. She had to think of something fast—the smoke thickened with each tortured breath.

Quickly examining him for breaks and burns, Katherine assessed that Thomas had suffered a blow to his head. Fortunately, she could find no bleeding or sign of broken bones. Grabbing him by the labels, Katherine slowly dragged him up the steps to the foyer. Stopping for breath, she shouted hoarsely, "Someone help me! Thomas is unconscious. I need help!" The sound of the grinding gears and the dying yacht drowned out her voice.

When no one responded, Katherine looked around for something with which to fashion a device for hoisting Thomas up the stairs. She knew she would not be able to carry him up the long, curving flight of steps alone. Finding nothing, she quickly stepped out of her panty hose and hastily tied them under his arms and around his body. Knotting them securely in a sort of harness, she stepped into it and adjusted the legs around her waist. Gripping the rail with one hand and his hair in the other, Katherine pulled and tugged until they reached the top. Thomas's feet thumped on each step as she struggled to drag him out of the smoke-filled lower deck.

"Help me, someone!" Katherine called again to the people massed on the listing deck. Her voice came in choking gasps as she tugged Thomas's lifeless body away from the stairs. Through the smoke and crush of people, she could not even make out the figures of Betsy and Roger. She hoped that they had escaped to safety with the others.

This time one of the waiters heard her voice and quickly

came to her aid. Lifting Thomas fireman style, he carried the
unconscious man to one of the waiting Coast Guard and police
vessels. Carefully, they lowered him overboard into Katherine's
waiting arms. As the last of the diners climbed aboard the rescue
vessels, the yacht shuddered and sank into the foaming Potomac.

"What happened?" Thomas muttered softly as the Coast
Guard vessel pulled into the harbor. "My head is killing me.
Have I been in a car accident?"

"Lie still, Thomas. You've suffered a blow to the head. You
might even have a concussion again. This time, I insist that you
have an x-ray. You were unconscious a long time. You weren't
in a car accident. The ship on which we were dining has sunk.
Don't worry about the others. Everyone is safely off the vessel.
We were the last ones to leave," Katherine said as she cradled
his head in her lap.

"I don't remember anything. How did I get out? My head
aches so badly that I know I didn't walk," Thomas replied as
Katherine cradled his hand in hers.

"Don't talk now, Thomas. It's enough that everyone is doing
fine. Lie as still as you can until we get you properly immobi-
lized," Katherine said as she tried to hold Thomas in a prone
position to prevent any movement. Without an x-ray she could
not really feel sure about her diagnosis. She hoped that he had
not suffered any kind of spinal cord injury.

"Thomas! Thomas!" a voice called from the back of the
crowd. Turning her attention to the back of the vessel, Katherine
saw Jasmine coming toward them. As he was loaded into one
of the waiting stretchers, Jasmine pushed her way through the
crush of people.

"Thomas, I was so worried about you. I tried to find you,
but the smoke was too thick. I searched as long as I could before
the flames forced me out," Jasmine cooed with considerable

concern in her voice. As she spoke, she totally ignored Katherine who stood beside Thomas's stretcher.

"Don't worry, Jasmine. I'm fine. Katherine saved me, and now she's insisting that I submit to an x-ray," Thomas responded with a look of pride at Katherine.

"We are so lucky to have her at Boxer, aren't we, Thomas? I just don't know what we'd do without her. She's so . . . multifaceted. As soon as they finish your tests, I'll have my driver take us to my house for a little rest before you return to work. You've had two nasty upsets lately. I want to make sure that you're absolutely all right. No one knows how to take care of a man better than I do," Jasmine declared as she wedged herself between Thomas and Katherine. From the look of determination on her face, everyone could see that she had no intention of allowing Thomas to slip through her fingers and into Katherine's arms. Katherine might have saved his life, but the man belonged to her.

Katherine shook her head at the audacity of the woman. Jasmine had run from the room with concern only for herself as the flames had leaped higher and threatened to block the exit. She had not worried that Thomas might lie on the floor unconscious or bleeding from a broken limb. She had cared only about saving her own hide. Now she was trying to play the devoted friend. She even wedged her way into the crowded ambulance for the ride to Boxer Hospital. She hoped that Thomas in his weakened state would see through the charade.

Just as Thomas raised his head to whisper his thanks to Katherine, an intense pain in his temple made him wince and groan in agony. Grabbing his head in both hands, he writhed from side to side as the tremor shot through him. Gasping for breath, he fell backward in a faint.

As soon as the ambulance stopped, Katherine gave the instructions for the orderlies to rush Thomas quickly to the first available MRI. Once inside the ER, she ordered a complete x-ray series. The results confirmed what she had suspected.

Thomas had suffered a massive concussion this time. He would require hospitalization for at least a few days.

Sitting anxiously by his side, Katherine waited until he opened his eyes. She had always thought that being a physician would help in times of medical emergency involving loved ones. However, she was quick to learn that nothing lessened the fear and concern. She was too distressed to pay any attention to Jasmine who stood beside her wringing her hands and sobbing quietly.

The hours dragged by with Katherine remaining at Thomas's bedside. Jasmine, claiming that she was too overcome to stay in the hospital any longer, had taken flight and gone home. She promised to return in the morning.

Watching her retreating back, Katherine could honestly say that she would rather sit all day and night in this uncomfortable evening gown than ever see Jasmine again. Thomas would need care when he awakened. Knowing Jasmine's recent history, Katherine did not think that she was the ideal candidate for the job.

Glancing at her watch, Katherine saw that it was six in the morning. She was physically and emotionally drained from the events of the night. Her body ached from the strain of dragging Thomas's heavier frame up the stairs. Her mind was exhausted from the constant monitoring of his vital signs and wondering when he would awaken.

Walking to the window to watch the sun rise over the buildings, Katherine tried to stretch the stiffness from her body. If she only had a change of clothes and her running shoes, she could slip out for a quick run. She would ask one of the nurses to sit with Thomas until she could return in about an hour. The run and the time out of the hospital would do her good. However, she didn't have them here and did not want to go home to get them. She would wait until he roused before leaving.

This was one of Katherine's favorite times of the day. The streets were quiet on Sunday mornings with only the sound of birds to disturb the silence. Even Washington seemed more at peace with itself when its sidewalks did not teem with people.

Peering over the closed window's edge, Katherine watched as a family of pigeons pecked at the ants that crawled along the hospital wall. Growing tired of them, she studied the ambling of a drunk in the alley. His staggering and lurching reminded Katherine of her own unsteady progress on the deck of the floundering dinner boat.

"I feel neglected. What's so interesting out there?" a slightly weak voice asked from the shadows behind her.

Twirling around, Katherine smiled and rushed to his bedside. Thomas was awake and obviously in good spirits. He reached out his hand as she approached.

"You gave me quite a scare, Thomas, but I think you'll be okay now. We'll order some follow-up x-rays in a few hours. I expect you to be back on your feet in a week or two," Katherine replied as she checked the monitor. All of his vital signs were normal.

"That was certainly a dance that will be recorded in the hospital's books of things not to do again. Did anyone else get hurt? My memory is sketchy at best. Who carried me off the boat?" Thomas inquired as he watched Katherine perform her duties as his physician. He only wished she would demonstrate less professional and more personal concern.

"Several of the guests were shaken up and almost everyone suffered some bruises and smoke inhalation, but you were the most seriously hurt. You'll be sore and bruised for a while. I dragged you out, which probably didn't help your condition much but was certainly better than letting you die," Katherine replied as she studied the array of purple and red marks on his face.

"My hero! I guess I owe you my life. Katherine, there's something we need to discuss. I might not remember much of what happened after the injury, but I do know that things weren't going too well with us before the crash," Thomas pleaded. He wanted to start a new page in their relationship.

"There will be plenty of time for conversation later. You need rest and I'm exhausted. I've been in this confining gown for long enough, too. Since you appear to be in pretty good shape, I'll leave you now," Katherine commented as she moved toward the door.

"But Katherine . . ." Thomas began only to be cut short by the door flying open and Jasmine rushing into the room.

"Thomas," she exclaimed, "you're awake!"

Fourteen

"What do you mean by saying that Thomas won't be able to assume his responsibilities for a while? He's an important man. He has a hospital to run. It's not possible," Jasmine argued with the neurologist as he tried to explain the reasons for his accurate diagnosis.

"Ms. Gaylord, I'm sure this is difficult for you as a friend of Dr. Baker's, but you have to face the facts. He suffered a severe head injury and is quite fortunate to be as healthy as he is. He's a strong man and will heal in time. Unfortunately, there is nothing anyone can do to speed things along. He needs rest and the support of those close to him," Dr. Foster explained one more time.

The conference room, which usually seemed so large when the entire staff met for its weekly debriefing sessions, appeared diminished by Jasmine's impatient pacing. She was not a woman who waited patiently for anything. Once she decided that she wanted something she usually went about getting it as quickly as possible. She wanted Thomas Baker, but now she would have to wait. Jasmine knew that the longer the delay, the greater the opportunity for Katherine to beat her to the punch.

Katherine sat quietly and watched Jasmine's agitation. She was not blind to Jasmine's intentions and the reasons for her impatience. She had heard all the rumors. In fact, Katherine and Thomas had chuckled over Jasmine's clever but very transparent schemes to win his affection. In the weeks prior to the dinner dance fiasco, she had sent flowers, candy, stadium tickets, and invitations to parties of both an intimate and formal nature. Thomas had thanked her for the items he could not return and declined all but the most formal and public of the invitations. The refusals had only caused her to redouble her efforts.

As Katherine listened to Dr. Foster, she was only partially aware of Jasmine's irritation. She had too much to think about to let Jasmine and her antics interfere with all she needed to do to help Thomas recover as quickly and completely as possible. She had the ER to run and the hospital, too, in his absence. The chairman of the board had already placed Boxer Hospital on her capable but tired shoulders. She was the only one who was sufficiently intimate with the fund-raising campaign to step into Thomas's shoes on such short notice.

As Dr. Foster spoke, Katherine allowed her mind to drift over the time she had shared with Thomas. They enjoyed so many of the same things from sleeping late, to reading the Sunday paper in bed, to picking strawberries on the nearby farms. She had hoped to spend the rest of her life with him doing those things that meant so much to them. She had wanted to bear children with him and to grow old beside him.

And, Katherine had wanted to show him that she could do his job at Boxer. The confidence of the board in her ability gave her the opportunity for which she had been waiting.

As soon as she could, Katherine excused herself and returned to Thomas. He had been moved from the intensive care unit to a private room on the neurology floor. He still complained of a dreadful headache, but, overall, he seemed in very good spirits. When she entered the room, Katherine found Betsy keeping him company. She gently patted her friend on the shoulder, and Betsy quietly slipped out as Katherine eased her tired body into the nearest chair.

Betsy had been spared the suffocating flames by being on the top deck when the yacht first went aground. She had suffered a broken arm from being thrown against one of the side railings as the yacht lurched at impact. She looked exhausted and in need of rest, but she had refused to leave Thomas unattended. Now that Katherine had arrived, she could go home.

"You should go home, Katherine. You look exhausted. What mischief is Jasmine cooking up? I wish she'd return to the farm. You'd have an easier time doing both of our jobs if she weren't here," Thomas said. He was feeling better already. Just looking at Katherine made him perk up. Like most physicians who were forced into the patient role, he did not like the confinement. Despite the pounding pain in his head, he wanted to be out of bed immediately.

"Don't worry about Jasmine. She's a pest, but she's relatively harmless as irritants go. The hospital is purring along and I have everything under control. I've made the appropriate statements to the press about your condition and your expected return date. Your job is to get as much rest as you need and leave the hospital concerns to me," Katherine replied, her eyes twinkling with the pleasure of running the hospital despite her fatigue.

"Are you saying, doctor, that you and Boxer don't need me?" Thomas asked playfully but with just a tinge of concern in his voice.

"I would never say anything of the kind. I enjoy the challenge of mixing it up with you. Who knows when I might want to lead another boycott," Katherine teased. "Now get some rest. You'll be back in your office before you know it."

"If you don't move me out of it while I'm not looking," Thomas called after her. He could hear her throaty laugh as Katherine walked down the hall.

For a while Thomas lay looking up at the ceiling. He could certainly see how he could be attracted to Dr. Katherine Winters. She was a spunky woman who seemed confident and self-assured. She definitely was brave. He did not know many people who would risk their lives to save someone else. Betsy had told him that Katherine dragged him from the burning yacht without any help. Thomas was quite impressed with her clear-headed ability. He decided that when he was discharged, he would make it up to her.

* * *

As Thomas reluctantly allowed himself to sleep, Katherine rushed to the ER to check on the rest of the patients. The exhausted staff of the hospital had treated almost everyone on the yacht for some form of smoke inhalation. Many of their colleagues had succumbed also. The most seriously affected had been hospitalized for the night. When she arrived, Katherine found very few casualties remaining.

Satisfied that everything was under control in the ER, Katherine thanked the staff for a job well done and dragged herself the few blocks to her apartment. She was so tired that she walked past a confused and insulted Mitzi who began to complain about the neglect in a voice used only by Siamese during times of distress.

"Mitzi, I'm so sorry. I'm exhausted. You must be hungry," Katherine muttered as she picked up the pouting cat. After a few minutes of scratching and a bowl refilled with her favorite food, Mitzi's usually sweet disposition had returned.

Drawing a bath of steaming hot water, Katherine lowered her tired body into the rose-scented bubbles. Every muscle had begun to ache from the effort of dragging Thomas's heavy body from the burning boat. Her hands bore scratches from clawing her way through the overturned chairs and broken dishes as she searched for him. Her soot smudged face showed the tracks of the tears Katherine shed when she thought she would never find him.

After toweling the water from her body, Katherine pulled the old familiar cotton nightshirt over her head. There was nothing more she could do for Thomas tonight. He was in good hands at Boxer. In only a few hours, she would have to resume the management of the hospital and needed her wits about her when she undertook that task again.

The next morning the entire hospital buzzed with conversation about the dinner dance, Thomas's head injury, and the no longer private relationship between Katherine and Thomas. Many had heard about Jasmine's behavior and the sultry tango. Those who had not heard were quickly brought up to speed by others who were eager to impart the delicious details of a story that appeared to be unfolding before their eyes. The usually long hot boring Washington summer suddenly had an air of anticipation and excitement. The fireworks in the Mall would not be the only ones blazing over the sweltering town in July.

Katherine did not like it one bit that her personal business had become public knowledge. She enjoyed her relative anonymity and considered the watchful eyes of Washington to be a gross intrusion into her private time. Yet, with Jasmine practically throwing herself at Thomas's head at the dance and in the hospital, Katherine had no choice but to smile and play along.

So on Sunday morning as she walked into Boxer Hospital to check on Thomas, she did not flinch when the lights from the television cameras glared in her eyes. She controlled her irritation when the reporter stuck his microphone directly into her face. She remained controlled and composed when his questions turned from the business of running the hospital for the recuperating chief of staff and delved into her personal relationship with Thomas.

Katherine's determination to rise above this annoying set of events remained constant until she arrived in Thomas's room to find Jasmine already there. At nine o'clock in the morning, Jasmine was busily spoon-feeding Thomas his oatmeal as if he were too sick to do it himself. Katherine had read his charts and knew that he was capable of caring for himself. If she knew, so did Jasmine. Yet Jasmine, in her impeccably tailored silk wrap dress that exposed her bosom and small waist, had decided to recline all over the "sick" man.

"What do you think you're doing, Jasmine?" Katherine asked in her coldest most professional tone.

"Why, Katherine, I'm feeding poor Thomas. You wouldn't want him to starve, would you? The poor, dear man is too stressed out from his ordeal to feed himself. I came here to make myself useful. So many of our fellow partygoers were hospitalized last night that I thought my services might be needed. Naturally, I came to Thomas's room first. An important man like Thomas needs all the care and support his friends and admirers can give at a time like this. I'd hate for him to regain his memory and find that no one was with him to share the moment. After all, dear, you weren't here," Jasmine cooed in a voice that made Katherine want to pluck out every one of her carefully coiffed hairs.

"We have nursing assistants to feed the patients, Jasmine. Besides, if you'd like to be of assistance, I'm sure that there are patients in worse shape than Thomas who would appreciate your ministrations. You might also want to make yourself useful in dealing with the press. The public relations department must be swamped with requests for statements. As a member of the board, I'm sure your talents would be of more good to the hospital in a PR capacity," Katherine said through teeth clinched so tightly that her jaws ached.

"PR? Well, maybe Thomas could spare me for a few minutes. I'll be right back to give you a shave as soon as I take care of those pesky reporters," Jasmine fluttered as she straightened her skirt and gave her hair a light touch.

Katherine and Thomas stared after her retreating backside as Jasmine scurried off to enlighten the public relations office on the proper way to cooperate with the press. As soon as the sound of her heels on the highly waxed tile floor died down, Thomas said, "I'm sure her heart is in the right place, but Jasmine is a bit trying on the nerves. Is she always like this?"

"Only when she's hunting . . . which is, as I remember, almost all the time," Katherine replied barely able to keep the snide tone out of her voice.

"Hunting? For what?"

"Foxes, jewelry, homes, a new husband . . . whatever it is that Jasmine feels at the moment will make her life complete. Right now, she's between husbands. According to the rumors, she's in the market for a new one and has picked out the likely candidate."

"Oh really? Well, she certainly hasn't given him much of her time lately. She was at the dance alone, so Betsy told me, and then here until late last night in an effort to keep me company. Now, she's back early this morning. The guy she's after must think she has forgotten him," Thomas commented as he accepted the electric razor that Katherine offered him.

"Not when you're the guy," Katherine answered. She kept a watchful eye on Thomas as she looked for his reaction.

"Me?" Thomas sputtered. Although Jasmine had been very solicitous, he had not imagined that she had set her net for him. "You know I can't abide horses. She can't possibly be interested in me. The last thing I want after a hard day at the hospital is to dress for dinner and spend the evening pumping hands and engaging in small talk."

"Well, consider yourself forewarned. You might want to have your defensive strategy in place before she corners you," Katherine commented, trying to sound playful when what she really wanted to do was protect him from Jasmine's claws.

Understanding the true meaning of Katherine's words, Thomas asked with a little smirk, "After I'm discharged, I thought we might spend some time together. That would keep Jasmine away from me."

Jokingly, Katherine replied, "I'm sure we can think of something that would keep you out of her clutches."

"When do you think my doctor will discharge me? I've about had it with this invalid role," Thomas asked as he looked longingly out the window.

"Probably tomorrow, but you'll have to remember to take it easy for a while. You might want to hire someone to stay with you, a housekeeper perhaps, for the first few days. You shouldn't do any unnecessary bending or lifting," Katherine advised sounding every bit like the doctor she was.

"I promise, Dr. Winters, I'll take good care of myself, but I might need a little help getting home. Might you be available for the job?" Thomas inquired playfully.

Taking his cue, Katherine laughed and agreed, "Gladly, Dr. Baker. Just let me know and I'll pull my car around front. I'd be happy to take you home and swing back with some takeout Chinese that you like so much."

"That sounds great . . . two treats at one time, an evening with you and good food. I'll give you a buzz as soon as I hear something definite. Where will you be? My office or yours?" Thomas asked, continuing the playful banter between them.

"Don't worry, I'll have Dr. Foster tell me. If you want to reach me for any reason, have one of the nurses page me. I've left my number at the desk. You can call me on your office number listed in the hospital directory. I'd better go now. You need to rest and I have a meeting to run. Besides, I have two jobs to do. I don't have the luxury of lying here with nothing to do," Katherine said as she eased her way out the door. She was relieved to see that Thomas appeared to be feeling so well.

Calling after her, he shouted, "Don't forget to order egg rolls. I wouldn't be so cocky if I were you. I won't be laid up for long."

As Thomas listened to the sound of Katherine's retreating steps, he was more determined than ever to press his idea about having them share the chief-of-staff position. She was definitely the most amazing person he had ever met. There was no challenge that did not appeal to her. She was a stunning administrator and a loyal friend.

Taking her seat at the conference room table, Katherine looked out at the familiar faces. Only a few months ago she had regularly held department head meetings in this very room. Now she was back as a substitute to finish the work begun by the man who had replaced her.

"Ladies and gentlemen, as you already know, Thomas has suffered a severe head injury that will prevent him from attending to his duties here at Boxer for a while. The board has asked me to step in for him until he can return to health and to the office that he has filled with such skill. Therefore, it is with mixed feelings that I outline the task before us as we continue the fund-raising effort he has started.

"I am aware that we have not always agreed with Thomas's plans, but their success cannot be argued. To date, he has already raised three quarters of the money initially targeted for this drive. It's up to us to bring in the rest in his absence. To that end, all activities will continue exactly as planned by Dr. Baker and the board. We will all do our parts to continue the success of his endeavors. We will not allow our personal misgivings or biases to interfere with doing what's right for Boxer.

"Despite the disastrous end to the dinner dance, we raised enough money over the two-day weekend to completely re-model the kitchen. Thanks to the contributions of our devoted patrons, the work will begin next week.

"Our past negotiations with Dr. Baker have proven that both of us were correct. We knew that we did not need to cut our staffs or reduce overtime to accomplish the required bottom-line results. We have proven as department heads that our concerns should first be to our patients, next to our staffs, and finally to the hospital. As front-line caregivers, our primary goal is to provide the highest quality attention to our patients that we pos-sibly can. We have done just that.

"As your colleague and peer, I say we have done a great job. Let's continue what we've already started. Good luck to all of us as we continue to bring Boxer into the twenty-first century," Katherine concluded, ending the short meeting. She had not planned to begin anything new; she merely wanted everyone to know that her charge had been to continue all of the successful work that she and Thomas had begun.

As she walked toward the ER and her in-box, Betsy matched strides with her. "You certainly put all of us on notice. I don't think anyone will question that Thomas's goals continue even though he is not on the job. I stopped by to see him this morning and except for a badly blackened eye and some nasty bruises, he looks pretty good for a man who was dragged up the stairs. He's certainly one lucky guy," she said.

"He's quite anxious to leave the hospital. I want him out of here, too, before Jasmine sinks her claws into him. I found her feeding him this morning. She will do anything to get a man once she has decided that she wants him. I don't need that headache on top of doing my job and Thomas's," Katherine commented as she flipped through the in-box. She sorted out the things she needed to handle immediately from the correspondence that would keep for a few days. Maybe by Friday Thomas would be sufficiently recovered to return to his office.

"I don't think she'll be any real trouble, but she could cause plenty of mischief. Stop by later if you have some time. I'm going home. My arm is throbbing a bit. If you need me, just call," Betsy said, walking toward the door. She hoped that Jasmine would be on her best behavior and not cause too much turmoil.

By lunchtime, Katherine had met with almost all of the members of the board including the other "Sisters" who ordinarily stayed away from the daily operation of the hospital. She had given interviews to several representatives of the press who were not satisfied with the prepared story presented to them by the public relations department. By the time she left the chief of staff's office for a meeting with Thomas's physician, Katherine felt as if she had never been away from the hectic pace of running the hospital.

Despite her fatigue, Katherine was relieved to hear from Dr. Foster that Thomas could leave the hospital the next day. He needed rest, but he did not need to stay in the hospital to get it. To Katherine's dismay, Jasmine had told him that she would be more than happy to care for Thomas at either his home or hers.

Arriving at Thomas's room, Katherine discovered a gathering of admirers showering him with attention as Thomas relished every minute. Nurses and doctors as well as board members had congregated to show their wishes for his rapid recovery. Of course, Jasmine perched on a nearby chair leading the parade.

"Katherine, isn't it wonderful that Dr. Foster says that Thomas can go home tomorrow? He'll be back to his old self in no time. I can hardly wait to drive him to my house in the country where he'll have only the best of care," Jasmine said, dripping sweetness with every word.

"I don't think going to your place would be such a good idea, Jasmine. It's awfully remote. I doubt that Thomas will have any side effects from the concussion, but he really should not be that far from a hospital. Besides, the board might prefer that he remain in town so that it can confer with him as necessary once Thomas does begin to recover," Katherine responded with her usual controlled attention to the meaning behind her words. She wanted Jasmine to understand that she would not allow Thomas to spend any time alone with her while in a weakened state.

As Jasmine began to speak, Thomas interrupted by saying, "I think Katherine has a point. Being here might actually speed my return to work. It might be wise for me to be where I can keep an eye on things." Although Thomas did not say it, Katherine immediately knew that he meant not only his job but her.

Jasmine could not contain her disappointment as she turned to Katherine and said with venom in her voice, "So that's why you sent me downstairs to public relations. You wanted Thomas all to yourself so that you could weave your little spell. Thomas isn't staying in town because of the board and his job. You want him here with you where you can keep an eye on him. You want to protect him from me. Don't think for a minute that your little plan will work. You might keep Thomas in town, but you can't stop him from seeing me. He's a grown man and from what I've seen of him, he's quite capable of charting his own course . . . and selecting his companions."

Before Katherine could think of something to say as all eyes in the room watched, Jasmine turned on her high taupe heels and marched out of the room. As she left, the others exchanged knowing glances. They had heard that Thomas was at the center

of a duel between two very determined and hard-working
women. Now that they had seen the conflict firsthand, they
could hardly wait to see how it resolved. They wondered who
would win, the wealthy board member or the hard-working acting former chief of staff and head of the ER.

After everyone had left, Thomas lay on his bed wondering
how he had managed to find himself the center of so much
attention. All he had done was suffer a head injury, get knocked
unconscious, practically die in a fire, and get rescued by one
of the women who now drew lots for him. He had to admit it
was certainly flattering in his diminished state to be so much
in demand. It certainly beat watching television all day. This
soap opera of his life was much more fascinating. Yet, he knew
that being in the middle could be a dangerous place to be. Both
of the women had a goal and both were determined to see it
through to fruition. He knew very little about either of them
although he suspected that Katherine's attention to his needs
came from a more genuine regard and affection. Betsy had told
him about Jasmine's history; she seemed determined to add his
initial to her long monogram.

Being the prize had its advantages and its disadvantages.
Thomas knew he would have to wait until the end of the story
to see which twist in the plot offered the most in personal satisfaction. He already had a suspicion. He hoped he was right.

Katherine, on the other hand, was rapidly growing tired of
Jasmine and her interference. With Jasmine, everything was
love and men. Although Katherine loved Thomas, she had other
priorities that took precedence over her relationship with him.
Right now, she was more concerned with the successful management of Boxer than with the possibility that Jasmine would
pose a stumbling block to her personal happiness. Katherine's
sense of duty and competition drove her to prove herself once
again. She had a job to do and did not need to be distracted
from it. Thomas had a place in her life, but he was not the center
of it at the moment.

Mentally returning Jasmine to the pile of issues she would

face at a later date, Katherine returned her attention to the task of running the hospital. Everything and everyone else took on a secondary position.

Fifteen

As soon as Thomas was out of the hospital, he began to feel better. The deep burgundy and navy carpets, the wooded blinds, the leather sofas with plaid afghans casually thrown over them, and the baby grand in the living room corner all felt comfortable. Being in his own surroundings with the relative quiet of home, restored his sense of balance.

Katherine insisted that he go to bed immediately. Thomas had enjoyed very little sleep in the busy hospital and was actually tired, so he did not resist her firm hand on his arm as she guided him upstairs. The muted navy and burgundy tones created the perfect environment for relaxation after the glaring lights and white walls of the hospital. The bedroom and its sitting room were comfortable with pleasantly overstuffed furniture without being feminine. He liked the bold masculine ambiance of his house. It was certainly more inviting than the sterile hospital room with its hard mattress and straight-back metal chair.

Katherine let herself out using the extra key Thomas kept in the vase at the front door. He had once offered it to her, but she had refused saying that their relationship had not progressed to that level. She had watched him drop it into the vase with a rather dejected look on his face. He said that all she had to do was take it whenever she felt ready.

Lying on his back in the tall brass bed, Thomas allowed the silence of the house to lull him to sleep. As he drifted off, he dreamed of a carnival ride with a beautiful woman with auburn hair. As he tossed in his sleep, Katherine's face came into view through the mist of slumber. As the feeling of contentment spread, Thomas smiled, pulled the covers up, and allowed himself to fall into a deep sleep.

Katherine spent her morning in meetings and with patients before rushing back to Thomas's house at lunchtime. As soon as she turned the key in the lock, she knew that he was awake. The sound of someone playing the piano greeted her at the front door. Following the lovely music, she found him entranced by the music that flowed from his fingers. Katherine stood motionless and listened as she had the first night he had played for her. The piano was one of the many refinements his mother had insisted that Thomas master. Like everything else he touched, he played with almost professional technique.

When he finished the piece, Thomas opened his eyes, smiled, and said, "Good afternoon, Katherine. I hope your morning wasn't too unpleasant. I spent a lovely time napping until the piano called to me to play it. I certainly don't envy you spending your entire day in the hospital."

"Oh, it's not all bad, you know. Your office is actually quite comfortable. It's not at all like the physicians lounge in the ER. You have plush leather upholstery, whereas, I have chrome and plastic. And how was your nap?"

"Not bad, I had a dream about riding a Ferris wheel with you. I even kissed you as we sat at the top. Not a bad way to spend an afternoon," Thomas replied with a little wink, which made him squint with pain.

"Any chance you might be hungry? I could fix you a quick lunch. I could whip up a couple of omelets in just a matter of minutes," Katherine said, ignoring the wink and the comment.

"I'm hungry but not for food. If you'll indulge me, I have this uncontrollable urge to take you into my arms. I hope you don't mind if I play along with it. As a physician, I'm confident that you would believe that each little step builds the foundation for bigger ones. You wouldn't want to deprive me of the sustenance my body needs for its healing," Thomas joked as he walked toward Katherine. Smiling, she stood near the entrance to the hall that led to the kitchen.

"I wouldn't mind indulging you for the sake of science and your recovery, doctor," Katherine responded. She was happy to see that Thomas's sense of humor had returned. In her heart she knew that it would not be long before he was restored to his usual self.

"Besides," Thomas whispered as he enfolded her in his arms, "I haven't properly thanked you for saving my life and my skin from that fire."

With that, Thomas pressed his lips in a warm gentle kiss on Katherine's. As he held her, Thomas felt a familiar wave of desire sweep over his body. His hands instinctively roamed the slope of her back and caressed the swell of her buttocks only to return to stroke the soft dewy skin of her throat.

Katherine sighed as her body relaxed under the spell of his touch. Thomas had always known the right spots on her body and now was no exception. As his lips tickled the tips of her ears and his fingers gently massaged her breasts, she clung to him and tried to push the memory of the past weeks from her mind.

As Thomas's fingers began unbuttoning her blouse, Katherine forced herself to remember his condition and the work that waited for her at the hospital. She would have loved to give herself to him, but his health and her in-box would not permit it. Besides, she did not want their lovemaking to come on the heels of his injury. She wanted Thomas in full control of his faculties when they resumed their relationship. She did not want him to come to her out of a feeling of obligation for saving his life.

Slowly pushing away from his hungry lips, Katherine smiled at Thomas and said in the same tone that he had used earlier, "As your physician, I'm afraid that as satisfying as this interlude promises to be, I cannot encourage you to continue. Your health is still too precarious and the bruising to your brain too extensive to allow you to continue along these wonderfully pleasurable lines. After a few more days of recovery have passed and you have stabilized more fully, if you continue to have these inclinations, you will find me more than willing to engage in these activities with you. Until then, I must insist that you rest and take nourishment, and that you refrain from physical activity."

"Although I cannot deny that this definitely falls into the category of physical activity, I must argue that I'm also nourishing my soul through my intention to . . . bond my inner self with yours. Doctor, surely you cannot deny your patient that element of his recovery," Thomas argued as the fingers of his right hand lightly brushed against the satin of Katherine's bra and the soft skin above it. All the time he spoke, his left hand gently stroked the inside of her thighs.

With her breath coming in little puffs, Katherine responded, "Dr. Baker, as your physician I can only say that I cannot be responsible for anything that happens to your health as a result of the activity that it would appear inevitable that we are about to undertake. I do encourage you, however, to proceed with caution. You are quite fragile at this time."

"Yes, doctor, I do agree with that statement. I find that I am about to burst from the ecstasy of the nearness of you and will undoubtedly exert great stress on all my bodily organs if I do not gain release. From the warmth of your flesh and the pounding of your heart, I gather that the physician is experiencing a need to heal herself as well," Thomas continued their light-hearted banter as he slipped Katherine's blouse off her shoulders. Quickly before she could think of yet another reason why they should not continue, he unsnapped her bra and threw it onto the pile of his clothing that already lay on the nearby chair.

Cupping her breasts in his hands, Thomas lowered his lips to her nipples and lightly teased them with his hot tongue. Katherine held his head and shoulders as the waves of pleasure ran through her body. Quickly she stepped out of her skirt and stood before him in only her panties. Thomas slowly traced the line from her breast down to the top of her bikinis with his lips. His fingers tugged at the thin fabric, eased it over her hips, and tossed it onto the floor as his lips continued their progress toward the thatch of auburn curls between her legs.

As his probing fingers found the throbbing button of pleasure, Katherine gripped his shoulders and shuddered as the flames of desire burned her flesh. She groaned as he massaged the little bud until it ached for release. She clung to him as his lips burned the inside of her thighs. She forgot her in-box and Thomas's health as thoughts of the much-needed release filled her mind.

"Thomas," she called through her parted lips, "Make love to me. Doctor's orders."

Rising, he pulled her onto the afghan that covered the wide sofa. Slowly, he lowered his body over hers until they almost connected. Looking into her upturned face he said, "Anything the doctor prescribes."

Lifting her hips to meet his, Thomas eased his aching manhood into Katherine's moist recesses. Instantly, they sighed and clung to each other. Their bodies rose and thrust in unison as they sought to provide each other with the needed release. Their hands and lips tickled and probed the tender spots known only to seasoned lovers as their bodies thrilled to the rivers of desire that coursed through them.

When they could endure the painful pleasure no longer, their movements increased in fury until even the ticking of the grandfather clock in the foyer was silenced by their whispered endearments. Clutching each other tightly, they merged until the tangle of limbs became indistinguishable and their hearts beat as one.

Lying spent and intertwined, Katherine and Thomas did not move for what seemed like hours. Slowly returning to the sound of the air-conditioning blowing through the vents, Thomas whispered so as not to break the feeling of tranquility that bonded them together, "I think we followed the doctor's orders perfectly, don't you?"

Chuckling Katherine replied, "Definitely. I hope we didn't overdo."

"No, as a matter of fact, I'm feeling remarkably well and hungry. How about making that omelet for me?"

"I'm hungry, too. You can make the salad while I whip up the omelet. I don't trust you out of my sight after that strenuous workout. You might need extra attention from your physician," Katherine answered as she slipped out of Thomas's arms and stooped to pick up her clothing.

"On second thought, let's forget about lunch. I can feel the need for more of my physician's healing touches already. This time, however, we're going upstairs. Coupling on this sofa might do wonders for my memory, but it's hell on the knees," Thomas said as he grabbed Katherine's hand and their clothing. As they walked across the cold marble foyer, the grandfather clock struck one. With a shrug, Katherine acknowledged that she would have to work late that night to compensate for time well spent.

When Katherine finally returned to the hospital, she found everyone bubbling with excitement. As the news of Thomas's injury spread, the "Sisters" had contacted major contributors from all over the country in an effort to reassure them that Boxer was in the capable hands of Katherine Winters, MD, during his recuperation. During their conversations, they asked each of them to write a check to the fund-raising campaign as a get-well greeting to Thomas and a show of gratitude and support to Katherine. The results had been most impressive as one pledge after the other arrived in the chief financial officer's office.

In their enthusiasm, the "Sisters" had commissioned the creation of a huge sign that highlighted the monies raised and the amount still needed. The newly erected display stood in the middle of the main lawn for everyone to see. The amount already in the Boxer coffers was staggering, and the percentage figure was overwhelming. With only ten percent of the objective unrealized, everyone knew that the hospital would soon begin the installation of its new technological advancements for which

Thomas had worked so diligently and from which Boxer would benefit.

Katherine was so immediately caught up in the chaos created by the press in their desire to report the results of the campaign that she had little time to think about her afternoon with Thomas. As she answered questions and gave the prepared statements thrust into her hands by the overworked members of the public relations staff, she only once had time to breathe in the smell of his cologne that still lingered on her clothing.

Even Jasmine, not to be outdone by the others, had made calls, wooed contributors, and spoken with praise for the bravery of her competitor. In fact, despite their interest in the same man, Jasmine did feel that Katherine was someone worthy of her attention. After all, she could certainly ride to the hounds with the best of them, and there was no denying that Katherine was brave. She had rescued Thomas from the fire while Jasmine, to her chagrin, had fled for her own safety. Reluctantly, she had to admit to herself that Katherine was a formidable opponent. She also remembered seeing Thomas's face when he looked at Katherine and the gentleness of the kiss he deposited on her lips at the carnival. Jasmine knew that she would have to work hard to replace Katherine in this match.

As Jasmine watched Katherine work the press, she decided that drastic actions would be the only means by which she could win Thomas. The disastrous dinner dance had put a stop to her plans to force a wedge between Katherine and Thomas. She concluded, as the warm summer breeze rippled the fabric of her dress, that it was time to resume her efforts. Thomas's injury was no excuse for inactivity. In fact, she might be able to use it to her advantage.

Slipping away from the hospital in late afternoon while Katherine worked, Jasmine drove quickly to Thomas's house. As she rushed up the stairs of his town house, she formulated a simple plan. She would throw herself on the man's loneliness and feelings of isolation. She would make herself indispensable. She would make him need her. As soon as she had Thomas securely hooked, Jasmine would reel him in and marry him before Katherine had a chance to figure out what had happened right under her busy nose.

As she rang the doorbell, Jasmine adjusted the front of her wraparound dress to emphasize the maximum amount of bosom exposure. She knew she had a stunning figure; too many men had whispered their appreciation for it for her not to know the impact her full bust, small waist, and luscious hips had on them. She would need all of her wiles to trap this one.

Thomas appeared neither surprised nor happy to see Jasmine as she stepped over the threshold. He had been enjoying the solitude of his piano after taking the nap Katherine had prescribed as a follow-up to their lovemaking. Something in the way Jasmine walked into the living room and assumed control of the keyboard told him that this would not be a relaxing encounter. A flitting glimpse of memory played before his eyes.

As he strained to bring the picture into focus, Jasmine played the first few cords of a fiery tango. Immediately, Thomas remembered the dinner dance, the feel of her body pressed against his, and the sultry music played by the quartet. A bright warning sign flashed "Danger" in his mind.

"Sit next to me, Thomas darling," Jasmine cooed, wiggling her buttocks over an inch on the piano bench. "We haven't had any time alone, really alone, since that weekend you spent at my house. If I remember correctly, you made quite an impression on everyone in your riding finery. Afterward, you showed me that you were certainly more than competent on the dance floor. We tangoed to this very music."

"I don't think I'll ever forget that weekend, Jasmine," Thomas replied trying to make light of his painful memory of his encounter with the horse and the direction the conversation was heading.

"Well, my poor dear, I can still feel the strength of your arms around me, smell the aroma of your spicy perfume, and savor the heat of your body burning into mine through our clothing. We certainly danced a nasty tango. My other guests are probably still talking about it. If you only had the music, I'd remind you of the way we moved," Jasmine purred the words as she seductively moistened her lips.

Before Thomas could respond, Jasmine rose to her feet and crossed the room. She had spied his stereo setup when she entered, and now she used it to set the stage to her advantage. Quickly selecting a disk from his sizable collection, she turned on the music. Immediately a violin began to play the same tango to which they had danced on the yacht. Crossing the burgundy and navy patterned carpet on her way to the large foyer, she threw open her arms and asked, "Would you care to dance?"

"I hope I don't step on your feet. My balance is still a bit off," Thomas replied as he joined her under the chandelier. Immediately, he heard the all too familiar warning bell sound in his head drowning out the melody of the tango.

"Dancing, riding a bike, and having sex are three things you never forget," Jasmine responded huskily as she pressed herself against him.

Taking Jasmine into his arms, Thomas skillfully negotiated a sensuous tango. With each step, the ringing of a warning bell sounded more loudly in his head. He could feel that dancing with Jasmine would lead to more than a pounding headache.

As the music stopped, Jasmine searched his face for signs of interest. Finding only confusion written on his handsome brow, she slipped her arms around his neck, pulled his lips down to hers, and proceeded to kiss Thomas in a way that would have set most men on fire.

At first, Thomas was too distracted by the clanging of the warning bell to feel the fingers that tightened in his hair and the teeth that nibbled on his lips. Suddenly, he wanted to know what there was about Jasmine Gaylord that had made so many men before him desire her and had caused Betsy to warn him about her.

She pulled him tighter, and Thomas relinquished his power to Jasmine as she continued to seduce him. He stood apart from himself and watched as she performed her magic. Thrusting her tongue between his teeth, she darted hot kisses around his mouth and lips accompanied by a slight sucking that pulled his tongue into her mouth. Her hands played along his back, shoulders, buttocks, and thighs at once kneading the muscles and tearing at them. Her pelvis writhed against his like an exotic dancer in the throes of a seductive number.

Almost against his will, Thomas's body responded to Jasmine's efforts. As his interest increased, so too did the tolling of the bell. Despite the pleasurable sensations that her actions caused to course through his body, Thomas could not give himself up to Jasmine. It was not the recent coupling with Katherine and the growing feelings of affection he had for her that kept him from giving in to the lustful desire that Jasmine aroused in him. He also saw something else . . . something even more frightening and sobering.

As Jasmine's hands moved to his crotch to stoke the fire that her gyrations had caused to spark, Thomas suddenly saw a flash of flames and heard the crackling of burning wood and fiber. Suddenly the smell of smoke filled his nose and the heat of the flames burned at his face. As Jasmine's fingers caressed his stiffening manhood, he looked into her face. He did not see the desire that filled it that evening and made her sigh and moan. Instead, the memory of an expression more compelling and more dangerous met his gaze. He looked into an expression from his memory banks, and he was filled with fear and disgust.

Thomas saw Jasmine's face filled with terror as she turned from him and fled the smoke-filled room. He saw himself shove her out of the way as a large portion of the ceiling crashed just inches from her head. He saw her glance at him briefly before turning her back on him, running toward the door, and leaving him to lie helplessly on the floor. The impact of the yacht's last pitch and the glancing blow of the ceiling tiles had caused him to lose his footing and tumble against one of the tables. He saw her retreating back as she fled to safety leaving him to die in the fire.

Grasping her shoulders, Thomas held Jasmine at arm's length

and tried to step away from her and her probing fingers. Her touch was no longer pleasurable but caused memories of pain to flood through his mind. Her kisses no longer excited his vanity but reminded him of her selfish acts. He no longer fought against his desire for her out of loyalty to Katherine and a foggy memory. Thomas found himself repulsed by the nearness of Jasmine, by the demanding nature of her fingers, and by the skillful determination of her kisses as they sought to control rather than love. And he remembered all the formerly blurred events of the evening of the dinner dance.

At that instant, the front door opened and Katherine entered carrying a bag containing take-out treats from the bistro near her apartment. She had let herself in using the extra key from the vase not wishing to disturb him if he were napping or playing the piano. She had hoped to recreate the perfection of their afternoon.

Seeing them together with Jasmine's fingers still locked in Thomas's hair and curled around the front of his trousers, Katherine cried out in shock and immediately dropped the heavy bag. Marmite de poule, asparagus almandine, and chocolate mouse spread over the tiles in a sticky, smelly combination of textures and fragrances. The mixture of scents and Jasmine's cloying perfume were enough to turn Katherine's stomach.

Looking from the mess on the floor to the shocked expression on Thomas's face and the look of triumph on Jasmine's, Katherine muttered, "I guess that is one prescription I do not need to write. You must be feeling quite recovered, Thomas, to take on two women in one day. I can see that I'm the third wheel here. I'm sorry to . . . ah . . . eat and run, but I really must be going. Don't see me to the door. You have your hands quite full."

"Katherine, wait! This isn't what you think!" Thomas shouted, stepping over the wasted remains of their evening together as the door slammed shut. Instantly, he realized that something far worse than the loss of his memory had just occurred. He had lost Katherine.

Rushing out into the warm summer night air, Thomas tried to catch up with Katherine but the horrible pounding in his head slowed him down. By the time he reached the sidewalk, she had driven away, leaving the angry glow of her car's taillights as a reminder that she had been there.

Feeling Jasmine's presence behind him, Thomas turned to look into her face. Once again in the glow of the streetlamps, he saw an expression that he did not like. This time terror did not disfigure her features. She smiled craftily as if gloating over winning a tennis match or a hunt. Whatever she was thinking, Thomas at that moment hated her for leaving him behind in the fire, for being too cowardly to help save his life, for planning this show to drive Katherine away, and for making him fall into her trap.

Suddenly remembering the hunt weekend and the incidents surrounding the dinner dance, Thomas saw that he had been the trophy at both events. Katherine had ridden to victory at the hunt and won the prize, but Jasmine had wedged an element of doubt between them. She had positioned him next to her at dinner and fawned over him all evening, making it obvious to all except Thomas that he was her reward. Katherine was to have been his date at the fund-raising dance, but Jasmine had monopolized his time during those fateful minutes before the yacht sank.

Jasmine had schemed to destroy their budding relationship tonight, too. She had known that Katherine would bring dinner to him after leaving the hospital. She had planned the tango and the seduction for a strategic time so that Katherine would find them together. Thomas's vanity had led him to assume that being the prize would be fun and rewarding. Now, he realized that it was quite painful and humiliating.

"Let her go, Thomas. Our evening together has only just begun. We don't need Katherine anyway. You're on the mend and the good doctor would only be in the way," Jasmine purred, stroking his shoulder and watching the remnants of her opponent vanish around the corner and out of sight. She linked her arm through his and led him back into the house.

"Please go, Jasmine. You've done enough for one night," Thomas said as he slipped away from her grasping fingers. The mess in the foyer reminded him of the chaos in his personal life.

"Are you throwing me out?" Jasmine demanded with shock in her voice. "No man has ever done that to me. Are you sure that's a smart idea? Don't forget that I'm a major contributor to the hospital that pays your salary."

"Boxer pays for my work but not for my soul. If you are vindictive enough to withdraw your generous pledges of support for the hospital because of me, I won't and can't stop you. You have to follow your own conscience just as you did the night of the fire as you left me to die on that yacht. I was a little fuzzy at first. The blow to the head stunned me more than I initially thought, but it's all coming back now. I remember the dancing, the dinner, and the press of your body against mine, but I also remember the sight of your fleeing back as you ran from that room. If it hadn't been for Katherine, I would have died in that fire. So, if you want to take your funds from the hospital, feel free. Boxer will survive just fine without your money," Thomas replied calmly as he opened the door for her.

Jasmine could not think of any way to deny what Thomas had said. Everything was true. She had fled, she had schemed, and she had plotted. Usually, her efforts paid off. However, this time she came up the loser.

"I wouldn't think of withdrawing my contributions. I'll just chalk this one up to experience. Not even I can win them all. Good night, Thomas. I'll see you at the next board meeting," Jasmine replied, as she stepped over the mess in the hall and into the night air with her usual undaunted confident stride. The events of the evening, Thomas's rejection of her, and Katherine's intrusion into her plans had not penetrated her protective shell or damaged her feeling of self-importance.

Thomas's head pounded as he cleaned up the remains of his

dinner from the foyer tiles. He had certainly made a mess of his relationship with Katherine. Now that Jasmine was permanently out of his life, he hoped he could make it up to her. Yet Thomas doubted that he would be able to straighten things out with Katherine as easily as he wiped up the spilled mouse.

Katherine had driven home with tears streaming down her cheeks. Rushing to Betsy's apartment, she unloaded her myriad of emotions on her friend. She could not remember when she had ever felt so helpless and hurt.

Throwing herself onto Betsy's sofa Katherine cried, "I had carefully protected myself from falling in love with any number of men who vied for my attention. I hadn't wanted to become involved with any of them. I was too busy with my career and I didn't want to get hurt by them. Against my better judgment, I allowed my feelings toward Thomas to grow until I couldn't stop myself from loving him. He had seemed genuinely fond of me, too. He said he loved me, and he acted like it, too.

"I knew I shouldn't have let myself love him," Katherine sniffled into her soggy tissue as she continued. "I put aside my goals in life and allowed my feelings for Thomas to direct my actions. I should have remained true to myself. Love hurts too much. I never should have allowed it into my life. If only Thomas hadn't come to Boxer, everything would be all right. I can still see him standing there entangled in Jasmine's web. We had spent such a lovely afternoon of lovemaking. How could he betray me like that?"

Betsy felt helpless to say or do anything for Katherine as her friend cried against her shoulder. She knew that Katherine had been very careful about allowing men into her life . . . at times too careful. Betsy worried that Katherine might never take the time to fall in love. Hearing the sobs that tore her friend's slim body, Betsy almost wished Katherine had not removed the barrier that separated her from Thomas Baker.

Finally, when Katherine began to calm down, Betsy made the

only suggestion that seemed a possible solution. Handing Katherine the last tissue in the box she said, "Forget about him.
You're stronger than both of them and twice as talented. Look
at the way you've worked two jobs and managed the hospital
single-handedly. You don't need him to be complete."

"Wait a minute. Aren't you the one who warned me against
going through life alone?" Katherine asked. Betsy's outburst of
liberal thought had totally shocked her. Her friend had always
been the kind of woman who believed that her life would not
be complete without a husband and children.

"Yes, I did, and I guess I was wrong. It is possible to be a
woman in a leadership position without relying on a man for
fulfillment. Watching you has convinced me that you are more
than capable of making it in this man's world. All you need is
faith in yourself and you'll be successful. This thing with
Thomas has upset you, but it can't defeat you. Shake it off,
Katherine. Go back to the hospital tomorrow and show them,
all of them including Thomas, who's boss. He'll drop that Jasmine woman as soon as he sees that you can stand tall and
strong without him and that he's not the center of you life,"
Betsy urged as she pushed Katherine toward the door.

"You are absolutely right. I will show him. Thank you, Betsy,
for reminding me of my goals. I knew I could count on you.
I'm not going to retreat or sound the horn of defeat. I did not
set out to win the heart of Thomas Baker. My goal was and will
always be to serve Boxer as the best hospital administrator possible. Nothing will turn me away from my original plan."

Sixteen

The next morning Katherine arrived in the ER with her resolve very much in tact. She had made up her mind that nothing would interfere in her plans to show the board that she should run Boxer on a permanent basis. She had allowed her feelings toward Thomas to sidetrack her efforts and to confuse her mind. However, she would not be derailed by him.

As usual the ER was a mass of humanity waiting for someone to cure its ills. Pulling on her white jacket, Katherine joined her team in assessing the needs of the sick and injured. A few required the simplest of treatment, such as the little boy with the dried pea in his nostril. Katherine merely grabbed it with sterile tweezers and pulled. The housekeeper thanked her and took the boy away amid a torrent of English and Spanish words intending to make him feel contrite for his behavior.

Some needed stitches to close knife wounds which they claimed were from peeling apples, but which Katherine recognized as the result of street fights. She quickly and expertly sterilized and sutured the area and sent them back to their neighborhood knowing that she would see them again in the ER. They neither thanked her nor looked back as they sauntered from the hospital.

Others, like one accident victim, required the efforts of Katherine and several surgeons to stabilize. Her car had careened off the road into an embankment before coming to rest against a cluster of trees. Fortunately, the woman had been wearing her seatbelt, which prevented her from crashing through the windshield. However, the angle of the car as it wedged itself against the tree had caused a branch to impale itself like a spear through her ribs and into her lung.

As Katherine examined the site of the wound, she asked incredulously, "How did this happen?"

John, one of the paramedics on the scene, explained as he shook his head in disbelief. He said, "The woman's car must have gone flying off the Teddy Roosevelt bridge into the ravine at considerable speed because when my partner and I arrived, we found the branch running through her just as you see it now. The only difference is that it was also connected to the tree at the same time. We had to use a chain saw to cut the branch from the tree. Then, we had to shorten it again so that we could remove the woman from the car. Boy, that was the freakiest thing I've ever seen. That woman was completely pinned to her car seat by that branch.

"For a while there, I was afraid that we'd have to bring the seat with us. When the fire department arrived, the men couldn't believe their eyes. They cut off the steering wheel and pulled out the seat. After that we lifted the woman and the branch onto the stretcher. It's the strangest thing I've ever seen. I'm glad I had a partner to see this one. No one would have believed me if I'd been alone."

Katherine and her team worked diligently to stabilize the woman before making the transfer to the operating room where the surgeons would remove the tree branch. She had heard about people running into fences and becoming impaled on pickets, but she had never seen anything like this in her ER tenure.

As she sat in the physicians' lounge, Katherine struggled with the words that would convey the story of her morning in the ER. None of the other cases gave her any difficulty, but the woman with the tree branch proved troublesome. Finally, she decided to state very simply that her team had stabilized a woman with a wooden spike through her chest. If anyone needed more information than that, she would provide it upon request.

Katherine was deep in thought when the door opened. She had enjoyed almost fifteen minutes of solitude before being interrupted by the intruder who stood beside the little desk waiting for her to look up from the report. When she finally finished the sentence, she laid down her pen. "Yes?" she asked as she picked up her coffee cup.

"Might I have a moment to speak with you?" Thomas asked.

Thomas had arrived at eight o'clock looking bruised but eager to return to work and to resolve the tension between them. He had made a terrible patient. Knowing that his agitation would only increase if he stayed away from the business of the hospital, Thomas had phoned Douglas Myers and told him that he would not need any more time at home to recover. The brief stay in the hospital and the even briefer one at home had been enough for him.

Besides, Thomas had decided as he watched Katherine drive away the previous evening that nothing would keep him from coming to work. His head still ached a bit, but he had to find the opportunity to set things right with her. He loved her and her energy. He knew from the set of Katherine's shoulders that she would not come to him again.

Seeing her so busy with the accident victim, Thomas had waited until things quieted down in the ER before he approached her. Now, as she sipped her cold coffee and scanned him casually, he wondered if he should have gone to his office instead of coming to see her. Katherine's demeanor was anything but inviting.

"Good morning, Thomas. I didn't expect to see you here today. You must be feeling much better," Katherine commented in much the same tone as she would have used with the most casual of associates but certainly not with a lover.

"Much better, thank you. If this is a bad time, I'll come back later, but I really need to speak with you," Thomas stated in a tone that was almost as flat as hers.

"I am rather pressed for time at the moment. I have a number of cases to finish and a meeting in a few minutes. Since you're here this morning, I assume you'll handle the staff meeting yourself. That takes one load off my shoulders and gives me a few more minutes down here. Perhaps we can talk after the meeting if that would be all right with you," Katherine offered as she set down her cup and picked up her pencil. Her movements signaled an end to the conversation.

Taking the none too subtle hint, Thomas replied as he left the room, "After the meeting would be just fine, Katherine. I'll see you in about thirty minutes."

Walking toward the elevator Thomas thought about the brief encounter with Katherine. He had not expected her to run to him with open arms, but he had not anticipated the complete freeze that she had given him. He had hoped that their talk later in the morning would undo the damage of the previous evening, but now he had his doubts.

Katherine returned to her work with difficulty. Although some of the feeling of betrayal had faded, she still smarted from the impact of seeing Thomas with Jasmine. She was fairly certain that Jasmine had initiated the interaction between them, but Katherine also knew that Thomas had done nothing to stop her. Surely he could have pushed her away. Instead, he seemed to be enjoying the attention.

Shaking her head, Katherine forced herself to continue her reports. Her life was much too complicated already without allowing Thomas to add one more dimension to it. The ER had always kept her so busy that she had little time to think about a social life. Thomas's arrival at Boxer had changed that. However, Katherine did not see why things could not return to their usual pattern if only she could remove him from her heart and refocus her efforts.

The rest of her morning progressed without setbacks as Katherine plowed through the mountain of paper on the small desk. Rising from her seat, she joined Betsy on their weekly walk to the conference room and the department chair meeting. Katherine could already tell that today's meeting would be one of the longest in her life.

"Good morning, everyone," Thomas greeted the assembled department chairs as they took their accustomed places around the table. As usual, Katherine sat directly opposite him at the other end. Although the others appeared oblivious to the friction between them, she could feel the waves of tension that traveled the length of the table.

"The first order of business is for me to thank all of you for your calls and good wishes. I'm still a bit shaky, but I'm definitely on the mend. That was some boat ride!" Thomas said amid a healthy chortling from the others who had also escaped from the eventful dinner dance.

He continued by saying, "I understand that the vessel has been examined by the fire department and pronounced repairable, which is indeed good news for our board member. He called last evening with word that the entire problem was the result of faulty wiring in the steering mechanism that shorted out the propeller system. The fire damage, although it appeared extensive to us because of all the smoke, was actually not as severe as he initially thought it would be. His business will be back in operation in about two weeks. In the meantime, his second craft will carry a full load every night rather than simply the overflow as needed.

"For our part, I understand from the banners and charts that Boxer made out pretty well despite a few torn evening gowns and a few bruises. I would like to thank all of you for doing your part to make it a successful fund-raiser. Thanks in no small part to Katherine, the kitchen repair is underway without disruption to our staff. Her foresight and determination certainly paid off. I applaud her dedication to the hospital and have communicated my appreciation to the board."

Thomas again paused in his discussion for a round of applause. Katherine was greatly moved as her colleagues rose from their seat and gave her a standing ovation. Even those who had initially opposed her and sided with Thomas realized the wisdom of her solution and joined in the acknowledgment of her devotion to the staff of Boxer Hospital. Smiling, Katherine graciously accepted their show of appreciation by inclining her head and offering her own applause to them in return.

"Continuing with our agenda . . . ," Thomas began as the applause faded and everyone settled into their seats once more.

The rest of the meeting progressed as was its usual custom with the department chairs giving updates on budget pictures and the efficiency of their personnel. Considering that Boxer was an exceptionally well-managed hospital, there were never any surprises. As the session drew to a close, Thomas asked for any suggestions for topics for next week's session. Receiving none, he adjourned the meeting.

As Katherine collected her things, Thomas beckoned and asked, "Katherine, might I have a few minutes with you before you return to the ER?"

"Of course, Thomas," she replied. Katherine no longer felt the need professionally to keep him at arm's length and had begun to address Thomas by his first name as did all the others. Regardless of the status of their social interaction, their professional life had reached a point of mutual respect that allowed the familiarity.

"Katherine, I'd like to see you tonight if you're free. We have many things to discuss, but this is not really the place for it. We've never managed to be alone here for more than a few minutes. I need to explain about Jasmine," Thomas said with an almost pleading quality in his voice. A less proud man would have resorted to that tactic.

"Thomas, you don't owe me any explanations at all," Katherine replied from where she stood at opposite end of the table. "Our relationship took an unexpected turn and appeared to be gaining momentum, but it obviously has reached the end of its purpose. We are both very busy professionals who should probably face the facts that we really don't have time for a personal life.

"I haven't cultivated one in all these years, and from your

resume it appears that you haven't had time for one either. I think we should chalk this experience up to the fact that we thought we could make an exception this time, but we were wrong. We're hospital administrators, Thomas. I don't think there's room in our lives for anything else.

"Besides, you'll be leaving soon. I can't risk the pain of finally forming a relationship only to have it end. I need to concentrate all of my energy on running the ER. It really is a full-time job. And, when you leave, I intend to again become the chief of staff of this hospital."

"I didn't think we came together out of convenience or loneliness or a need to experiment with something that has been easy for others but difficult for us," Thomas rebutted softly. "I was drawn to you because of your spirit and commitment. I admired those qualities in you and thought that you might direct them toward making a relationship work with me. I'm fully aware, probably more than most, of your professional aspirations. However, I don't understand why the two must be mutually exclusive. I would think that becoming involved with someone who is also devoted to the cause of providing quality health care would make the relationship healthier."

Hesitating for only a moment, Katherine replied, "Perhaps the problem is, Thomas, that you and I are committed to the same organization. We both want to be in charge of Boxer. That makes for a very competitive situation between us, which has not helped the progress of our relationship one bit. As soon as we reach out to each other, the hospital and our ambition step between us. It won't work, Thomas."

"Are you sure that you're not upset because of what you saw with Jasmine? If you are, let me assure you that nothing happened with her. I am not in the least attracted to her, not now, and not ever," Thomas added in the hope that perhaps he had touched on the real cause of Katherine's hesitation.

"No, it's not Jasmine. I was angry with you when I discovered you in a rather compromising pose with her. I was hurt. But, I'm not anymore. I thought about it and realized that the reason

I felt betrayed . . . I guess that's the right word . . . betrayed, was that you and I have worked so hard for Boxer that I thought we were on the same page in all aspects of our life.

"I realize that we've had our differences, but the goal was always the same. We both wanted only the best for Boxer. Finding Jasmine wrapped around you as she was definitely upset me, but the realization of the identity of the third party in this relationship does not involve her.

"No, Thomas, our problem has nothing to do with Jasmine. The one thing that unites us and keeps us apart at the same time is the very thing that we each love more than we could ever love each other. The obstacle to our relationship is Boxer."

As Katherine's words echoed off the conference room walls, Thomas sank into the chair at the head of the table. His head throbbed more from the reality of what Katherine had just said than from the injury. Looking at her standing so proudly behind her chair, he knew that she was right. They were opposing ends of the same table, contradictory opinions with the same purpose, and mirror images of the same profile. Katherine was absolutely correct. Boxer gave them purpose.

"But, Katherine, I love you," Thomas replied as if the strength of his conviction would change the force between them.

"And I love you, Thomas. But that emotion alone isn't enough when that other presence still exists," Katherine responded slowly shaking her head.

"Then, I'll leave Boxer. I'd rather not have this hospital if I can't have you in my life," Thomas declared. His voice was filled with the emotion that played across his sad, bruised face, making it difficult for Katherine to tell which had disfigured him more—the accident or the pain of their relationship.

"You can't leave here any more than I can. You haven't finished what you set out to accomplish. You haven't seen the hospital enter the new age of technology. There's much more here for you to do. No, Thomas, that's not an option, and deep down in your heart you know it," Katherine commented softly.

She really did not want to add to his misery by stating the obvious.

"Then I guess this discussion can come to no purpose and can solve none of our problems," Thomas reluctantly conceded. Slowly, he straightened his body until he stood his full height. Thomas looked the part of the wounded warrior who knew that he had just lost a crucial battle.

Gathering her files, Katherine carefully placed them inside her briefcase and clicked it shut. The sound added a final period to their session. Walking to the door, she stopped and looked back at the man she loved. The conference room telephone rang, ending any further conversation.

The rest of the summer passed with Katherine and Thomas seeing very little of each other except for the usual department chair meetings. The restoration of the kitchen had progressed even more smoothly than expected. Because of quick thinking on the part of the hospital's main engineer, the crew had hung a temporary suspended ceiling that blocked off even more of the noise enabling them to work in round-the-clock shifts. Since most of the occupants of the floor directly above the kitchen were office staff with the exception of one corner, few people were inconvenienced by the hammering and banging. After two weeks, the hospital unveiled its newly renovated space to the delight of the board members and neighbors who had taken Boxer Hospital to their heart.

As the autumn weather settled over Washington, Katherine and Betsy resumed their favorite pastime of hiking through Great Falls. They packed lunches and sometimes rented bikes for part of their trek. Katherine thought of including Thomas in her activities, but she changed her mind. The love she felt for him now occupied a safe spot in her heart. No longer did it require energy to push him from her mind after moments of enjoying the memory of the feel of his kisses and his arms. She did not want to awaken the pain that had taken possession of her being after the fateful staff meeting. Katherine was not over Thomas; she simply knew how to love more wisely now.

As she trekked through the woods, Thomas took long drives in his sports car. He loved the autumn when the leaves changed colors and the air felt crisp. Driving through the countryside with the top down and the warm fall air on his face was one of his favorite pastimes. He enjoyed the nip in the air that told him that winter would not be far away.

Sometimes, Thomas wished he could share the moments with Katherine, but he knew that the timing was not right for them. He had carefully stored his love for her in a compartment in his heart. When the time was right, he would pull it out again. For now, he was content in knowing that he loved and was loved in return.

The restoration of the kitchen was not the only project that had progressed ahead of schedule. The new technology wing of the hospital would be completed in the spring. Thanks to fund-raising suggestions from Katherine, Thomas had been able to raise all the money the hospital needed to secure the builder and supplies for the project. All the equipment had been selected from the newest technology on the market and only waited for a firm delivery date.

As late fall turned into winter and then into spring, the hospital community started gearing up for the grand opening of the new wing. Committees decorated the inside and the outside of the building with plants, flowers, balloons, and streamers. They even planned to replicate the carnival that had been so successful as a fund-raiser and community event during the summer. They all remembered the kiss on the Ferris wheel.

Katherine and Thomas had convinced themselves that no one was aware of the affection for each other that they shared and hid. They thought that since they were keeping their distance from each other, no one had noticed the longing glances that flew from the ends of the conference room table, the lingering touches when papers passed between their hungry fingers, or the sudden change in their demeanor when the other entered the room. They thought that they had concealed their love from their all-knowing colleagues with as much success as they had hidden it from each other.

Betsy began to put their plan into action as soon as she discovered that Katherine had scheduled herself into a slot in the skeletal crew assigned to work the day of the carnival. She immediately contrived with Thomas's secretary to find a way to get them alone together. She knew it would not be easy to arrange, but she had to do something to force these two to reach out to each other. Thinking that the unveiling of Thomas's rejuvenation project might be the perfect day to inspire them to make a stab at revitalizing their relationship as well.

The weather in Washington in April could be temperamental, but the spring had been so lovely that everyone hoped that the sun would shine on the hospital's special weekend. Forbidding anyone to mention the word "rain," the committee members placed signs all over the neighborhood that would encourage all but the stodgiest members of the community to attend. Even the weekend highlights section of the paper listed the event in bold type as the spring fling not to be missed.

As one of the hospital's department chairpersons, Katherine proudly took her place on the platform beside her colleagues and listened as Thomas gave a short welcome and then he and Douglas Myers, the chairman of the board, cut the ribbon. The wing for which they had all worked so hard to raise funds was officially open and ready for patients.

Joining the others on the official tour, Katherine marveled along with them at the beauty of the gleaming machinery and the sparkling floors. She knew that no other hospital in Washington owned this particular MRI machine or this special hydrotherapy device. None of their competitors could provide their patients with such incredible state-of-the-art diagnostic care.

Thomas glowed with satisfaction as he watched the board members gingerly touch the machinery with an almost reverent respect for each nut and bolt. Even the most reluctant among them now welcomed the new technology that moved Boxer from a conservative, reliable caregiving institution into the arena of the super-hospital ready for any emergency or ailment.

The press, usually callused and difficult to impress, appeared genuinely moved by the changes in Boxer. They hid their usual cynicism and refrained from asking redundant questions for which Boxer's top-notch public relations department had already provided them with the answers. Instead, they clicked their cameras nonstop and recorded the comments of awestruck visitors.

Escaping from the crush inside the technology wing, Katherine joined the larger assembly on the lawn. As the warm, spring sun lay across her shoulders, she nibbled a sticky candied apple and waited her turn on the Ferris wheel. Laughing happily, she watched trick riders on unicycles and men on stilts entertain the revelers.

Slipping into the vacated car, Katherine barely noticed that someone had joined her on the seat. She would not mind sharing the view of the hospital and the happy neighbors with a stranger. After all, everyone had come to have a good time and to wish the hospital staff well in the new wing.

Turning toward her partner, Katherine gasped and then smiled "Why, Thomas, I thought you would be too busy posing for the photographers to take time out for a ride. Let me be among the first to congratulate you. The new wing is stunning. The architects' vision is even more remarkable in its completed form. You should feel very proud," Katherine said as she regained her composure.

"Correction, we should feel proud. Everyone in the Boxer community contributed to the successful construction of this remarkable technology wing. It never could have come to be a reality if we had not all pulled together. You were especially helpful, Katherine. I've told the board on many occasions that

I never could have pulled this off without your insights into the personalities of the Boxer constituents," Thomas corrected gently. He felt strangely nervous being alone again with her.

"It is the most beautiful hospital I've ever seen. The new wing fits perfectly and looks as if it has always been a part of the original Boxer. It doesn't disrupt the line of the original structure in the least. It's a little late to ask this, but are we ready for all this new technology?" Katherine queried as she surveyed the grandeur beneath them.

"Everyone has been attending classes geared to making them ready for this moment. What they don't know now, they'll acquire as they become more comfortable with the equipment. It's clear from the number of people down there that the community was ready for the change. We'll have to rise to the challenge now that we've thrown down our own gauntlet. Besides, we have to stay at least one step ahead of our competition. For too long this hospital has been in the middle of the pack. Now, Boxer is the leader, but you don't stay there by becoming complacent. Keeping the personnel inspired is the next step," Thomas quipped with a little smile. He loved the idea that his hospital would lead the way for many others to follow.

"How can they not be inspired? Just look at his place!" Katherine gushed.

As the Ferris wheel began to move giving them a bird's-eye-view of the hospital, Thomas placed his hand over Katherine's. The feel of her skin was even softer than he remembered. Her nearness made him feel more light-headed than the view from the top of the ride. It had been so long since he had touched her that Thomas felt himself being pulled to her as if they were part of a magnetic field. Together, they surveyed the hospital that they loved so dearly. This time, Jasmine was nowhere to be seen.

"Katherine, marry me. I've been offered a professorship at the university, and I'm thinking of taking it. It's time I settled down, and Washington seems to be the perfect place for me. Now that my work at Boxer is done, I'm free to take a different fork in the road," Thomas said without a trace of the teasing that usually passed between them.

"You could leave Boxer, Thomas? I'm surprised," Katherine replied, avoiding his question.

"I guess I've realized that a few plaques and lot of marble can't keep me warm at night. If leaving here is the only way I can have you in my life, then that's the move I have to make. But you've skirted the question. I love you, Katherine. Will you marry me?" Thomas pressed his request again as he lifted her hand to his lips.

Just as her lips began to form the answer, the ride came to a stop and the voices of the crowd burst their perfect moment. Smiling sweetly, Katherine motioned to the line of people who waited for them to vacate their place in the car. "The ride's over. We have to get out," she said softly.

"If it's not my secretary calling to interrupt our time together, it's a line of people waiting to ride the Ferris wheel. Have dinner with me tonight, Katherine. We need to finish this discussion. Let's go to our little bistro. How's seven o'clock for you?" Thomas asked as he steered her through the crowd.

Before Katherine had the chance to answer, they were separated by the mob of surging people anxious to board the ride. Laughing, she waved her hand high over her head and gave a thumb's up, which she hoped he could see.

The afternoon was a great success. From the noise and the activity in and around the hospital, it appeared that everyone in the neighborhood, the nearby university, and the Washington, D.C., area stopped by to view the new wing, eat cotton candy, and ride the Ferris wheel. The Public Relations Department had scheduled a press conference as the close of a perfect spring day.

As the staff, board of directors, and members of the press assembled in the hospital's auditorium, Katherine looked at all the happy staff members. She was surprised at the number that had managed to get away from their duties, but she knew that all of them wanted to be part of this special day for Boxer.

Katherine understood their enthusiasm, especially since she had walked the picket line with most of them. She had shared their dreams and their fears. Now it was time for them to share in the fulfillment of those of the hospital.

As Douglas Myers approached the podium, loud applause rang through the room and the cameras flashed wildly. His usual shy, retiring demeanor had been transformed into that of a smiling celebrity as he represented the hospital that they all loved and had helped make the leader in patient service and now technology.

Raising his hands Douglas began his carefully rehearsed speech, "Ladies and gentlemen, it is with great pleasure that I close today's activities in celebration of the grand opening of Boxer's new technology wing. Our community of physicians, supporters, and friends has made this day one that we will long remember and cherish for the good feelings that we have shared and the foundation for the new beginning we have laid. We have come a long way in the history of this hospital from a medium-size neighborhood care facility, to a major institution, and now to a leader in technology.

"As most of you know, we have been engaged in a search for a new chief financial officer for the last three months without success. We wanted someone with vision and passion as well as a sound financial background. We looked for someone who could continue to work with the chief of staff in promoting the image of our hospital to our community and the world.

"We found many candidates with the financial expertise we wanted but none with the emotional commitment that would provide the kind of leadership Boxer draws from its people. We had become fearful that we would never find the right match until it dawned on us that our search was misdirected. We should not have been looking outside the hospital but inside. We already had the best person for the job on our staff. Last evening at a specially convened closed-door meeting, the board met to rectify our error.

"Before we leave here today, I want to announce another first for Boxer Hospital. By unanimous vote, I am pleased to confer the position of chief financial officer on Dr. Thomas Baker, who, as of today, will no longer serve as the chief of staff of Boxer Hospital. Dr. Baker, if you'll come forward please."

Thunderous applause greeted a stunned Thomas as he approached the front of the auditorium and shook hands with Douglas Myers. Thomas was genuinely moved by the outpouring of affection as he thanked first the board and then the assembled staff. For the first time in his illustrious career, Thomas finally had found a home.

Again raising his hands to signal for silence, Douglas Myers spoke to the crowd. "This is truly a day of firsts," he said, as he scanned the faces that waited impatiently for him to finish so that they could congratulate Thomas on his promotion. "The tradition at Boxer and at all hospitals is to conduct a formal candidate search for replacement when positions become available. However, the board decided that in this case no search could possibly uncover a more perfect candidate to fill the position of chief of staff here at Boxer. We need someone with energy, drive, and commitment. We need someone whose devotion to this hospital would be unquestioned regardless of the difficulty of the decisions.

"Therefore, it is my pleasure to announce that the new chief of staff for Boxer Hospital is Katherine Winters, MD. Dr. Winters, would you please join us."

This time the crowd went wild. Cat calls, shouts of "Brava," and deafening applause mixed with the glare from the camera lights as Katherine, propelled by the many hands that patted her on the back, made her way to the front of the room. She could barely see for the tears of happiness that filled her eyes and clung to her lashes. Her heart beat so loudly that she could hear it above the din.

Shaking first Douglas Myers's hand and then Thomas's, Katherine joined the chairman of the board and the new chief financial officer for their first official photograph. Standing between them, Douglas Myers raised their arms in a sign of unity and recognition. Smiling, Katherine searched the crowd for her ER staff and dear friends. Finding Betsy standing among them, she mouthed a tearful "thank you" for their love and support.

The board members on the sidelines applauded with equal vigor. They had been divided in their loyalty with some of them supporting Thomas's plans and others siding with Katherine. Now, however, after the success of Katherine's plans and Thomas's vision, they all agreed that these two certainly knew how to structure a fund-raising campaign and a revolutionary goal that would put other hospitals to shame. Even Jasmine looked pleased with the changes. As she linked her arm through Roger Paulsen's, it was clear that she had set her sights on someone else.

"Ladies and gentlemen, allow me to introduce our new one-two punch!" Douglas Myers shouted as he caught the enthusiasm of the crowd. He actually beamed and appeared more confident in the presence of the staff than usual.

Katherine had never shaken so many hands or been slapped on the back so many times or kissed so many cheeks in her entire life. Not even her family's excitement at her medical school graduation could compare to this. As the flood of people continued to swell before her, she tried to see Thomas in the crowd. Standing on her tiptoes, she could barely spot him towering over the men and women who pressed around him. Giving up, Katherine returned her attention to the people who anxiously waited to express their well wishes.

The rest of the afternoon passed in a blur of photographs and receptions. Every committee associated with the hospital hosted a tea for Katherine and Thomas. Although they shared the spotlight, they never had a moment together. Someone was always spiriting them away to yet another function.

By the time Katherine was finally on her own, her feet hurt from standing all afternoon and her face ached from smiling. Her throat felt sore and scratchy from all the talking, and she was exhausted from the attention. However, she would not trade the day for anything in the world. She had never felt so happy.

* * *

Walking home with Betsy, Katherine looked up at the April sky. Not a cloud had marred the opening festivities. Not a drop of rain had fallen on the carnival. Everything had been perfect. She could not have ordered more wonderful weather.

"Well, kid," Betsy said with emotion in her voice as they rode up on the elevator together, "you did it. You're the chief of staff of Boxer Hospital. How does it feel to have the job you've wanted for so long? I'm so proud of you that I could burst!"

"I still can't believe it. I guess it will seem real to me when I report to my office on Monday. After all this time, all this work, it's finally mine. But, you know, there's still one more thing that I want. And at seven o'clock tonight, I'm going to make that mine, too," Katherine answered as she slipped her key into the lock and opened her apartment door.

"So the ride on the Ferris wheel worked," Betsy grinned and gloated. She was proud of her matchmaking.

" 'What do you mean?" Katherine asked as Mitzi brushed against her leg. The cat did not care if Katherine were the new chief of staff, all she wanted was her dinner.

"Oh, nothing much, just a few of your loyal friends got tired of waiting for you to do something and we sort of took matters into our own hands. We engineered it so that you and Thomas would have to ride in the same car. Good thinking, ha?" Betsy responded with her fingers stuck in her imaginary suspender straps.

"Did Thomas know about this?"

"Sure, he was more than happy to go along. He's been trying to see you for some time, but he said that you were always too busy. Well, you're not too busy now. You have thirty minutes to get dressed. Don't be late. This might just be the most important night of your life," Betsy added as she shoved Katherine inside and closed the door.

"Thanks, Betsy!" Katherine shouted.

"Don't mention it. Just remember that I'm a size ten in maid of honor dresses," Betsy cried as she left Katherine to feed the cat, shower, and dress in record time.

Katherine arrived at the bistro five minutes late but looking stunning. She wore a simple black long-sleeved wool dress with a single strand of pearls and pearl button earrings. Instead of pulling her hair up in an efficient ball, she allowed it to tumble around her shoulders. Tonight she was a woman in love and not a physician or the newly appointed chief of staff.

Thomas spied her as soon as she entered the restaurant. Rising, he greeted her with a big smile and a warm kiss on the cheek. The love he had for her was so clearly written on his face that Katherine felt like throwing herself into his arms. If his reception had been less enthusiastic, she would have felt miserable.

"Well, Thomas, we're finally alone. What was it that you wanted to discuss?" Katherine asked playfully as she fingered her pearls and gazed into his watchful eyes.

"You know perfectly well what it is. I've waited to be alone with you for quite some time, Katherine. You know how much I love you and how completely I need you in my life. There's nothing standing between us now. Boxer Hospital has made it so that there are no longer any obstacles to our happiness together. For the third time today, I'm asking you. Will you please marry me?" Thomas asked with his hands enclosing hers.

Just then, the telephone rang at the little appointment desk in the corner. Looking at each other, Katherine and Thomas broke into gales of laughter that startled the other guests and caused them to stare quizzically. Gaining control of themselves, Thomas repeated, "Come on, Katherine, say yes. You'll never find anyone who loves you more than I do or needs you more. I'm a mess without you. I can't even propose without something interrupting me. Put me out of my misery. Katherine, please . . ."

Afraid to delay too long for fear something else would interrupt their moment, Katherine responded, "I love you, Thomas. I would be honored to become your wife."

Slipping their arms around each other, they kissed. This time they did not hear the sound of the telephone.

COMING IN OCTOBER . . .

FOOLS RUSH IN   (1-58314-037-9, $4.99US/$6.50CAN)
By Gwynne Forster
When Justine Montgomery discovers that her long-lost daughter has been adopted by journalist Duncan Banks—and that he's looking for a nanny—she enters into a web of deceit and divided loyalties with her new employer. Their fragile trust and unexpected passion force them to risk everything to claim a love they never thought possible.

SECRET PASSION   (1-5831-0425-5, $4.99US/$6.50CAN)
By Layle Guisto
Stalking victim Julia Smalls moves to Chicago to start a new life—one without terror. Her boss is suspicious of her secrecy but no one can deny their sizzling attraction. When strange accidents start happening, Julia believes her past has come back to haunt her and must make the choice between her life . . . and the love of her life.

FALSE IMPRESSIONS   (1-58314-038-7, $4.99US/$6.50CAN)
By Marilyn Tyner
After Zoe Johnson stumbles onyto a plot to steal high-tech software, she unwittingly becomes the inventor's hostage. He thinks she's a thoef . . . but she thinks he's stunningly attractive. As the weeks go by, both truth and an unexpected desire unfurl as the couple are thrown into a perilous game that could rob them of their lives—and their love.

A SURE THING   (1-58314-048-4, $4.99US/$6.50CAN)
By Courtni Wright
ER physician Katherine Winters finds she must compete bitterly with Thomas Baker for the chief of staff position at her hospital. Yet she can't help being fiercely drawn to the attractive doctor. For his part, Thomas finds Katherine irresistible. Can their desire melt bitter rivalry into love?

Available wherever paperbacks are sold, or order direct from the publisher. Send cover price plus $2.50 for the first book and $.50 per each additional book for shipping and handling to BET Books, c/o Kensington Publishing Corp, Consumer Orders, or call (toll free) 888-345-BOOK, to place your order using Mastercard or Visa. Residents of New York, Washington, D.C., and Tennessee must include sales tax. DO NOT SEND CASH.

Coming Soon from Arabesque Books . . .

__ONE LOVE By Lynn Emery
   1-58314-046-8 $4.99US/$6.50CAN
When recovering alcoholic Lanessa Thomas is thrown back with
Alexander St. Romain—the only man she ever loved and the one she
hurt the most—they must battle bitter distrust and pain to save their
second chance at love.

__DESTINED by Adrienne Ellis Reeves
   1-58314-047-6 $4.99US/$6.50CAN
When Leah Givens eloped as a teen, her father forced her to leave her
new husband immediately. But now, thirteen years later, her one and
only is back. Now, they must decide if they are strong enough to heal
the scars from years of separation and build a love that is destined.

__IMPETUOUS by Dianne Mayhew
   1-58314-043-3 $4.99US/$6.50CAN
Liberty Sutton made the worst mistake of her life when she gave sole
custody of her baby to its father. But when she meets executive Jarrett
Irving, and unexpectedly is given a chance to reclaim a life with her
child, she must reconcile her troubled past with a future that promises
happiness.

__UNDER A BLUE MOON by Shirley Harrison
   1-58314-049-2 $4.99US/$6.50CAN
Knocked unconscious and left to die, Angie Manchester awakens on
an exotic island with handsome Dr. Matthew Sinclair at her side—and
no memory of her identity. Thrown together by chance and danger,
but drawn by overwhelming desire, the two must take cover in the
island's lush forest where they succumb to a passion that comes but
once in a lifetime.

Call toll free **1-888-345-BOOK** to order by phone or use this coupon
to order by mail.

Name _____

Address _____

City _____ State _____ Zip _____

Please send me the books I have checked above.

I am enclosing	$_____
Plus postage and handling*	$_____
Sales tax (in NY, TN, and DC)	$_____
Total amount enclosed	$_____

*Add $2.50 for the first book and $.50 for each additional book.
Send check or Money order (no cash or CODs) to: **Arabesque Books, Dept.
C.O., 850 Third Avenue, New York, NY 10022**
Prices and numbers subject to change without notice.
All orders subject to availability.
Visit our web site at **www.arabesquebooks.com**

NEW ARABESQUE ROMANCES . . .

ONE LOVE by Lynn Emery
1-58314-046-8   **$4.99**US/**$6.99**CAN
When recovering alcoholic Lanessa Thomas is reunited with the
only man she ever loved, and the man she hurt the most, Alexander
St. Romain, she is determined to ignore her passionate temptations.
But when Lanessa's hard-won stability is threatened, both she and
Alex must battle unresolved pain and anger in order to salvage their
second chance at love.

DESTINED by Adrienne Ellis Reeves
1-58314-047-6   **$4.99**US/**$6.99**CAN
Teenage newlywed Leah Givens was shocked when her father tore
her away from bridal bliss and accused her husband Bill Johnson of
statutory rape. His schemes kept them apart for thirteen years, but
now Bill's long search for his lost love is over and the couple must
decide if they are strong enough to heal the scars of their past and
surrender to their shared destiny.

IMPETUOUS by Dianne Mayhew
1-58314-043-3   **$4.99**US/**$6.99**CAN
Four years ago, Liberty Sutton made the worst mistake of her life
by granting custody of her newborn to her married lover. But just
as handsome executive Jarrett Irving enters her life, she's given the
chance to reclaim a life with her child. Trying to reconcile a troubled
past with a future that promises happiness will take luck and the
love of a good man.

UNDER A BLUE MOON by Shirley Harrison
1-58314-049-2   **$4.99**US/**$6.99**CAN
After being attacked at sea, Angie Manchester awakens on an exotic
island with amnesia—and Dr. Matthew Sinclair at her side. Thrown
together by chance, but drawn by desire, the puzzle of Angie's identity and Matt's own haunted past keeps a wall between the two until
the vicious thugs return. Forced to hide in the lush forest, their
uncontrollable passion finally ignites.

Please Use Coupon on Next Page to Order